angel

Katie Price is one of the UK's top celebrities. She was formerly the glamour model Jordan and is now a best-selling author, successful businesswoman and star of her own reality TV show. Katie is a patron of Vision Charity and currently lives in Surrey with her three children.

Praise for *Angel*

'A page-turner . . . it is brilliant. Genuinely amusing and readable. This summer, every beach in Spain will be polka-dotted with its neon pink covers' *Evening Standard*

'The perfect post-modern fairy tale' *Glamour*

'*Angel* is the perfect sexy summer read' *New Woman*

'A perfect book for the beach' *Sun*

Praise for *Angel Uncovered*

'Glam, glitz, gorgeous people . . . so Jordan!' *Woman*

'A real insight into the celebrity world' *OK!*

'Brilliantly bitchy' *New!*

'Celebrity fans, want the perfect night in? Flick back those hair extensions, pull on the Juicy Couture trackie, then join Angel on her rocky ride to WAG central' *Scottish Daily*

Praise for *Paradise*

'A fabulous guilty holiday pleasure' *heat*

'Go on, run yourself a bath full of bubbles and indulge in this page-turner.' *Now*

Also by Katie Price

Non-Fiction
Being Jordan
Jordan: A Whole New World
Jordan: Pushed to the Limit
Standing Out
You Only Live Once

Fiction
Crystal
Sapphire
Angel trilogy:
Angel
Angel Uncovered
Paradise

angel

Katie Price x

arrow books

This edition published by Arrow Books 2011

2 4 6 8 10 9 7 5 3 1

Copyright © Katie Price 2006; Rebecca Farnworth 2006

Katie Price and Rebecca Farnworth have asserted their right under
the Copyright, Designs and Patents Act 1988 to be identified as the
authors of this work.

This book is a work of fiction. Names and characters are the product of
the author's imagination and any resemblance to actual persons,
living or dead, is entirely coincidental.

First published in Great Britain in 2006 by Arrow Books

Arrow Books
Random House, 20 Vauxhall Bridge Road,
London SW1V 2SA

www.randomhouse.co.uk

Addresses for companies within The Random House Group Limited can
be found at: www.randomhouse.co.uk/offices.htm

The Random House Group Limited Reg. No. 954009

A CIP catalogue record for this book
is available from the British Library

ISBN 9780099553151

The Random House Group Limited supports The Forest Stewardship
Council (FSC), the leading international forest certification organisation.
All our titles that are printed on Greenpeace approved FSC certified paper
carry the FSC logo. Our paper procurement policy can be found at:
www.randomhouse.co.uk/environment

Mixed Sources
Product group from well-managed
forests and other controlled sources
www.fsc.org Cert no. TT-COC-002139
© 1996 Forest Stewardship Council
FSC

Typeset by SX Composing DTP, Rayleigh, Essex
Printed and bound in Great Britain by
CPI Bookmarque Ltd, Croydon, CR0 4TD

Chapter 1

Birthday Girl

'Come off it, Angel, there's no way you can go clubbing dressed like that!' Gemma exclaimed.

'I always dress like this,' Angel replied, surprised. 'What's wrong with it?'

She looked at herself in the mirror and frowned. She was wearing her usual uniform of jeans, a baggy T-shirt, a dark-green hoodie and, her one concession to going clubbing, flat gold pumps. Her long brunette hair was loose and cascaded wildly down her back and the only make-up she was wearing was mascara.

'Where do I begin?' sighed Gemma. 'Please borrow something of mine and let me do your make-up. It's your birthday, for God's sake; we're supposed to be celebrating!'

'Okay,' shrugged Angel, not really bothered what she looked like, just glad to be going out with Gemma and knowing also that once Gemma had set her mind to something, resistance was futile.

'You know I've always hated my birthday, so it's no big deal. Who cares what I look like?'

'It *is* a big deal, and tonight you are going to pull.' Gemma had been itching to get her hands on Angel, knowing that it wouldn't take much to make her friend look gorgeous. It was always a mystery to Gemma that Angel was so completely unaware of how beautiful she was. There was no other way to describe her. She had the most amazing green eyes, fringed with lashes so long they could easily have been false; her lips were full and sensuous, the kind so many women spent a fortune on collagen trying to imitate; her skin was golden brown and flawless, except for the odd freckle, which only added to her beauty; and as if her face wasn't stunning enough she had a knock-out figure, curvaceous, with a great pair of boobs, long slim legs and an enviably flat stomach. Not that anyone ever got to see any of that under Angel's shapeless tops and baggy jeans. That was something Gemma was determined to change.

She immediately started pulling clothes out of her wardrobe. Gemma's middle name should have been 'fashionista' – she worshipped fashion and no trend ever passed her by. She owned most of Topshop's current collection so there was a lot to choose from: shrugs, wrap dresses, puffball skirts, polka dot tops, shorts. She picked up each garment and held it up against Angel, who was lounging on the bed and flicking through one of Gemma's many

2

celeb mags. Finally, Gemma settled on a sexy scarlet T-shirt with a low-cut neck and sweet puffed sleeves and a pleated denim miniskirt.

'Right,' she ordered, 'put these on. Sexy and simple – perfect. And borrow my Wonderbra as well, to give yourself some cleavage.'

'But I never wear skirts,' protested Angel, picking up the garment and feeling slightly alarmed by how short it was.

'It's about time you did, then.'

Angel reluctantly pulled off her clothes, fumbled with the push-up bra and slowly slipped on the skirt and T-shirt. She smoothed down the skirt, then hesitantly looked at herself in the mirror. At first she felt self-conscious about how much of her body was on display, but as she took in the whole of her reflection, she couldn't help smiling. She straightened her shoulders and lifted her head, the light catching her hair and a glint in her green eyes. The Wonderbra had given her an amazing cleavage. She didn't look too bad, did she?

'Wow, you look fantastic!' Gemma exclaimed, fussing with one of her sleeves. 'Now, let me get started on your face. What have you got on at the moment?'

'Nothing,' replied Angel, turning round in front of the mirror, checking out the outfit. 'Just some mascara.'

Gemma laughed. 'You're the only girl I know who would even think of going clubbing without wearing any make-up!' She dragged her over to her dressing table, which was piled high with beauty products – foundations, blushers, powder, eye shadows, concealers, lipsticks, Gemma had it all – and made her sit down. Before Angel had the chance to protest she grabbed a pair of tweezers and started attacking Angel's eyebrows.

'Ouch,' yelled Angel in pain. 'What the fuck are you doing?'

'Something you should have done years ago.'

'Well, it bloody well hurts, you sadist!' wailed Angel.

'Don't you know anything, Angel? The eyebrow is crucial. It frames the face; why do you think most stars have their own personal brow-shaper?' Gemma said, sounding exactly like the beauty page of a celebrity magazine. 'At the moment you've practically got a monobrow. I'm doing you a massive favour – you should be grateful.'

Several painful minutes later, she was done. 'I could go on, but that'll do for now.'

'Let me have a drink first,' Angel demanded. 'I need something for the pain.'

'Lightweight,' laughed Gemma, passing her a bottle of Smirnoff Ice.

Angel closed her eyes as Gemma got to work on her, quite enjoying the sensation of Gemma's cool fingers on her skin. Ten minutes later, she finally allowed Angel to look at herself in the mirror.

An unfamiliar face stared back at her, glowing

and shimmery, full lips parted in an uncertain smile, eyes huge and sparkling.

'God, is that really me?' Angel exclaimed, hardly believing the transformation. She'd always thought she was fairly ordinary: not a minger, but not a stunner either. But the girl staring back at her looked really good. Gemma hadn't put on a lot of make-up, simply accentuated Angel's beautiful eyes and lips and given her cheeks a sexy glow.

'You look amazing, Angel,' Gemma said gleefully. 'You know what I think? You look like a model.'

'Are you having a laugh?' Angel demanded, staring at her friend. She must be taking the piss. So she looked much prettier made up for a night out, and she had to admit that she liked this new Angel, but there was no way she had the looks to be a model.

'No, I'm not!' Gemma retorted. 'Mum and I are always saying you should.' But she could see that this was pushing it, so, glad she'd made some progress with Angel tonight, she quickly changed the subject.

'Now for some shoes!'

'Can't I just wear my pumps?' Angel pleaded.

'No, you can't. Here, try these.' And Gemma thrust a pair of red strappy sandals into Angel's hands.

'I'm never going to be able to walk in these, never mind dance,' Angel grumbled, as she fastened the straps. *Gemma is definitely a sadist*, she thought as she tottered unsteadily round the room. She could count on one hand the number of times she had worn heels, preferring her Timberlands or her pumps.

'There's a first time for everything,' Gemma said completely unsympathetically, putting on her own make-up. 'How do I look?'

'Gorgeous as ever,' replied Angel, relieved to be out of the spotlight and thinking that her friend was easily the prettiest girl she had ever known. Gemma was petite, with long, glossy, black, poker-straight hair, a heart-shaped face and the deepest blue eyes. She looked fragile, someone you wanted to shelter and protect, but she was actually as tough as old boots, and when some older girls had tried to bully Angel in primary school it was Gemma who had stood up to them and told them exactly where to go. She had been looking out for Angel ever since.

She was standing in front of the full-length mirror now, fiddling with her hair. 'What do you think, Angel, up or down?'

'Definitely down, it looks amazing.'

'And so do you, Angel, you are so going to meet someone tonight,' Gemma said. 'That Craig from college who does media studies is going and I know he really fancies you.'

'Well, I'm not interested in him,' Angel replied.

Gemma's dad called up telling them to get their arses into gear.

'Angel, you have got to face facts – Cal has been going out with Melanie for nearly a year. Get over it!'

The Cal in question was twenty-one-year-old, drop-dead gorgeous, well fit Callum Bailey, whom Angel had been hopelessly, secretly and madly in love with for as long as she could remember. She knew him because he was her older brother Tony's best friend. His dad had walked out on him when he was two and Cal had had a rough time since then. His mum was an alcoholic and, with his dad gone, love and stability had largely been missing from his life. His salvation had been football and the Summer family. Angel's dad, Frank, was the coach for the local youth team and had taken Cal under his wing, treating him practically like another son. So Cal spent nearly all his time at her house, which was good because she got to see him but bad because he appeared to be oblivious to her feelings and, instead of seeing her as a potential girlfriend, treated her like a kid sister.

'Never mind me and Cal, what about you and Tony?' Angel answered back. The two of them had been flirting on and off for the last three months. Tony was shy around girls and didn't seem able to make the first move, even though Angel had told him time and time again that Gemma was interested.

'All right, I know,' Gemma admitted. 'I haven't had sex for so long I'm probably a virgin again. But you're not much better. People will start to think we're bloody lesbos if we don't score soon.'

It was true, Angel thought – she was in a sexual slump. Today, May 28th, she was seventeen and she'd only had one serious relationship so far – Greg, a shy but cute lad from her school. They'd gone out for three months before having sex. And while Angel hadn't been expecting the earth to move, she had been seriously disappointed all the same. Greg had been a virgin too and it was all a bit rushed – two minutes, if Angel remembered right. After that, they did it a few more times, with little improvement – which only increased her frustration; if Greg knew anything about the female body, he wasn't letting on and Angel had got fed up with nipping off to the bathroom for a bit of DIY after yet another crap shag. She'd only started going out with Greg to get over her feelings for Cal but there was fat chance of that. It only intensified how she felt because she could just imagine how good Cal Bailey was in bed, though she didn't need to imagine – she knew how good he was. One night, when her parents were away, Tony had a party. Cal and Mel had stayed round her house and Angel got to hear everything, and judging from Mel's moans of delight, which Angel heard through her bedroom wall, Cal knew exactly what he was doing.

After Angel had split with Greg she'd gone out with various other lads, but it never lasted more than a couple of weeks. They all followed the same pattern: they'd go out clubbing, Angel would pretend she was having a good time, the lad would kiss her, she'd kiss him back because she felt she had to and then she'd make some excuse and go home. Then they'd meet up again for a drink and things would go a bit further, but she'd never gone as far as having sex with them, however good-looking the lad in question was. There was no getting away from it – Cal was the only one she was interested in.

'Are you girls ready for that lift?' Gemma's dad, Bill, called up the stairs, jangling his car keys. 'The taxi service wants to sit down and have a drink, so can you put a move on?'

The two girls raced downstairs. Bill was a total sweetie who would do anything for his daughter. Angel couldn't help comparing him to her dad, who only seemed to criticise her these days.

'Let's have a look at you,' called Jeanie, Gemma's mum, from the living room.

Gemma walked in first and her mum looked her up and down fondly as if passing judgment on her daughter. This was a family ritual whenever Gemma went clubbing. Finally, Jeanie said, 'You pass just about, but do you actually call that a skirt?'

'Come off it, Jeanie, when you were Gemma's age your skirts were much shorter,' teased Bill.

'Cheeky bastard!' exclaimed Jeanie. 'You never had a problem with it.'

'Right, Angel.' Gemma pulled her reluctant friend through the door. 'It's your turn for the inspection.'

Angel walked slowly into the room, still getting used to her heels. Jeanie and Bill, expecting to see Angel in her usual casual uniform, were speechless.

'You think I look too tarty?' Angel said anxiously, wrongly interpreting their silence. 'I told you not to put too much make-up on me, Gemma.'

'No, love, you look gorgeous,' Jeanie finally said. 'Gemma's done a great job, I couldn't have done it better myself.' Jeanie owned a very successful beauty salon in Brighton, so Angel knew she meant what she said.

'Just you look after her,' Bill warned Gemma, and Angel smiled at him. When Angel found out last year that she had been adopted, Jeanie and Bill had been the only people, apart from Gemma, she could talk to about her feelings.

'Enjoy yourselves, girls,' Jeanie said. 'And if you can't be good, be careful.'

Angel and Gemma giggled. '*Mum!* We are so not going to have sex with anyone the first time we meet them! Don't wait up, we'll get a taxi.'

The two girls had to queue to get into Creation, which was two minutes from the sea, and even though they shivered in the cool May air, chatting and giggling, for once Gemma didn't mind the wait. She stood back a little to watch every man do a double-take the moment he laid eyes on Angel. It wasn't that she was wearing more revealing clothes than anyone else – there were lots of girls wearing considerably less than her – but none of them looked as sexy and beautiful as Angel. Not for a second did Gemma feel jealous of Angel; she was genuinely glad to see her friend looking so stunning. For too long had she been hiding behind her baggy T-shirts.

Inside, the club was warm and noisy and they made a dash to the ladies to brush their hair, which had been dishevelled by the strong wind blowing off the sea, and touch up their lip gloss. Then they headed for the bar. Suddenly, Gemma gripped Angel's arm.

'Tony's over there!'

Angel looked at the other end of the bar, where her brother was waiting to buy a drink.

'Oh my God. I didn't know he was going to be here,' she exclaimed, half nervous, half excited. 'Do you think Cal's here, too?' But her question was immediately answered when her brother moved aside, and there was Cal, handsome and sexy, his dark eyes coolly surveying the scene, leaning against the bar, casual in his low-slung Ted Baker jeans and tight black T-shirt showing off his gorgeous body.

Angel's heart started racing and she froze.

'Come on.' Gemma pushed her friend forward. 'I want to see your brother. And I want Cal to see you.' She walked purposefully over to where the lads were standing, with Angel trailing reluctantly behind her.

'Hi, Gemma!' Tony smiled, obviously delighted to see Gemma. 'Would you and your friend like a drink?'

Gemma laughed and then dragged Angel in front of her.

'It's your sister, stupid! I've given her a make-over.'

Tony stared at her. 'Bloody hell.' Just as he was about to go on, Cal joined the group. He said 'Hi' to Gemma, looking appraisingly at Angel as if to say *who's this?* and then did the same double-take as every man in the room when he realised. 'Angie? You look so different!'

Angel could feel herself blushing, wishing she was dressed in her jeans and T-shirt even though the look on Cal's face told her clearly that he was glad she wasn't.

'So,' said Gemma cheekily, 'are you going to get us that drink, then?'

'Of course,' replied Tony, totally under her spell. 'I owe Angie a birthday drink, so what do you both want?'

'Two double Bacardi and cokes, please,' said Gemma, winking at Angel as Tony turned towards the bar.

As the four of them sipped their drinks it rapidly became clear to Angel that tonight was the night

Gemma and Tony were finally going to get it together. She knew that Gemma was frustrated with all the flirtatious conversations that seemed to go nowhere. Gemma wanted Tony Summer and judging by the way he was hanging on to her every word, gazing into her eyes, that looked like a definite possibility. The two of them were talking and laughing together intimately and with the music blaring out across the club it was impossible for Angel and Cal to join in their conversation.

'Is Mel here?' Angel asked him. His überbitch girlfriend was a footballer's wife in the making, with her fake tan, fake nails and designer clothes. Angel had been convinced when they first started going out that it wouldn't last more than a couple of months. Cal had always been wary of intimacy and always ended up dumping his girlfriends when they tried to get too close to him and wanted more commitment. Angel would never make that mistake. But for some reason, Mel seemed to be lasting longer than the rest, the cow.

Cal didn't catch what she said at first and had to duck down so she could make herself heard. She breathed in his scent and closed her eyes.

'No,' he replied, his cheek grazing hers. 'She's got some big family meal and I didn't want to go.'

He was staring right at her, and instead of dropping her gaze Angel shook back her long hair and stared right back at him. Cal was easily one of the best-looking men she had ever seen. His father was Italian and Cal had inherited his colouring – olive skin and jet-black hair which he always wore short. He had an incredibly handsome face, perfect features with beautiful brown eyes that could appear distant at times and full of passion at others. His was the kind of face that stopped you in your tracks, made you want to take a second, a third look at the dark-haired, handsome man, and by then you were probably lost. Angel was most definitely lost. The small scar just below his right eyebrow, a souvenir from a collision on the football pitch, only made him sexier, more desirable. She took a sip of her drink and looked around the club, feeling slightly bolder. Next to her she felt Cal move and they both watched Gemma and Tony walk over to one of the sofas, clearly wanting to be on their own.

'I'm really hoping Tony will finally ask Gemma out,' Cal shouted over the music. 'I'm so sick of him going on about her.'

'Yeah, I know what you mean,' Angel replied more quietly, wanting him to bring his face close to hers again and thinking longingly of Cal asking her out. *As if*.

'How are things going at the club?' she asked in a louder voice. Cal was a professional footballer who played for the local team, but Frank always said that with his talent he was destined for bigger things.

'Not bad, but I'm kind of ready to move on now.'

'I can't see you playing for Brighton for much

longer,' she agreed.

'What have you decided to do?' he asked her, bending down to her again.

Wow, Angel thought, *we're actually having a conversation and for once he isn't speaking to me as if I am just Tony's younger sister.*

She had another month left at college and she really wanted to go to art school, but her parents weren't keen. They wanted her to take a subject like business studies, where she was guaranteed a job at the end of it. Her face fell as she thought of it. She actually didn't have a clue what she wanted to do, but found herself saying, 'I'd like to do fashion design, I'm just not sure if I can fund it at the moment.'

'Really? I had no idea you were into that kind of thing.' Cal was looking at her again with definite interest.

'There are lots of things you don't know about me,' she said flirtatiously, spurred on by the way he was staring at her.

'You're right. You suddenly seem all grown up.'

'Well, it *is* my birthday today,' Angel replied, secretly wishing that he would kiss her.

'Happy Birthday, then.'

As they sipped their drinks, Angel couldn't believe that she was this close to the man who had filled so many of her dreams.

The Pussycat Dolls' 'Don't Cha' blasted out.

'Well,' said Cal finally. 'D'you want to dance?'

'Okay,' Angel replied, trying to sound casual, and the pair of them put down their glasses and headed for the dance floor. Angel already knew that Cal was a good dancer; she had spent long enough watching him from the sidelines of some club or other. Tonight was the first night he'd noticed her in that way, and she couldn't believe her luck. She followed him onto the dance floor, still feeling awkward in her heels. She rapidly became aware of envious glances from other women being levelled towards her; they would love to have been dancing with Cal. As the Dolls sang their hearts out, Angel thought *I bet you wish your girlfriend looked like me tonight, Cal?* The dance floor was heaving and Angel was frequently pushed against Cal.

'Sorry,' she shouted as yet again some tanked-up lad shoved into her and she practically fell onto Cal.

'No worries,' he grinned back, steadying her. His hand remained on her lower back for a second and Angel felt a shiver of excitement at his warm touch on her bare skin.

They danced closely, the club around them shrinking to just the two of them, and gradually Angel relaxed. Dancing in heels wasn't so bad after all. She kept sneaking glances at Cal when she thought he wasn't looking, and smiled to herself. Her birthday night was turning out so much better than she had expected.

'Another drink?' Cal mimed and Angel nodded. He took her hand and led her towards the bar. Once they had pushed their way there Angel was expecting him to let go of her but instead he draped his arm possessively around her shoulders, pulling her close. Angel so loved him touching her. Drinks in hand, he pulled her towards one of the dimly lit corners.

'Let's go somewhere a little more quiet,' he shouted above the music. They sat down on one of the sofas, as far away from Tony and Gemma as possible.

'You're a great dancer,' he said, giving her a slow, sexy smile.

She smiled back and was just about to return the compliment, but she didn't need to say anything. His hands were on her face and he gently pulled her towards him.

'You look so sexy, birthday girl,' he murmured, his thumb caressing her jaw-line softly. 'How come I never noticed this before?'

Before Angel had time to reply, he started kissing her. As she had known he would be, Cal was a fantastic kisser. The feel of his lips on hers, the taste of him, was so exciting. She pressed her body against his and kissed him back, praying that she was doing it right, hardly able to believe that she was kissing him at last.

After a few minutes he pulled away from their embrace and looked at her.

'What are you doing to me?' he murmured, running his hands through her tousled hair.

'Why? Do you want me to stop?' she murmured back.

By way of an answer he once more moved towards her, this time showering her neck with tiny kisses and slipping his hand under her T-shirt.

Neither Greg nor any of the other lads she'd been out with had ever made her feel like this. Angel was on fire as Cal expertly caressed her skin, her breasts. She slid her hands under his T-shirt and started touching his smooth skin. Then she ran her hand across his flat, hard stomach and dared to move further down. Drink and desire made her bold.

He pulled her on top of him so she was sitting on his lap and could feel his erection rubbing tantalisingly against her.

'God, I want you,' he murmured in her ear.

They kissed again, harder and deeper, and Angel could feel herself losing control, caring about nothing but his mouth and the feel of his hands on her body. But suddenly Cal abruptly pulled away, whispering urgently, 'Christ, Tony and Gemma are over there!'

Angel turned and across the room she saw Gemma looking at them, raising her eyebrows, but Tony clearly hadn't seen them. Cal pushed Angel off him and frantically straightened his T-shirt.

'What was I thinking?' he muttered. 'You're

Tony's little sister. And I'm with Mel.' And to Angel's horror, he got up and walked off without giving her a second glance. She sat in stunned disbelief for a few moments, trying to get a grip. *What the hell was that about?* She saw Gemma waving and reluctantly got up to join her.

Gemma looked like the cat who'd got the cream. Tony must finally have asked her out because the two of them were all over each other for the rest of the night. Cal was nowhere to be seen until two o'clock, when, to Angel's extreme discomfort, she found herself sharing a taxi home with him. Gemma and Tony were entwined in each other's arms, whispering and giggling, while Angel and Cal sat opposite each other in stony silence. Angel tried to occupy as little space as possible in the taxi, desperate not to touch Cal's long legs. She folded her arms, shivering as she looked out at Saturday-night Brighton, the lights of the pier sparkling in all their kitschy glory, the groups of clubbers roaming the streets. She felt totally humiliated by Cal's reaction. What was wrong with her? Was she only good enough for a quick grope in the dark?

'You two are very quiet,' Tony suddenly put in.

'Just knackered, mate,' Cal replied coolly.

'What's your excuse, Angie?'

'Pissed,' Angel muttered, wishing she was anywhere but here.

First stop was Gemma's.

'See you later,' Angel mumbled, getting out of

the car and deliberately not looking at Cal. She was forced to wait by the front door as Gemma and Tony shared a passionate goodnight kiss and she willed herself not to look back at Cal. After the longest minute of Angel's life, Gemma prised herself away from Tony.

As soon as she had shut and locked the front door Gemma turned to Angel, bubbling over with curiosity.

'So what happened with you and Cal. He was all over you!'

'I'll tell you in bed,' Angel muttered, longing to cover her head with the duvet and forget the night had ever happened.

'I can't believe it! What a total bastard,' Gemma exclaimed ten minutes later when Angel told her what had happened. As they always did when Angel stayed with Gemma, the two girls were sharing Gemma's double bed. Angel felt so cold she'd had to put on a jumper over her pyjamas, and even clasping the hot mug of tea Gemma had got her from downstairs, she still kept shivering.

'I feel so embarrassed, Gemma, how am I ever going to face him again? Why did he treat me like that? He practically pushed me onto the floor, he was so desperate to get away from me.'

'I'm sure he was just pissed,' Gemma said, trying to reassure her. 'And maybe he felt guilty – he is going out with Mel, after all.'

'He didn't seem that pissed. It was more like he

felt ashamed to be seen with me, that I wasn't good enough.'

Gemma looked at her friend and her heart ached to see her looking so crushed.

'God, I'm sorry, Gemma,' Angel finally said tiredly. 'I haven't even asked you about Tony.'

Gemma had been looking forward to telling Angel all about her night, but the last thing she wanted to do was go on about her happiness.

'I'll tell you in the morning. Just try and forget about tonight. It's Cal's loss, honestly. Look at you tonight. I bet every bloke in the room wanted you.'

But Angel couldn't sleep; she kept replaying what had happened over and over in her mind and each time her feelings of humiliation and rejection intensified. At four, her mobile phone beeped; she had a text message. She reached for it on the bedside table.

It was from Cal. For a delirious moment before she opened the message she thought he might be apologising, then she read it.

Angie please don't tell anyone about tonight. I was pissed and it shouldn't have happened, sorry. Cal.

She switched off her phone and buried herself under the duvet, curling up in the foetal position. *Think of all the good things,* she told herself, *think about going to art college, think about getting your own place.* But it didn't work. The tears silently streamed down her cheeks as she pressed her face into the pillow. Finally, at six, she fell into a fitful sleep.

At nine in the morning, Jeanie brought the girls tea and toast in bed and laughed at the exhausted pair.

'Too many Bacardi and cokes, I'm guessing,' she said, misreading Angel's pallor for a hangover. Angel nodded and forced herself to smile.

'It's a lovely day,' said Jeanie, pulling back the curtains and letting the sunlight stream in.

Gemma groaned and pulled the duvet over her head but Angel sat up.

'Jeanie, I know I've asked you this before but why do you think my real mum gave me away?'

Jeanie looked surprised. 'What made you think of that again, love?'

Angel shrugged. 'I suppose birthdays make me feel sad. I wonder if my real mum thinks about me.' What she didn't add was that her encounter with Cal had left her feeling so hurt that she longed for reassurance.

'All I know from Michelle and Frank, and I'm pretty sure it's all they know too, is that your mum was only a teenager and she couldn't cope, so she had you adopted when you were six months old. She wanted a better life for you, Angel, it's not that she didn't love you.'

She can't have loved me that much, Angel wanted to reply, *if she gave me away*, but realising this conversation was only going to depress her even more, she changed the subject and asked, 'Would it be okay if I went riding?'

'Course, love, if you think you're up to it.' Jeanie had taught Angel to ride when she was eight years old and always let her borrow her horse, and over the years Angel had become a very good rider.

Gemma was in no fit state to join her, so Angel cycled up to the stables on her own. Gemma lived in a large Victorian house with a huge garden in an expensive area in Brighton. Bill ran his own building company and that, along with Jeanie's successful beauty salon, made them comfortably off and a lot wealthier than Angel's family – not that that ever bothered the two girls. Angel lived five minutes away in a small terraced house with a tiny patio, but she liked the area as it was only ten minutes from the city centre and the sea. The narrow streets were lined with brightly painted houses, except the Summer's house. Frank refused to paint their house anything other than white, even though as a child Angel had begged him to paint it pink or at least blue after Chelsea, the football team she supported.

The stables were at the top of a particularly steep hill near the racetrack. Angel loved the stunning view across the whole of Brighton and the sea. Once she arrived, out of breath from cycling, she tacked up Storm and set off. It was a beautiful morning and as she galloped across the fields she shouted out, 'I don't need him!' startling Storm so he went even faster. It was often her therapy to ride and talk to herself, sing and shout – sometimes she felt so full of emotion she just had to let it out. An hour and a half later, she trotted back to the stables, hot and sweaty but slightly calmer. But as the stables came into view her peace of mind was shattered for there, leaning against his car, was Cal. Angel bit her lip and forced herself to look calm. She acted as if she hadn't seen him, rode up to Storm's stable and dismounted.

'You didn't reply to my text,' he said, not looking at her.

'I didn't think I needed to,' she replied, addressing her comments to Storm as she unbuckled his saddle and heaved it off.

'I just didn't want it to go any further.'

'It won't.' And somehow Angel found the strength to add, 'To be honest, Cal, I can't even remember what happened, I was so pissed.' She finally raised her eyes and looked at him. He looked momentarily annoyed, as if she had insulted him by not remembering every detail of his embrace, but then the shutters came down and he shrugged. 'So we're cool then?'

Angel nodded and carried on untacking Storm. *Just keep busy*, she told herself, *he'll be gone soon.*

'Okay, see you around, Angie.' Cal got into his car and Angel willed herself not to look at him drive off. When she was certain he couldn't see her she buried her face in Storm's neck, willing the humiliation and hurt away.

Chapter 2

The Morning After

'Did you have a good time last night, Angie?' Michelle called out to Angel as she let herself into the house.

Bollocks, she thought, she was hoping to slip upstairs to be on her own. She didn't want to talk about it – the memory was still too raw. But she forced herself to go into the living room. Her mum was curled up on the sofa. Angel took in her pretty face, pale and drawn and un-made-up her long, blonde, highlighted hair in need of a wash and her shapeless T-shirt and scruffy jeans in place of her usual well-coordinated outfits. *Oh God, here we go again*, she thought.

Her mum was having one of her blue days. Michelle had these regularly and they always happened around this time of year, as her own baby daughter had died on May 25th – three days before Angel's birthday. When Angel was feeling particularly bitter about being adopted she wished her mum and dad had been given another baby, someone with a different birthday.

'It was okay,' Angel replied, and then, keen not to continue the conversation, added, 'D'you want a cup of tea?'

Michelle nodded and Angel, glad of an escape, wandered into the kitchen.

'I'll have a cup if you're making one,' Frank said, coming in from the patio.

'Dad,' Angel turned to Frank, who was washing the soil from his hands – he'd been planting up pots for Michelle – 'can't you get Mum to go and see someone, she's really down again.' Angel felt she'd had this conversation a million times before.

Her dad sighed. 'I've tried, you know I have.'

Maybe not hard enough, Angel couldn't help thinking. Her mum had been on anti-depressants for as long as she could remember, but even with medication she still suffered bouts of depression. It made everyone in the house feel as if they were walking on eggshells, especially Angel, who hated seeing her mum so unhappy and felt powerless to help her.

Angel made tea, then went upstairs to her bedroom with a slight feeling of guilt. But she was feeling bad enough herself without having to deal with her mum's depression.

In contrast to the rest of the house, which had magnolia walls and neutral carpets, Angel's room was a riot of colour and clutter. Every inch of wall space was covered with pictures. Her own artwork:

huge oil paintings of stormy seas, calm seas, the sea at sunset (Angel had a bit of a thing about the sea); pictures of the men she fancied: Brad Pitt (in his younger days, before being a dad took its toll); Jesse Metcalfe, the hot gardener from *Desperate Housewives*; the footballer Freddie Ljungberg and Mickey Waters from the boy band Wanted. She didn't think much of his music but she thought he was fit. There were photographs of her and Gemma pulling faces in photo booths, horse riding aged nine, dressed as vampires for trick-or-treating, dressed outrageously in identical red tutus, their hair dyed red for Comic Relief.

There were photos from her family holidays. Every year the Summers went to Malaga in Spain and stayed at Jeanie and Bill's timeshare villa and every year, until he was seventeen, Cal came too. She, Tony and Cal had had the best times together – hanging out on the beach, swimming, water skiing, hiring pedaloes, playing frisbee, sneaking out to bars, the boys ordering beers and smoking when they knew Frank wasn't around. But by the time the boys were fifteen, they didn't think it was cool having eleven-year-old Angel tagging after them, so she was left to her own devices while they tried to chat up girls their own age. Unfortunately for Angel, Cal was always successful and at some point in the holiday she'd be confronted with him locked in a passionate snog with some English girl he'd met.

Now, that her glance fell on a picture of him

that she'd taken as he walked off the pitch with Tony after a match his team had won, thanks to Cal's three goals. She remembered calling out his name and how he'd looked straight at her, smiling. It was one of her many fantasies about him to imagine that he was smiling just for her. But now as she flung herself down on her bed, disturbing Prince, her chocolate-brown Labrador, and reached for her iPod, she didn't want to see him. *Screw you, Cal Bailey*. She pulled the photo off the wall, intending to rip it up and chuck it in the bin, but found she couldn't, so she stuffed it into her bedside cabinet along with all the other things she could never throw away – tickets from gigs and programmes from football matches, and several horoscopes torn from magazines which suggested that Geminis and Scorpios might be the perfect match (she was a Gemini and Cal was a Scorpio). Wanting to vent her anger at him somehow, she ripped up the glossy pages and threw *them* in the bin.

There was a knock at her door.

'Come in,' she called and Tony wandered in.

'Hello, lover boy,' she teased. Tony looked both embarrassed and pleased with himself.

'I'm going out for a drink now with Gemma, and I wondered what you were doing.'

Angel shrugged. 'I've got coursework to do.'

'I just wanted to check that you weren't going out, because you know Mum's in one of her moods,' Tony said.

Angel sighed. 'No, I'll be here.'

'Maybe you could make dinner? I don't think Mum's eaten anything all day.'

Even though Tony was right, and the two often took it in turns when Michelle was feeling low, Angel could have done without it.

I'm not feeling so good myself, she wanted to say, but as that would have involved an awkward explanation about Cal, she simply agreed to make pasta. Frank was a disaster in the kitchen.

'Thanks, Angie,' her mum said wearily as Angel put a bowl of spaghetti bolognese in front of her, 'but I'm not hungry.'

'Come on, Mich,' Frank urged. 'You've got to eat something.'

'I'm going to bed,' Michelle said, getting up from the table. 'Thanks for making it, Angie. I'm sorry to be so useless.' Her voice trailed off into tears as she shuffled out of the kitchen.

Frank and Angel looked at each other. This was all too familiar. They could expect the next two weeks to be like this. Michelle would have to be off work from her part-time job in the florist's and the whole house would be subdued until she went to the doctor and had her medication adjusted, or something just clicked back.

Frank cleared his throat. 'Had any more thoughts about what you're going to do when you finish next month?' Angel was at the local

FE college taking art A-level and a BTEC in performing arts, neither of which would have been her dad's choice of subject for her.

Angel groaned inwardly. Having a conversation with her dad about her future career prospects was about as pleasurable as having a Brazilian bikini wax.

'I still want to do art.'

'I know you're good at painting and stuff but what kind of job will you get at the end of it?' Frank persisted. He'd always had his life mapped out – football was his passion but he was never good enough to be a professional, so when he got too old to play in the Saturday league, he took up coaching and worked for Bill's building firm.

'I don't know,' Angel answered, pushing her pasta round her plate, her appetite gone. 'Fashion design, maybe. I think if I go to art school it will help me make up my mind.'

Frank tutted. 'Bloody expensive way of finding out.'

Angel knew exactly what was coming next: the Frank Summer lecture. 'We can't give you any money, Angie. If you did something like Tony, something where there was definitely a job at the end of it, you know we'd help you. But I can't afford giving you a loan and you not being able to pay it back three years down the line, when you've got no job.'

'So it's got nothing to do with the fact that I'm

not your real daughter but Tony's your son?' Angel burst out suddenly, sick and tired of having to hide her emotions, and feeling hurt because Frank had helped Tony out with his course fees.

Prince heard the edge in her voice and sloped over to lay his head on her knee.

'Don't be so stupid,' Frank exclaimed angrily. 'And keep your voice down, I don't want your mum to hear you. She's upset enough as it is.'

Angel bit her lip to stop herself shouting back. Why did her feelings always have to take second place to everyone else's in the house? It wasn't her fault that their baby daughter had died; she hadn't asked to be adopted by them. She got up from the table, taking her plate with her and dumping her uneaten spaghetti in the bin.

'I've got coursework to do,' she said, leaving the kitchen and going back upstairs.

She grabbed her portfolio and pencil and made a start on her drawing, but it was hopeless, she couldn't concentrate. She threw down her pencil in frustration, then opened her jewellery box, searching for her birth certificate. She opened the pale pink document, staring at her real name – Angel Adams. When Frank and Michelle finally told her she was adopted, on her sixteenth birthday (what a great one that turned out to be – *not*), and after she'd stopped crying and shouting, she told them that she wanted to be called 'Angel'. She could tell that her mum didn't have a problem with it, but

Frank said it was a bloody daft name and that he'd still call her Angie as that's what she'd been to him for the last sixteen years, a comment which Angel had never really forgiven him for.

The bombshell about the adoption confirmed why she'd always felt like an outsider in her family. She was so different from the others. They were practical and seemed to know what they wanted, whereas she was passionate and needed more reassurance. And however much her parents said that they loved Tony and her equally, in her heart she didn't believe it. Tony was their real son so they must love him more. She reached for her mobile, about to text Gemma and find out what she was up to, then she remembered she was out with her brother.

'Bollocks,' she said out loud, her bad mood worsening. She was stuck here for the rest of the night. It was at times like this she longed to meet her birth mother. Maybe when she met her, everything would make sense; she would find the love she had always longed for and she wouldn't feel alone anymore. But she knew she couldn't look for her until she'd left home as Michelle would never be able to deal with it.

She lay back on her bed listening to her iPod, deliberately selecting songs which fitted her blue mood, starting with Mariah Carey's 'I've Been Thinking About You' (no change there then), 'We Belong Together' (yes, Cal, when are you going to wake up to that?), Christina Aguilera's 'Beautiful',

Alicia Keys' 'Fallin', Sugababes' 'Too Lost In You' and Whitney Houston's 'I Have Nothing'. Finally, when even she was ready for a track that told her she'd survive, she chose Sugababes' 'Stronger'.

And all the time, thoughts of her family and Cal chased round her head. What was it with Cal and her birthdays? It was on her sixteenth that they'd ended up having a furious row, just after she'd found out she was adopted. It had been such a huge shock to her and had left her feeling vulnerable and emotional, and furious that she hadn't been told before. Unfortunately it was Cal who received the brunt of her anger. The two of them had ended up alone in the living room and Cal had said, 'I heard the news. You're so lucky, Angie. I wish my mum had had me adopted. I'd have loved parents like Frank and Michelle.' Angel had looked at him, not believing her ears, and suddenly the anger she'd been trying to contain had reached boiling point. She'd sprung up from the sofa and before she'd realised what she was doing she'd slapped Cal hard across the face.

'Hey, calm down,' Cal said, clearly surprised by the force of her reaction and holding a hand up to his face, where a livid red mark was already showing. 'I was just trying to help.'

'Well, don't bother,' Angel had shouted. 'Fuck off back to your fucking perfect girlfriend and leave me alone!'

A year on, the memory still had the power to

make her squirm. *Yes, Angel*, she said to herself, *you should give tips on how to get a man – hit him and then tell him to fuck off . . .*

But one thing was certain, she decided, trying to push that memory out of her head – whatever Frank said, she was going to go to art school. She was going to get a job and save up and when she'd finally got enough, she'd move out and get a place of her own, maybe with Gemma, and then she could finally start living her life and stop feeling that she could never be herself.

'How are you feeling about Cal now?' Gemma asked Angel as the two girls walked out of college.

'I'm still really pissed off about what happened,' Angel admitted. 'And I really want to hate him for what he did, but the worst thing is I just can't, it's doing my head in.'

'I know what you mean,' Gemma said sympathetically. 'What you need is some retail therapy.'

Angel laughed; shopping was Gemma's answer to everything and usually she would have said no, but she was feeling reckless, she needed a change. She was sick of all her clothes. That Saturday night had been like a wake-up call. So she agreed to hit Gemma's number-one favourite destination – Topshop.

Gemma was like a Tasmanian devil, rushing round the store and grabbing garments that caught her eye. When she was happy with her selection the two headed off for the changing room and squeezed into one of the cubicles. She had Angel try on shirt-dresses, flirty little skirts, sexy halter-neck tops, shrugs, low-rise cropped jeans. With every item she tried on, Angel felt a surge of confidence. She wasn't being vain, she really did look good.

'You look great in everything,' Gemma told her. 'I think you should get them all.'

'Don't be stupid, I can't afford all this!' Angel said.

'Get a store card then,' Gemma whispered wickedly.

'No way!' Angel exclaimed. 'I'll never be able to pay it back.'

'Come on, you got some birthday money, didn't you?' Gemma persisted.

'Yeah, but I was supposed to be saving it for art school,' Angel replied.

'Do you really want to go around all summer in your jeans and crappy old T-shirts when you could be wearing these?' Gemma held up a pair of mini silver shorts that Angel had especially fallen in love with. 'Or this?' Gemma picked up a cute green and white polka dot boob tube. 'Or this?' Gemma reached for a slinky green shirt-dress. 'And how could you walk away from this?' she said finally, picking up a gorgeous little red pleated mini and waving it in front of Angel.

'You bastard!' Angel joked, knowing that she was not going to be able to resist. But she didn't get too carried away, choosing items that she could wear in the day time – well, except for the silver shorts, which would be hard to get away with except in a club, but she just had to have them.

'Oh my God!' Angel exclaimed as they walked out of the shop and into the late-afternoon sunshine. 'I can't believe I just bought all those things.' Plus, Gemma had insisted she buy a string of red beads, a long gold chain, several bracelets and a sweet scarlet handbag. 'I need a drink! Let's get a beer.'

'All in good time,' Gemma promised. 'But first we'll go and see Mum and get you that manicure she promised you for your birthday. And then, Cinderella, we will get a beer.'

That night as Angel curled up in bed, Prince snoring gently on her bedroom floor, she couldn't help smiling at how the day had turned out. At the salon Jeanie had cracked open a bottle of wine to celebrate Angel's birthday and the three of them had gossiped, giggled and bitched away a couple of hours. Mainly about Mel, who used to go to Jeanie's salon until one day she'd accused one of the staff of burning her during a bikini wax and threatened to sue, even though there had been nothing wrong with the temperature; it was just the kind of person Mel was.

'He's bound to leave her soon,' Jeanie assured Angel, knowing all about her obsession.

'He definitely will if he sees Angel in her silver shorts!' Gemma exclaimed. 'You've got to wear them next time we go clubbing.'

Angel was glad Jeanie and Gemma had such confidence in her ability to attract Cal. Even though she felt better than last night, she was still smarting from his rejection. Just before turning off her light she pulled open the drawer in her bedside cabinet and reached for the photo of Cal, unable to go to sleep without one final look at him.

Chapter 3

Summer Loving

In the weeks that followed, Angel tried to put all her energy into completing her art coursework and preparing for her final exams. She so wanted to do well. Frank still insisted he wasn't going to fund her. All her life he had drummed into her the importance of not getting into debt and Angel worried that if she took out a student loan, she might never be able to repay it, especially doing a subject as uncertain as art. Gemma had no such worries. Her parents were going to pay for her to do a beautician's course.

'Your mum and dad are well tight,' Gemma told her friend. 'Can't they see how talented you are?'

Angel shrugged; the two of them had talked about this so many times before, and there really wasn't anything more to be said. Her parents were never going to change their mind.

But even though she was working hard, and when she wasn't working she was off riding, she couldn't help thinking of Cal. She frequently dreamt of him – intense erotic dreams where he didn't push her away. Now that she had kissed Cal, her desire for him had increased so it was like a physical ache at times. She tried to avoid going to places he was likely to be, but Brighton wasn't that big a city and she often saw him when she was out clubbing. He'd be with Mel, who clamped herself to his arm and wouldn't let him out of her sight, and even if Angel was certain that he'd seen her, he never came over and said hello, so she kept her distance.

Angel and Gemma couldn't stand Mel. She was always dressed head to toe in designer labels because her property developer daddy was loaded and always gave his little princess what she wanted. Mel was no stunner and it took a lot of effort and money to get her there. She went to the hairdresser's twice a week to get her long blonde hair blow-dried, she was permanently tanned because she made frequent trips to a spray booth, her nails were fake square-tipped French-manicured, her teeth had been bleached and she was never seen without full make-up. She was stick thin with large boobs and although she denied it, Gemma and Angel were convinced they were silicone. 'You just can't be that skinny and have tits,' Gemma was fond of pointing out. She and Cal had been together for nearly a year and everyone knew that she was desperate for him to marry her. Neither Gemma nor Angel could understand what Cal saw in her and questioned Tony at length to try and find out. But Tony insisted she was gorgeous, what was their problem?

'It must be her big tits,' Gemma said to Angel. 'What else could it be?'

'Well, it's not her personality, is it?' replied Angel. Mel was the most uptight, high-maintenance woman the girls had ever met, and Angel laughed, imagining what it must be like going out with someone like that. Actually, Angel did have a theory about why Cal was with Mel, but it wasn't one she really wanted to share with anyone, not even Gemma. She believed Cal was with Mel because her money represented success and security to him. All his life Cal had struggled to escape his own impoverished upbringing and put as much distance as possible between his alcoholic mother and himself. Being with Mel probably made him feel safe and in control.

'Perhaps she's really good at blow jobs,' Gemma giggled.

'Oh, come on, can you really imagine Her Majesty going down on anyone? She'd be too worried about smudging her make-up,' Angel replied, exploding into giggles herself.

'Oh my God, Angel,' Gemma managed to splutter through her laughter. 'You actually cracked your face!'

It was true – since her birthday, when she'd got off with Cal, Angel hadn't felt much like laughing.

But gradually the humiliation had worn off and something good had come of the experience. It was as if a light had been switched on inside her and now, instead of wanting to wear shapeless clothes that hid her body, Angel chose more revealing outfits. She started to take more care over her appearance and wore make-up, and because she was so beautiful even just applying mascara and a bit of lip gloss made her look absolutely stunning. As a result, every time she went out she was pursued by men wanting to buy her drinks and ask her out. But she never saw anyone who interested her enough – no one seemed as special as Cal.

That is, until she started working as a lifeguard on Brighton beach. She had left college and had got a place to study art. The thought of working in a call centre or an office filled her with dread, so when she saw the lifeguard job advertised, she jumped at the chance. At least that would be the summer sorted out and maybe something else would pop up by the autumn. She had always been a strong swimmer and easily passed the test. On her first day, she found herself face to face with an extremely handsome man. He was very nearly as hot as Cal, with Mediterranean good looks, broad shoulders and a warm smile.

'Hi, I'm Juan,' he said, and to her great surprise bent down and kissed her on each cheek. Laughing at her reaction he explained, 'It's how we say hello in Spanish.'

'I'm Angel,' she managed to reply.

'Yes, I think you are!' He gazed at her and Angel stared back, taking in his chocolate-brown eyes and good-looking face and then sneaking a look at his very toned and tanned body. She was now *very* glad she hadn't taken a job in a call centre!

She quickly found out that Juan was studying English at one of the many language schools in Brighton and planned to open his own bar back home in Malaga. He was twenty, easygoing, extremely flirtatious and exactly what Angel needed. Halfway through their first day together, Tim, their long-haired, hippy supervisor, came over and told them there would be a rescue simulation later in the day and he wanted Angel and Juan to take part.

'What do you think will happen?' Angel asked Juan.

'You drown, I rescue you and then I get to give you the kiss of life.'

Angel giggled; if any of the English lads she knew had said that it would have sounded dead cheesy, but coming from Juan, with his delightful broken English, it actually sounded incredibly sexy. If he was going to be the rescuer then she wouldn't mind doing a bit of drowning.

The pair flirted their way through the rest of the day. The weather wasn't particularly hot so the beach wasn't crowded and there really wasn't much to do. Angel had imagined herself spending her days gazing out to sea and dreaming about Cal, but there wasn't a chance of that with Juan, who, desperate to practise his English and flirt with Angel, talked non-stop. He wanted to know everything about her and expressed complete surprise when she let on that she didn't have a boyfriend.

'I cannot believe it!' he said. 'In Spain, this would never happen! Such a beautiful girl, are these English men blind?' Angel couldn't help laughing at him.

At four o'clock, Tim turned up along with some of the other lifeguards.

'Right then, Angel, I want you to swim out five metres and pretend to get into difficulty. Juan, you will then sound the alarm and rescue her, following the procedures we've learnt.'

Angel quickly stripped down to her red swimsuit and walked down to the sea; there she kicked off her trainers and dived straight in. It was bloody freezing! She gritted her teeth and swam out. Once she thought she had gone far enough she stopped, turned to face the beach and started treading water, shouting out, 'Help!' Immediately Juan tore off his T-shirt and ran into the water.

Top banana! thought Angel. Even from a distance Juan had the most gorgeous body. *He can rescue me any time!*

Juan quickly swam out to Angel with a very impressive front crawl. Angel grinned at him but he was obviously playing things by the book as he told her not to panic, ordered her to hold onto the float and started towing her back to the shore. As soon as he could stand he scooped her into his arms and carried her onto the pebbles. He laid her gently on the ground and put her in the recovery position. Then he leant over her and started massaging her heart, put his finger into her mouth as if to remove any obstruction and knelt down and put his lips against hers. Angel froze, feeling embarrassed by the other lifeguards eyeballing them, but also intrigued. She closed her eyes, trying to imagine that they weren't surrounded by ten other people and that Juan was going to kiss her properly. Then Tim called out, 'That's it, well done,' and pressed the button on his stopwatch.

Rather reluctantly, Juan took his mouth away from Angel's and helped her to her feet, putting a towel round her shoulders as by now she was shivering.

'That was pretty much perfect, Juan; I hope the rest of you were watching that. Thanks, Angel, for doing your bit. You'd better have a hot shower, you look frozen!'

That night Angel went on and on to Gemma about how gorgeous Juan was, and how much she fancied him.

'More than Cal?' Gemma teased.

'Differently to Cal,' Angel replied. 'Juan's my holiday romance and maybe something more, who knows?'

The two girls sat on Gemma's bed as she experimented putting make-up on Angel for her beautician's course. Now that she had finished college, Angel spent even more of her time at Gemma's. There just didn't seem to be a good reason to go home. She would only have to put up with her dad nagging her about taking a proper subject. Though, of course, she only got to spend time with Gemma when she wasn't out with Tony. Luckily for Angel, his sports physiotherapy course kept him extremely busy, so she still got to see lots of her friend.

To her surprise, Angel was loving the summer. Suddenly they were in the grip of a heatwave and while so many other workers were trapped inside, longing to be outside, Angel got to spend all her time at the beach in the company of the delicious Juan. After a week of working together, he asked her out for a drink after work. Angel had no hesitation in agreeing. He was such good fun to be with and she loved the way he made her feel so good about herself – he was always complimenting her, telling her how *bella* she was. As soon as their shift finished Angel sneaked into the toilets of one of the many bars lining the sea front and changed. She put on a tiny black halter-neck dress that gave maximum exposure to her tanned back and legs and a pair of high wedge sandals that made her legs look even longer. A quick coating of mascara and liner and a slick of berry-coloured lip gloss and she was ready. Juan looked suitably impressed as she stepped out of the bar. He had swapped his work clothes for a pair of faded jeans and a white T-shirt and dark glasses. Angel was expecting that they would hang out by the sea, but Juan had other ideas.

'You deserve to go somewhere special,' he said and he whisked her off to the chic Hotel du Vin for champagne cocktails.

'God!' Angel exclaimed, looking at the price list. 'Can you afford these?'

He shrugged. 'My mother sent me some extra money. I want to spend it on you, Angel.'

Two cocktails later, Angel was enjoying herself enormously. They were flirting nicely and, almost imperceptibly, Juan had edged closer to her and put his arm round her shoulder.

'Why don't we go back to my flat, Angel? I really want to kiss you and I don't think the people here will approve.'

Angel smiled – she liked his directness and she wanted to kiss him too.

As soon as they got outside Juan pulled her into a doorway and started kissing her passionately. *Good*, Angel thought to herself, *very good. Eight out of ten*.

Back at his flat the kissing continued and the caresses started. Juan ran his hands all over Angel's body, sending shivers of delight rippling through her. He undid the halter-neck top of her dress and started caressing her breasts, first with his hands, then he kissed her nipples, gently sucking them so Angel felt a white-hot flame of desire ignite within her. As he kissed her nipples he started caressing her through the silk of her thong. It was exquisitely pleasurable and Angel found that she didn't want him to stop, and she helped him slip off her underwear. He showered kisses on her stomach and moved further and further down her body, ending up his journey between her legs.

'Oh God,' Angel moaned. It was so good, all her being was concentrated on the meeting of his tongue against her flesh. She didn't want him to stop and gave in to the sheer pleasure. Minutes later, he brought her to the most intense and satisfying orgasm of her life.

When she came to, he was clearly ready for more, and she felt so languid and satisfied that she couldn't resist running her hands all over his body. She pulled off his T-shirt and started kissing his chest.

'Angel, I have, how you say, preservatives?'

'You what?'

'Condoms.'

'Oh.' She was momentarily jolted out of her post-orgasmic haze. It was all happening a bit too fast. 'There is something I can do for you,' she said, reaching down and unbuttoning his jeans and moving down the bed.

*

'Hiya, Angel, we're having a few beers down there, by the West Pier, d'you want to join us?' Gemma and Tony stood in front of Angel and Juan's lifeguard tent.

'That would be great, we finish in ten minutes,' Angel replied.

It was the end of another blisteringly hot summer's day. Even at six p.m. the sun still felt strong and the beach was packed. Angel's hair was full of natural bronze highlights from the sun and she was a deep golden brown. Instead of her all-in-one costume she had taken to wearing a tiny red bikini.

'It doesn't affect my ability to save anyone,' she told Tim defiantly.

'I'm sure it doesn't, but I expect there'll be a queue of lads waiting to be rescued,' he said wryly.

At six o'clock precisely, when they were off duty, Juan picked Angel up in his arms and raced into the sea with her. She squealed in outrage as he dropped her into the water. She retaliated by dragging him under and the two splashed playfully around, he threatening to undo her bikini, she pulling at his trunks, their tussle ending with a very salty and passionate snog. Finally, the prospect of a cold beer lured them out of the water. As they walked over to where Tony and Gemma were sitting, Angel's stomach did a somersault, for there, sitting down and drinking beer, were Cal and Melanie, who had obviously seen Angel and Juan's display in the water.

'I'll get the towels,' Juan said, jogging back to their station.

Angel shook back her long wet hair and took a deep breath.

'Hi, Cal, hello, Melanie.' Cal's upper body was bare and he was wearing green camouflage combats. He looked very, very good. *Don't think about it*, Angel told herself sternly. *He's a bastard.* It was the first time she'd spoken to him since they'd met at the stables nearly two months ago when he'd wanted her to pretend that their encounter at Creation hadn't happened. But much as she wanted to hate him for how he'd treated her, she found it impossible. The only emotion she felt was an overwhelming attraction for him.

The überbitch was wearing a pink kaftan top trimmed with sequins, a white bikini and shed-loads of make-up.

'How are you, Angie?' Cal asked.

'Good thanks,' she replied. At that moment Juan appeared and wrapped the towel round Angel. She realised he had never met Cal and Mel and so introduced them. It did make her feel good being able to introduce this very good-looking man as her boyfriend. She wanted Cal to realise that other men found her attractive. For a second they did the alpha-male thing and sized each other up, then

Juan shook Cal's hand and kissed Mel. *Must remind him not to do that again*, Angel thought, seeing how impressed the überbitch was with Juan's Latin good looks.

Gemma, who'd been hovering around anxiously, handed them each a beer and they sat down.

'You're very brown, Angie. Is it spray-on?' Melanie asked snidely.

Angel laughed. 'No way, I couldn't afford that. This is all real.'

Mel's face fell slightly. 'Had your hair highlighted, haven't you? Looks good.'

Angel shook her head and Juan pulled her towards him. 'No, she's all real, all of her, my beautiful, beautiful Angel.' And ignoring all the amused looks from the others, he kissed Angel on the lips.

'And why do you call her Angie?' Juan demanded. 'Her name's Angel.'

This really wasn't something Angel wanted to go into right now in front of an audience. 'I'll tell you later, babe,' she whispered, running her hand possessively down his back and kissing him.

'When you two have finished, I've got some news about Cal,' Tony put in.

Oh my God, thought Angel, *he's going to marry the überbitch*. Her heart sank.

'Chelsea are going to sign him.'

'Oh my God!' Angel squealed. 'That's fantastic!' And without really thinking about what she was doing she rushed over to where he was sitting, her towel falling off her in her haste, and bent down to hug a very surprised Cal.

She suddenly became aware of their bare skin touching and pulled away as if she had been burnt.

'Cal, that's brilliant news! I'm so pleased for you,' Angel exclaimed, and she truly was. She knew how talented Cal was and she knew how ambitious he was. She was also hugely relieved that he wasn't engaged to the überbitch.

'Cheers, Angie.' He smiled back at her. 'I won't be in the first team straight away, but it's great to be in the squad.'

Mel's eyes were boring holes into Angel through her designer shades and Angel swiftly moved back to her place next to Juan.

'So when do you start?'

'Next week,' Cal replied.

'Yeah, we're throwing a party for him at the club,' Tony added.

He looked delighted at his friend's news but Angel knew it must be hard for him. Tony dreamt of playing professionally but it had never happened for him and never would and she really felt for her brother.

'Mel's organising the party, Angel.' Gemma's mouth twitched. 'It's going to be a fancy dress one.' She took a quick swig of her beer to stop herself catching Angel's eye.

'I'm planning to start a business organising parties and thought this would be good practice,' put in Mel grandly.

'What's the theme?' asked Angel.

'Hollywood stars.' Mel was obviously proud of such an original idea.

'Fantastic – Juan, you can be Antonio Banderas!' exclaimed Angel.

'Yeah, but I don't want you looking like Melanie Griffith!'

'Cheeky bastard,' Angel teased. 'Do I look like Melanie Griffith? Although she wasn't bad before she became obsessed with looking young and skinny.'

Juan put a hand up to Angel's face and considered her.

'You will have to be Brigitte Bardot or Marilyn Monroe. Or maybe Pamela Anderson, but your breasts are much more beautiful.'

Angel squirmed with embarrassment. 'He's Spanish, got no inhibitions!' she explained in mock horror, seeing the looks on everyone's faces.

'So what do you think, everyone, Bardot or Monroe?' Juan persisted.

'Monroe,' Gemma put in.

'Yeah,' agreed Tony.

Juan looked at Cal questioningly. Cal cleared his throat. 'Yeah, Monroe,' he mumbled. Angel sneaked a look at Mel, who had a face like thunder – she hated anyone else getting compliments.

'Who are you going as?' Gemma asked Mel innocently.

'Actually, *I* was going to go as Monroe,' Mel replied sniffily. 'I thought I told you that, Cal.'

Cal looked mortified at his mistake and much as Angel would have loved to see an argument between them, Juan put in, 'Well, Angel can go as someone else then – there are so many possibilities for her.'

'Anyway,' said Cal, clearly desperate to change the subject, 'who wants to get something to eat?'

Angel claimed that she and Juan were broke, which wasn't strictly true, she just didn't think she could bear being with Cal and Mel any longer. The others said their goodbyes and got up to leave and Angel and Juan stayed on the beach, finishing their beers. As the others walked away Angel pulled Juan into a passionate embrace. Partly she was doing it because she wanted to and partly because she wanted to flaunt her lover in front of Cal. She couldn't resist looking at the party walking along the promenade as she kissed Juan.

Bingo! she thought to herself, seeing Cal turning round and staring back at her as she deliberately pressed her body into Juan's.

'So how do you know Cal?' Juan asked as the two of them packed up their things.

'I've known him for years,' Angel tried to say as casually as possible. 'He's just a friend.'

*

Three weeks into their romance and Juan still hadn't persuaded Angel to have sex with him, despite his best efforts. But by the time Cal's leaving party came round, Angel had decided that she wanted to go further with Juan. She knew that he was just a summer fling who would soon be gone, but she liked him a lot. She trusted him and he had already proven himself to be a skilful lover. And after the crap sex with Greg, Angel thought she deserved him.

They had spent the week before the party scouring the second-hand clothes shops to find a gangster-style suit for Juan, who was going to go as Al Pacino in *The Godfather*. Angel still didn't have an idea of who to go as, but then they came across an amazing playboy bunny costume in a dress hire shop. Juan persuaded her to try it on as a laugh, but when she checked herself out in the mirror she knew that would have to be her costume. The black satin all-in-one fitted her perfectly, showing off her curves and long legs. So what if Mel's theme was Hollywood stars? Angel wanted to make an impact.

'Sit still, can't you!' Gemma ordered Angel as she tried to stick on her false eyelashes while Angel was fidgeting.

'Gemma,' Angel moaned, 'if you're going to be a beautician you really need to learn how to talk to your clients properly!'

'I'm certain I'm never going to have a client as

difficult as you,' replied Gemma. 'Now for the lips.' Gemma surveyed her handiwork; Angel looked ravishing.

'Gemma!' Angel squealed, catching sight of herself. 'That is so cool.'

She loved the way that Gemma's make-up subtly but skilfully made her look sexy, and she practised fluttering her false eyelashes and pouting with her sexy glossed lips.

'I definitely think you should go blonde soon,' Gemma said to her friend. 'It would really suit you.'

When Juan came to pick her up he couldn't believe his eyes; he kept going on and on about how beautiful she was. *He is so good for my ego*, Angel thought to herself, thinking he also looked pretty hot in his pinstripe suit, with his smouldering brown eyes and handsome tanned face.

She was dreading the next part of the evening. Before the party she and Juan were going to meet her parents. She had warned him that her dad might be offhand and distant with him, but in the end it wasn't like that at all. Frank had already had a few drinks. He and Michelle were won over by Juan's perfect manners and charm and when her dad discovered his passion for football, as a life-long Barca fan, he had no problem in seeing him as Angel's boyfriend. And for the first time her parents seemed to notice that their daughter was a beauty. Her mum actually insisted on getting out the camera and taking a picture of her.

'He's very handsome,' Michelle told her daughter, sitting on her bed and watching as Angel put the finishing touches to her make-up in her bedroom mirror.

'Yes, he's lovely,' Angel agreed.

'You are being careful, aren't you, love?' Michelle whispered, looking anxiously at her daughter.

It took a second for Angel to realise what she was talking about as she and her mum never had *those* kinds of conversations.

'Of course, Mum,' she insisted, desperate not to go into details. 'Don't worry about it.' If she wanted advice on contraception, her mum was the very last person in the world she would have asked. 'Come on, the taxi's here and you know Dad doesn't like to keep it waiting.'

The party was well under way by the time they arrived. Angel immediately spotted Gemma and grabbed Juan by the hand as she rushed over to see her friend. Gemma was dressed as Catwoman and looked amazing; Tony was Batman and looked self-conscious. Juan went to get the drinks and Angel found herself scanning the room for Cal.

'He's over there,' Gemma told her friend, knowing exactly whom she wanted to see.

Angel looked to the far side of the room. She knew that Melanie had persuaded him to go as Brad Pitt in *Troy* and she so wanted to laugh at Cal, figuring that it would help her get over her attraction to him, but tonight wasn't going to be the night. He was indeed dressed as Brad Pitt, but whereas most men would have looked ridiculous in the Ancient Greek get-up of a leather skirt and leather body armour, Cal looked heart-stoppingly gorgeous and got to show off even more of his fit body than usual.

'Oh no,' Angel whispered to Gemma. 'I so wanted him to look a complete tit.'

'Don't worry,' Gemma told her. 'Just you wait until you see Mel.'

Suddenly she came into view. Mel had gone for Monroe in a big way, with the peroxide-blonde wig, the startlingly red lipstick, the white fifties-style dress. But her features weren't good enough to carry it off and instead of being sexy she just looked overly made-up and tarty.

'She looks well minging!' Angel said gleefully to Gemma, starting to enjoy the evening. Juan appeared with their drinks and when he told them it was a free bar everyone cheered up even more, knocked back the first round and sent Juan back for refills. Angel was longing for Cal to notice her but so far he seemed oblivious to her presence and was constantly surrounded by people congratulating him on his news, so she took to the dance floor with Juan instead. He spun her round, took her in his arms and generally showed off with her. Angel was aware that they were the centre of attention but for once she didn't care. She was with a gorgeous man who adored her. When Juan took her into his arms and kissed her, her mind was made up.

'Come on,' she whispered in his ear. 'Let's go.' And she led him outside the clubhouse and away from the crowds.

'Where are you taking me?' Juan asked her.

'It's a surprise, but I think you'll like it.'

They walked across the deserted football pitch. There was a full moon in the August night sky and it was almost as if the pitch was floodlit. Angel took off her shoes and walked barefoot, enjoying the feeling of the grass against her feet. They came to the groundsman's hut and Angel felt above the doorframe for the key, which she knew was kept there, as it had been one of hers and Gemma's hiding places when they got tired of watching the match. Inside there was just a table and chair, and a cleanly swept wooden floor. Angel took off Juan's jacket and laid it on the floor, and told him to turn around. She unzipped her bunny costume and slipped it off, along with everything else. Only when she was naked did she tell him to turn back round and she stood before him with the pale moonlight shimmering on her naked body.

'I'm ready now,' she whispered huskily.

Juan pulled her towards him and kissed her deeply, then whispered, 'Oh, baby, I've been wanting to make love with you for so long.'

Some time later Angel and Juan slipped back

into the party. Juan went to the bar to get them a drink to celebrate and Angel found herself face to face with Cal.

'Hi, Brad,' Angel exclaimed. 'Love the skirt!' She laughed, seeing Cal looking so obviously embarrassed by his costume.

'Yeah, well, it wouldn't have been my choice, bunny girl.'

Feeling emboldened by the alcohol and by having made love with Juan, Angel moved closer to him and said, 'So what do you think of my outfit then?'

Cal looked at her in the same way he had in the club all those months ago, with such desire that Angel's heart almost skipped a beat. 'Angie, I wanted to say before, I'm really . . .' But at that instant Mel joined the couple, looking less than pleased to see them locked in intimate conversation.

Angel broke the awkward moment by saying, 'I was just complimenting Cal on his skirt, almost as good as Brad's.'

The shutters had come down on Cal's face and he was back to keeping her at a distance once more. He smiled briefly but his eyes gave nothing away.

Mel put in bitchily, 'And you seem to be doing your best to be a Playboy tart, I mean, bunny, with that lovebite on your neck. And did you know your zip's undone?'

Angel was mortified and couldn't look at Cal.

Fortunately Juan came to her rescue. He put their drinks on a nearby table and whispered, 'Come on, let's dance some more,' and Angel was able to hide her confusion. Before she hit the dance floor she made an emergency trip to the Ladies with Gemma and borrowed some of her concealer for the offending mark on her neck and got her to zip up her costume.

'Yes,' she replied to Gemma's raised eyebrows. 'We did it, and it was good.'

'I'll need a full report tomorrow,' Gemma answered, smiling at her friend's boldness.

An hour later the party was drawing to a close. The music stopped and Tony stood behind a microphone. Immediately, Angel had butterflies for her brother because she knew how shy he was. He cleared his throat nervously, then began his short and sweet speech, talking about how well Cal had done and what a good friend he had been and how they were all going to miss him, concluding with: 'I just wanted to thank everyone for coming here tonight. I know you all, like me, want to wish Cal all the luck in the world at his new club.' And with that he thrust the microphone at Cal. Cal's speech was a little longer than her brother's and he took time to thank people who had been involved in his playing career, especially Angel's dad, whom he credited with putting him on his path to success. Frank blushed but looked pleased when Cal made everyone give him a round of applause.

'I also want to thank Michelle for cooking me all those meals and washing my kit; Tony for being such a good friend and Angie for putting up with me round her house so often.' At the mention of her name Angel started and found Cal looking straight at her. She stared back at him, feeling her heart pounding, but he swiftly moved on to thank Mel for organising such a great party. Gemma tried to cheer Angel up by pretending to throw up. Angel gave a small smile but after the euphoria of her passion with Juan, she found herself gripped with sadness at the prospect of Cal leaving Brighton. Who knows when she'd ever get to see him again. While it had been torture seeing him from time to time, that was better than nothing. There was no getting away from her feelings – Juan had been a wonderfully generous and sensuous man to make love with, but Angel couldn't help wishing that it had been Cal. She had tried burying her feelings for so long but now, fuelled by alcohol and a sense of loss, she felt her passion for him rise to the surface. Tears stung her eyes. She was desperate to leave the party before her emotions got the better of her but her mum and dad had other ideas and were deep in conversation with Gemma's parents.

And then suddenly Cal was in front of her again. 'Angie, I just wanted to say goodbye and good luck with your designing.' And he leant over and kissed her lightly on the cheek.

'Thanks, Cal,' she replied, amazed that he'd remembered her ambitions, thrilled that he had kissed her. 'And good luck at Chelsea, though you won't need it.'

Cal again looked as if he had something else to say but Mel the limpet magically appeared at his side. *She must have an inbuilt radar*, thought Angel bitterly. *Every time a woman comes within kissing distance of Cal she gets her bony arse over there.*

'See you then, Angie.'

'See you, Cal.'

Chapter 4

Angel's Delight

Suddenly the summer that Angel had thought so full of promise had lost its charm. She had imagined saving up all the money she'd need for the first year of her course, but so far, by the end of August, she'd only got enough for her first term. Gemma was now spending most of her free time with Tony so Angel hardly got to see her and she sorely missed her best friend. But, above all, she missed Cal. It had never just been about his good looks. She was in love with him, with his passion, his determination, his irresistible charm. And she loved him for all the emotions she sensed he kept back and which she wanted to unlock. In Cal she recognised a kindred spirit.

She tried to suppress these feelings, lose herself in her relationship with Juan. But their sweet little romance was about to be blown apart. Angel had noticed him becoming ever so slightly distant but as he still said he loved her at least ten times a day, she thought nothing more about it. Then, one night after work, Juan said he couldn't meet her, that he was tired and needed to have an early night. Something didn't ring true to Angel and when she went home she found she couldn't relax. She phoned Juan but his mobile was switched off – also very unusual. Refusing her mum's offer of supper, she got back on her bike and cycled round to his flat. She rang the bell but there was no answer and there was no light on. More and more she felt something wasn't right and by now she was desperate to see Juan. She decided to try all his favourite haunts. It had started to rain and Angel was soaked through but she couldn't give up and go home until she had found him. *I'm being silly*, she tried to tell herself. *He's just gone out to get something to eat*. But the feeling of unease wouldn't go away.

It was at the third restaurant she tried that she finally tracked him down. He was sitting at a table in the window, wearing a suit and looking more handsome and groomed than she had ever seen him. He was alone. She felt a huge surge of relief and was about to tap on the glass and alert him to her presence when a beautiful Spanish woman walked over to his table and sat down. Angel's stomach lurched; this wasn't so good. *I could get on my bike now and leave and ask him about it in the morning*, she thought, *or I can go in there and find out what's going on*. Never one to run away, Angel wiped the rain from her face and pushed open the restaurant door. Immediately one of the waiters came over, saying, 'I'm sorry, miss, we are fully booked.' Angel shook her head and walked over to Juan's table. The beautiful woman looked at her questioningly, then Juan turned round, going pale under his Mediterranean tan.

'Angel? What are you doing here?' he exclaimed, looking supremely awkward.

'I could ask you the same. Aren't you going to introduce me?'

Juan looked as if he wanted the floor to open up and swallow him.

'Um, this is Rosa.'

Rosa looked at Juan, then at Angel, obviously realising that something was going on.

'I'm Juan's fiancée,' she finally said, slowly. 'And who are you?'

Angel looked at Juan, speechless. All right, so she hadn't imagined being with Juan for ever, but to discover that she was simply his English bit on the side was incredibly hurtful. She mustered all the dignity she could.

'You'd better ask Juan,' she said, trying not to cry, then she turned on her heel and ran out of the restaurant and into the rain.

'Everything okay, Angie?' her mother asked her at breakfast the following morning, taking in her daughter's subdued expression and red-rimmed eyes.

'Fine,' Angel mumbled, trying and failing to force herself to eat any cereal. Realising she wasn't going to be able to eat anything, she got up from the table.

'I'm going to work early today so I'll see you later,' Angel said to her mum.

'Have a good day then,' her mum replied anxiously, obviously at a loss to know how to get Angel to open up.

The first thing Angel did when she arrived at work was track down Tim and tell him that she didn't want to work with Juan any more.

'Oh, have you little lovebirds had a tiff, then?' Tim couldn't resist taking the piss; she and Juan had been the talk of the lifeguards all summer.

'Actually, I just found out that he's engaged.'

That shut him up. 'I'll put you with Julie.' Angel didn't look at him, just nodded her thanks, grabbed her bike and set off along the cycle path that ran by the sea. Working with Julie meant that she'd be at the opposite end of the beach to Juan, a good mile separating them, and with any luck she wouldn't have to see him. She had been furious last night, unable to decide whether the situation with Cal or with Juan was more hurtful and humiliating, and even now, in the early morning August sunshine, her anger had lost none of its intensity. *How dare he treat me like this?* She was humiliated, hurt and very, very angry. Juan had never promised her any long-term commitment, but neither had he so much as hinted that he might already have a girlfriend, never mind a fiancée. She hated the fact that he'd lied to her.

All morning she stomped around, needing to be busy so as not to brood over him, but there really wasn't much to do as a lifeguard and she could hardly wish for an emergency just because her heart was broken. And Julie was one of the nosiest women Angel had ever met and wouldn't stop asking her questions about Juan, probing into their relationship. She knew immediately that something was up, but Angel refused to tell her, saying instead that Tim had wanted to move people around. She couldn't bear the thought of Julie's beady eyes lighting up when she heard about Juan's betrayal. Gossip for Julie was better than sex. *Though, maybe*, thought Angel to herself, *she's just had really bad sex.* Then she furiously tried to banish all thoughts of sex, but an image of Juan kissing her rose up in her head, and even though she hated him for what he'd done, part of her already missed the intimacy she'd shared with him.

'Excuse me, miss, can you tell me where the nearest restrooms are?'

Angel looked up at the middle-aged American woman and could tell even at a glance that this was someone who'd had a lot of work done. She must have been in her late forties, but there wasn't a line on her face, her boobs were as perky as an eighteen-year-old's, her lips looked collagen-plump and her teeth dazzling white.

Angel gave her directions but the woman seemed in no hurry to leave.

'I guess this is your summer job?'

'Yeah,' Angel replied, reluctant to make small talk.

'So what will you do after the summer?'

Angel frowned, wishing the woman would mind her own business, then shrugged. Hell, even talking to a complete stranger was better than enduring Julie's endless questions.

'I'm hoping to go to art school, but I haven't saved up enough money yet so I'll have to get another job.'

'Hmm.' The woman didn't seem to be listening but was staring intently at Angel's face as if sizing her up. Then she reached inside her designer bag, pulled out a card and held it out to Angel, who read *Carrie Rose, Agent.*

'Just so you know, I'm not a weirdo. I run a model agency in London and I would love to see some pictures of you.'

Angel laughed. 'Seriously?'

'Seriously. You are one good-looking girl. By the way, what's your name?'

Angel clambered up from her plastic chair, much more eager now, and shook the woman's hand.

'I'm Angel.'

Carrie smiled, or at least gave a Botoxed impersonation of a smile, and said, 'Well, your parents had the right idea. You sure look like an angel. In fact, there's no time like the present. I'm going to get my partner down here to shoot a roll straight away.' And she flipped up her mobile and started talking.

'Great,' she said, ending the call. 'He can be here in ten minutes.'

Angel looked at her watch. 'I'll just have to see if Julie can cover me.'

When Angel told Julie what was planned she pulled a face.

'Actually, I was supposed to be meeting Juan for lunch, he's just texted to ask me,' she said slyly, watching Angel's reaction out of the corner of her eye.

Bitch, thought Angel. 'Great, then he can tell you all about his fiancée and you won't have to ask me. And you weren't going till one, were you? So as soon as the photographer gets here and we've finished, you can go.'

While they waited, Carrie told Angel to brush out her hair. When Angel said anxiously that she didn't have any make-up with her, Carrie whipped out mascara and started layering Angel's lashes, then dabbed a bit of Elizabeth Arden Eight Hour Cream on her lips.

'I've never done any modelling before,' Angel said. 'How will I know what to do?'

'Just do whatever Ryan asks and don't worry, you'll either have it or you won't.'

Finally Ryan arrived, laden down with photographic equipment. He was a browner, male version of Carrie and his teeth were so white they nearly blinded her. *What is it with these people?* Angel thought. While Ryan set up his tripod, Carrie told Angel to take off her sweatshirt and shorts and stand by the shoreline in her red bikini. It was a cloudy day and Angel couldn't help shivering slightly. Finally Ryan was ready and he started calling out instructions: he wanted her hand on her hip; he wanted her pouting at the camera; he wanted her smiling, running her fingers through her hair; he wanted her to stick her boobs out more; he wanted her kneeling. Instead of feeling nervous, Angel found herself enjoying the experience. But then Carrie came over to her.

'It's looking great, Angel. What we'd like you to do now is take your top off and we can shoot some topless ones.'

This was not what Angel was expecting. Her apprehension must have shown on her face because Carrie rushed to reassure her. 'Just a few tasteful ones, Angel.'

'I'm not sure I feel comfortable doing that,' Angel replied. It might seem like a small thing to Carrie but to Angel, who had only just got used to feeling good about her body, it seemed like a big leap to take. And she wasn't at all sure she wanted to take it with Julie watching her every move, a look on her face like a slapped arse, and with people strolling past on the promenade.

'Well, of course it's up to you,' Carrie replied. 'But with your looks you'd be crazy not to – you'd make a perfect glamour model. And didn't you say that you wanted to save up money for your college course?'

'I think I need time to think about it,' Angel answered. 'Could I let you know on Monday?' Sensing that it really would be pointless to argue with Angel, Carrie pointed to her business card, which Angel had left on her towel.

'Make sure you call me. From what I've seen so far, I think you've definitely got what it takes. You could do so much better than this, Angel.' Carrie gestured at Brighton beach as if it was a shanty-town. 'Seize the moment.'

'So have you got any message to give to Juan?' Julie crept over and asked once Carrie and Ryan had gone.

Angel smiled sweetly at her. 'How about "fuck you"?'

Julie flushed with anger and marched off. But Angel couldn't help noticing that it was hard to flounce off in a huff on a pebbly beach, and she longed to shout out that Julie's cellulite was wobbling.

The rest of the day passed in something of a haze. Instead of brooding over Juan, Angel now had a whole other world to think about, a world that seemed to have opened up to her completely out of the blue. Looking at Carrie's card again, Angel felt a bubble of excitement about her prospects. She just needed to get her head round the topless bit. She wished she could talk it through with her mum and dad but knew they would freak out at the thought of her doing any topless modelling, as would Tony. Gemma was the only one she could talk to and she wasted no time phoning her and asking her to meet up after work.

At six she was unlocking her bike and preparing to cycle to Gemma's when Juan jogged up beside her.

'Hello, Angel.'

She gave him the briefest of glances and then looked away coldly. He looked sad and defeated, not at all his usual joyous self.

'I've got nothing to say to you,' she muttered and she carried on unlocking her bike, intending to ride off and ignore him.

'Please, let me talk to you, just for a minute.'

Angel gave a deep sigh. 'Okay, but I haven't got long.' She pushed her bike along the sea front at a swift pace, Juan falling into step next to her. The distance between them seemed alien; she was so used to the feel of his arm round her.

'I should have told you about Rosa.'

'Too fucking right!' Angel exclaimed, forgetting her intention to play it cool.

'When I met you I thought you and I were just going to have fun, not be serious. But then I fell in love with you. And I couldn't tell you about Rosa, because I didn't want to lose you.'

Angel glanced at Juan. He looked miserable. *Good, serves him right*, she thought.

'I'm going home at the end of the week and I don't want to leave with this bad feeling between us. I hurt you and I'm sorry and I want you to know that if there wasn't Rosa, there would only be you, it's just that we've been engaged for a year and our families are expecting us to get married. And I know that much as I love you, you don't really love me.'

They had both stopped walking. Juan was looking pleadingly at Angel. She shifted uncomfortably. He was right. And it really didn't seem like he had set out to hurt her deliberately. She thought suddenly of Cal and of how he had wanted her to pretend that nothing had ever happened between them. Hurt as she was, she knew Juan wasn't the love of her life. She could tell him to piss off or they could end the summer as friends. Her choice.

'You really hurt me, Juan,' she said finally. 'I felt so close to you and I trusted you.'

'Please forgive me, Angel, I don't want to go back home and think that you hate me. You are so precious to me.'

'I don't know if I forgive you yet, but I don't want us to be enemies,' Angel said, smiling at his flowery speech. She would miss him.

Juan took her hand and kissed it. Then they hugged. Angel was the first to pull away.

'*Adiós*, Juan, I hope everything goes well for you.'

'And for you, Angel, and I know it will.'

Angel got on her bike and cycled away, dodging all the rollerbladers and dog walkers. Tears welled up in her eyes. She probably wouldn't see Juan again but it wasn't, after all, the worst thing that had ever happened to her. She would get over him.

That night, Gemma was surprised to see Angel's smiling face. She had thought she'd be consoling a heartbroken friend but instead she found Angel full of excitement at the day's events.

'So what do you think I should do about this modelling stuff? Should I do the topless shots?' Angel asked.

'Definitely,' Gemma replied quickly. 'There's nothing wrong with it, you've got a beautiful body, why not use it? It's not like they're asking you to do porn or anything, after all.'

'And it would be great if I could earn some money as a model.' With the lifeguard job paying so little, she knew now there was no way she could fund her college course unless something else came up. And maybe she could even get a place of her own with Gemma. For the first time Angel had a feeling that life had definite possibilities for her. There was a big, wide world out there just waiting for her, a world where she mattered, where no one made her feel guilty and where she could seize her own future. She had been spotted!

'I'm sure this is the start of something big,' Gemma told her, glad to share Angel's exciting news. 'Haven't I always said that you should be a model?'

They drank and giggled their way through the evening and Angel crashed at Gemma's that night, after both girls consumed far too many cocktails. Luckily, the next day was a Sunday and Angel didn't have to work. Gemma's mum brought them breakfast in bed, then she and Gemma went to the stables to check on Storm. In the afternoon, the two girls lay on the sofa, painting each other's nails and watching *Lost* on DVD, and eventually Gemma's dad got a takeaway curry for them all and Tony joined them for dinner.

'You're so lucky,' Angel sighed as they curled up in Gemma's double bed that night.

'Why?' Gemma asked.

'Your mum and dad love you so much.'

'Yours love you too, Angel.'

'I'm sure they do in their own way, it's just that I've never really felt it. It's like they're doing their duty but they don't really love me for who I am. I bet they wish they'd adopted someone else.'

Gemma was silent for a few minutes, but in the

darkness she hugged her friend, then told her, 'I'm sure that's not true. And, anyway, I love you for who you are.'

Angel smiled, then said cheekily, 'You bloody lezzer! And I don't know if I'll be able to talk to you when I become rich and famous!'

Gemma threw a pillow at her head by way of an answer.

'Okay, Angel, tilt your head back slightly and smile,' Ryan called out as Angel posed, dressed only in her red bikini bottoms. It wasn't anything like as scary as she had imagined. In fact, in the impersonal setting of the hotel room, with the camera focused on her and Ryan calling encouragements, Angel found to her surprise that the role of the sultry topless model came to her quite easily. Carrie was in seventh heaven and at the end of the shoot declared dramatically, 'Girl, you've got it. I'll know for sure when I see the pictures but I'm almost one-hundred-per-cent certain. I'll call you in the next couple of days.'

For the next two days Angel lived in a glorious state of anticipation. Every time her mobile rang she prayed it was Carrie, but by the end of the third day she had started to doubt that anything was ever going to come of it and disappointment had set in. But at six o'clock, just as she was sitting down to supper with her mum and dad, her mobile went.

'Can't that wait?' Frank said in exasperation as

Angel immediately leapt from her seat and grabbed her phone. He hadn't been overly impressed when Angel told them about being spotted by an agent at the beach.

Not bothering to reply, Angel answered her phone. It was Carrie.

'Angel,' she exclaimed, and Angel quickly moved further away from the table so that her parents wouldn't hear every word of Carrie's excited babble. 'I love the pictures, love them! Love them! And the great news is I've just had a call from a photographer and he needs someone for a shoot tomorrow – are you up for it?'

Angel was temporarily speechless, then managed to splutter, 'Really?'

'Yes, really,' Carrie repeated indulgently and laughed. She promised to text her the details, telling her that she would need to be in London by midday, and said goodbye quickly.

'Good news, love?' Michelle asked as Angel came back to the table, her face glowing with excitement.

'I think so! Carrie wants me to join her agency and I've got a shoot tomorrow afternoon!'

Michelle looked pleased for her daughter and went to hug her, but Frank was stony-faced.

'And what kind of photographs will they be then? Because I'm not having you posing half naked.'

'They'll be glamour shots,' Angel replied, wondering herself what exactly that meant. 'Carrie said they would be tasteful, probably swimwear.' That last bit was definitely a lie – Angel knew that she'd be posing topless for some of the photos, but Frank would go ballistic if she told him that.

'Um,' Frank replied, managing to convey disappointment and disapproval in one tiny word.

Feeling too excited to eat, Angel excused herself from the table and raced round to Gemma's, where her news was received in a far more positive way than at home. The two stayed up for ages, speculating about what might be in store for Angel tomorrow.

'You don't think it will be any more than topless, do you?' Angel asked anxiously, voicing what had been on her mind since Carrie called.

'Well, if they ask you, just don't do it,' Gemma said. 'And whatever you do, don't agree to anything before you find out exactly how much you're getting paid. And don't sign anything you're not sure about,' she added firmly.

Angel's head was spinning. 'I wish you could come with me,' she said longingly, feeling very nervous.

'You'll be fine,' Gemma reassured her. 'Just be strong, and enjoy it – after all, what have you got to lose?'

The next day, as Angel traipsed up three flights of stairs to the photographer's studio, she tried to hold onto Gemma's wise words. She had been expecting to walk into a modern, luxurious studio and instead found herself in a run-down building somewhere in West London. At last she arrived at the door and, mustering all her courage, she rang the buzzer. It was flung open by a jolly-looking man in his fifties, dressed in jeans and a denim shirt and in the middle of an animated conversation on his mobile. He mouthed 'Angel?' and gestured her in. *He doesn't look like a serial killer or a pervert*, thought Angel with relief, then scrapped that thought because what was a serial killer supposed to look like? He would hardly be wearing a sign on his shirt advertising the fact that he liked to kill people and chop them up into tiny pieces, then eat them for dinner washed down with a glass of Chianti!

As the man talked on, Angel took in her surroundings. She was in a large studio with a camera set up on a tripod at one end in front of a large white screen. Everywhere she looked the walls were covered with pictures of women, or, to be more precise, topless women. Angel had never seen so many pairs of breasts all at once. She panicked. These women all looked so beautiful and glamorous, she suddenly felt incredibly self-conscious. And intimidated. How could she possibly compete with those perfect tanned bodies, groomed hair and immaculately made-up faces? And, she couldn't help noticing, bigger breasts. She turned round and looked at the door. She still had a choice: she could go now, right this minute, back to Brighton, back to Julie and her job as a lifeguard. Back to a life without possibilities. Or she could stay here and see what happened. For a split second she was tempted to run, but just as she started moving the man finished his phone call and came rushing over to give her a huge hug and kiss her on both cheeks.

'Angel! I'm Richard. And you've saved my life. Thank you so much for coming in at such short notice, darling.'

Angel had to smile at his exuberance; he was so over the top and flamboyant.

'Now, I've got Danni coming in to do your hair and make-up any minute now, so why don't we have a coffee while we wait?'

Angel rarely drank coffee but she felt too shy to say so, so she forced down the stuff quickly. Her stomach gurgled loudly in response. She'd been too nervous to have breakfast or lunch. She hoped Richard hadn't noticed.

'Hungry?' Richard asked kindly.

Angel nodded.

'No breakfast, no lunch?' he asked again.

Angel nodded again. He sighed. 'You girls, what are you like! We're going to be working hard for the next couple of hours and I don't want you fainting on me. I'd better make you a sandwich.'

As Richard busied himself in his tiny kitchen, situated in a corner of the large studio, Danni arrived with a large make-up case. Angel had been praying that she would be someone friendly, someone to put her at ease. Luckily, Danni couldn't have been nicer. She was an attractive twenty-something Aussie, with a dry sense of humour and a laid-back attitude. While she unpacked her case, unhurriedly getting out pots and tubes, pencils and lipsticks, Angel felt herself starting to relax. These were nice people, so open and friendly, so *normal*. Surely nothing bad was going to happen. Richard presented her with the sandwich and watched her as she ate it, ordering her to finish every last crumb. She was only too happy to obey – she really was starving and never usually skipped meals. When she had taken the last bite and the last sip of water, Danni got started on her face.

'People like you make my job so easy,' she joked, smoothing foundation onto Angel's skin. 'You've got such a perfect complexion, you lucky girl!'

Angel blushed; she still wasn't used to getting compliments from strangers. As Danni expertly worked on her face, Angel sat back and enjoyed the feathery strokes on her face. There was something very soothing about being made up, surrendering control to someone else, someone who so obviously knew what she was doing. She closed her eyes at Danni's request and when she opened them she was stunned at the transformation.

The girl staring back at her looked so much older that Angel hardly recognised her shimmery, glamorous reflection, so much more polished and sexy, almost like one of the girls from the photographs.

'You look great,' Danni told her reassuringly, seeing her confusion. 'Stunning.'

Richard wandered over to take a look. 'You look gorgeous, darling, well done. Now pop along to the dressing room and choose some underwear and a pair of shoes and we can get started.'

As soon she walked into the dressing room and saw the piles of underwear Angel's nerves started up again. *Oh, God, what if I can't do it, what if I don't look right?* she fretted, rifling through the underwear and at a complete loss to know what to wear. There were thongs and knickers of every colour and of every material: lace, satin, silk, cotton, Lycra. *I'll give this one a miss*, Angel thought to herself, picking up a tiny leather G-string studded with diamante and hastily dropping it.

'Don't worry,' Richard called in to her. 'It's all clean!'

In the end, Angel went for a shocking pink lace thong and matching bra and slipped on a pair of gold stilettos. Before going back into the studio she looked at herself in the mirror, tossed back her long hair and took a deep breath. 'Just go for it, you've got nothing to lose,' she told her reflection, willing herself to be strong. She marched back into the studio confidently, as if she always paraded around in next to nothing in front of total strangers, and took her place in front of the camera. There were no props to hide behind, just her, a white backdrop and Richard looking through the lens at her. This was it.

'You look fabulous, darling!' Richard called out. 'Love the pink and gold combo, now let's get started.

'Hand on your hip, look at the camera, that's it, stick out your boobs a bit more, smile and hold it.' And as he clicked away and shouted out encouragement, Angel's nerves disappeared. Instead of worrying about whether she was doing the right thing she found that she was enjoying herself. She concentrated on getting the pose right, breathing in slightly, pushing out her boobs, cheekily pulling the side of her thong, thinking only of the camera.

After fifteen minutes, Richard called out, 'Ready to try some topless shots now, darling? I'm loving what you're doing.'

To her own surprise she didn't hesitate, she just shook back her hair, undid her bra, whirled it round her head and then tossed it to the far side of the studio – much to Richard and Danni's amusement.

He continued to call out instructions but Angel found that she knew what to do almost instinctively. She smiled, turned, pouted, shook her hair, played with different poses and attitudes. She could tell from Richard's smile that she was doing well.

An hour and a half later, after several changes of underwear and make-up retouches, they stopped.

'Fabulous,' Richard said simply. 'I don't get a girl like you very often. You've got real star quality, Angel, a natural talent.' He must have seen her doubtful smile because he hastened to add, 'And I promise you, I don't say that to all the girls, very far from it, as Danni will tell you.'

Danni nodded enthusiastically, giving Angel a smile and thumbs-up. Angel was on cloud nine. It was such an amazing feeling, discovering that she was good at something and being praised for it. She had never felt that special. And here she was, doing what thousands of girls would envy her for. And to her huge surprise she had loved every minute of the experience.

'Don't you think I'm a bit flat-chested for this type of modelling?' she asked anxiously. She couldn't help comparing her 32B breasts with the 32DDs all around her.

'No, you're perfect just the way you are and don't let anyone tell you otherwise!'

As soon as she left the studio she called Gemma and filled her in on how the shoot had gone. She was in a bubble of happiness on the train back to Brighton; she wanted to smile at everyone.

The bubble burst as soon as she stepped through her front door. Still fired up by what she'd done, Angel raced into the kitchen where Frank, Michelle and Tony were having dinner.

'They liked me! I'm going to be in the paper next week!' She stood in front of them, grinning excitedly, and looked at them expectantly.

Frank angrily pushed his plate away. 'You should have asked us first,' he said loudly. 'Who are these people, taking advantage of a young girl like that?'

Angel looked at him, feeling her happiness drain away. Trust him to bring her down. But he wasn't finished. 'And what kind of photos are they, anyway?'

'Bikini shots,' she answered defiantly. But she wasn't able to meet his eye and he stared at her.

'Angie. Tell me the truth. Are you doing topless modelling?' He moved over to where she was standing and grabbed her shoulders, forcing her to look at him. 'Are you?'

'Jesus Christ, Angel, you're not topless, are you? I don't want every lad at college looking at your tits,' Tony put in furiously.

Angel stared angrily at her dad and her brother, then looked at her mother, who was helplessly watching the scene between her husband and daughter. Angel shrugged bitterly. What had she expected their reaction to be? They were only thinking of themselves. They had never seen her for who she really was and what she could do. And they couldn't see what a difference it could make to her life.

She turned on her heel, blinded by her tears. 'You can't stop me,' she shouted back, catching her mother's stricken expression. 'I'm doing it and that's it.'

*

For the next three weeks, Angel stayed at Gemma's and travelled to London every day for more shoots with Richard. The paper had loved the first pictures of Angel and booked her to do a whole week of Page 3, which was very unusual on the glamour circuit. A Hollywood film about a stripper was about to open in London and the paper wanted their own take on the film, with Angel performing her own striptease for the readers. She couldn't believe her luck when Carrie gave her the news.

'This is a massive break, darling,' Carrie had told her on the phone while Angel was at Richard's. 'I've a hunch that you'll be going places very soon.'

Angel laughed. 'I'm already going places, Carrie,' she replied, thinking that she could be stuck in some boring dead-end job and instead she was having the most fun ever.

'This is just the beginning, take my word for it,' Carrie answered. 'Speak to you later, darling, I have to fly now.'

Angel was still smiling to herself as she slipped into her first outfit of the shoot – a purple and black corset, suspender belt, stockings and a black lace thong – and checked out her appearance in the dressing-room mirror. Danni had put Angel's hair up and given her smoky eyes and red vampy lips.

'Ooh, very Moulin Rouge,' Richard exclaimed as she walked into the studio. 'I love it, darling!'

'So do I, *dahling*,' Angel answered cheekily.

Richard laughed. 'You're learning, now get your arse over here and we can get going.'

Angel was having a ball. She had such a good rapport with Richard and he loved the fact that she had so many ideas of her own about how she should look. The two of them bantered and joked their way through the shoot. The paper wanted Angel to remove an item of underwear each day so that on the last day she'd be naked. *Talk about a steep learning curve*, Angel thought; it was less than a month ago that she had worried about posing topless and now here she was, about to reveal all, or nearly all. She was lying on a white fur rug on the studio floor, stark naked and trying to find the best position to pose in which wouldn't reveal everything she had.

'I think it's best if I'm on all fours, sideways to the camera, with one knee slightly in front of the other so you can't see my you-know-what.'

Richard looked through the lens and called out, 'That's the one, hold it. Perfect.'

If only the rest of my life could be going as well as my work, Angel thought as she travelled back to Brighton on the train. It was such an exciting time for her, but there was a pit of loneliness inside her, the sad realisation that none of her family seemed to want to share her good fortune and be happy for her. Neither Tony nor her dad were speaking to her. Although Angel was used to her dad's disapproval, it still smarted to be cut out so completely, and Tony's was doubly hurtful. They were so different but they had always got on well, looked out for each other and been a part of each other's lives. Now she felt adrift, completely isolated from the family. Her mum came round to see her at Gemma's one night when Frank was at football training, but it wasn't a very good meeting. Michelle was upset about the rift and anxious to make up with her daughter, but she didn't have any suggestions about how to heal things.

'What about doing fashion modelling instead, love?' she asked. 'I don't think your dad would have a problem with that.'

Angel sighed. 'I've already told you, I'm not tall or skinny enough to be that kind of model, and anyway, I love what I'm doing now. There's nothing wrong with it, it's not like I'm doing porn!'

It was so frustrating, why didn't they get it? But as far back as she could remember, it had always been the same – whether it was her passion for riding or her artistic ambitions, her mum and dad simply didn't understand her. She might have guessed that she couldn't expect any support from her parents with her modelling ambitions.

'You really want this many?' The newsagent looked dubiously at Angel as he counted out ten copies of *The Sun*. Angel nodded, trying to be casual. 'Yeah, someone I know is in it,' she said, all the while trying to contain her excitement. As soon as she got out of the shop she opened the paper at Page 3. Her first ever photo shoot in a national paper. She couldn't move for a minute, spellbound by her own picture. She laughed delightedly as she raced back to show Gemma. They spread the paper out on the living-room carpet, alternately staring at the pictures of Angel and laughing hysterically.

'I can't believe it's you!' Gemma kept saying.

'I can't believe it's me either!' It just didn't seem possible that she was in the paper and was going to be looked at by millions of people! Gemma wanted her to take the day off so they could celebrate, but Angel had several castings in London, which she knew she couldn't miss. Reluctantly, she got her things together and headed off to the station. On the train her thoughts turned to Cal. She wondered if he had seen her picture and, if he had, what did he think? Would he see what she so wanted him to – that the girl from Brighton was now a woman?

It had been two months since she'd said goodbye to him but her feelings for him hadn't changed. She still wanted him, still loved him. He was in regular contact with Tony and her dad – they had both been up to watch him play for Chelsea reserves last night, but he hadn't asked Angel. All she knew was that his football career was going from strength to strength and he was still with Mel. According to the local gossip grapevine, she was desperate for him to ask her to move in with him in London and so far he hadn't.

Chapter 5

London Calling

My first house, Angel thought happily as she padded around the tiny one-bedroom flat in Belsize Park in North London, putting up photographs of her and Gemma in an attempt to make it feel more like home. She was renting the flat from Carrie, who had offered her a very reasonable arrangement, because although her modelling career was starting to take off, she was hardly loaded. Her mum hadn't wanted her to go and had begged her to stay but Angel's mind was made up. It was time for a change and she had to seize the opportunity she'd been given. It was time to say goodbye to the old Angel and embrace the new.

Her dad had sat in silence during the drive to the station but at the last minute he hugged Angel tightly to him and gruffly told her to take care of herself. And she had made things up with Tony, as Gemma had threatened to dump him if he didn't stop being so uptight about his sister's choice of career. So it was with a much lighter heart than during the past few weeks that she came to London. And here she was now, in the capital. Close to Camden with its great weekend market, which Angel loved browsing through to discover a vintage top or dress, something that no one else would be wearing, and within walking distance of Hampstead with its chic bars and cafés. She was close to Hampstead Heath, so she could get away from people and noise and cars and escape into open space if she wanted to. The first few days, she couldn't wait to go exploring, getting such a buzz from being on her own, in her own flat, in the city. She felt free as she walked around. There were no memories here and no people to remind her of the past and the small world she had left behind. But it was also strange, suddenly being free to do whatever she wanted – she could go to bed whenever, wake up when she liked, eat whenever she wanted without her mum nagging her to come down from her room. It was both liberating and terrifying.

But Carrie kept nagging her to go out socialising.

'Listen, darling, it's not enough to be good at your job, there are hundreds of other girls out there who are models. In order to stand out you need to get noticed by the press, make a name for yourself,' she told, or rather ordered, her when Angel dropped by her office.

Since the pictures of her striptease had appeared in the paper, she'd become a hot property and Carrie was keen to cash in on her success. Practically every other day Angel had a casting or a shoot. Today she'd done a shoot for a lingerie catalogue with three other glamour girls and it had been a real eye-opener.

One of the girls, Andrea, a dead ringer for Thandie Newton, was lovely, down to earth, funny and not at all full of herself. The other two – Lisa and Vicki – were absolute bitches who had made it their mission to be as unpleasant as possible to Angel from the minute she had walked into the studio, barely bothering to say hello to her, and looking her up and down as if she was something they'd stepped in.

'How long have you been modelling for, then?' demanded Lisa when they were in the dressing room, getting ready. She was an overly made-up blonde, who would have been pretty if she hadn't looked as if she was trying so hard.

'Nearly two months now,' Angel replied.

Lisa sniffed dismissively. 'It must be beginner's luck then, you getting on Page 3 so soon. Don't expect it to last, though.'

'Who thought up your name?' asked Vicki, the other model, a blonde clone of Lisa.

'No one, it's my name,' Angel answered, not liking the way the girls were looking at her. It made her feel as if she was back in the school playground.

'Leave her alone, you two,' Andrea called out. 'You were new to this game once yourselves, about a hundred years ago!'

The blonde clones shot Andrea an evil look and then tottered out onto the balcony together to have a cigarette and no doubt carry on with their bitching.

'Ignore them,' Andrea told her. 'They're just jealous. And while they're having a fag let's grab the best thongs.'

Angel was very relieved that Andrea was there because Lisa and Vicki didn't get less bitchy during the shoot. There were snide little digs about her hair (*'Brunette – isn't that a bit last season'*), her nails (*'Oh, we didn't know the natural look was in'*) and her breasts (*'Ever thought of having a boob job?'*). But Angel had the last laugh when Dawn, the photographer, a very straight talker, used her and Andrea more than the other two and told Vicki she'd put on weight.

As Angel and Andrea walked out of the studio together, they swapped numbers. 'You'll have to come out with me and the girls one night,' Andrea said. 'Not all models are like that pair of witches!' Angel was glad for the invite. Apart from Cal, who she wouldn't have dreamt of phoning, she didn't know anyone in London.

But she didn't want to be bullied into socialising by Carrie. Now, she shrugged, looking at Carrie across her desk. Going out and clubbing was one thing with Gemma, in a place where she knew people; it was another thing entirely to do it in a huge city, without friends nearby.

Carrie fixed her with her piercing blue eyes (which Angel was convinced were blue contact lenses) and said, 'This is non-negotiable, Angel, I really need you to get out there.'

She didn't need to add, *or I'll drop you*, but her meaning was clear.

'Okay, I'll do my best,' Angel replied, irritated that Carrie had started attaching conditions to their working relationship. But she owed her so much, she quickly reminded herself. Surely it wouldn't be too much to ask to go to a few parties.

'You don't have to do anything,' Carrie answered. 'One of my girls can't make it to the film premiere of the new James Bond movie tomorrow night, so why don't you go? And there's an after-party. Turn up, get yourself photographed, I'll be happy.' And she thrust the invitation at Angel. 'It will be very good for your profile.'

Angel spent the run-up to the event worrying about what to wear. She wasn't earning that much money yet so couldn't afford to blow it in designer shops. In the end she scoured the second-hand boutiques in Camden and found a sexy black silk Chinese-style dress, which fitted her perfectly and emphasised all her curves, with splits up each side showing off her tanned slim legs. Angel reasoned that she was known for showing off her breasts, so tonight she'd keep them covered up and show off her legs instead.

That done, she had her hair cut and coloured. She was still brunette, but now had gold and bronze highlights running through her hair. 'Just to give you a bit of a lift, darling, and your hair some extra depth. Not that you really need it, because you look sensational,' said Jez, a seriously camp hairdresser and a complete sweetheart, recommended by Danni.

Then it was off to get her nails done – Angel's least favourite part of grooming as she was a closet nail-biter. The glamour models she'd met so far all had nails that were nearly as long as Tanya Turner's, which Angel thought was hilarious and not her at all. She couldn't imagine how they actually did anything like put on a pair of tights without laddering them or inserting a tampon (ouch, best not to think about that one), or why any man would want a set of talons like that near his tackle . . . She preferred her nails short and natural-looking, but today she made an exception and had them painted scarlet.

Finally, back home in the bath, came the removal of practically all her body hair. In her line of work it would have been career suicide to show off stubbly armpits or even a hint of a pube. When she first started Angel had tried waxing, but she couldn't wait for the hairs to grow back, plus having a Brazilian wax, however good the results, was one of the most excruciating experiences of her life, and one that she never wanted to repeat – she couldn't imagine childbirth to be any more painful than that. Finally, a hair-free (well, practically, except for a landing strip) Angel called up Gemma in a panic, worrying about going to the event on her own.

'Pull yourself together!' Gemma told her, just a few minutes before the car was due to pick her up. 'It'll be a laugh.' But Angel didn't feel much like laughing when the car dropped her off at the end of the red carpet and she was confronted with having to walk down the whole length of it to get into the building. She hung back a bit, temporarily overwhelmed by the crowds of people waiting behind the crash barriers, shouting out the names of the stars whose attention they wanted to attract. Everywhere she looked were glamorous, beautiful women in evening dresses and handsome men in suits, familiar faces from the film, music and TV worlds – *Oh my God, was that Madonna, she was so tiny!* In a daze she also saw Elle Macpherson, Sharon Stone, Victoria Beckham looking gorgeous in her Roberto Cavalli, Christian Slater and the hot gardener from *Desperate Housewives*. She was half hoping that none of the waiting photographers would notice *her*, but no such luck.

'Angel, over here,' one of the photographers called out, a cry taken up by several others of the pack, and she found herself automatically smiling for the cameras as they flashed in front of her. *This wasn't so bad*, she thought with relief, slowly making her way into the huge cinema foyer, which was packed with celebrities. A wave of shyness came over her again and she suddenly felt that she had no right to be with all these famous people. She was just a young girl from Brighton. But then she noticed a woman whose only claim to fame was the famous married footballer she had slept with and then told the world about in graphic detail. *Well, if she's here, I shouldn't feel bad. At least I've been invited because of my work!* Angel thought, perking up. She despised anyone who would sell a story about someone they had been involved with – to betray someone who had trusted them seemed the lowest of the low.

She made sure she was sitting as far away as possible from the kiss-and-tell woman in the auditorium. She looked in vain for anyone she knew, vowing that next time she had an invitation to one of these events, she would take someone with her or refuse to go. She had wanted to bring Gemma but Carrie said she only had one ticket. The film was good, but Angel was too aware of her surroundings to be able to lose herself in it. Next came the party at Sugar's, an exclusive club in Mayfair. Once again, Angel had to steel herself to go in, feeling intimidated by the crowds of glamorous people all chatting and waving to each other. Clearly, everyone knew someone here. Luckily, just as she was contemplating turning round and going home, she bumped into Andrea.

'Hiya, babe,' she exclaimed, giving Angel two air-kisses, the obligatory welcome of anyone in the celeb world, as Angel was discovering. 'How are you?'

'Glad to see you!' Angel replied with relief. 'I don't know anyone here at all. I feel like a right Norman No Mates, I'm about to go home.'

'Don't be daft, come and meet my friends,' Andrea exclaimed and quickly introduced Angel to the group she was with, which included two footballers, a TV presenter and a soap star. At first, Angel felt very shy and tongue-tied – she had never been around such famous people before, but gradually she found her feet and before she knew it she was chatting to Thierry Henry and Freddie Ljungberg about how the season was going. At first she could tell they thought she was just another bimbo glamour girl, but because Angel knew her football it wasn't long before they had revised that opinion. But just as she was enjoying the banter, the blonde clones, Lisa and Vicki, turned up and, looking at Angel through narrowed eyes, tried to slide in between the two footballers.

'Nice dress,' said Vicki, sounding as if she thought it was anything but nice. She herself was wearing a turquoise satin slip dress, which her boobs were bursting out of.

'Thanks,' Angel replied, then dropped her voice and whispered sympathetically, 'How's the diet going?'

Vicki turned scarlet with anger under the layers of fake tan and Angel realised that she'd better back off – it wasn't as if she thought she had any chance with the footballers. And even though it would have been fun watching Lisa and Vicki trying and failing to get their attention, she pretended she needed the bathroom and slipped away from the group. The club was packed and she had to weave carefully through the throng of people. Suddenly her way forward was blocked. A boyishly good-looking blond man stood right in front of her, making no attempt to move. She tried to slip around him, muttering apologies, but he blocked her escape attempts. Finally, she looked up and said, more loudly, 'Excuse me, can I get past?' His smiling face looked familiar and Angel realised with a jolt that he was Mickey Waters. *The* Mickey Waters, lead singer of the boy band Wanted.

'Actually, no, I don't think you can,' he said. 'I was just about to come over and talk to you.'

'Oh,' Angel replied, in some confusion. 'Do you know Andrea then?'

'Nope, I wanted to meet you.'

Angel felt a shiver of excitement run down her spine. Mickey was incredibly handsome, and such a star! She had never met anyone so famous before. Wanted had been around for a year and taken the charts by storm, having more singles going to number one in their first week than any other band since The Beatles.

Angel looked at him, not quite able to grasp the fact that someone who could talk to anyone here was seeking *her* out. He insisted on buying her a drink and they spent the rest of the night together, huddled in a corner, chatting and flirting and oblivious to everyone around them. He was extremely easy to talk to, confident and charming. He reminded her a little bit of Juan and she realised how much she had missed having that male attention. Mickey had seen her photos and wanted to know all about her, how her career was going, where she was living, what she thought of London. In turn, Angel asked him about the band. She had never met a pop star before.

'But I haven't asked you the most important question yet,' Mickey said teasingly towards the end of the night. 'Do you have a boyfriend?'

Angel shook her head quickly. 'No, no, I'm single. What about you?' she added hesitantly, suddenly very much wanting only one answer.

Mickey slowly nodded. 'Me too.' The two of them smiled at each other. *God, I really fancy him!* thought Angel, surprised at the intensity of her feelings. He was lovely, warm and funny. And he was gorgeous, with pretty-boy looks, intensely blue eyes, blond hair and a muscular body, which looked pretty fit all over, if his chest was anything to go by. She was getting quite a good look, as his shirt was unbuttoned to just above his waist.

'Want to get out of here?'

She nodded, still unable to believe her luck. The best-looking, most famous guy in the club had been talking to her and her alone all night. She'd noticed girls all around them throwing her envious glances, and Vicki and Lisa were skulking close by, watching jealously. Only Andrea had occasionally given her a thumbs-up, smiling at her encouragingly.

'Fancy coming back to mine? I've got a great view from my apartment and we could have a drink.' He took her hand as they made their way out of the club. Outside, Angel breathed in the fresh air, glad to be away from the noise and the crowds. Part of her thought, *Yes, why not?* But the other side thought, *I bet he doesn't just want to talk. And if he really wants me, he can wait.*

She shook her head firmly. 'I've got a shoot tomorrow afternoon, I really should go back and get some sleep.' She looked at her watch, hardly believing that it was already half past two in the morning.

'Okay, well at least let me give you a lift back and I can get your number and stuff.' He smiled easily, pointing at his limo waiting by the kerb. *No harm in that,* Angel thought as she got in. As soon as the door was shut, Mickey pulled her towards him and started kissing her. *Wow, what a fantastic kisser.* Her head was still saying to hold back, to wait, but she was helpless against the desire building up within her as Mickey started caressing her. And suddenly her body was saying *yes, let him, this feels so good.*

Finally she pulled away, tried to control her breathing, and murmured, 'What about the driver?'

'He can't see us through the screen and, anyway, he's paid to keep his eyes on the road.' Mickey unbuttoned her dress and stroked her nipple, slowly, tantalisingly, then bent down and started kissing each one, which provoked a powerful chain reaction in other parts of her body. She moaned with pleasure as Mickey touched her thigh, gradually moving higher and higher until his fingers brushed against her French knickers and began caressing her. She felt herself unfurling, yielding to his touch, and became temporarily oblivious to her surroundings, to everything but Mickey. Suddenly, the driver stopped and Angel was jolted out of her haze of lust. She pulled away from Mickey and hastily rearranged her dress, saw that they'd braked for a red light. If Mickey was disappointed he didn't show it, instead he smiled and leant closer to her, whispering, 'That was just a taster.'

That night, for the first time in ages, Angel didn't go to sleep thinking of Cal. Instead, as she closed her eyes she allowed herself to imagine that she was back in the limo with Mickey. And this time they didn't stop . . .

When Angel woke up the next morning, the first thing she did was reach for her phone. Yesss! There was a text from Mickey. He must have sent it as soon as he got in: *How about dinner tonight x*. Angel thought about being cool, waiting another couple of hours or so in order not to look too keen, but she was so excited she couldn't hold back. *Yes x*, she texted back. And then, desperate to talk to someone about Mickey, she called Gemma, even though it was still early. She was expecting her friend to be pleased for her, but after she'd revealed what had happened and how much she thought she fancied him, Gemma didn't say anything for a moment, then, sounding cautious, said 'I don't know, Angel, I think he's got a bit of a reputation. And you always see pictures of him falling out of a club, looking pissed. Just watch yourself.'

'Oh, come on, Gemma, he didn't seem like that!' Angel replied crossly. 'And I thought you'd be pleased that I'd finally met someone else.'

'I am,' Gemma said soothingly, realising that she should have been more enthusiastic. 'I just don't want you to get hurt.'

'I'm only going out for dinner with him,' Angel replied, exasperated. She had been hoping for a good old gossip about Mickey, discussing all the juicy details, but here was Gemma, pouring cold water on the whole thing. They talked about other things for a minute, then, in order to end the conversation, Angel pretended she had to get ready for the shoot, because she didn't want to show how angry she was with her friend. It wasn't until she'd stomped off to the gym to burn off some anger and a fair amount of sexual frustration that she calmed down.

She had a shoot with Richard in the afternoon, this time for one of the other tabloids, which Angel enjoyed because she got to be slightly more adventurous with her poses. Today was about what lingerie to wear for a mini-break with a new lover and Angel had great fun posing in sheer pink camisoles and French knickers, saucy leopard-print bras and matching briefs, and a scarlet lace bra and matching thong. Richard had brought in some furniture, so she reclined on the pink velvet sofa for several shots and then sat at the cute white dressing table.

Over the last two months she'd grown really fond of him, and loved working with him. She found herself confiding in him about Mickey as Danni touched up her make-up in between poses.

'He sounds lovely, darling, but just be careful. You know what these pop stars are like,' Richard said protectively.

'Oh, not you as well!' Angel groaned. 'I've just had my best friend giving me earache about him!'

'It's because we care about you, isn't that right, Danni?' Richard replied.

'Yep, and I know you won't want to hear this,' Danni said, 'but he has got a bit of a reputation with women – he seems to collect glamour girls, so make sure you're not just adding to his collection.'

'Okay, okay,' Angel grumbled. 'But please,

please will you help me sort out my make-up before I go and meet him at the restaurant?'

'I will if you promise to drink more water in future, especially after a rough night. It's the best thing when you're knackered and means I won't have to slap on so much concealer in future,' Danni said.

'Yeah, yeah, whatever,' Angel muttered. Danni was always telling her to use this product or that product and to be honest she couldn't see what difference it made. When she was twenty she'd start worrying about her skin, in the meantime, so long as she took her make-up off every night, what was the problem?

'You look gorgeous,' Mickey told her, as she slid into her chair, Hakkasan's maître d' hovering nearby.

'Thanks,' Angel replied shyly, 'I've got a good make-up artist.'

Mickey smiled. 'I reckon you look just as good with it all off.'

Angel blushed, secretly thinking, *Well that's not something you're going to see for a while*.

The restaurant's famous cocktails were amazing and the food was delicious, but Angel hardly touched it. She was sitting forward on the edge of her seat, leaning into Mickey across the table, totally wrapped up in him. He was like a breath of fresh air, entertaining, funny and charming. She would never have imagined someone so famous being so completely normal and down to earth. He knew everything about the celeb scene in London, who was going out with who, who had done what, who'd slept with who, and he had accepted her immediately as a member of that scene, too. By the end of the meal, Angel couldn't help herself. She was falling for him.

'So what happens now?' Mickey asked as they settled the bill. Angel had insisted on paying half and even though Mickey hadn't wanted to let her, she wouldn't take no for an answer.

'I'm flying to Spain tomorrow for a shoot and I've got a really early start, so I'd better get home,' Angel replied, longing instead to go home with him.

She was instantly rewarded with Mickey groaning, 'Don't do this to me! Come back to mine.'

Angel shook her head. 'It's not that I don't want to, it's just—'

Mickey cut in. 'You're treating me mean to keep me keen – believe me, Angel, you don't need to, I'm already keen,' and he leant over the table and kissed her. Angel felt her resolve melt the moment his lips met hers, and just as she was trying to think about a way to accept his invitation after having said no already, Mickey stopped, leaving her desperate for more. She looked at him, her cheeks flushed, but he just shrugged and said, 'It's up to you, babe.'

The evening had lost a little of its shine as they stepped out of the restaurant, hand in hand.

Trying to look unconcerned, Angel worried about Mickey. *Am I doing the right thing, making him wait? Or will I push him away?* She stopped just outside the door, wanting to reassure Mickey that she did really like him and that she would love to see him again, but just as she was about to speak a photographer leapt out into their path, temporarily dazzling the couple with the flash, and then legged it down the street.

'Oh no!' Angel exclaimed. Now their first date was going to be out in the open for everyone to see and talk about. She had only just come to terms with people staring at her in the shop or on the street and whispering. Having a paparazzo follow her was a completely new experience, and although Carrie was always onto her about getting more exposure, she hated the idea of her private life opened up for everyone to see.

'Glad to see my manager got something right for once,' Mickey said, sounding pleased.

'What do you mean?' Angel demanded.

'Well, I told him we'd be here and he tipped off the photographer. I thought the publicity would do us both some good. The papers are bound to want the story.'

Angel let go of his hand abruptly. *What? Is this all I am, some juicy publicity? A bit of totty for Mickey to be seen out with?*

'Hey, what's the matter?' Mickey asked, as Angel started walking, slowly at first, then more quickly.

She had no idea where she was going; she just knew she had to get away. He ran after her, but Angel refused to stop, feeling furious by now.

'I don't like being used, Mickey.' She rounded on him when he'd caught up. 'If all you're looking for is publicity, fucking leave me out of it.'

'Babe, I wasn't – I thought it would be good for both of us.'

'I hardly know you and I don't want to be in the papers for this.' And, seeing a taxi driving towards her with its light on, Angel held out her hand to hail it.

'Don't go now, please, I'm sorry I fucked up. I really like you, Angel, don't go,' Mickey pleaded. But Angel had already opened the door and jumped in. She didn't look back as the cab pulled away.

She felt completely deflated when she let herself into her flat a little later. The evening had started so promisingly and she really thought she had something special with Mickey. But clearly he didn't feel like that. The thought of him making a public display of their relationship, reducing it down to a bit of calculated publicity, made her feel like a fool. The only consolation was that she hadn't slept with him. She turned off her mobile, took a long shower and got into bed, where she lay awake for a long time before finally falling into an exhausted sleep.

'You were right to warn me about Mickey,' Angel said miserably, having spilt the whole story of what had happened the night before to Danni. They had flown to Malaga that morning, where Angel was modelling swimwear for a tabloid spread looking ahead to the next summer's range, and Danni was putting the finishing touches to her face. Angel trusted Danni and often found herself confiding in her. She'd come to rely on her for advice – not only did she know everything there was to know about the business, from which glamour girls to watch out for to which photographers were arseholes, she was also good at cutting through the crap and sizing up a situation.

'Come on, Angel, don't let him get to you,' Danni replied sympathetically.

'I just hate feeling that he was using me. That I didn't matter to him, that I could have been any girl,' Angel muttered, trying not to move her face too much while Danni applied the blusher.

'Well, forget him, there's plenty of other men out there who won't behave like that wanker.'

'Hmm.' Angel wasn't convinced. So far, she had a crap track record when it came to choosing men: Cal had wanted her briefly in the nightclub, then pretended nothing had ever happened between them, Juan turned out to have a fiancée, and now Mickey. Men were bastards, she decided.

'Chin up,' Danni told her firmly. 'Just take a look at yourself, you look fab.'

Angel smiled as she surveyed Danni's handiwork in the mirror. She did look good – her skin bronzed and flawless, false eyelashes giving her sultry, sexy eyes, and a shimmer of gloss emphasising her full lips. She shook out her long hair. She was here to do a job and only that mattered.

The day was a great success. She was feeling more and more confident as she modelled, and while she posed round the turquoise pool in a variety of bikinis she pushed all thoughts of Mickey out of her head, concentrating on perfecting her sultry come-and-get-me-if-you-dare stare and sexy pout.

The photographer was full of compliments as he moved around the set, shouting instructions and encouragements. 'You should be doing the lad mags, Angel,' he finally said at the end of the shoot. 'They'd absolutely love you.'

'Yeah, well, I wouldn't expect that so soon, I've only just started,' she replied, secretly grateful for his compliments on a day like today.

'Don't be so modest, it won't get you anywhere in the world you're in,' the photographer joked, gesturing to his assistant to start packing up the gear. Angel smiled. She would love her career to take off, but she certainly didn't expect it to happen overnight.

She didn't get back home until midnight, and once she closed the door of her flat all the buzz from the day seemed to drain out of her. She was exhausted from travelling, from smiling and posing all day – and from the disappointingly empty answerphone. She checked both her home phone and her mobile again, but there were no messages – only one from her mum calling to say hello. She sank onto the sofa and kicked off her heels. It was all very well telling everyone that she didn't want anything more to do with Mickey, but all she could think about was his hand on her thigh, his kiss, his eyes looking into hers. She groaned, pushed herself off the sofa and wearily wandered into the bathroom and then to bed.

She was woken at ten by the doorbell. Still half asleep, she stumbled to the door and opened it, only to be confronted by an enormous bouquet of the most beautiful pale pink roses, which completely obscured the delivery man, who had to lean to one side to say, 'Shall I take these in for you, love? I've got quite a few more to bring in from the van.'

Angel nodded, then watched in amazement as the man proceeded to bring in three more equally huge bouquets – one of red roses, one of white, one of yellow, spilling onto every surface of her tiny living room.

'Somebody likes you,' the delivery man joked, as he handed Angel the card and left.

I don't know what your favourite colour is – hopefully one of these is right. So sorry about the other

night, I was an idiot. I've tried to stop the story.
Please say you'll see me again. Mickey x.

It was the most full-on apology she had ever received and while it didn't make up for what he had done, at least it showed he was sorry. She paced up and down for a few minutes, wondering what she should do. The thought of not seeing him again filled her with disappointment. She did want to see him again, very much. Finally, she picked up her phone and called him, her heart beating wildly.

'Thanks for the flowers, Mickey,' she said quickly when he'd picked up, sounding sleepy. 'They're gorgeous, and—' she paused, taking another deep breath and daring herself to go on '—for future reference, my favourite colour is pink.'

'Does that mean you'll see me again?' Mickey asked hopefully, much more awake.

'I could meet you this morning, if you're free?'

'Just tell me where.'

An hour later Angel and Mickey were sitting in a café on Hampstead High Street. Mickey hadn't arrived empty-handed, the first thing he did was give Angel a perfect single rose in pale pink.

'You're being very charming,' Angel joked. No one had ever sent her flowers before, let alone four bouquets in one day.

'I want to charm you,' Mickey said seriously, looking into her eyes. 'I really do. It's been ages since I've felt about someone the way I feel about you. I meet so many girls in my job, and most of them are lovely, but you're in a different league.'

He gazed at her with his incredibly blue eyes, in a way that sent a shiver down her spine. *Is he telling the truth?* Angel wondered. He seemed completely sincere and she wanted to believe him.

They spent the next three hours in the café, chatting and laughing, reading the papers together and pointing out fellow clubbers and celebrities to one another. Once again, Angel couldn't believe she was now part of this world, but Mickey explained relationships, networks and personalities. He apologised again for the paparazzo incident, explaining that his manager was always at him to get publicity and had simply worn him down that day. He listened sympathetically when Angel complained that Carrie was exactly the same, but suggested that maybe it was preferable to drop the media a hint and control the situation, rather than being caught out when you least wanted it. Angel said spiritedly that she didn't want it at all. After the misery of the last two days, Angel was elated. She loved being in Mickey's company. The sexual tension between them was so intense. Every time their legs touched by accident, Angel felt a frisson of excitement. She really, really liked him.

One latte became two; then they were hungry and had to order sandwiches. Finally they left the café, but neither was in any hurry to separate and when Mickey suggested they go for a walk on

Hampstead Heath Angel was only too happy to agree. It was mid-October and an unusually bleak, cold day, but Angel didn't feel the chill. Mickey put his arm round her and she was buoyed up with excitement and anticipation.

'I need to ask you something,' she said as they paused at the top of Parliament Hill Fields to look at the spectacular view of London. 'People have told me you've got a bit of a reputation as a womaniser, and that I shouldn't trust you. Are they right?' She looked him squarely in the eye.

He laughed. 'There have been quite a few girls, I admit, probably because I've always been on the lookout for that someone special.' *Someone like you*, Angel longed for him to say, but instead he asked, 'How about you?'

His question jolted Angel back into reality. 'I guess I'm like you, I'm looking for someone special,' she said evasively – she could hardly mention Cal at this point.

And Mickey, as if reading her mind, pulled her close and kissed her. Angel wrapped her arms round his neck, eyes closed, returning his kiss with fierce passion. *God, I can't believe it. I really, really like him*, she thought, giddy from the intensity of his kiss.

By four, they had walked far enough; it was getting dark and both reluctantly admitted that they were half frozen.

'Let's go and have tea somewhere posh,' Mickey

suggested, and Angel was pleasantly surprised when he hailed a taxi and asked to go to the Ritz. Relaxing in the Ritz's luxurious tearoom, Mickey ordered sandwiches and cakes, and he also insisted on a bottle of vintage Cristal.

'Thanks for a magical day, Angel,' he said, clinking his glass against hers and giving her his special smile. Angel couldn't speak, just put her head on his shoulder and smiled to herself.

Chapter 6

Head Over Heels

That night she went home alone again. Apart from a passionate goodnight kiss, Mickey hadn't tried to go any further, even though Angel now secretly wanted him to. The next day, there was a piece about them in several of the tabloids, with one paper printing the picture of them hand in hand, accompanied by the headline MICKEY'S ANGEL. Reluctantly, she spread out the paper, but she barely had time to read it before Carrie was on the phone to her.

'Darling, fabulous news about you and Mickey Waters. I couldn't have planned it better myself. He is gorgeous and it's going to do your career no end of good.'

Angel wasn't happy to hear Carrie talking about her feelings and her new romance in such a calculated way, but Mickey's words from yesterday rang in her ears and she was savvy enough to realise that her refusal to stay out of the media wouldn't get her anywhere. She had chosen this career and she now had to play the game by their rules. However much she disliked it. So she just mumbled something about it being early days and avoided Carrie's eager questions about her and Mickey.

As soon as she flipped shut her hot-pink Motorola RAZR, Mickey called. 'I'm so sorry, Angel, I did try to get the story pulled and my manager called the paper, but they weren't having any of it. I promise it won't happen again.'

'It's okay,' Angel replied, considering the picture and thinking how good she and Mickey looked together. 'I'm cool about it now, actually.'

Mickey was in the studio for the next week, in recording sessions that lasted well into the night, so he had no time to spend with Angel. But he called and texted her every moment he was free, telling her how much he missed her and how much he wanted to see her. On Thursday he told her to keep the weekend free because he had a surprise for her. With every call and every text, Angel felt them growing closer; she always wanted to talk to him, was disappointed when half a day went by without a phone call. She couldn't wait for the weekend. She felt a little guilty, because she had promised Gemma a girly weekend in London, which she now had to cancel. Gemma said she understood, no problem, but Angel could tell she wasn't very happy. Gemma had always been there for her and Angel had never had to let her friend down before, but this was special, wasn't it? She wanted to tell Gemma all about Mickey, how wonderful he was, how good he made her feel, how great they were together. But very quickly Gemma said she had to get back to work. Angel put down the phone with mixed feelings, torn between anticipation and regret. She and Gemma had always shared everything, and now all of a sudden they seemed to be growing apart. Why couldn't she just be happy for her? For once, everything was going well in her life.

Never in a million years could Angel have guessed what Mickey had planned for them – a weekend in Paris. She had always dreamt of going there and she couldn't believe it when he told her to pack for two nights and be ready at seven a.m. for the car to pick her up. She could barely sleep all night, fizzing with excitement at the thought of being with Mickey for two whole days, in the most romantic city in the world.

'I've missed you so much, babe!' Mickey exclaimed as she got into the car, immediately putting his arm round her and kissing her.

'And I've missed you,' Angel replied, pulling away a little, suddenly shy at being so close to the famous singer. But her shyness quickly melted as Mickey held her close. She was so excited as they got out of the car at Waterloo and headed across the station concourse to the Eurostar check-in. She didn't even mind when Mickey stopped to sign a couple of autographs for some young girls, but then she froze, convinced she had heard the whirr of a camera rewinding behind her.

'Hey,' she exclaimed, spinning round and seeing a photographer staking them out a couple of metres away. Immediately her smile disappeared and she pulled her baseball cap down over her face.

'Come on, Mickey, there's a photographer, let's get on the train.' She didn't want some paparazzo making money out of their romantic weekend.

'Chill out, babe,' Mickey answered, not sounding at all bothered, but Angel grabbed his arm and pulled him towards the platform.

As soon as they boarded the train and settled down into first class, Angel anxiously scanned the seats around them, checking that the photographer wasn't following them. Mickey laughed when he saw her worried expression.

'He's not on the train, babe, he just got lucky. Now let's have some champagne and you can tell me what you've been up to.' A glass of champagne later, snuggled up close to Mickey, chatting, flirting and kissing, Angel forgot all about the photographer. Instead she had butterflies of excitement at what would happen when they arrived at their hotel.

Mickey had booked them into the Ritz, telling her their suite was the one Princess Diana had always stayed in whenever she came to Paris. Angel felt a delicious shudder of apprehension as they were shown to their luxurious suite. This was it, then, but to her surprise there were two bedrooms adjoining the huge living room.

'See,' Mickey whispered, wrapping his arms round her, 'I didn't make any assumptions.'

Angel half wanted to stay there. It felt so good being held by Mickey, but he had other ideas and whisked her down to a tasty lunch of lobster and frites (both of them giggling when the snooty maître d' raised an eyebrow at Mickey's request for ketchup). Then he insisted that they start their tour of Paris by going up the Eiffel Tower.

'You're okay to walk, aren't you?' he asked as they left the hotel.

'God, yes, I want to walk!' Angel exclaimed. 'I can't wait to see Paris.' They wandered along the busy streets with their arms round each other, taking in the sights, looking in boutiques and stopping every now and then to steal a kiss.

'Do you know what, babe?' Mickey asked her, as they stood on the fifth level of the Eiffel Tower, looking at Paris spread out beneath them, putting his arm round her, and pulling her close to him. 'I wouldn't want to be here with anyone else but you.' Angel took a deep breath. All her life it seemed she had been hiding her feelings, but she wasn't going to any more. She shook back her long hair and tilted her chin defiantly. 'And I wouldn't want to be here with anyone else but you,' she said, turning round to kiss him.

By the time they returned to their hotel suite, walking back through the brightly lit streets, Angel's mind was made up. She wanted Mickey, wanted him more than anything, and she couldn't wait another minute. She knew she would have to make the first move, having played hard to get until now, even though she would have preferred him to.

'I'm going to have a bath,' she told Mickey as he poured them each a glass of champagne. She filled the bath with bubbles and lit candles and deliberately left the bathroom door open. After she had quickly cleaned her teeth, making a face at the combination of champagne and toothpaste, checked out her appearance in the mirror and arranged her hair into a ponytail, she undressed and stepped into the bath. She waited a few minutes, before calling softly, making her voice low and husky, 'Mickey, can I have some more champagne, please?'

A moment later, he came in, carrying the bottle of vintage Cristal. Angel held out her glass and looked at him from underneath her lashes while he filled it up. 'Thanks,' she whispered, taking a sip. Then, 'It's a very big bath.'

'Yes, it is,' he agreed, smiling.

'I just wondered,' She said, taking another sip of champagne, 'if you wanted to get in with me?'

'Well,' he replied, 'I could, but I don't want you to take advantage of me.'

'You cheeky bastard!' Angel exclaimed, and, feeling a surge of confidence, added, 'Get your kit off and get in here!'

Mickey needed no further encouragement. He ripped off his shirt, revealing his firm, toned torso, unbuttoned his jeans and let them fall to the floor, pausing for a moment in his white Calvins, which gave a pretty good impression of what they might contain, then slipped them off too. Angel was impressed. Then, in all his gorgeous, tanned, firm nakedness, Mickey got into the bath with Angel. He lay back opposite her, his legs trapping her on either side, and the two of them contemplated each other through the steam and the bubbles. Angel was dying to touch him; she smiled at him shyly and that was all it took for Mickey to sit up and pull her towards him. She moved into his arms and they kissed hungrily.

His hands were sliding over her body, caressing her breasts, moving further down, slipping between her legs. *God, he's turning me on*, Angel thought as he teased her, and she in turn touched his smooth skin, running her hands across his back, then his firm stomach, and then dared herself to go further.

'God, I want to fuck you,' Mickey groaned as she caressed him.

But they were fighting for room to move, water spilling out of the bath and drenching the marble floor. Mickey took her hand and pulled her up. 'Let's go into the bedroom.'

Not caring that their bodies were still dripping wet, they fell onto the huge double bed. Mickey carried on his tantalising exploration of her body, kissing her breasts and caressing her, sending ripples of pleasure through Angel as he moved down her body, kissing her stomach, her thighs and ending up between her legs. As his tongue circled her, Angel moaned, conscious of nothing but the feel of his tongue against her. She was close, but wanted to touch him, feel him, taste him.

'Come here,' she said breathlessly, pulling him up the bed. Once she had him where she wanted she began her exploration of *his* body, showering his skin with kisses, moving down his body until she gently took his cock in her mouth.

'That feels so good, babe,' Mickey groaned, closing his eyes with pleasure.

After a few minutes he murmured, 'Come here,' and he pulled Angel up beside him. He picked up his glass of champagne and the two of them took turns to take sips, gazing at each other, flushed with desire, but only for a moment. Mickey put down the glass and then he was on top of Angel, pressing his body against hers. She arched her back, pressing against him, wanting only to feel him inside her. Just when she thought she'd scream if he didn't give her what she wanted, he slid inside her.

It felt so good. She wrapped her legs around his body and kissed him deeply.

'God, you feel so good,' he groaned, thrusting

into her. Then they switched, so she was on top and his hands were caressing her, bringing her closer and closer to orgasm.

'Condom,' she said suddenly, feeling that he too was getting close. For a second he looked as if he couldn't stop, then he reached under the pillow for the condom and ripped open the wrapper with his teeth. Now Angel could let go, surrender to the feeling building up in her. She closed her eyes and tilted back her head.

'Yes,' she moaned as the orgasm rippled through her body.

'Oh, God, yes,' Mickey echoed as he reached his own.

Laughing and breathless, Angel collapsed beside him.

'That was so fucking good,' Mickey whispered. 'You're so fucking sexy.'

'So are you,' Angel whispered back.

That night they made love all over the luxurious suite – on one of the elegant sofas, on the ridiculously thick carpet ('We're shagging on the shagpile,' Angel had said, giggling) and on the bed again. Sex with Juan had been sweet, but this was in a different league, maybe because Angel felt more experienced, freed from any inhibitions. She loved seeing how much her body turned Mickey on, loved touching him, kissing him, tasting him. She discarded any fears she had that Mickey was after a quick shag when they finally curled up together on the huge double bed in the early hours of the morning, exhausted but unable to let each other go.

'I think I'm falling in love with you, Angel,' Mickey murmured to her.

'Really?' Angel couldn't keep the smile off her face. She had always wanted a man to be as open and passionate as she was, and here he was, right next to her. 'I'm falling in love with you, too,' she whispered, turning round to kiss him on the lips.

They spent most of the next day in bed, leaving themselves just half an hour to catch the train and no time to explore Paris. But Paris would always be there to come back to, and making love with Mickey had been the most intoxicating experience of her life. That night, Mickey and Angel took a taxi back to Mickey's penthouse overlooking Hyde Park, in one of the most expensive and exclusive areas in London. Inside the enormous living room, everything screamed pop star – from the floor-to-ceiling windows, the heavy cream silk curtains, the huge expensive-looking white leather sofas, the white carpet that Angel's heels sunk into, the giant plasma-screen TV, covering most of one of the walls, the life-size black and white photograph of Mickey walking down a New York street, copying the classic James Dean pose, black coat slung round his shoulders, hands in pockets, looking moody; the hundreds of CDs and DVDs spilling off the shelves and scattered on the floor, the five framed gold discs occupying centre stage above the ultra-modern, minimalist fireplace. There was a purple pool table, a set of weights and an exercise bike and the room still didn't feel cluttered.

'What an amazing place,' she exclaimed, looking round and seeing the stunning view across the park and the London skyline. 'I'll never be able to have you back to my tiny flat!'

'Come and see the bedroom, it's got a different view.'

Different, Angel thought appreciatively as Mickey ripped off his clothes and pulled her onto the bed with him, and altogether more satisfying . . .

Two days later, pictures of them in Paris appeared in a paper. Angel was puzzled. 'That photographer we saw in the station must have followed us then, but how the fuck did he know we were going?'

Mickey shrugged but avoided looking her in the eye. 'It's a pisser, babe, but you know what it's like, he probably just got lucky – maybe he did get on our train.'

'Very lucky,' Angel answered, reading the article, which seemed to have an awful lot of information about their trip – from which hotel they'd stayed in to what they'd had for lunch to how they'd spent the whole of Sunday in bed. Angel thought for a moment. Finally, she shrugged and put it out of her mind. She was in such a blissed-out state that she couldn't worry about anything other than when she was next going to see Mickey. And that was how she spent the next two months.

The lovers were pretty much inseparable. Angel practically moved into his apartment, going home only to collect clothes and her post. Mickey introduced her to his world and she loved it. Every night they would be out socialising – either at a hip club or restaurant or going to a launch party or an awards do. It was like being caught up in a whirlwind of pleasure, but the best bit of all was experiencing it with Mickey. She was in that loved-up state where you can't get enough of the other person, where nothing else matters except being with them.

But not everyone shared their happiness. One night when she was out clubbing with Mickey, she bumped into Lisa and Vicki in the Ladies.

'Oh, hi, Angel,' they chorused insincerely, as Angel emerged from the cubicle. The two models were busy layering even more make-up onto their already overloaded faces.

Angel managed to smile, then stood next to them, checking her own appearance (a slick of lip gloss was enough for her), wanting to get away from them as soon as possible. But just as she was turning to go, Vicki spoke. 'Still with Mickey?'

'Yeah,' she replied, thinking, *What's it to you, you pair of slappers?*

'Oh?' answered Lisa. 'I heard that he'd dumped you.'

'Well, you heard wrong,' Angel snapped.

Lisa and Vicki smirked knowingly. 'Don't expect it to last that much longer,' Vicki replied, a look of false concern on her face. 'Mickey doesn't stay with anyone that long. He likes to play the field, doesn't like to be tied down.'

'Oh, piss off, the pair of you,' Angel said, walking towards the door. 'You're just jealous.'

The girls laughed louder this time. 'Don't be stupid,' Lisa exclaimed. 'We know all about him, Vicki's shagged him.'

Not giving them the satisfaction of a reply, Angel marched out of the Ladies without giving them a second glance, but inside she was fuming. She managed to contain herself until they got into the car; she really didn't want Lisa and Vicki seeing that they had upset her. But as soon as Mickey closed the door, she was on his case.

'I've just seen Vicki.'

'Who?' Mickey replied casually.

'You know, that glamour girl you shagged,' Angel answered, raising her voice.

'Oh, *her*,' Mickey replied, smirking. 'Yeah, I had a one-night stand with her ages ago, but to be honest, babe, I can't remember anything about it. I was single and pissed, and she threw herself at me. I just remember waking up and thinking, Jesus, who's that lying next to me? She kept phoning me and texting me afterwards but I never saw her again, I promise. I'm not interested. She was a mistake, it didn't mean anything. I love you.'

While Angel didn't exactly think it was great that Mickey had had one-night stands, she was relieved. Vicki might have shagged him when he was too drunk to remember, but it was she, Angel, who was having a relationship with him. And he loved her and she loved him. So she resolved to put Vicki right out of her head, and ignore the silly tart if she ever saw her again.

Her career seemed to be really taking off – she had never been busier or more in demand. She was inundated with offers of work – two tabloids had a bidding war over getting Angel to sign an exclusive deal for the next three months, which would be worth a lot of money. She finally landed the coup of a shoot with *Tackle*, one of the biggest lad mags. One of the Formula One teams booked her as one of their girls – a wildly glamorous job, which involved dressing up in a skintight scarlet catsuit, posing for five minutes with the drivers during the press call, drinking quite a bit of champagne and hanging out with some seriously gorgeous drivers. Plus, there was talk of an advertising deal with a leading mobile phone company.

Carrie had been right about the press interest – things had definitely picked up since she had been openly linked with Mickey. People were fascinated by her and wanted to invite her to all the celeb parties, launches and premieres. She had become a household name and she and Mickey were a regular feature in celeb mags and the tabloids. They were the golden couple of the moment and the press couldn't get enough of the beautiful glamour girl and the successful singer who seemed to have found true love at last.

But her success wasn't only down to her blossoming romance with the pop star; that had just been a starting point. Quickly, the papers and magazines were starting to wake up to Angel's star quality. But there was a price to be paid for her growing fame. More and more often, when Angel was out shopping or going to the gym, she was photographed, both by paparazzi and passers-by and their bloody camera mobiles. Angel had spent enough time poring over celebs in mags herself, ogling stars who had been caught out looking minging, without their make-up on, wearing pikey clothes, stuffing their faces with a Big Mac and fries. At first, she had thought that being snapped looking a bit rough would be the worst thing because people would be able to see what you looked like when you rolled out of bed. But that turned out to be the least of her concerns. What bothered her more than anything was the feeling that no area in her life was private any more, because there was always a photographer waiting to capture the moment and sell it.

She put up with it for a while, but finally plucked up courage and complained to Carrie about it. Her agent just laughed. 'It goes with the territory, darling, and you'll get used to it. The time to worry is when they're not photographing your every move!'

She had a point, but Angel wasn't so sure. She took to wearing the celebrity uniform of large shades – Chanel rapidly becoming her favourite – whenever she went anywhere.

The other thing that was starting to seriously bug her was the size of her breasts. At 32B she felt they were on the small side for a girl in her line of work. Whenever she compared herself to the other girls their breasts looked so much bigger, so much sexier, and even though Angel was constantly being told by Richard and Danni and everyone else she worked with that she had a perfect figure, she couldn't help wanting to change. So telling no one, not even Gemma, she made an appointment for a consultation at a clinic. She wouldn't rush into having a boob job, but she definitely wanted to find out what her options were.

At the end of November she had a shoot booked with Richard for a Christmas special. They had such a giggle, arranging the fake snow around the studio, decorating the Christmas tree and arranging presents underneath it. Angel had posed on a sledge dressed in a red Santa's hat, a red G-string and nothing else, topless in front of the Christmas tree in white fur-trimmed shorts and white thigh-high boots and finally as an underdressed Angel in a silver sequinned thong and a halo. But by five o'clock she was desperate to finish so she could see Mickey.

'How much longer,' she groaned, pulling off her halo and rubbing her head where the wire had pressed against her.

Richard laughed. 'Come on, my little love-struck bird, just half an hour, then I promise I'll let you go.'

'Oh God, I can't wait that long!' she exclaimed, almost unable to stand still a second longer.

'Ah, love's young dream,' put in Danni from the sidelines. 'I can almost remember that feeling.'

'You two are so cynical!' Angel said in mock disgust. 'I'm in love!'

'Well, you've lasted longer than any of Mickey's other girls,' Danni said, obviously meaning it as a joke and immediately regretting it as the smile vanished from Angel's face.

'Sorry, I was just kidding, Angel,' Danni said quickly.

'It's okay,' Angel replied, but it wasn't. Danni's comment had hit a nerve, a real area of insecurity. Since she'd been seeing Mickey she couldn't fail to be aware of the long line of women before her – soap stars, girl band singers, glamour girls – Mickey's affairs were well documented in the tabloids and Vicki and Lisa's bitchy remarks hadn't helped. Angel felt some of her excitement about seeing Mickey leave her. Maybe she was stupid to have told him she loved him. But that was the kind of person she was: if she felt something, she had to let it out. She concentrated on the photo shoot, wanting to get it over with and see him, and feel reassured.

'Hey, babe,' Mickey said as she let herself into his apartment. He was lying on the white leather sofa and she rushed over to him, threw herself on top of him and kissed him as though her life depended on it.

'I missed you!' she declared, when they came up for breath.

'It's only been a day!' he laughed. And as she lay down on the sofa next to him and nestled her head on his shoulder, he added, 'You'd better go and get ready, we're due at the restaurant in half an hour.'

'Can't we cancel and stay in?' Angel said, feeling disappointed – she'd forgotten about the dinner and all she wanted to do was be close to Mickey.

'Nope, we're meeting Sam and the others, remember?'

But when she and Mickey turned up at Nobu, it wasn't just the other members of the band. Dinner with the four of them would have been fine as Angel liked them all. Tonight, though, there was also their manager, several people from the record company and various girlfriends, so the quiet informal dinner Angel had been expecting turned into a table of fifteen. She ended up next to Sam, who she got on well with, but it was Mickey she wanted to be next to. She couldn't help thinking back to the conversation with Danni and Richard and she kept looking over at him, willing him to give her a smile. But he was too busy talking to the guy from his record label and barely looked at her all evening. Angel tried hard not to, but she couldn't help feeling neglected.

After dinner Angel was hoping to have Mickey to herself, but he invited everyone back to his penthouse for a drink. As soon as they got in, he cracked open the Cristal and turned up his state-of-the-art Bose stereo, gave her a brief kiss and moved among his guests. Angel tried to talk to some of the other girlfriends but found she had little in common with them, their only topics of conversation being the designer clothes they wanted to buy, the designer clothes they had just bought and bitching about various celebrities. She wandered aimlessly around Mickey's apartment, sipping her champagne, looking around for him. She finally found him in the bedroom. She watched, surprised, as he knelt by the bedside table, busy tidying a tiny heap of powder into a line on the glass top. Mickey was doing cocaine. Angel wasn't naïve. She knew perfectly well that for a lot of people in their circle, coke was normal. She'd already suspected that Mickey was an occasional user, but had never said much about it because she didn't think it was a problem. But she'd never actually seen him do it.

'Babe!' he exclaimed. 'D'you want some?'

Angel shook her head mutely.

'Oh, come on – one little line isn't going to hurt you, and it might put a smile on that beautiful face of yours.' He got up from the bed and kissed her. 'I'm sorry that all these people are here, but I had to invite them, you know how it is.'

Angel wasn't sure that she did know how it was. All she knew was that she wanted to be alone with Mickey, and half the penthouse was full of strangers.

'Come on, babe,' Mickey repeated. 'Give it a try, I guarantee you'll like it. And when everyone's gone, I'll make it up to you, I promise.' He kissed her again.

Thinking about it later, Angel had no idea what prompted her to say 'yes' to the white line Mickey prepared. She'd never had any interest in it, generally thinking coked-up people were tossers. But tonight was different. She'd been feeling vulnerable, feeling that everyone was waiting for them to break up, expecting a big story of heartbreak and misery any day now. All of a sudden, she felt defiant. *What the hell*, she thought, *I have to get through the next few hours somehow.*

'Okay,' she replied. Mickey sat her down and showed her how it was done.

A few minutes later, she had to agree with Mickey: she felt much, much better. She suddenly didn't mind that the flat was full of people; she grabbed a bottle of champagne for herself and made sure that she was sitting next to Mickey, included in all his conversations, and she giggled and chatted the next few hours away, all her insecurity gone. When the guests finally went at five, Angel was still feeling lively and quite drunk. She dragged Mickey into the bedroom, pulled off her clothes, then poured champagne over her naked body.

'I tried coke for the first time,' she declared drunkenly, 'now it's your turn to do something for me. Lick that champagne off me!'

Mickey didn't need to be asked twice.

Chapter 7

A Reality Check

'I think he might be *the one*!' Angel declared. Gemma was peering into H&M at Oxford Circus, analysing the display. Mickey was away promoting the band's new single in Germany. He had wanted Angel to come, but she'd thought it would be nice to have Gemma to stay for the weekend, repair their friendship a little.

Gemma turned and looked at her sceptically. 'You haven't known him that long, how can you be sure?'

'Because of how he makes me feel.' Angel's face lit up and she took Gemma's arm and wandered into the shop. 'We're so close. It's not just about sex, you know, although that's shit-hot. It's so much more.'

'So how do you feel about Cal now?' Gemma asked hesitantly.

Angel stopped, not caring about any of the other shoppers pushing to get by them. She shook her head as if she could shake off the feeling. 'I don't know,' she finally said. 'I guess I'll always feel something for him, but what's the point? He doesn't care about me and I'm with Mickey now. He loves me, Gemma! Can you believe that? And I love him!' Angel looked at her friend, her eyes shining, her face radiant. Gemma didn't look convinced.

'I don't understand why everyone's got a problem. Maybe when you come up the next time you can meet him and you'll see what I mean?' Angel suggested. She was so happy to see her friend. She hadn't realised how much she'd missed their friendship since she'd left Brighton, and she didn't want to fall out again.

Initially things had been a little strained between the two girls. They spoke and texted regularly but only ever had brief conversations, and they had barely seen each other these past four months. Gemma had been busy with her beautician's course, Angel's work schedule was packed, and when she wasn't working, much as she missed Gemma, she wanted to see Mickey. But she had decided this weekend was all about them and, after sharing a bottle of wine at Angel's flat, they had hit the shops together for an afternoon of retail therapy, gossiping, window-shopping and trying on clothes.

Now the two of them turned up at the exclusive Old Bond Street, to the Gucci store, where Angel wanted to buy Mickey's Christmas present.

From the minute they walked into the shop, Gemma's mood changed. Usually she would have been in her element in such a place, being a retail queen, but now she just stood there looking serious.

'Which one do you prefer?' Angel was pointing out two watches in the display cabinet. 'I like both of them.'

Gemma shrugged. 'Which one's the cheapest?'

'I don't really care,' Angel said absentmindedly, trying to decide between the two of them. 'I want to buy him something really special.'

'Don't you think two grand is way too much to spend on someone you've only just met?' Gemma muttered, checking her mobile phone while Angel asked the assistant to get the watches out for her.

'I know it seems a lot, but I've earnt really good money lately,' she said, a bit defensively.

'You should be saving it for yourself,' was Gemma's terse reply as she walked away from Angel and pretended to be studying some of the jewellery. Upset by Gemma's attitude, Angel quickly paid for one of the watches. The two girls were quiet as they left the store, their earlier carefree mood gone.

'Shall we get something to drink?' Angel suggested.

'Sure,' Gemma replied offhandedly. Angel had planned to take her to the St. Martins Lane Hotel, but seeing how she reacted to the Gucci experience,

Angel worried that she would look too flash. But it was the only place she knew around there, so she waved over a cab. She hoped that Gemma might cheer up after a Strawberry Daiquiri, but even after the second one she still seemed distant. Angel couldn't believe that this was happening, she had always been so close to Gemma. In desperation she blurted out, 'I've really missed you and I'm sorry I haven't seen you much lately.'

'Well, that might be about to change,' Gemma said slowly. 'Tony and I are moving to London after Christmas. He's going to work for Spurs, as a physio, and I've got a job as a beauty therapist.'

'Oh my God!' Angel exclaimed. 'That is just the best news, why didn't you tell me sooner?'

Gemma hesitated for a moment, then said, 'To be honest, I didn't know if you'd be that bothered. You seem so busy with Mickey and your new celeb friends and your posh bars.' She gestured at the expensive-looking chic interior of the the Light Bar.

Angel felt awful. 'I'm so sorry if I've given you that impression. You're my best friend and you always will be.'

Finally Gemma looked at her, her smile genuine. 'And you're my best friend, too.'

That night Angel couldn't sleep. She kept thinking about what Gemma had said. *Perhaps I have been too caught up with Mickey*. She felt awful. She'd never wanted to be one of those girls who drop their friends the moment they have a boyfriend. *I'm not going to do it any more, Gemma is too important to me.* And Angel thought about how she'd neglected her family. She spoke to her mum once a week on the phone, but as her mum didn't really ask about her work the conversations were usually fairly strained with lots of observations about Angel's new flat, about Prince, about Gemma and Tony, some comments about Frank's work and the current season. If by any chance her dad answered the phone, he barely said a word and just handed the receiver to her mum. Clearly, he still had a problem with Angel doing glamour modelling. Every time her mum asked her to come and see them Angel replied that she was busy, which was true, but deep down she knew she could have found the time if she had wanted to. Nor had she invited her mum up to London to see her, even though she knew her mum really wanted to but didn't like to ask. And she hadn't even told them about Mickey, but had let them find out from the papers. Tossing and turning, Angel felt cut off from all that she knew, all that was familiar to her, and, although she could never move back home, she missed feeling part of a family just as she missed being with her friends. She resolved to contact her mum the next day and arrange a visit.

But the following night Mickey was back and Angel forgot about her mum and her new resolutions for Gemma. He called her as soon as he got home.

'Come round now, babe,' he pleaded with her. 'I've missed you.'

'It's only been two days!' she laughed, secretly pleased to hear the urgency in his voice. Deciding to give him a cheeky surprise, she put on her sexiest black underwear, complete with stockings and heels, and simply wore her pink trenchcoat over it, drawing the belt tight round her waist so as to avoid flashing the taxi driver. Instead of using her key to open the door to Mickey's penthouse, she rang the bell. When he answered she gave him her most seductive smile and stepped inside. He went to put his arms round her, but she held up a hand and said, 'Wait, I've got a surprise for you.'

She opened her coat and let it fall to the floor, giving him her come-and-get-me-if-you-dare look. Mickey needed no more encouragement. He picked her up and carried her to bed.

'Next time I go away, you've got to come with me,' he said, after they'd made love. 'I don't like imagining what you're getting up to when I'm away.'

Angel laughed, thinking he was joking, but he suddenly gripped her arm. 'I'm being serious. What did you do? Who did you see?' he demanded, his voice loud and harsh.

Angel twisted to pull away from him. 'I told you! Gemma came to stay. We went shopping, had dinner, then went back to mine.' Angel was reeling from Mickey's behaviour, his tone of voice. She had never seen this side of him and she really didn't like it. She looked at him as he lounged moodily on the bed. Then a nasty little thought struck her. 'Are you sure you haven't got a guilty conscience yourself, and you're accusing me of something *you've* done?'

'Don't be fucking stupid,' Mickey snapped, but he wouldn't look at her.

Angel felt sudden tears sting her eyes; she had been so looking forward to seeing Mickey and now he was behaving like a complete twat. She looked at him lying back on the bed, his hands crossed behind his head, staring at the ceiling as if he didn't give a fuck about her. She quickly got up from the bed and miserably started picking up her underwear and coat, putting them back on.

Just as she was about to leave, Mickey seemed to come to his senses.

'I'm sorry, babe, don't go,' he called after her, getting up from the bed and walking towards her. Angel paused, her hand already on the doorknob. She half thought of leaving anyway, feeling so hurt by the way he'd just treated her, but he seemed so down that she relented. She let him put his arms around her. 'I'm sorry,' he said softly. 'My manager gave me a really hard time in Germany and I was taking it out on you; I shouldn't have.'

'What was the problem?' Angel asked.

'I'll tell you some other time, I'm too knackered

to talk,' Mickey replied evasively. 'But please don't go, come back to bed.'

'Fine,' Angel replied. But it wasn't fine. She felt vulnerable and unsure of herself and Mickey.

That night she had the most intense dream of Cal. She was frantically searching the streets of Brighton for him. One minute she was running after him down by the sea, seeing him walk away. However fast she ran, she couldn't catch up with him and every time she tried to call him, no sound came out of her mouth. Then she was in the club where he'd kissed her and she was trying to push her way through the crowd of dancers to get to him, but again she couldn't get near him. She woke up crying, filled with wild, desperate longing for him.

'Hey,' Mickey said sleepily, cradling her in his arms. 'It's okay, babe. I'm sorry about last night, don't be upset.'

Angel wiped away her tears, relieved that Mickey thought she was crying about him.

'Listen, I've been meaning to ask you for ages, do you want to spend Christmas with me and my mum and dad? They really want to meet you.'

'I'd love to,' Angel replied, surprised. The fact that he'd asked her made her feel better almost instantly. It was such a small thing, really, but it showed that he was committed to her and that she was part of his life. She closed her eyes and put her head on Mickey's chest, willing herself to forget the dream. *It was only a dream*, she told herself, *nothing more; it doesn't mean anything*.

But as hard as she tried to tell herself that, in the nights that followed, images of Cal came flooding back into her mind, and feelings that she'd thought she had buried.

'You don't mind about Christmas, do you, Mum?' she asked later that day, when she called Michelle to tell her the news.

'No, love,' her mum replied, sounding sad. 'But you will come down after Christmas, won't you? Bring Mickey, we'd love to meet him.'

Angel agreed half-heartedly. She had a feeling that her dad wouldn't approve of Mickey one little bit.

The remaining weeks before Christmas passed in a flash. For the first time in her life, Angel actually had money to burn and she went mad buying presents for her family: she got her mum a voucher for a day's pampering at an expensive spa hotel in Brighton, because her mum never treated herself to anything; for her dad she bought a digital camera; for Tony an Xbox; and for Gemma some Chanel sunglasses and a make-up case from MAC. She had photo shoots, went to loads of Christmas parties and sent out Christmas cards, caught up in the rush before the holidays. The morning of Christmas Eve, Mickey collected her and her huge stash of presents and drove her to his parents. They lived in Wood Green, North London, in a tiny terraced house on a street that had seen better days. Angel was surprised. After Mickey's amazing penthouse she was expecting something a lot more upmarket, and hadn't she read that celebs always bought their parents large new houses when they made it? The only thing that set Mickey's parents' house apart from its neighbours was the gigantic illuminated Father Christmas climbing up the side of the house and the flashing icicles hanging along the window frames. *Classy*, Angel thought, *not*.

Mickey had already told her that they had encouraged his singing talent from when he was five, devoting all their free time to ferrying him to singing and drama lessons and to singing competitions, and once she stepped through the front door Angel quickly realised that Mickey was indeed the apple of his parents' eyes. They clearly adored their son – the living room was like a shrine to him, every surface and practically every inch of wall was covered in photos of him and nothing was too much for them. From the moment they arrived, Mickey didn't have to lift a finger. His mum, Sandra, made them both sit in the living room while she brought in an endless supply of drinks and snacks and Angel tried to ignore the garish artificial Christmas tree, changing colour in the corner, and the mini tree on the mantelpiece which burst into 'We Wish You a Merry Christmas' every time someone walked past it.

Angel had been feeling a little apprehensive about meeting his parents – she knew how close he was to them – but she soon relaxed. There were none of the tensions she associated with her own family. She had wondered what the sleeping arrangements would be, and was pleasantly surprised when Mickey showed her their bedroom, complete with a double bed. It would be lovely cuddling up to Mickey on Christmas Eve.

'Love you,' Mickey whispered as he held her later.

'You too,' Angel replied happily.

She wasn't quite so happy the next day. Things started to go downhill when they unwrapped presents. She had been so excited about giving Mickey his watch and he was suitably impressed.

'Babe! That's awesome, thank you so much!' he exclaimed, hugging her.

'Is it real?' his mum asked. A question that, frankly, Angel thought, was bang out of order.

'Yes,' she replied, trying not to sound offended. Mickey then handed her a small package. Inside was a set of lingerie, red and quite cheap-looking. 'Oh,' she said, and she couldn't keep her face from falling. It wasn't at all the kind of thing she would wear, and to have to open it in front of his parents was embarrassing.

'Thanks,' she said, stuffing it back into its wrapping. She hadn't expected him to spend a fortune on her, but surely he could have bought her something a little nicer?

'You can model it for me later,' Mickey said, winking at her and causing Angel to turn away to hide her irritation. His parents gave her an M&S toiletries set (*which was going straight to a charity shop*, Angel thought). She had bought them a huge box of handmade Belgian chocolates and two bottles of champagne. To try to shrug off her disappointment, she left the room to phone home and wish everyone a happy Christmas. As she spoke to her mum, she suddenly felt homesick hearing all the familiar voices in the background talking and laughing. Her parents took it in turns with Gemma's to have Christmas lunch at each other's house and even with her away it remained a firm tradition. Despite Frank's tendency to be strict, Christmas Day was always a laugh: everyone stuffed their faces, drank too much and then played charades.

Her mum passed her on to Gemma. 'What did he get you then?' was practically her friend's first question.

'Some gorgeous underwear,' Angel replied, trying and failing to impress her friend.

'Agent Provocateur? Coco de Mer?' Gemma asked excitedly.

'No, I'm not sure where he got it,' Angel lied.

Gemma's 'Oh' spoke volumes.

As she returned to the living room, Angel tried to pull herself together, telling herself sternly that it was the thought that counted. But that was the trouble: cheap, tacky underwear didn't seem like such a good thought. Her mood didn't improve when she offered to help Sandra in the kitchen and then spent the next three hours peeling veg and washing up while Mickey and his dad, Dave, sat on the sofa drinking beer. Angel couldn't help comparing it with her house, where everyone always mucked in to help on Christmas Day, even her dad. Mickey's mum talked non-stop about Mickey, how wonderful he was, how talented, how handsome, and while Angel agreed with a lot of what she said, even she had to draw the line when Sandra declared that Mickey was one of the best singers in the country. *No but yeah but he's got crap taste in presents*, was what she wanted to say, hearing Mickey and Dave laughing in the living room.

By the time Christmas lunch was served, the men were half drunk and Angel's mood had worsened. Conversation revolved entirely around Mickey and while Angel didn't expect to be the centre of attention, a bit of interest from his parents would have been welcome.

'Must have done your career no end of good, going out with Mickey,' Dave said at one point. 'All that publicity from going out with a pop star, I bet you could hardly believe your luck!'

That was so the wrong thing to say to Angel that she was too stunned to reply for a second. Then, when she was about to retort angrily that she was doing just fine before she met him, Mickey said,

'Actually, Dad, we've both done well out of it. I'm just glad she's with me.' And he took Angel's hand and kissed it. She had barely a second to smile at him when Sandra exclaimed, 'Ahh! Isn't he romantic?'

God, get me out of here! thought Angel, not knowing how much more Mickey-worship she could take. After lunch, the men fell asleep in the lounge while Angel and Sandra cleared the table and washed up. Angel felt stir crazy; she was someone who liked to be doing something and sitting around the house was seriously doing her head in. She waited for half an hour and then changed into her tracksuit and told Sandra she was going jogging. The cold December air revived her and she ran for half an hour, belting to the park and up the hill, trying to tire herself out for a long evening ahead.

'Mickey's upstairs,' Sandra told Angel when she got back, and, grabbing a glass of water, Angel went to the bedroom. There she was shocked to discover Mickey snorting a line of coke. He started when he heard the door open.

'Thank Christ, it's only you!' he exclaimed with relief, pretending to sink back onto the bed in shock.

Angel shut the door behind her. 'Why are you taking that?' she demanded.

'I just fancied a little pick-me-up, babe, do you want some?'

Angel shook her head, frowning. Yes, she had agreed to once at the party last month, and she had done it one other time at a club a couple of weeks ago, but Christmas Day at his parents' house was hardly the time or place.

'I thought you only took it when we went clubbing.'

Mickey shrugged. 'I just do it every now and then, but it's not a problem, babe, honestly.' He held out his hand and when Angel took it he pulled her onto the bed beside him.

'My parents are watching TV, aren't they?' he whispered, kissing her neck. Angel nodded.

'Well,' Mickey whispered again, undoing her zip and putting her hand on the bulge in his jeans, 'I've got another Christmas present for you.'

Should I be worried about Mickey's drug-taking? Angel wondered afterwards as she showered. It shocked her that he had taken coke on Christmas Day with his parents downstairs. How often was he doing it when she wasn't watching? Would he have told her if she hadn't caught him at it? Angel was uneasy. It was something she was going to have to watch, she decided. She knew very well that he occasionally took coke when they went clubbing. But when she had asked him about it the other day, feeling that one line was enough for her, whereas he would do five or six, he had just laughed it off and kept saying he didn't have a problem. She stared at her reflection thoughtfully, listening to the sounds of the TV and Dave's loud laugh drifting upstairs.

Mickey was on good form for the rest of the night. True, he drank a fair bit, but she didn't catch him sneaking upstairs for any more fixes and, as if making it up to her, he stayed close to her for the rest of the night as they all watched TV. But she was disappointed on Boxing Day. Mickey had promised to come with her to Brighton to meet her family, but when they woke up he complained of having a sore throat. 'I think I'd better stay here, babe, I feel really rough,' he croaked feebly from the bed.

Angel couldn't help feeling hurt; she had made the effort to come to his family's and endured two whole days with them. And he really didn't seem ill to her – a slight cold, maybe. *Typical bloke*, she thought crossly, *thinking he had man flu*.

'Well can I borrow your car, then?' she demanded, pissed off with him. 'Because how else am I going to get down there?'

She could tell that he really didn't want her to borrow it – it was a bright red Porsche 911 and his pride and joy – but the alternative would be to come with her and he obviously wanted to do that even less.

She could tell her parents were surprised that Mickey wasn't with her, but, as usual in her family, no one said what they really thought and it was brushed under the carpet. She had been dreading seeing her dad, but he treated her no differently than he always did: he gave her a hug and asked her how she was and then changed the subject to football. But it was such a relief to be home, away from the claustrophobic atmosphere at Mickey's, and to get a bit of TLC from her mum, who insisted on cooking Angel's favourite dinner of roast chicken and roast potatoes, even though Angel said she didn't have to as she must have spent enough time cooking on Christmas Day.

While Michelle was busy in the kitchen, Angel found herself alone in the living room with her dad.

'So how's Mum been lately?' she asked, keeping her voice low so Michelle couldn't overhear.

'Oh, you know, the usual, up and down,' her dad answered. 'She's missed you.'

'I know, I will try and see more of her, it's just I've been so busy,' Angel replied, feeling guilty.

'We've all missed you. Prince has been pining,' her dad added, watching Angel stroke the Labrador.

'Really? Sorry, boy,' she said, patting him. 'I've missed him too,' she said, 'but there's no way I could have him in London with me at the moment. My flat's tiny and I'm hardly ever in.'

'Why don't you come back home, then?' her dad replied, almost as if he missed her. Angel felt uncomfortable. This wasn't how they usually talked to each other.

'Oh, I couldn't, I have shoots every day,' she

replied, more breezily than she felt. 'I'd spend all my time commuting.'

Seeing that they were nearly on the dangerous topic of her work, Angel quickly changed the subject and asked if he had seen Cal lately.

'Yeah, he dropped round the day before Christmas Eve.'

'Is he okay?' asked Angel, her heart beating a little faster, as it always did when she was thinking of Cal.

'I think so – he's doing well at Chelsea – he's been on as a sub for the first team a couple of times. I got the feeling that things aren't great between him and his girlfriend – what's her name again?'

'Mel,' Angel replied, trying hard to suppress a look of delight.

'Never understood what he saw in her. Too vain and too much make-up. I don't know, I used to wonder why . . .' Her dad trailed off, looking embarrassed all of a sudden.

'Wonder what?' Angel asked, now more surprised than uncomfortable at the turn the conversation was taking.

'Why you and he never got together. You always seemed to have so much in common,' her dad managed to say, his face flushed with the rare effort of talking about emotions.

Angel could hardly believe her ears. 'Cal's never been interested in me! And anyway, I've always thought he was way out of my league.'

'Don't be daft, you're worth a hundred of that Mel girl.'

Had he been drinking? Angel wondered, but was chuffed nonetheless. It was so out of character for her dad to talk like this, but she loved him being protective.

'I know Cal has always had a soft spot for you, because you both, you know . . .' Again, her dad trailed off.

'Were abandoned by our mothers?' Angel put in bluntly.

'Well, yes,' her dad said awkwardly and switched on the TV. Angel sank back into the sofa. She'd had no idea her dad had thought about her and Cal like that. She chewed her thumbnail, ignoring Danni's orders to leave her nails alone, absentmindedly watching the game. Talking about Cal's mother made her recall the incident she had always blamed for the barrier that had gone up between her and Cal.

It had been Cal's first game as a professional for Brighton a couple of years ago, and the whole Summer family had gone along to cheer him. Angel knew that Cal had asked his mother to come as well, but when she looked around the stadium, Angel realised she hadn't shown up – probably too drunk to make it. Later that day, Angel had walked in on Cal and her dad, clearly in the middle of a heart-to-heart.

'Why does she always do this to me, Frank? She

promised she would come and watch me play and I really thought that this time she would. How fucking stupid of me.'

Seeing Cal's face, Angel froze, stunned to see such a display of raw emotion from him. Cal looked up at her, his eyes brimming with tears. Frank said quickly, 'Give us a minute, Angie.'

Angel had turned on her heel and run upstairs. She knew what a big deal the game had been to Cal and she wished she could say something to comfort him. But when they met over dinner later that night with the rest of the family, Cal wouldn't even look at her. He completely ignored her.

While the others went into the living room, Cal and Angel cleared the table. Clearing her throat, Angel had said, 'Cal, I just wanted to say that I'm really sorry that your mum didn't turn up today.'

Cal carried on with what he was doing. 'Don't be,' he replied harshly. 'She's just a fucking loser. Count yourself lucky to have such great parents.' And with that he left the room. From that moment on, the easy familiarity between them was over. Cal obviously regretted that Angel had seen him break down and made sure he was never alone with her again. He broke off all contact with his mother, moved into a studio flat and focused all his energy on football and on breaking as many girls' hearts as he could. For a while, after the scene Angel had witnessed, Cal continued to come round to the Summer house several nights a week and always for

Sunday lunch, and she couldn't help but think he sometimes blamed her for taking her family for granted when things between her and her parents got strained. Then he met Melanie and started spending less and less time with the Summers and more with Mel. And their encounter in the Brighton club had changed things once more, making it almost impossible for them to talk normally.

Angel stayed in Brighton for two days, and while she didn't see Cal, she got to see lots of Gemma. Being with her, seeing Jeanie and Bill, brought home to her how very much she had missed hanging out with her friend.

'God, I can't wait to move to London in a couple of weeks, it'll be so great living near you again. So, come on, how's it going with Mickey?' Gemma asked as they nipped upstairs to her bedroom for a gossip.

'Good, I think,' Angel said cautiously. 'I can't wait for you to meet him.'

'If you like him, Angel, I'm sure I will,' Gemma replied, equally carefully.

The image of Mickey snorting coke in his parents' house came to Angel. She sighed. *Not if Gemma knew about that*, she couldn't help thinking to herself.

Back in London, Angel made several big decisions. She bought a tiny flat in Hampstead – a top-floor apartment, which she had fallen in love with for its roof garden and wonderful view of the Heath. That done, and the move over with, she decided to take the plunge and have a boob job. She told Carrie not to book her any work for a month.

'Darling, you won't regret it, I promise,' Carrie gushed when they met up. 'Nearly all my girls have had them done. I've had mine done and I love them. See?' She thrust out her chest and Angel was forced to look at Carrie's silicone-enhanced boobs. Not exactly thinking that Carrie was her role model, Angel smiled politely and simply said, 'Yes, they look great.'

But no one had prepared her for quite how painful it would be after the operation. She came round from the anaesthetic in total agony. She looked down, expecting to see a change that would make all this pain worth it, but she couldn't see anything because of the bandages. In fact, her breasts looked smaller. *Oh God, what have I done?* she thought miserably.

She wanted to call her mum to come and pick her up and take her home, but couldn't because she hadn't even told her about the op. She hadn't told anyone except Mickey. He had come with her to the private Harley Street clinic, but he couldn't be there when she came round because he had a gig and couldn't cancel it. The last thing Angel heard before she went into the operating theatre was Mickey promising to be round first thing in the morning. The trouble was, Mickey didn't do first thing. He didn't do morning, full stop. He didn't turn up until midday, by which time Angel was feeling thoroughly sorry for herself.

'Sorry, babe, I overslept,' he said as he sauntered into her room. 'But I've got you a present.'

Angel perked up; perhaps it would be a lovely little something, say from Tiffany's? Or Gucci or Chanel? It was a pink teddy bear. Angel had no great love of cuddly toys, but she pretended it was just what she needed to cheer her up. He checked with the doctor, packed her bag for her and took her home where he tucked her up on the sofa and spent the next two days looking after her. When she finally took off the bandages, she definitely noticed a difference and Mickey seemed very impressed, although she told him he could look but not touch until the scars had healed.

'I can't believe I just said that! It makes me sound like Frankenstein's monster!' she exclaimed.

'It's not the most romantic thing you've ever said to me, but I understand,' he answered, giving her one of his usual cheeky grins.

On the third day she felt strong enough to call up Gemma and ask her to come over.

'Be gentle with me,' Angel told her when she opened the door, 'I've just had surgery.'

Just as she'd predicted, Gemma hit the roof. 'I can't believe you did that,' she said furiously. 'You had great boobs. I don't understand – now you're going to look like a clone of everyone else. I bet it was Mickey's idea, wasn't it?'

'No, it wasn't!' Angel retorted angrily. 'He had nothing to do with it whatsoever, it was my decision.'

'Well, I think you're bloody mad to have had them done.'

'That's easy for you to say,' Angel shouted back. 'You've got big boobs!'

Suddenly they looked at each other and burst out laughing.

'I can't believe we're arguing about boobs!' Gemma said. 'Let's have a look at them, then.'

Angel gingerly lifted her sweatshirt and carefully took off the extremely unglamorous sports bra she had to wear until the scars had healed.

'Not bad,' Gemma admitted. 'But mine are still bigger,' she said gleefully.

While Gemma might not approve of her boob job, she definitely agreed with Angel's next plan, which was to go platinum blonde. Even though Angel was fairly new to modelling, she knew that a change of image, particularly one as dramatic as going blonde, was bound to get her even more publicity. 'You won't regret it,' Jez assured her as he expertly brushed the bleach onto her hair, which he wrapped up in strips of tin foil – *so not a good look*, Angel thought as she looked at her reflection – half alien, half Nora Batty.

'Blondes definitely have more fun,' Jez sighed theatrically. 'When I had mine done, I was inundated with offers. It was exhausting.'

Angel laughed. 'I don't want any other offers, I'm doing this for my work.' Even so, it was a shock when she looked at herself in the mirror several hours later, once her hair had been washed and blow-dried. She looked so different. But she liked it. She liked everything that made her different from the girl she'd been in Brighton.

Chapter 8

You Again

One year later . . .

Although she'd been part of the celebrity scene for over a year now, Angel hated walking into clubs on her own. It was something she always tried to avoid, even if it meant getting there late or waiting for a crowd of acquaintances to disappear into. She didn't like the feeling that people were staring at her – it made her feel paranoid and ill at ease. She had agreed to meet Gemma at Sugar's, but when she arrived at the club her friend was nowhere to be seen. She forced herself to get out of the cab, put on a confident smile and saunter in, despite feeling anything but self-possessed. She walked purposefully over to the bar and ordered herself a vodka and tonic. She checked her watch. *Please hurry up, Gemma*, she thought to herself. There was nowhere to sit and the last thing she wanted to do was to stand alone at the bar – she felt far too conspicuous. She shook back her long platinum-blonde hair and took out her phone, pretending to be texting.

'Angie?' She started at the familiar voice and looked up, almost not daring to believe it. There, next to her, was Cal. Angel's stomach did a somersault, a double back-flip and several cartwheels. She'd seen him play often enough – his picture was splashed all over the back of the tabs, as he was now a rising star in Chelsea's first team – but she hadn't run into him once since they'd both been in London. And here he was, looking better than ever, giving her a warm smile.

'Hi, Cal,' she managed to reply, her throat suddenly feeling dry and her heart racing wildly.

'I nearly didn't recognise you with your blonde hair, you look amazing.'

'Thanks,' Angel replied, her smile matching his in warmth. 'I'm the new improved model.' *And you don't look at all bad yourself.*

'So, who are you here with?' Cal asked.

'I'm waiting for Gemma. But you know her, always late.'

Angel's phone suddenly alerted her that she had a text message. 'Oh, there you go, they've only just left, they're going to be at least another half hour.'

'Can I buy you a drink while you wait? Looks like my friends are late as well, and you could fill me in on your meteoric rise to fame.'

Angel frowned at him, hoping he wasn't taking the piss. 'Okay, cool,' she answered, trying desperately hard to sound relaxed, but feeling the exact opposite.

They ordered drinks and she followed Cal to a sofa that had suddenly become free. As they passed a large mirror Angel surreptitiously checked out her appearance. She was wearing one of her favourite outfits. A tight black vest trimmed with lace, a black satin mini that had a shocking pink net underskirt, so she looked like a very naughty ballerina, and pink strappy sandals trimmed with Swarovski crystals. As usual, her legs were bare and golden brown. She sat down on the sofa and crossed her long legs, conscious all of a sudden that her skirt was so short it barely covered her bum. Cal sat beside her.

'Cheers.' He chinked his drink against hers. Angel felt light-headed with excitement at being in his company again. She couldn't help remembering the last time they had been alone together at a club, how his hands had felt caressing her body, the feel of his lips on hers. She blushed and she could sense Cal's gaze on her as she sipped her drink. Gathering her confidence and cool, she breathed in deeply, deliberately trying to push out her breasts a little as she did so, wanting him to notice that it wasn't just her hair that had changed.

'Tony told me that you're living in Hampstead now.'

'Yeah, I bought a flat there last year. I love being by the Heath, I need the space. I mean, I love

London, but I do miss the sea and the countryside.' She was aware that she was babbling, but couldn't help it. She was still trying to get her head around the fact that he was here, in her favourite club, talking to her, laughing with her.

'That's such a coincidence – I've just bought a house there, too.'

'Oh, you flash bastard!' Angel joked, thinking, *Does that mean I'll get to see you then?*

'Well, I'm sure the way you're going, it won't be long before you can get any house you want.' He paused, then said, 'So are you enjoying it all?'

Angel reflected. 'I think so. I mean, there are some things I don't like – never knowing what the papers are going to come out with next – but I suppose I've got to accept that. Did you read that story about the boy who was supposed to be my first boyfriend? He was in the same year as me at school and I don't think we ever said a word to each other, and we never spent any time alone, but apparently I gave him the best blow job of his life!'

'To be honest, I've stopped reading the papers,' Cal replied. 'Too much crap. But your work's going well, isn't it?'

'I love the modelling bit,' Angel said. 'All the travelling and stuff . . .' She trailed off, not wanting to babble again.

Cal looked at her. 'The camera certainly loves you.'

Angel smiled. 'Thank God for airbrushing.'

Cal stared straight into her eyes, causing Angel's heart to beat faster.

'I'm really pleased it's turning out so well for you, Angie.'

'And for you, Cal.'

For a moment, the noise of the club receded and there was only Angel and Cal, on the sofa, looking at each other in the dim light. Everything faded: Mickey, Mel, the other people around them. Angel leant forward expectantly, and she was certain that she wasn't imagining it. The sexual tension between them was back. She was so conscious of her body, and of his, and she felt on fire with every minute that Cal kept looking at her in the way she had remembered so clearly from the Brighton club. All of a sudden, she wanted to move near him, to touch him. She shook her head, trying to rid herself of the mental image, then leant back and smoothed her hair behind her ears. Across the space, her eyes met his again. God, she wanted him so much—

'I'm so sorry we're late!' Gemma's voice cut the silence, breaking the spell of intimacy between them. Angel could have groaned with disappointment. She had been dying to see Gemma, but now all she wanted to do was be alone with Cal. Nonetheless, she plastered a big smile across her face and got up to hug her friend. Her brother gave her a quick peck on the cheek. She could tell by the look on his face that the skirt was a bit much for him. He seemed to have accepted her job, even complimented Angel on some of the coverage, and he rarely made any comments about her dress, but every now and then he reminded her all too much of their dad.

There were no free chairs, so the four of them had to squash up on the sofa. Angel found herself pressed against Cal, but every time she tried to inch away he seemed to move closer to her, so in the end she gave up. She watched him talk, simply enjoying his company and his conversation. The four of them were getting on so well, chatting away so easily, that for a fleeting moment Angel allowed herself to imagine what it would be like if Cal and she were a couple. They talked their way through work, family and friends and somehow the conversation turned to the future. Gemma, who had managed to down two large vodkas very quickly and was already a little drunk, declared, 'Did you know that Angel is amazing at reading palms?'

Angel looked at her friend like she'd gone mad and the men laughed disbelievingly.

'An amazing bullshitter, more like!' exclaimed Tony.

But Cal said, 'Go on, then,' holding out his hand to Angel. 'Read mine.'

Despite knowing nothing whatsoever of palm reading, she took it, pretending to study it. When his fingers touched hers, she felt a flash of desire so intense that it took her breath away for a second.

She carefully ran her fingers over his palm, tracing the lines, trying to regain her composure.

'Come on, Mystic Meg, what do you see?' Cal teased.

I see you with me, Angel wanted to say, but instead she muttered something about him having choices to make in his love life.

'Well, that's true, isn't it?' Tony said. 'You've split up with Mel.'

Angel's imagination went into overdrive. What, Cal was single? Then she realised with a jolt that she was not. For the first time all night, she thought about Mickey. Remembered that she was with him. Her boyfriend. A wave of guilt crashed over her as she looked around the club, seeing if he was anywhere in sight. He'd said he couldn't meet her until later. Oh God, he couldn't be here already? She didn't think she could take him and Cal in the same room. Her thoughts were racing. Meanwhile, Cal had moved on.

'Okay, let me read yours now.' He took Angel's hand in his, gently running his fingers across her palm. Gemma and Tony were whispering, lost in conversation of their own and oblivious to their friends.

'I see that you're going to meet someone, or maybe you've already met him, and when you get together it will be the most intense experience of your life. And you know what?' At this point Cal leant into her and whispered in her ear. 'I think he'll feel it, too.' For a second they stared at each other and Angel willed him to share her feelings.

But suddenly the moment was shattered. 'Babe!' Mickey shouted across the table, trying to be heard over the music. 'I'm sorry I'm late.'

Immediately, Cal moved away from Angel. Mickey leant across the table and kissed her on the lips. Any other time, she would have been thrilled to see him. Now the kiss felt like a betrayal of the intimacy she'd just shared with Cal. She introduced Mickey to everyone, noticing how he and Cal sized each other up. And as Cal shook Mickey's hand she couldn't help thinking how boyish Mickey looked compared to him. There were only a few years between them but Cal seemed so much older, so much more sophisticated, so much more of a man, as he sat back on the sofa, coolly observing her boyfriend.

'I'm just going to grab a seat,' Mickey said.

'No, don't bother, mate. I've got to go,' Cal called out, getting up, 'See you later,' he said to the group.

Please look at me, Angel willed him, *please*. But he walked away without a second glance at her.

Later, when Mickey was chatting to some of his friends and Tony to his, Angel and Gemma analysed her meeting with Cal.

'He just likes knowing that he could have me if he wanted to,' Angel finally said. 'He's probably like that with loads of women.'

'I'm not sure,' Gemma replied. 'I saw the way he

was looking at you. It was so intense. I think he really likes you.'

'Likes me or likes knowing that I like him?' Angel couldn't help feeling bitter. Every time she saw Cal it stirred her up, put everything out of kilter, made everything else seem so insignificant.

'I always let him do this to me,' she exclaimed. 'And it's got to stop! I've got a boyfriend – a gorgeous, sexy boyfriend, who adores me! I don't need Cal! Let's get another drink. Fuck Cal!' she declared, holding up her glass to Gemma's. 'Who needs him?'

When she stumbled into the Ladies with Gemma later, she bumped into Andrea. 'Hey,' she exclaimed. 'How did it go in the States?' Andrea had just returned from a month out there.

Her friend hugged her warmly. 'Great, but knackering. You'll have to go sometime. How's Mickey?'

'Good,' Angel replied as Gemma slipped back into the main room, waving to Angel. 'Really good.'

Andrea looked at her for a moment, and seemed on the verge of saying something, then thought better of it. She turned to go. 'Great. Let's meet up soon, I'll text you.'

The rest of the night passed in a blur of vodka, hysterical giggling fits with Gemma, some crazy dancing and then back to Mickey's for wild sex. But lost as she was in her passion for him, at the moment she climaxed there was only one man she was thinking of. And it wasn't the one she was with.

Now Angel knew that Cal lived in Hampstead, she felt even more haunted by thoughts of him. Every time she went out, even if it was only to buy milk or a paper, she kept thinking that she'd run into him. *I can't live like this*, she told herself sternly after thinking for the tenth time that she'd caught sight of him in the street and her heart had missed a beat.

Work was a great distraction and she was now busier and more in demand than she had ever been, and she loved it, it gave her such a buzz. She was booked in for shoots practically every other day and Carrie had just landed her another lucrative contract with one of the red-tops, which meant she was rarely out of the papers. Her deal with the mobile phone company had come through and her half-naked body was plastered all over the capital, her hot-pink mobile up to her ear, white towel slipping from her body and very nearly exposing her breasts, with the slogan: 'A little something with all-over coverage'. The ads were so successful she was signed up to do another year for them; she was also signed up as the face (and body) of a major lingerie chain (Angel was convinced it was her new boobs that had got her the deal). And the press and the celeb mags couldn't get enough of her and Mickey. Wherever the couple went they were photographed. There were whole articles devoted to analysing their body language, their clothes, where they went out, who they hung out with and whether they would get married. It wasn't long before *OK!* started showing an interest in the golden couple, and Angel found herself signed up to do regular interviews and photo shoots with them. Mickey loved talking about their relationship and no question seemed too intimate to him. He happily divulged details of their sex life, how often they made love and where. All of which Angel found embarrassing and very irritating – especially as Mickey seemed to want to make love with her less and less lately, and if he did he wanted a big performance. He wanted her to dress in sexy underwear, he wanted to be tied to the bed and spanked, or he wanted her to be tied to the bed. He bought her a selection of uniforms from Ann Summers and Angel found herself having to dress as a naughty nurse, a pervy policewoman and a cheeky air hostess. Angel loved sex with him and was happy to do the odd bit of role-play, but that's all Mickey seemed to be into these days. He never wanted to make love with her for herself any more, and on more than one occasion he said that he really wanted to have a threesome, something Angel wasn't at all certain that she wanted to try.

'Come on, babe, do me your sexy look.'

Angel stepped out of the shower and found herself staring into the lens of a digital recorder, with Mickey behind it. Immediately, she grabbed her towel.

'What are you doing?' she exclaimed crossly.

'I want to make a film of us, babe. Go on, do it for me.' He put down the camera and kissed her. 'Go on.'

Angel sighed. She had been posing for the camera all day. She had been looking forward to chilling out with Mickey, maybe getting a takeaway and watching a DVD together. But evidently he had other plans.

'Tonight is my fantasy night – next time it will be yours, babe. I promise.'

'Okay,' Angel muttered.

Then Mickey reeled off a list of his demands: she had to put on her black lace basque, stockings and a thong, she had to go into the bedroom, lie on the bed and touch herself while Mickey filmed her, then he would join her on the bed with the camera still rolling and she would give him a blow job, then they'd have sex – he'd let her know what positions. Mickey had it all planned out.

'I'm not really in the mood,' Angel started saying, her eyes scratchy with tiredness. She'd had such a full-on day pleasing everyone else, answering questions, moving this way and that. This was the last thing she wanted to do. But Mickey quickly handed her a glass of champagne and laid out a line of coke for her. Usually Angel would never touch coke if they were staying in together and she only very rarely did it when they were out, but with everything going on, she felt completely strung out, wired and exhausted at the same time. She was going to need something to get her going. She did the line and sipped her champagne. A few minutes later, she started perking up and got ready for her starring role in Mickey's film. *Or should that be 'best supporting actress'?* she thought later, as Mickey lay beside her, asleep. There had been no doubt about the real star of Mickey's film. Angel had barely touched herself before Mickey got onto the bed next to her and told her to suck his dick. After that he gave her body the briefest of caresses before telling her to turn over as he took her from behind. He wanted maximum exposure for himself, so he put the camera at the side of the bed. *I didn't even have an orgasm*, Angel thought bitterly, as a very satisfied Mickey snored next to her.

'Does Tony ever ask you to do stuff like that in bed?' Angel asked Gemma when the two of them caught up over lattes in a Hampstead café on one of Angel's rare afternoons off. 'Oh, gross,' she then exclaimed in horror. 'Forget I asked that – he's my brother, I really don't need to know!'

Gemma laughed. 'Well, we do like the odd game. I'll leave it there . . . But, Angel, if you didn't want him to film you, you should have said no. Why didn't you?'

Angel frowned. 'I don't know. It seems so

important to him. And I don't want him to go off me, I suppose.'

Gemma snorted in disgust. 'What happened to girl power? You don't have to do everything your boyfriend asks! And if he goes off you because of it, then he's not worth it.'

She was about to carry on her tirade and then caught sight of Angel's face. Her friend looked so vulnerable and tired.

'Hey,' she said, softening her approach. 'It doesn't matter, so long as you enjoyed it in the end.'

'I suppose so,' Angel replied and then grinned, shaking off the moment of sadness. 'And it is very funny watching Mickey watch himself on film when we have sex. He takes his performance so seriously and he gets this expression on his face like he's such a stud!'

'You're kidding!' Gemma exclaimed.

'Nope, he's put up a huge plasma screen in the bedroom.'

The two girls gigged hysterically. It did Angel good to laugh. She'd been brooding about Mickey, but chatting to Gemma now it all just seemed like a bit of fun. She would say to Mickey that she didn't always want to make a home movie when they had sex. And if he didn't like it, well, that would be tough.

'Anyway, I've got some news for you.' Gemma beamed at her friend. 'I can't believe you haven't noticed.'

'What – are you pregnant?' Angel exclaimed.

'Don't be silly, look!' And Gemma held out her left hand, showing off a very gorgeous, very large, princess-cut diamond engagement ring.

'Oh my God!' Angel squealed. 'I can't believe I didn't see it! That is such good news.' She got off her seat and flung her arms round her friend, tears in her eyes. 'I'm so happy for you! I want to know all the details. How did he propose? When are you going to get married?'

As Gemma chatted away, Angel felt mortified that she'd spent twenty minutes moaning about herself and hadn't even noticed Gemma's ring. Really, she couldn't have been happier at the news.

'Now, we're having two engagement parties: one's just a dinner with the family and the other will be a big party at a club, with all our friends.'

'What, my family as well?' Angel's good mood evaporated. Although things had calmed down, she still slightly dreaded spending time with her dad in case he started having a go at her about her work.

'It'll be fine.' Gemma paused. 'We've also asked Cal, because he's going to be best man.'

'Oh?' Angel perked up again.

'Yeah, and, sorry, bad news: he's got a new girl-friend, Simone Fraser off *Hollyoaks*. She's coming too, Tony already invited her and I couldn't do anything about it. But you can bring Mickey.'

'Great,' Angel muttered. 'Perhaps he'd like to bring some of his home movies. Help break the ice.'

'Don't worry,' Gemma soothed her friend, 'I'll make sure you're at the opposite end of the table.'

'So, tell me about Simone.' Angel couldn't resist asking. She might have guessed that Cal wouldn't be single for long.

'She's pretty, if you like that kind of thing, dark-haired, quite a good figure – of course, she's nowhere near as pretty as you,' Gemma said loyally. 'And she's the biggest bitch I've ever met.'

'What, a bigger bitch than the lovely Melanie?'

'Yep, and she clings to Cal like a drowning man clinging to a lifebelt – won't let him out of her sight, just like Mel.'

I can't blame her for that, Angel thought to herself wistfully.

'How is the Cal obsession these days?' Gemma asked sympathetically.

'Still pretty bad. Although today was the first time in ages that I didn't think I was going to bump into him in Hampstead, so maybe I'm getting better. But now you've said he's going to be there at the dinner, I'm obsessing again. God, how sad am I!'

Chapter 9

Encounter
at the Royale

Angel took one last look at her reflection. She had rapidly become notorious in the tabloids and celebrity magazines for the revealing clothes she wore. Tonight was no exception. She was dressed to thrill in her black designer corset, which emphasised her tiny waist and pushed up her breasts so they looked as if they might be tantalisingly released at any moment from their silk confines. A minuscule black satin kilt skirt accompanied the corset; it was barely decent and showed off her long, lean, tanned legs to devastating effect. She completed the outfit with a pair of delicate silver Gina sandals with sky-high heels and a platinum necklace with a diamond-studded letter A around her neck – the first thing she had bought for herself when she had started to make it as a model.

'You'll do,' she told her reflection, practising her

trademark pout in the mirror before slamming her door and running down the stairs and into the limo below where Mickey was getting impatient. She hadn't seen him for three weeks because he'd been in the States with the band trying to break into the charts, and she had missed him. She couldn't wait to see him again. Absence definitely made the heart grow fonder – she even forgave him for his filming exploits.

'I was going to ask what took you so long, but now you're here I understand. You look stunning, babe.' He leant across to kiss her and slid one hand up her thigh. God, he was gorgeous! Those blue eyes, that boyishly handsome face, and that to-die-for body. He could easily give Brad Pitt a run for his money. She just loved running her hands over his muscular chest, across his six-pack and on, slipping her fingers under the waistband of his Calvins and . . . But, suddenly aware of the limo driver eye-balling them in the mirror, Angel pulled away. 'Save it till later,' she whispered tantalisingly.

'Oh, I will,' Mickey murmured. 'God, I've missed you.'

Outside the club in Mayfair, there was a long queue of people snaking round the block, waiting to enter. The Royale had only just opened and had rapidly become *the* place to be seen. Mickey and Angel got out of the limo and walked straight to the front of the queue – as VIPs they were assured immediate entry. Angel felt sorry for the people waiting out in the cold, and even though she'd become one of the country's most photographed women in the last year or so, she still found it strange to be treated as a celebrity. While part of her enjoyed the perks of being able to jump the queue, the other, more sensitive, side couldn't help feeling slightly guilty for her good fortune, as if she hadn't quite deserved it. She could still remember what it felt like to queue in the pouring rain, dying to get into the club you'd been longing to go to all week. Mickey had no such qualms. He revelled in his fame and frequently asked for favours – free designer clothes, free jewellery, haircuts and beauty treatments, free tickets for this and that – on the basis of who he was.

Inside the club Mickey steered Angel towards the VIP lounge, quickly attracted the waitress's attention and ordered a bottle of vintage Cristal. As they sat down on the purple velvet sofa, Mickey said, 'I've got the perfect little something to go with the champagne.'

When the bubbly arrived, Mickey filled both their glasses to the brim. He rapidly drained his, while Angel sipped hers a little more slowly. Then Mickey got up, pulling her up from the sofa. 'Follow me, babe.' They wove their way through the clubbers to the men's bathroom. After checking that the coast was clear, Mickey quickly pulled Angel inside one of the cubicles and locked the door. Expertly he laid out two lines of coke on the cistern lid. He took the first, then looked at Angel expectantly. She hesitated, not really feeling the need for it tonight, but he moved around to make room for her and all of a sudden it seemed silly to refuse. She bent down to take hers and instantly felt the drug take a hold of her, mixing deliciously with the champagne. Mickey sat down and pulled her on top of him, passionately kissing her, his fingers roaming around her body.

'Did you miss me, Angel?' he whispered.

'Very much,' She shivered as his hands slowly found their way underneath her skirt. She could feel his hardness against her thighs and suddenly she wanted to feel him inside her. As if he read her mind, he slipped his hand up her skirt and caressed her through her silk thong. Angel bit her lip to stop herself from moaning. He unzipped his trousers, slipped her thong to one side and entered her. The coke made the sex feel incredible, and even when she heard the bathroom door open Angel didn't want Mickey to stop. Until she heard one of the men speak.

'Fuck me, it's hot in there!'

She froze.

It was Cal and her brother. Jesus Christ, could they have arrived at a worse moment? 'Stop!' she whispered urgently in Mickey's ear, making as if to get up.

'Can't, babe, I'm so close,' he gasped, thrusting deeper into her. Music from the club was playing in the bathroom but even so, Angel thought there was no way the two men could fail to know what was happening just a few feet away from them. Mercifully they left just before Mickey let out a strangled 'Oh God!' Angel didn't feel remotely turned on any more and as soon as he'd finished, she made him check that the bathroom was empty before she straightened her clothing, reapplied her make-up and sprayed on her perfume.

'God, I definitely need some more champagne now,' exclaimed Angel as they sat back at their table, pouring out two more glasses, and she prayed that Cal and her brother hadn't realised she and Mickey had been the ones giving the performance in the bathroom. He gave her a curious glance. 'What do you care who heard us in the bathroom, babe? Anyway, if you want any more of the other stuff, I've got plenty on me.'

Angel was already regretting having taken the one line; hearing Cal and Tony outside had been such a comedown. She sipped her champagne, realising that Mickey was still waiting for an answer.

'I'll be okay, Mickey.'

He shrugged, 'You only have to ask. Come here and give me a kiss.'

But just as Angel leant across to kiss him, Mickey pulled away. To celebrate the opening of the club, a number of 'real' people had been allowed into the VIP area and one of his many female fans was demanding an autograph. Mickey never liked to disappoint, especially if the fan in question was a looker. Angel watched him flashing his most winning smile at the girl, registered the look of total delight on her face as he kissed her, and felt a certain amount of dismay as Mickey saucily proceeded to sign his name across the girl's tight pink T-shirt, right across her breasts. The girl in pink was quickly joined by several other girls, all desperate for a piece of Mickey. Angel smiled to herself, thinking, *Let them have their bit of fun. I'm the one who'll be going home with him – not them.*

Her reverie was interrupted when she was spotted by some of her many male admirers and she found herself having to smile away at the lads surrounding her and to sign the pictures they thrust at her. One lad tore off his shirt and demanded that she sign his chest, then four others followed suit. The fans were the part of fame she was least confident about. True, she could strip for the cameras and pose in nothing more than a smile and a strategically-placed hand or prop, but somehow, being surrounded by all the men and women wanting to talk to her, to touch her, to have their picture taken with her, sometimes got too much. After enduring her admirers for some ten minutes, she decided she'd had enough.

Mickey was still doing the fan thing – he never seemed to mind how many girls wanted to talk to him. She tried to catch his eye and let him know what she was doing, but he was still kissing and signing. She shrugged, picked up her pink leather bag and headed out to the Royale's roof garden.

Angel leant against the railing and gazed at the London skyline before her, mesmerised by the many lights glittering extravagantly in the distance like so many diamonds. *Or maybe that was the coke talking*, she thought. Much as she loved living in London, part of her missed Brighton, missed seeing the sea every day. She was a girl who definitely needed space. It was colder than she'd realised and she shivered in the cool March air and turned to go back inside when a familiar male voice called out to her.

'Hi, Angie.' She span round and there was Cal. He walked over to her and kissed her cheek.

'Cal. How are you?' *Please don't let him know it was me in the bathroom*, she prayed again.

'Warmer than you, I should imagine.' He made a show of looking her up and down and Angel's face burnt with embarrassment.

'You're wearing even less than when I saw you last time. Does your mum know you've come out looking like this?' he said teasingly.

Oh God, she thought, *why was he always able to do that?* Why did the outfit she had put on so confidently earlier that night, that she had thought made her look good, suddenly feel all wrong? She looked at him, trying to cool her flushed face with her hands. He leant next to her against the railing, stylishly dressed in an impeccably-cut designer suit.

She felt flustered and on edge and, instead of returning his banter, she became defensive.

'Well, it depends which mum you mean, doesn't it? I'm sure my real mum wouldn't mind what I wore.'

Cal laughed. 'I was just kidding. You look . . .' He was obviously searching for the right word.

Sexy was the one Angel longed for him to find, failing that, *gorgeous* would do, too. Instead, she had to make do with:

'You look exactly how a successful glamour model should look.'

'Cheers, Cal,' she replied wryly. 'And you look . . .' she paused as he had and sized him up '. . . exactly how a premiership footballer should look.'

He laughed. 'Touché, Angie.'

She frowned. 'No one calls me that any more, I meant to tell you when I saw you the other month.'

'Well, Tony does and so does your dad. And I've known you since school and you've always been Angie to me.'

'Yes, but it's not my name and I've always hated it. I've never understood why Mum and Dad couldn't call me Angel – that's the name my real mum gave me.' Much to her horror she felt tears start to well up in her eyes. Oh God, the last thing she wanted to do was to cry in front of him. She turned away and pretended to be studying the view, frantically blinking the tears away. Suddenly she felt Cal slip his jacket, still warm from his body, over her shoulders.

'You look frozen.'

'Thanks,' she said in surprise, touched by his concern.

'Anyway . . .' He was now much closer to her, leaning forward on the railing, and she instantly became all too aware of his firm muscular body, and the scent of his aftershave – still Hugo Boss No 1, she realised. 'Who are you here with?'

'Mickey,' she answered.

'I didn't know you were still seeing him. Tony thought you might have broken up.' Was it Angel's imagination or did his voice suddenly seem colder?

'No,' Angel replied. 'Why would you think that? He's just been away in the States.'

There was a slight pause. 'I know it's none of my business, but do you really think he's such a good idea, Angie? I mean, Angel?'

'What do you mean?' she demanded, rounding on him furiously. He was well out of line.

Cal took a step back but bravely opened his mouth again, obviously about to launch into a character assassination, when someone called his name.

Angel and he both turned at once – it was hard to say who was more relieved at the interruption. Cal's soap-star actress girlfriend Simone was stalking across the roof deck towards them, clearly put-out to discover him deep in conversation with another woman, especially one as scantily clad as Angel.

'Cal, I've been looking for you everywhere, darling,' she said petulantly when she reached them. She slipped a possessive hand round his waist, looking daggers at Angel.

Cow, thought Angel. Gemma was right, she seemed an even bigger bitch than Mel.

'Simone, this is Angie – sorry, Angel.'

'Oh, hi,' Simone managed, giving her a once-over with ice-cold eyes.

'Cal, we're supposed to be at Silver's now.'

'God, yes, I forgot. It was good to see you again, Angie – I mean, Angel. Sorry, I must try and remember that.'

'And you, Cal.' She slipped off his jacket ready to hand it back.

'No, you borrow it – your mum would never forgive me if you caught pneumonia.'

Simone now looked as if she could have cheerfully thrown Angel off the side of the building, but Angel gave her most dazzling smile and put the jacket back on. 'Thanks, Cal. I'll give it to Tony the next time I see him.'

Simone and Cal were just about to go back inside the club when Mickey staggered onto the roof garden. His eyes were glazed and it looked like he'd spilt champagne on his jeans. He stumbled straight into Cal, who had to step sideways to avoid getting knocked over, but Mickey barely apologised, just staggered over to Angel and put his arms round her. She looked over at Cal, embarrassed that her boyfriend was making such a twat of himself, and mouthed 'sorry', but Cal shrugged and was gone before she knew it, with Simone clinging to his arm.

'Babe, we're going on to Johnny's now.' Mickey was drunk and more coked up than when she'd left him. She looked at him coldly. All the desire she had felt for him earlier had gone.

'Okay,' she replied, trying to keep the irritation out of her voice. 'I think I'm going to head home, I've got an early shoot.'

She couldn't help noticing that Mickey didn't seem too concerned that she was leaving. As they walked down the stairs into the main area of the club, picking their way through the crowd of people drinking, dancing and chatting, he had to lean heavily on her arm just to stay upright. He walked her to her limo, swaying unsteadily, and just as she was about to get in, he whispered, 'Have you got any cash on you, Angel?'

'Yeah – a couple of hundred,' she answered, her heart sinking.

'Could you lend me some? I'm totally out and I owe Johnny.'

She really didn't want to. Despite earning good money, she was still conscious of what she was spending and she'd already spent more than she'd intended to this month. Reluctantly she opened her bag, pulled out a wad of cash and silently handed it to him.

'Cheers, babe.' He stuffed it into his pocket

without looking at it. 'I'll call you in the morning.'
He gave her a quick kiss and slammed the door shut,
walking over to his car without a second glance.

Angel sank back into the leather seat as her car
sped away, winding its way through back streets
and quiet neighbourhoods towards Hampstead.
The euphoria of the night and her coke-filled good
mood seemed to have deserted her. She looked out
into the darkness. This wasn't the first time Mickey
had asked to borrow money – in fact, over the last
two months she'd probably lent him close to five
grand. She couldn't understand why he needed it –
surely he was loaded? He had the flat that must be
worth at least a million, the Porsche, a recording
contract. What was going on? He never seemed to
have any cash on him and there was always some
excuse or other about his credit cards not working,
a royalty payment about to hit his accounts, and so
on. It didn't add up.

Oh, for God's sake, she told herself, *you'll get it back*.

But would she? She thought of Cal as she
snuggled deeper into his jacket, breathing in his
scent. She couldn't imagine him borrowing money
off anyone, least of all his girlfriend.

The following morning Angel woke up with a
pounding headache and a horribly dry mouth – an
eight on her personal hangover scale. Not good,
not good at all. Very bad, in fact.

'Shit, shit, shit, I never should have drunk so

much,' she groaned to herself as she forced herself out of bed and into the bathroom. She studied herself in the mirror, squinting in the bright light. She looked like crap; there were violet bags under her eyes and she hadn't bothered to take off her make-up from the night before. She ran a shaking hand through her limp hair – her hair was having a seriously bad day. *God, I hope Danni can put me back together again*, she prayed, as she alternated hot and cold water in the shower in an attempt to give her circulation a boost and shake off the hangover.

There was only one thing for it – the Coca Cola and white-bread toast cure. Three slices later, washed down with an ice-cold glass of Coke and a couple of paracetamol, she was starting to feel a little more human. She could actually move her head without being blinded with pain. She was just brushing out her damp hair when her door buzzer went. She padded over to the door and looked at the monitor entry-phone video. Her heart missed its usual beat when she saw Cal standing downstairs.

'Hi,' she buzzed down to him.

'Hi,' he buzzed back. 'I left my wallet in my jacket. Okay if I get it?'

'Sure,' she replied, trying to sound casual. Cal was the last person in the world she wanted to see this early in the morning and with such a raging hangover. She buzzed open the downstairs door. She left her front door ajar and raced into her bedroom, where she grabbed the nearest clothes –

a pair of pink Juicy Couture tracksuit bottoms and a tight white vest. There was no time for make-up, so she had to content herself with dabbing on a bit of lip gloss.

'God, have you only just got up, lazy bones?' Cal exclaimed, as he walked into the living room, taking in her hair still damp from the shower. 'Some of us have been up and training for the last three hours,' he added.

'Here's your jacket. I didn't realise I had your wallet as well, otherwise I'd have stayed longer at the club!' she said teasingly. He grabbed it from her and slung it on the sofa, their fingers brushing against each other in the exchange. Despite her pounding head, she felt a jolt of excitement at his touch.

'Would you like a drink?' she asked him. 'A coffee, I mean, or some water?'

'A coffee would be great,' he replied.

He followed her into the kitchen, which was too small for two people, really. As she busied herself making him a cafetière of coffee, she felt very conscious of him standing next to her, especially since she wasn't wearing any underwear and she couldn't help but notice that her nipples had sprung to attention and were showing through her thin cotton vest.

'Hung over?' he asked sympathetically, noticing the can of Coke and the half-eaten toast.

'Yeah,' she sighed. 'Please don't give me a hard

time, though. I feel like shit and I've got a shoot in a couple of hours. Thank God for make-up!' She rubbed her aching face with her hands, smoothing down her hair and taking a deep breath. The kitchen felt suddenly claustrophobic.

'Actually,' Cal replied, 'I've always thought you look great without all that stuff.'

'Come on,' she said wearily, 'look at me, I'm in a right state!'

'No, you're not, you look very natural, very pretty.'

Wow. This was new. Angel wasn't used to getting compliments from Cal, and she could feel herself blushing again, which reminded her of their awkward conversation last night. She sighed, handed him his coffee and he followed her into the living room. They sat at opposite ends of her brown leather sofa and Angel turned to face him, tucking her legs up and clasping her hands over her knees, trying to hide her conspicuous nipples.

Cal shifted about uncomfortably, taking a sip of his coffee, putting it down, taking it back up. She realised he wanted to get something off his chest. Oh no, she thought, sneaking a peek at the clock. *Here we go again.* And sure enough . . .

'So, I was about to ask you last night how it was going with Mickey,' Cal finally said, sounding serious.

'Oh, that. It's going great, really great,' she said breezily, giving him a bland smile. She squirmed a bit when she remembered Mickey borrowing yet more money from her, but pushed that firmly to the back of her mind.

'It's just, you know, he's got quite a reputation.'

'For what?' she challenged, looking him squarely in the eye.

'Well . . .' Cal paused, looking slightly awkward. 'Drugs and women, mainly.'

'Oh, come on,' she scoffed, 'you should know better than to believe everything you read.'

'It's not what I read, Angie, it's what I've been hearing from friends. Apparently it's quite a habit he's got. He's a coke addict, Angie. You really, really don't want to get involved in all that.'

He looked at her intently, his face open and worried. She blushed again, liking his concern, but then she shook her head firmly. She refused to believe all that about Mickey. Images came to her, unwanted images of Mickey chopping up lines, laughing maniacally and she quickly got up, walking over to the window. She felt Cal's eyes on her back and turned around, joking feebly, 'I'm not going to answer you if you keep calling me Angie.'

He changed tack too quickly for her hung-over brain to click into action.

'OK, Angel, no more jokes. Are you taking drugs?' His voice was firmer now and he looked her straight in the eye.

If she hadn't been so tired, she would have

known this was coming. Trying to be casual, she laughed it off. 'Oh, come on, who isn't these days, for God's sake!'

But he didn't smile, just gave her a long look. 'I'm not, Angel, and none of my friends are.'

'Look,' she sighed, sinking back into the sofa, 'I just do it every now and then when I'm out, it's not a big deal, honestly. I'm not addicted or anything, I can take it or leave it.'

He leant closer to her, his face serious. 'Trust me, Angel, you may think that now, but sooner or later you won't be able to just take it or leave it any more. Take it from me, it will fuck you up for sure.'

'Oh, come on, Cal,' she groaned in exasperation. 'Give me a break! I'm a model. It's part of the territory. Sometimes I just need a little something.' *So what? What's the big deal?*

'If Tony knew, he'd go ballistic. You know that, don't you?'

'Well,' she retorted coolly, 'Tony doesn't need to know and I'd appreciate it if you didn't tell him.'

She got up off the sofa to bring the conversation to a close. God, this was turning out to be a bitch of a day. When he didn't move, she walked over to the fireplace, as if she'd been meaning to all along, and rearranged a picture frame. Her head was spinning. Why was he having a go at her? And since when had Cal ever cared about what she got up to?

She turned back to face him. 'Hey, Cal. I'm not

going to come over all Danniella Westbrook, if that's what you're worried about.' She tilted back her head and pointed at her nose, moving closer to him. 'See, it's all still there.' Snapping her head back down, she swayed a bit, then realised with a start how much of her body she had exposed. Her breasts were practically in his face and her Juicy Couture bottoms, which had seen better days, were slipping down her slender hips, very nearly revealing quite a bit more than she intended. She swiftly hoisted them up and crossed her arms.

She'd meant it as a joke, but he didn't seem amused.

'I know all about addiction from my mum, if you remember,' Cal said.

'Oh, and how is she?' Angel asked, thinking that Cal would lose the moral high ground now as he probably hadn't seen his mum for ages.

'Doing much better, thanks, she's finally agreed to get treatment for her alcoholism. I've arranged for her to go to a clinic and last week she actually came and watched me play.'

'Oh, that's good,' Angel mumbled, torn between feeling happy for Cal and resentment that he was having a go at her. She changed the subject again.

'So how's Simone?' she finally asked.

'She's great,' he replied abruptly, got up and put his cup on the coffee table. As if on cue, his mobile started ringing. He pulled it out of his pocket and flicked it open impatiently.

'Hey. Yes, okay. I'll be with you in half an hour. See you.'

'Does that mean the lecture is over?' Angel demanded, still annoyed at having been spoken to like a child. He'd made her feel like Kevin the teenager – she almost felt like stamping her foot and saying, 'It's not fair!'

'Temporarily,' he said abruptly. 'But you're not off the hook. I'm just going to meet Simone at the gym.' Angel frowned at the thought of the two of them working out together. 'Thanks for the coffee, Angel, and I hope your hangover gets better,' Cal said as she opened the door for him. He turned to go, but suddenly reached out and gently touched her arm. 'I didn't mean to give you a hard time,' he said, much kinder now. 'It's just, you're Tony's little sister. I don't want any bad shit happening to you.'

So that was how he saw her. How stupid of her to imagine it was anything else. She moved abruptly away, taking a hold of the door.

'I'm perfectly capable of taking care of myself, and I don't need you preaching at me,' she snapped, starting to close the door. He just shrugged, unimpressed, and she immediately regretted her quick words. She shouted after him, 'Have a good workout with Simone.'

'Thanks,' he called back cheerfully. 'I might give you one sometime. Although—' she could see him pause on the stairs and raise an eyebrow '—you'll have to promise to wear something a bit less revealing than that. See you tomorrow night at Tony's engagement dinner, Angel.'

The conversation left her reeling. She walked slowly back into the lounge. Maybe all his talk about drugs was a sign that he genuinely cared about her? She felt annoyed again about the way he was being negative about Mickey. She loved Mickey. She looked out of the window, catching a last sight of Cal's long legs striding down the road. God, he was gorgeous. And so confusing. When she turned, her eyes fell on his jacket, still slung over the back of the sofa. She ran back over to the window but he was already getting into his car. *Oh well*, she thought, *I can give it back to him at the dinner. Simone will freak.* She smiled at the thought. And then she couldn't resist – she held the jacket to her face and breathed in deeply, lost in the smell of his aftershave one more time.

Chapter 10

A Shoot, a Dinner and a Goodbye . . .

Angel had her outfit for the engagement dinner all planned out – a simple little black dress with diamante straps, which was long enough for her dad not to raise an eyebrow, sexy without being tarty, and a pair of black satin Gina thong sandals with diamante trim. She was going for understated make-up and wearing her long blonde hair loose. She had tested the whole kit out in front of her bedroom mirror, analysing her reflection and thinking, with some satisfaction, that that cow Simone wouldn't be able to look down her nose at her this time. She was booked in to do a shoot during the day, but she'd make it back home in plenty of time to change for the evening. Before she left, she laid everything out on her bed, ready and waiting for her. She slammed her door shut, mentally preparing herself for a long day and an even longer evening.

The shoot was for the cover of *Tackle* – an eight-page spread of pictures of her, along with an interview. This was a big deal, Carrie had said more than once, and it showed better than all the jobs she'd recently done that she was going places with her modelling. Angel wanted everything to be perfect. Jez had touched up her roots the day before, and she had gone to bed early in order to have a healthy glow and had been drinking mineral water all morning, for once mindful of Danni's instructions. But from the minute she arrived at the studio, everything went wrong. Danni had left a message to say she had food poisoning and couldn't make it and the magazine had booked Stephan instead, an arrogant idiot who seemed to have no idea how to make the most of Angel's features and who refused to listen to her ideas either. She ended up caked in heavy make-up, which she thought made her look like a drag queen, and Stephan piled her hair high up on her head, making it look like a pineapple. The stylist appeared to have done nothing more than grab a handful of underwear, and Vince, the photographer, looked like a right surly bastard.

Jesus Christ, thought Angel, gritting her teeth as she considered herself in the mirror, dressed in a red satin basque, a red fur-trimmed thong and black patent thigh-length boots. *I look like a hooker!* She paused for a moment, trying to think. Should she call Carrie? No, it was too late, she had to get on with the shoot. She tottered into the studio.

'So, how do you want me?'

'I thought we'd start off with these?' Vince held up a pair of handcuffs and ordered the stylist to cuff her to the bed.

'Ow!' Angel exclaimed as the metal pinched her skin. The stylist barely apologised, just stepped to the side, watching her indifferently.

'Okay, baby,' Vince called out, 'I want you to writhe around and lick your lips.' Angel rolled her eyes – she hated being called 'baby' – but she did as she was told. Then it was off with the cuffs and he ordered her to slip a hand inside her thong and half close her eyes. Then he wanted her on all fours on the bed, pouting at the camera and thrusting her arse into the air. She did everything he asked for without complaining, but felt increasingly uncomfortable and angry. She hated the way he wanted her arranged like some porn star. It was so tacky. She especially didn't like doing all this in front of the two male journalists from the magazine who had turned up to watch the shoot, their beady little eyes feasting on Angel's beautiful body.

When Vince was satisfied with what he'd got, he told her she needed to change into the next outfit. *God knows what that will turn out to be*, thought Angel grimly, *a rubber bondage suit?* She pulled herself together and marched over to the photographer.

'Before I do anything else, Vince, I'd really like to see the Polaroids,' she said firmly. He looked like he wanted to refuse her request, but when she didn't back down, he reluctantly handed her a pile. Angel flicked through the pictures with an expert hand. Finally, she looked up at Vince, fixing him with a furious look.

'I look like shit!' she exclaimed. 'I'm supposed to look sexy, but not like I'm advertising a sex chatline! There's no way I'll go with these pictures. You've done it your way, now please can we try it mine? Then we'll see what looks better.' She ignored his pissed-off expression and stalked back into her dressing room. She slammed the door, marched into the tiny bathroom and started wiping off the layers of make-up. She hated when photographers didn't want to hear her opinion and treated her like some dumb bimbo. She'd been in the business long enough to know what worked and what didn't.

When she emerged from the bathroom, calmer and with a clean face, she asked Stephan to give her a kind of Bardot look with dark, smoky eyes and pale glossed lips. He pursed his lips dismissively, but did what he was told. She waved away the stylist, rifling through the piles of underwear and finally settling on a pair of white lace French knickers and a white silk camisole. She found a diamante collar, which she put round her neck, and she took down her hair and wore it loose. When she came back, the two journalists looked suitably impressed. She looked sensational. The white set off her gorgeous, tanned limbs and her white-blonde hair and it was a thousand times sexier than the garish red underwear.

She started her shoot by kneeling on the bed in the vest and knickers, looking dreamily at the camera, then started experimenting, first with removing the camisole and covering her breasts with her long blonde hair, then taking off the knickers but putting the vest back on and lying on her stomach, so the camera got a shot of her long, tanned legs and pert bum. Finally, after ordering the two men from the magazine out of the room, she took everything off except her diamante necklace and lay back against the pillow, with her hair fanned out and with her hand covering her.

'And? How does it look?' She was in a better mood now, pleased with herself for taking a stand. She wrapped herself in the sheet and padded over to Vince, who was considering the Polaroids.

'I think we'll go with the white,' he replied casually. That was it, no apology for wasting her time, no acknowledgment that she'd been right all along. She allowed herself a tiny smile and turned to go, when he said, 'But I want a different backdrop and different bedding, so the stylist will have to go out and get it right now.'

What? He was doing that just to piss her around, wasn't he? He couldn't take the fact that she'd openly humiliated him by doing the shoot her own way. Bastard. Angel checked the clock on the studio wall: four o'clock already. This really was the longest day in history. She took a deep breath, faced him and tried to keep her voice even. 'Okay, but I have to finish by half past six, it's my brother's engagement dinner and I can't be late.'

'Sure, whatever,' said the photographer. 'We'll be done by then.'

Of course, they weren't. The stylist didn't get back until half past five and then took for ever sorting out the bed. Vince made Angel do all the poses again, even though she was convinced that her first shots were the best ones, and she was getting angrier by the minute, sure that he was doing this out of spite. At half past seven, they were finally done. She had just twenty minutes to get to the restaurant and absolutely no time to go home to shower and change.

'Oh God, what am I going to do,' she groaned, running into the changing room without giving the photographer another glance. The stylist took pity on her and lent her a vintage silver sequined shrug, which she suggested Angel wear over the white camisole, along with her low-rise jeans and her silver Ginas. Angel brushed out her hair, applied some clear lip gloss, and left on her dramatic black eye make-up. A dash of her favourite Chanel perfume and that was it. She hoped the silver shrug would make it look as if she'd gone to some effort, but she knew her dad wouldn't approve of the jeans or the amount of cleavage she had on display. He, like Gemma, had not liked the idea of her having a boob job and the last thing Angel wanted to do now was draw attention to her breasts. At least she had had the foresight to tuck Tony and Gemma's engagement present in her bag when she'd left that morning: first-class Eurostar tickets to Paris and a weekend at the Ritz. She knew that Gemma had always wanted to go to Paris but that Tony had never got round to taking her. Perhaps, if she flashed the envelope around a lot, it would take everyone's attention away from the fact that she was underdressed for the Savoy.

She felt her stomach knotting with anxiety as she sat in the taxi, contemplating a quick hit-and-run on one of the shops they passed. But there was no time, really, she was already going to show up seriously late as it was. And she had so wanted tonight to go well. Her parents had only met Mickey a few times and she sensed that her dad hadn't taken to him. She paid the taxi and raced into the restaurant, oblivious to the admiring looks of the other diners as she ran to her table.

'About time, too,' was all her dad said when she arrived breathlessly. He and her mum were sitting at one end, opposite Gemma's mum and dad, Jeanie and Bill. Tony, Gemma, Cal and Simone were grouped around the other. There were two empty chairs.

'Sorry,' she said, bending down to give him a quick kiss and then kissing her mum. 'I was doing a shoot and although I said I had to leave on time, it completely over-ran. Isn't Mickey here yet?'

Her dad shrugged and she looked at Tony, who shook his head. *Fuck*, she thought. The evening couldn't have got off to a worse start as far as she was concerned.

'Lovely to see you, Angel,' Jeanie said, getting up to give her a hug.

'Looking lovely as ever,' put in Bill kindly. Angel smiled at both of them gratefully, and greeted the rest of the table, but the air was decidedly tense as she slipped into her seat.

To make matters worse, she found herself sitting opposite Cal and Simone. Taking in Simone's chic black Galaxy dress and very subtle make-up, she wished that she was wearing her black dress. Why, oh why, she cursed herself, had she not just taken her outfit to the shoot, just in case?

Cal smiled at her. 'What was the shoot for, then?'

'*Tackle*,' she replied.

'And you wore?' asked Simone, arching a perfectly shaped eyebrow, her voice heavy with innuendo.

You really are a cow, thought Angel again. It seemed to be the only thing Angel could think in her presence. She turned sideways, so that only one half of the table could hear her.

'I wore a smile, and this,' she replied, touching her diamante collar.

'Oh, God,' groaned Tony. 'Don't let Dad hear you!'

'Don't you mind posing nude?' Simone persisted.

Angel shook her head. 'It's my job. It's what I do. And it's not like I show everything! I'd never do any top-shelf stuff!'

'I can't imagine it,' Simone exclaimed. 'I'd be so embarrassed!'

'But you're an actress,' put in Gemma, smiling at Angel. 'Haven't you ever had to take your clothes off for a role?'

'No, I have not!' replied Simone – *a little too hotly*, thought Angel. 'I have a no-nudity clause in my contract.' *Hmmm*, Angel wondered, *perhaps Miss Goody Two Shoes has some skeletons hidden in her cupboard?* Many actresses started out doing topless modelling to pay the rent. Why would Simone be any different? With any luck, a celeb mag would get hold of photos one day soon, and then her smug, self-satisfied expression would be wiped right off her face.

'So where's Mickey? Held up in the studio?' demanded Simone loudly, obviously keen to change the subject while still trying to find something that would get Angel into trouble.

'Probably,' said Angel coolly, not rising to take the bait but taking a large sip of her champagne instead.

'I saw the match last weekend, Cal. That was a great goal, but then their defence was woeful, wasn't it?' She addressed Cal directly, openly excluding Simone. So she showed up half an hour late and her boyfriend still wasn't here, keeping everyone from ordering, and she wasn't dressed for the occasion, but that didn't mean that she wasn't more than a match for Simone, the cow.

Simone giggled, ignoring the jibe. 'Don't tell me you're interested in football, Angel?'

'Of course she is,' Cal retorted. 'Look at who her dad and brother are – and you were even quite a good little player yourself, if I remember correctly, weren't you?'

'I don't know if Dad would agree with that.' Angel smiled, enjoying Cal's defence of her and the sulky look on Simone's face. But her mini-triumph was short-lived. Her dad grumpily called out from the other end of the table that they'd give her fella ten more minutes and then they'd be ordering, with or without him.

Angel nodded. 'He'll be here, Dad,' she said, but under the table she crossed her fingers and prayed that Mickey would get here any minute now.

Mickey finally arrived when they were halfway through the starters. He made a great show of greeting everybody, double-kissing all the women, including Michelle, who blushed, and ostentatiously shaking the men's hands. Finally he gave Angel a kiss on the lips and sat down, saying with a disarming smile, 'I'm so sorry, everybody, I was held up in the studio.'

Angel was very aware of Tony, Cal and her dad sizing up Mickey. She knew her dad would absolutely hate the way he was dressed – a white shirt unbuttoned to the chest, showing off his tanned, smooth skin, jeans that hung so low he showed off his tight white Calvins, and brilliant white trainers that had clearly never been used for any real exercise. She also knew that Mickey's carefully tousled dark-blond hair with its highlights and his heavy silver bracelet and selection of rings would go down like a lead balloon with her dad, who was of the old school when it came to male grooming, considering anything other than deodorant down-right poofy. Sensing their disapproval, Angel started being deliberately attentive towards Mickey, fussing over him, sharing her starter with him and pouring him a large glass of champagne.

'Thanks, gorgeous.' He looked at her with his blue eyes and Angel almost forgave him for being late. She had hoped that she and Mickey could fade into the background and that the focus would be on Gemma and Tony, but Mickey then committed another *faux pas* by going to the bathroom just as the main course arrived. Frank was always hot on manners and he narrowed his eyes at Mickey's retreating figure, frowning at the underwear showing above the waist of his jeans.

'Relax,' Gemma whispered. Angel smiled grate-fully at her. Gemma was always sensitive to how other people might be feeling, even at her own engagement dinner.

'I'm sorry, Gemma, Mickey and me seem to be getting everything wrong tonight.' She looked up and saw Cal staring at her thoughtfully. She raised her eyebrow. 'Oh shit,' she exclaimed, remembering. 'I meant, bring your jacket back tonight, you left it on my sofa the other day.' Out of the corner of her eye, she saw Simone grit her teeth.

'Don't worry, I've got plenty of other ones.' He was deliberately casual.

'Yes,' Simone put in abruptly, 'but isn't that the Alexander McQueen that I bought you?'

'It's okay, I promise I won't sell it,' Angel said teasingly. But Simone didn't crack her face.

By the time everyone had practically finished their main course, with the exception of Simone, who had eaten nothing but a few mouthfuls of grilled fish and a couple of vegetables, Mickey still hadn't returned to the table. Angel felt her face growing hot again. Where the hell was he? Just as she was trying to think of a way to slip away unnoticed and track him down, Mickey appeared, his smile more dazzling than before. He sniffed several times and Angel could see Tony and Cal frowning at each other.

'So, Mickey,' Cal asked as Mickey sat down, 'how's life with the band?'

'It's great,' Mickey replied. 'We're touring next month and the tickets are already sold out.'

'Oh?' said Angel. Touring? That was news to her.

'Yeah, babe, we're going to be travelling all over. You can come with us if you like.' He kissed her. She pulled away slightly, feeling annoyed at him for springing this on her so casually, and in front of everyone. She realised with a pang that they hadn't actually been talking much lately. Suddenly she felt depressed – the shoot had been such hard work and then she'd let everyone down at the dinner table. She took a sip of champagne, trying to pull herself together.

'Actually, Mickey,' Angel fought to keep her voice down so Cal and Simone couldn't hear, 'I'm working.'

'Well, I'm sure you can surprise me and warm up my bed on some of those lonely nights.'

Typically, her dad chose that moment to look up from his plate and caught the last bit. He frowned again and Angel tried to think of a way to bring the conversation back to something more socially acceptable.

'How's Prince, Mum?' she called across the table.

Her mum's face immediately fell.

'What is it?' Angel tried to quell the rising sense of panic.

Her mum looked at her sadly. 'I'm really sorry, Angel. We had to have him put down yesterday. I took him to the vet's because I was worried about him, and he said it was cancer and it would be cruel to leave him suffering any longer. I tried to call you but I only got your voicemail. I really didn't want to leave a message about something like that. And I didn't want him to suffer.'

Angel felt the room dissolve around her, helpless

as tears started spilling from her eyes. Ignoring the other people at the table, she said, her voice trembling with barely suppressed emotion, 'You should have waited, Mum. I should have been there when he died. Why didn't you tell me?'

Her mum looked upset, but her dad clenched his jaw and turned on her. 'Don't shout at your mother,' he hissed, trying to keep his voice down. 'She tried to call you. It's not our fault if you can't be bothered to pick up the phone and ring home. We told you a couple of weeks ago that he wasn't himself, that he seemed ill, but you didn't bother to come home and see him. Probably too busy with your precious shoots, going out with your precious boyfriend.'

'Dad – don't—' Tony tried to cut in, while Jeanie and Bill looked uncomfortable to be caught up in a family row. But Angel couldn't hold back any longer. She got up, knocking over a champagne glass in her confusion, and ran out of the room.

In the Ladies, she shut herself in a cubicle and sobbed bitterly. She couldn't believe that she hadn't had the chance to say goodbye to Prince. He'd been with them for ages, always her friend, even when everyone else seemed to be having a go at her. She buried her face in her hands, knowing she had neglected him lately. Yes, she'd been busy, but she could have made the time to go and see him. She sobbed again.

After a few minutes, there was a gentle knocking

at the door. 'It's me, Gemma. Are you okay, Angel? Please come out.'

Angel sniffed, wiped away her tears and reluctantly opened the door and came out. Gemma immediately hugged her. 'I'm so sorry, babe, I know how much he meant to you. Your parents should have told you. They didn't even tell Tony, he's really upset for you.'

Angel sniffed, pulling away to get a tissue. 'I'm sorry, Gemma, I'm ruining your night.'

'Oh course you're not!'

'It's just, I feel I failed him. I should have been with him when he was put down. I keep thinking of his brown eyes looking for me and wondering why I wasn't there.' She tried to wipe her tears away.

'I'm sure he didn't know what was going on,' Gemma said soothingly. 'And your mum was with him. She loved him as much as you did.'

'Do you think so?' Angel stared at her reflection miserably.

'Come on, let's sort you out.' Ever practical, Gemma pulled out a pack of cleaning wipes from her bag and started removing Angel's black eye make-up, which had run dramatically down her face, streaking her cheeks.

'Do you want me to put some of my stuff on you?' she asked kindly.

Angel nodded, hardly caring, but not exactly wanting to face the others in such a red-eyed, dishevelled state. Expertly Gemma started brushing on eye shadow, applying liner and adding powder, blusher and lip gloss. Within five minutes, Angel was transformed, her vampish eye make-up replaced with much subtler tones that emphasised her beautiful green eyes and long lashes. She was still sniffing but looked much calmer now.

'Thanks so much, Gemma, you're a star. Sorry about all this.' She caught a glimpse of her reflection. 'That looks great!' She blew her nose carefully, so as not to destroy Gemma's handiwork. 'You're so talented, Gemma.' She considered her face thoughtfully. 'Hey, I've got an idea,' she said suddenly, some of the old sparkle back in her eyes. 'Would you like to be my make-up artist? Danni's going back to Australia next week and it was such a disaster doing the shoot without her today.' It would be wonderful to have someone she totally trusted working for her.

Gemma didn't have to think about it twice. 'Are you serious? I'd love it! I'm so bored of working in the salon – it'd be great to go freelance.'

When she returned to the dinner table, Mickey put his arm round her and Cal mouthed, 'Are you okay?' across the table, looking at her sympathetically. She nodded back, not trusting herself to speak without crying again. But Cal seemed to understand how she was feeling without further explanation and in an obvious attempt to deflect attention away from her he filled up his glass and passed the bottle round, saying, 'I think we should have a toast for Gemma and Tony –

the happy couple.'

'Good idea,' Jeanie seconded, and everyone raised their glasses. 'To the happy couple.' Gemma smiled, leant closer to Tony, and slowly the hum of conversation started up again.

For the rest of the meal, Angel was subdued. Her mum came over after the toast and hugged her, saying again how sorry she was, and Angel just hugged her back. After that she smiled and made the occasional comment for the sake of appearances, but all she wanted was to get home, curl up in bed and cry for her beloved dog. She was drawn reluctantly back into the conversation when Gemma told Tony that Angel wanted her to work for her.

He looked sceptical. 'Are you sure there would be enough work for Gemma to make it worthwhile for her?'

Angel was annoyed. When would they start taking her seriously, for God's sake? 'I've got shoots booked for the next six months,' she said, somewhat put out, 'and if I'm not busy I can always introduce Gemma to some of the other models I know.'

'Well, I don't know if I like the thought of her having to travel that much, and it's not like she'll need the money once we're married.'

'What, you want her waiting at home for you?' she asked dismissively. 'Shopping for designer clothes and getting her nails done? The perfect footballer's physio's wife!' Angel couldn't stop herself sounding snide.

'There's nothing wrong with being a housewife,' her dad put in from the other end of the table.

Angel shrugged. 'Yeah, but I'm sure mum would love to have done something else as well, wouldn't you?'

Her mother smiled, but before she could answer, her dad cut in. 'No, she wouldn't. She had enough to do bringing up you and your brother.'

'And waiting on you hand and foot,' Angel muttered under her breath.

'What was that?' her dad said.

'I'm sure you're right, Dad,' she said sweetly.

By now they were on to dessert. Angel's appetite had left her and for once she didn't order anything. Instead, she drained her champagne and asked the waiter for a double vodka. Her father raised an eyebrow, but she didn't care. The only thing that brought a smile to her lips was seeing the look of longing on Simone's face as Cal ate his sticky toffee pudding – though whether it was for the pudding or Cal it was hard to tell. That woman really needed to eat more and stop obsessing about food!

She was so lost in thought that for once she didn't pay much attention to Cal, noting only that Simone clearly couldn't keep her hands off him, constantly touching his arm or smoothing back his hair, although Cal appeared not to notice. At one point he stretched out his long legs and accidentally brushed them against Angel's.

She was startled. 'Sorry,' he said immediately, smiling at her.

'It's okay,' Angel smiled back tiredly.

'Oi,' Mickey joked, catching on to the situation, 'are you playing footsie with my bird? Keep your hands off her, she's all mine!' And he pulled Angel towards him and wrapped her in his arms. She leant against him, needing the comfort. He held her close for a second, then whispered, 'Can you pay for me, babe? I'm clean out of cash.'

'Sure,' Angel replied, moving out of his embrace and praying that Simone and Cal hadn't heard him. Her dad asked for the bill and Angel winced to think of him working out in painstaking detail who owed what. She couldn't bear to pay for Mickey in front of everyone.

'It's okay, Frank,' Cal called out, as if he'd heard her silent plea. 'It's my treat.' Everyone cheered and clapped, another toast was made to Tony and Gemma, and Angel finally remembered to present the happy couple with her envelope. Gemma was thrilled. She couldn't thank Angel enough, and even Tony looked pleased.

Then, at last, Angel could escape. She hugged her parents and her mum whispered, 'Hope you have a good night, love. Come and see us soon.' Fearing that she might break down again, Angel nodded, then made an excuse about having an early start, said a general goodbye to everyone and followed Mickey swiftly out of the restaurant.

Mickey got into the cab and Angel was just about to climb in after him when she felt a hand on her arm.

'I'm really sorry about Prince,' Cal said quietly. She straightened up, unable to bear another moment of anyone's sympathy.

'I suppose you think I'm pathetic getting so upset about my dog,' she muttered.

'Not at all. I was gutted when mine died. Take care.' And he leant over and kissed her on the cheek, lingering there for a moment and whispering in a low voice, 'And don't forget what I said the other day. Just look after yourself, okay?' Then he called out, 'See you, Mickey.'

'Thank Christ that's over,' Mickey exclaimed, throwing himself back into the seat. 'God, your parents are uptight! Well, your mum's okay, I guess, but your dad's like a bloody throwback to the nineteen-fifties. I kept expecting him to say it was grim down pit!'

'Yeah,' Angel had to agree. 'But it didn't help that you were an hour late. Where the hell were you?'

He looked pained at her annoyed tone. 'I told you, I was in the studio. I've got a lot to do before this new tour – my manager's been giving us all hell because we lost money in America.'

Angel was feeling too upset to ask him more. They spent the rest of the drive in silence and once they were inside Mickey's luxury flat he poured them each a large vodka and set out a couple of lines. Angel couldn't help remembering Cal's warning.

'I don't really want anything else,' she said.

'Come on, babe, it will do you good.'

'Can't we just go to bed?' All Angel wanted to do was curl up in his arms and feel comforted.

His face looked set and when he spoke it was as abruptly as before. 'You go, babe, I need to unwind.'

Angel pulled off her clothes and climbed into bed, too emotionally exhausted to take off her make-up. Usually she slept without any clothes on but tonight she felt cold and shaky and reached out for one of Mickey's T-shirts. What was going on? Their relationship seemed to have got stuck in a rut. They weren't talking much, they hardly saw each other and she could barely remember the last time they'd had sex. She heard him move around in the living room and longed for him to come and join her. She wanted to feel his arms around her, to hear him say that everything was going to be all right, that he loved her. But Mickey didn't come to bed and when she finally went looking for him two hours later, she found him passed out on the sofa. She threw a blanket over him and contemplated lying next to him, but there wasn't room. She slept badly and woke early. Finding Mickey still asleep, she let herself out of the flat and got a taxi home. Only once she had closed the door behind her did she give in to the tears.

Chapter 11

Falling Angel

'And what's your favourite sexual position, then, Angel?'

Angel sighed as she looked at Colin, the twenty-something lads-mag journalist who needed to lose weight, get a haircut and learn that it was rude to stare as he openly ogled her cleavage. The interview was supposed to be accompanying her shoot with *Tackle*, but she really wasn't in the mood for a saucy exchange with a hack. In any case, Angel was struggling to remember when she'd last had good sex with Mickey. Lately he had been too out of it for anything apart from the odd quickie in a club bathroom, just before he took one line too many. But Angel knew that was not what the readers of *Tackle* would want to hear.

'There are so many, Colin, so many different things that I like. Sometimes I like to go on top, sometimes I like the plain old missionary, sometimes I like it on the edge of the bed, sometimes I like it from behind, sometimes I like riding bareback flicking the peanut – if you know what I mean.' Colin nodded and scribbled away in his notebook, and Angel smiled to herself, wondering if he did. 'Or I like being a slut with a nut,' she continued. 'It all depends on my mood. And sometimes I like to be the dominant one and sometimes I like to be dominated.'

'Oh, so are you a bit of a dominatrix?' Colin agreed a bit too eagerly, his eyes taking on a weasely gleam.

'I don't mean bondage or anything, darling. Dressing up in a rubber suit and mask really doesn't do it for me. What I mean by dominant is that sometimes I like to devise the scenario in bed or somewhere else and sometimes I like the man to tell me exactly what he wants.'

'Would you ever have a threesome?' Colin asked hopefully.

Angel was reminded of Mickey's repeated requests that she try it for him and her heart sank. 'That would depend,' was all she decided to say.

'On what?' Colin persisted.

'On my mood and on the people involved.' She leant forward to pick up her phone from the coffee table, giving Colin a further eyeful of her magnificent breasts. 'Let's just say that I'm not ruling it out.

'And now I really have to go, Colin – you've got enough haven't you?' *Christ, I wish he'd bugger off!*

She got up from the sofa, making a big show of checking her watch.

'Yeah, you've given me some great stuff. Just one last question: if you could sleep with anyone, who would it be?'

Angel smiled coyly. 'But I'm already with Mickey, the man who fulfils all my fantasies.'

'Okay, but if you weren't, who would it be?'

Cal was the only man Angel ever fantasised about, but she could hardly reveal that to the world. 'I don't know . . . Freddie Ljungberg. He's well fucking fit.'

She practically had to frogmarch Colin to the front door to get rid of him. When he'd gone, she decided to head off to the gym. She hadn't done any exercise for ages, not that she ever liked to do that much, but her agent kept nagging her, saying that she wouldn't get picked up by the Americans unless she did. Angel had been blessed with good genes: she was naturally slim, plus all the sport she'd done when she was growing up – swimming, riding and football – had given her a toned body, and to the envy of nearly every woman she knew she'd never really had to work at keeping in shape. But she'd been burning the candle at both ends lately, drinking more than was good for her, and she knew she could do with a bit of work.

God, this is so boring, she groaned to herself as she got on the cross trainer and started the machine up. *Come on, you bleeding endorphins, kick in and give me some kind of rush*. She managed twenty minutes and was just drinking some water when she looked across the gym and saw Cal, just ten feet away from her. He was running on the treadmill, a look of steely determination on his handsome features. *Hello*, thought Angel. *This gym session has just got a whole lot better.* She hadn't seen him since the engagement dinner and though she still felt sad about Prince, she felt more together, more up for an encounter with Cal Bailey. She smiled to herself, walked over and got on the machine next to him.

'Hi,' she said, starting up the machine into a brisk walk. He nodded hello.

'Can't you go any faster?' she teased.

Cal gave her a sideways look. 'Two more miles and I can talk to you.'

Angel smiled and sped up herself. She'd always been a good runner and with Cal next to her she felt a surge of energy. They ran side by side with Angel matching his speed, but when she sneaked a look at his treadmill's display she realised that it was no achievement at all as he'd already run five miles. Ten minutes later, Cal started slowing down. Secretly relieved, Angel started her cool-down programme as well.

'So,' said Cal, turning to face her at last, 'I didn't know you were a member here.' He stopped, wiped his face and took a drink of water.

'Yeah, well, I've been letting things slide a bit.' She saw Cal take in her slim, tanned limbs in her skin-hugging Lycra shorts and cropped top.

'Yep, looks that way. So what's next?' he asked her as they both headed to the water fountain.

'Well, I was going to have a swim,' she said, thinking that she was actually bloody knackered and needed a lie down.

'You lightweight! Tell you what, I'll give you a workout if you want.'

It seemed too good an offer to refuse, but Angel regretted her decision almost immediately as he had her performing a punishing series of sit-ups on the exercise ball, then got her to use some of the weight machines she loathed. She particularly objected to the one that worked the inner thigh.

'Please stand to the side while I'm doing this!' she begged him, forced to hold the position with her legs spread wide open.

'It's okay,' he replied, 'I've seen it all before. Twenty more.'

'God, you're a sadist.'

After thirty minutes using various machines, Angel finally persuaded him to go for that swim. She quickly showered, plaited her hair and then considered her swimwear. She could wear her black sports costume, which killed her curves and flattened her breasts, or she could wear her white bikini, which had completely the opposite effect. There was really no contest – it had to be the white bikini. She slipped it on and made her way to the poolside. Cal was already ploughing up and down the fast lane doing a flashy front crawl. Angel pulled down her goggles, opted for the medium lane and dived in, determined to beat him, which she did quite easily. When she and Cal both ended up at the same end, he gestured for her to stop, smiling through the water running down his face.

'I didn't realise you were such a good swimmer!'

'There are lots of things you don't know about me, Cal,' she replied, pleasantly aware that Cal's attention was focused on her white bikini.

'I'm beginning to realise that. Three more, then a steam?'

He took off in the water, closely pursued by Angel. For a while she hung back, letting him think that he was in the lead, then she effortlessly overtook him. Three lengths done, she pulled herself up onto the side, took off her goggles and made a show of considering her nails as Cal pulled up.

'Okay, you win,' he said grudgingly.

Angel laughed. 'You are such a bad loser!'

The steam room was deserted. They flopped down on opposite benches, stretching their legs out. Angel couldn't help taking surreptitious glances at Cal through the steam. God, he had such a fantastic body – sexy biceps that she longed to kiss, long muscular legs, just the right amount of hair on his chest, with a washboard stomach. And she didn't even want to think about the dark line of hairs running from his navel into his shorts. She closed her eyes and imagined walking over to him, kissing him, caressing him, gently peeling off his trunks and revealing his—

'Fuck me, I'm roasted,' Cal exclaimed. 'I've got to get out of here.'

She opened her eyes as Cal headed out of the steam room. *Too bad . . .*

'See you upstairs?' he asked in the doorway, framed by the steam swirling around him.

'Sure.'

'Jesus – what is it you women do all that time?'

Angel sat down opposite Cal, who had two empty coffee cups in front of him.

'Just stuff, you know – hair, make-up, moisturiser, blah blah . . .'

Cal grimaced at her. 'Well, at least you weren't as long as Simone usually is.'

'And how is the lovely Simone?' Angel asked, trying to keep her voice even but secretly wanting Cal to start bitching about her.

'She's great, really great.'

Bugger that, thought Angel, reaching for the menu.

'I'm starving. I'm going to have a tomato and mozzarella bagel, and do you think they do chips here?'

Cal laughed. 'Of course they don't, it's a gym!'

It was such a treat to be spending time with Cal. She had always thought he had this way of making the person he was with feel so special. He asked her all about her work and seemed genuinely interested in her ambitions. Angel couldn't help comparing him with Mickey, whose main topic of conversation tended to be himself. She and Cal seemed to be getting on better than they had in ages. Then Simone appeared at their table.

She was immaculately dressed in a black designer tracksuit and trainers, her long brown silky hair pulled back in a ponytail, her lips lightly glossed. Completing the ensemble was a very sulky look on her face. She ignored Angel, immediately bending down and draping her arms round Cal.

'I didn't know you were coming to the gym, darling. Why didn't you call me?'

'I'm sorry, babe, it was a spur of the moment decision.'

'Well, will you come and work out with me now?'

Angel snorted. 'What, with all the exercise he's just had?'

Simone clenched her jaw and looked furious, finally acknowledging Angel with a brief nod. Cal smiled, obviously realising he needed to defuse the situation.

'I bumped into Angel on the treadmill.'

'Oh?' said Simone coldly. 'I would have thought you rarely exercised standing up, Angel.'

Angel smiled right back at her. 'You're so right, sex is good exercise, but every now and then even I like to go for a run or a swim. And, as Cal will tell you, I'm very good at swimming.'

'You went swimming?' Simone spat out the words.

'Yeah,' Angel replied, gathering her things together. 'It was really lucky that I remembered my bikini. And then we hit the steam room. God, it's hot in there.'

Simone's expression was not so much chewing a wasp as swallowing a swarm. Angel decided to make a swift exit.

'Cheers for the workout, Cal, and I'll see you both at Gemma and Tony's party tomorrow night.' She was already out the door, throwing both a casual wave.

'See you, Angel,' Cal called after her.

Simone was still too angry to speak.

Angel was not looking forward to the engagement party. Tony hadn't spoken to her since the dinner, and, despite Gemma's denials, Angel knew he hadn't forgiven her for showing up late and then making a scene. And he clearly didn't approve of Mickey. So as she was getting ready, she felt tense and apprehensive.

'Chill, babe,' Mickey told her, rubbing her shoulders. 'It's just a party. And it's at Sugar's, your favourite club.'

Angel sipped her mineral water while she considered what to wear. She had just bought an amazing silver dress with a low-cut back. It was gorgeous! And although it revealed quite a bit of flesh it didn't flaunt too much cleavage, so it shouldn't annoy her brother. She'd just started on her make-up when Mickey wandered in and handed her a glass of champagne.

'Thought this would help you to relax.'

'Cheers, but I really want to watch how much I drink tonight.'

'It's just one glass, babe,' Mickey said.

He's right, Angel told herself, *I really do need to chill*. She drank the champagne. It tasted a little strange, but she had just cleaned her teeth. Twenty minutes later they were in a taxi on their way to the club. The press was out in force tonight and Angel and Mickey got out of the taxi among an explosion of flash bulbs.

'Over here, Angel,' the photographers called, asking for her and Mickey to pose together. Mickey immediately put his arm round Angel and gave the photographers what they wanted, and Angel flashed her trademark pout.

Inside the club, Angel led Mickey over to where Gemma and Tony were standing. Gemma was delighted to see Angel and hugged her and Mickey. Tony just about managed a smile and hello. A waiter went past with a tray of champagne and Mickey took a glass for him and Angel.

Angel put hers back. 'Actually, I think I'm going to get a glass of water.' As she walked over to the bar and leant against it, trying to attract the bartender's attention, she felt a wave of dizziness.

She swayed a bit, feeling giddy and light-headed. *God, I can't be drunk*, she thought, confused, *I've only had a glass*. She was just sipping her water when Mickey came and found her.

'Babe, I've just had a text from my manager, we've got an urgent meeting, I'm really sorry but I've got to go.'

'Do you have to? We've only just got here.'

'Yeah, it's a bummer, but I do. It's about our new recording contract so I've got to be there, babe.'

Angel reached out to hold onto Mickey's arm. 'It's just that I feel a bit weird, kind of dizzy. I only had one glass of champagne, didn't I?' She held on to him as the room lurched beneath her feet. 'Seriously, Mickey, can you find me somewhere to sit down? I feel so strange.'

Mickey smirked. 'Oh yeah, I should have told you, I put a little something in your drink just before, to calm you down. It's a pisser I've got to go, because having sex on this particular number is fucking fantastic. We'll do it another time.' She started to protest, but he just kissed her cheek and was gone.

Angel wanted to feel angry but found she couldn't summon the energy. The room had steadied itself and she was starting to feel very, very mellow. She smiled to herself and carried on sipping her water. A group of footballers from Chelsea suddenly surrounded her. Usually she would have hated so many men crowding round her, but tonight, in her altered state, she loved the attention. They were all so lovely and she felt so dreamy. She let the men kiss her on the cheek, take pictures of her with their phones and buy her a drink and she sat down at their table.

'I've got to ask you, Angel,' said one of the men, a cocky good-looking lad with a shaved head and a diamond earring, 'how do your tits feel?'

Angel laughed and thrust her chest forward. 'I think they feel fucking fantastic.' Before she could think about it, she grabbed his hand and pressed it to her right breast. 'What do you reckon?' She smiled cheekily.

'You're right,' he said in delight, hardly believing his luck. 'They do feel good.'

Who knows what might have happened next, but suddenly Angel was aware of someone behind her. The good-looking lad immediately removed his hand from her breast and mumbled an apology. Angel turned round and found herself face to face with a very serious-looking Cal.

'Angel, I need to talk to you.'

'Oh? But I'm having fun with these boys. Why don't you join us?'

But Cal took her arm and pulled her to her feet.

'So masterful!' she said sarcastically, leaning against him for support. Cal didn't answer, but marched her to the deserted upstairs part of the club and sat her down on one of the sofas in a dark, empty corner of the room.

'Are you drunk? Tony would go mad if he saw you behaving like that at his engagement party.'

'Oh, hello, Cal, how are you? And no, I'm not drunk. Mickey said he put something in my drink. I didn't know, though, so don't shout at me.' It didn't come out quite as clearly as that and Angel had to repeat herself several times before Cal understood.

'You'd better have some water,' he said abruptly, and he went off for a few minutes and returned with a bottle of water and a glass, which he filled for her. 'Come on, drink this. I can't believe Mickey did that to you. I told you to be careful.'

'I feel fine, honestly,' she protested, putting the glass down. 'Actually, I feel great. I don't often get to spend time alone with you.' Her voice had become low and, she thought, very seductive, and she moved closer to Cal. Then, and it was like having an out-of-body experience, she found herself moving further towards him and kissing him. At first Cal resisted, but then it seemed to her that he gave in and kissed her back. Angel pressed herself against him. God, Mickey was right, she felt amazing, incredibly turned on. She pulled away from the kiss and slid onto the floor so she was kneeling in front of Cal. As she started trying to unbuckle his belt, Cal grabbed her arms and tried to stop her, but Angel was being very persistent.

'What the fuck's going on here?' All of a sudden Tony was standing by the sofa, looking absolutely furious. 'What the fuck are you doing, Angie? Leave him alone, you're embarrassing him and yourself!'

It probably would have been a good idea not to say anything, but as Cal pulled her up, Angel shouted, 'Fuck off, Tony, we're enjoying ourselves!'

'Get real! You threw yourself at him and Cal's too polite to tell you to fuck off, you stupid cow. What the hell have you taken, you're clearly off your head.'

'I'm not off my head, and it's not my fault anyway. Mickey gave me something, that's all.'

'You're so selfish, you ruined my dinner and now you're ruining my party. You're just a waster like your mother.'

'What?' Angel finally managed to get up from the floor and faced Tony.

'Just leave it, Tony,' Cal called out warningly.

'No,' Angel said. 'I want to know what he means about my mum.'

Tony looked at her and gave a harsh laugh. 'Mum and Dad didn't think you should know what your real mum was like. They told you she was a teenage mum, too young to look after you. Bullshit – she was a junkie. And you're turning out to be quite a chip off the old block.'

Suddenly Gemma was there. 'Stop it, Tony, you've said enough.' Tony looked as if he had plenty more to say, but stormed back downstairs.

Angel found that she was shaking. 'I never knew

that. Oh, God, Gemma, is that true? Am I like her?'

'No,' her friend said firmly. 'I think you need to go home and forget about tonight. Mickey was well out of order putting that in your drink.'

'I'll take her home,' Cal said quietly.

Suddenly Angel was overcome with shame. 'No, I can get a taxi on my own.'

'No way,' replied Cal firmly. 'We'll go out the back so the photographers won't see you.'

Angel was incapable of walking on her own and finally, trying unsuccessfully to support her to the exit, Cal picked her up, told her to put her arms round his neck and carried her down the stairs. Angel closed her eyes; everything was spinning madly and she could see two Cals. Outside he managed to get her into a waiting taxi and sat next to her. And that was all Angel could remember.

She woke up with a splitting headache and a mouth that felt like she'd been eating cotton wool. She gingerly raised her head from the pillow and lowered it back down again immediately. Oh, God. She felt spectacularly bad. She closed her eyes and groaned, desperately trying to remember what had gone on the night before, but could only recall walking into the club – the rest was a complete blank.

'How are you feeling?'

Angel's eyes sprang open. There, standing next to her bed, was Cal, drinking coffee and looking handsome as ever.

'What are you doing here?' she croaked, suddenly aware that she was naked under the duvet, except for a pair of briefs. She pulled the cover tightly around her.

'Don't you remember? I brought you home last night.'

'Why?' Angel asked in astonishment.

Cal looked at her, puzzled. 'You really don't remember?'

'No,' Angel replied, feeling more and more anxious about what had happened. 'I remember arriving at the party and seeing Gemma and Tony and that's it.'

'Mickey put something in your drink, and let's just say it had a bit of an effect on you. I thought it best if I brought you home. I was going to go back to the party, but I really didn't want to leave you. You were so totally out of it.'

'Oh my God.' Despite her splitting headache, Angel sat up.

'You left Tony and Gemma's party and didn't go back?' She groaned. 'Tony's going to kill me.'

'He's cool about it. He didn't want you left on your own in the state you were in. Listen, I'm going to make some tea and toast, you need to eat something.'

Angel lay back down in bed carefully. She felt so awful she didn't even care what she looked like. What the hell had she done last night? She had a horrible feeling that she must have disgraced herself in some way.

The doorbell went. It was Gemma.

'How is she?' she heard her friend asking Cal in the hallway.

'Okay, I think, just a bit disorientated,' he answered.

Too bloody right, Angel thought. Then Gemma walked into her bedroom, her face concerned.

'Hiya, Angel, how are you feeling?'

'Like shit,' replied Angel. 'And I don't know what the hell's been going on – did you know that Cal's here?' At that moment the man himself walked into the bedroom, carrying a mug of tea and a plate of toast.

'Cheers, Cal,' Angel managed to mutter.

'Listen, I've got to go to training. Don't worry about last night, I've already forgotten about it.' He gave Angel the briefest of smiles, said goodbye to her and Gemma and was gone.

Angel sat up and put on her robe. Gemma sat on the bed next to her and handed her the tea.

'Oh my God, Gemma, what have I done?'

'Drink the tea and I'll tell you. And it's okay, everyone knows you were off your head and it wasn't your fault.'

With a mounting feeling of dread, Angel drank the tea.

'Okay, you've got to tell me what Cal was doing here.'

Gemma gave a deep sigh and told her everything. When it came to the part where she revealed what Angel had been trying to do to Cal when Tony found her, Angel gave a cry and covered her face with her hands.

'I can't believe I did that. Oh, Gemma, I know I never had a chance with him before, but now, God, he must think I'm a complete whore.'

'I'm sure he doesn't, Angel, he wouldn't have brought you home if he did. He was really worried about you – we all were.'

'I can't remember him bringing me home at all. And he must have undressed me! I feel so embarrassed!'

'Forget Cal, there's something else I need to tell you.'

As Angel looked at her friend, she had a sick feeling in the pit of her stomach; she had never seen Gemma looking so serious.

'You can't remember what Tony told you last night, can you?'

Angel shook her head. 'I don't even remember seeing him.'

'He was very angry when he saw you with Cal, and he told you about your mum.' Gemma reached out and held onto Angel's hand. 'Angel, it's not good news, are you sure you want to know?'

'You've got to tell me,' Angel replied urgently.

An hour later, when Angel felt she had no more tears left to cry, she forced herself to get up and take the bath Gemma had run for her. She felt shell-shocked by the news that her mother had been a heroin addict. Within just a few minutes, her secret picture of her real mother had been ripped apart. She hadn't been a teenage mum too scared to bring up a daughter on her own, who had always regretted giving her baby up for adoption. She was an addict who had abandoned her daughter without a second thought. Angel had dreamt of being reunited with her mum one day, discovering that they were soul mates, finding the unconditional love she had never felt at home. Now, that dream was shattered. Angel felt more miserable than she ever had before. *What was the point of any of this?* she thought as she looked round her perfect bathroom with its very expensive walk-in shower and the huge Victorian bath with the authentic silver taps she had chosen so carefully. What was the point of her perfect flat in the perfect location? What was the point of her career, of being famous, if you didn't feel loved? She sank onto the floor, crying bitterly.

'How are you feeling?' Gemma asked as Angel emerged some forty minutes later.

'I still feel like shit,' she sighed, her eyes puffy, her face pale. 'Can we go for a walk on the Heath? I need to clear my head.'

As soon as they left the streets behind and walked in the fresh air, surrounded by trees and open space, Angel started to feel slightly better. She had been silent for most of the walk, lost in thought, but finally she spoke.

'Gemma, I'm going to find my real mum. I've wanted to do it for ages, and now I've got to know the truth.'

'Are you sure?'

'I don't think I can feel any worse than I do at the moment. I find out my mum was a junkie and probably still is. That I was off my head and disgraced myself in front of the man I've been in love with for years, ruining any possible chance I might ever have had with him. What can be worse than that?' Angel grimaced. 'Come on, let's walk to that café and have a drink. But, please, promise me again that Tony was the only one who saw what I was doing?'

'Promise,' replied Gemma, thinking that now would not be a good time to tell her that she'd let a complete stranger grope her breast.

Chapter 12

All At Sea

For the next few weeks Angel tried to keep as busy as possible. The moment she was alone she started obsessing over what had happened that night with Cal. Mickey was away touring the UK with the band and she hardly got to see him. Whenever they spoke on the phone, all he did was go on and on about his career, how the band were dragging him down. Wanted seemed to have peaked and now they were on the slide and not selling records as they used to. Mickey was desperate for a solo recording contract, but so far no one wanted to sign him. Angel was getting a little pissed off massaging his ego, when he never seemed that interested in *her* work. Gemma was busy planning the wedding and working extra hours to pay for it, so Angel only got to see her when they were working together on shoots. If she ever had any free time during the day, she'd go to the gym – a different one from the one where she'd met Cal, though. She just couldn't face him quite yet. Or she'd go riding for hours. She bought a new horse, Star, and kept him at a stable a few miles from where she lived. As always, riding was great therapy for her, a chance to escape the anxiety and pressure. She made sure her social diary was packed: nights out with her glamour girlfriends and Jez, her fantastic hairdresser. Every single invitation for premieres, charity parties, or new product launches that Carrie passed on to her, Angel forced herself to go to.

She also had plenty of work on, for which she was grateful. As well as her regular tabloid and lad-mag shoots, she was chosen as the face of an Italian designer label specialising in watches, jewellery, sunglasses and jeans. For the first shoot she was flown off to the Maldives.

'It's a hard life,' Gemma said as the pair of them sipped their Slippery Nipple cocktails in their five-star water bungalow and looked out at the dazzling blue Indian Ocean after the photo shoot on the white sandy beach.

During a rare day off, Angel set into motion her plan to meet her birth mother, contacting the relevant agencies. She was told it could take several months and there was no guarantee that her mother would want to see her. But Angel had a feeling that she would.

Mickey was not much of a support during this time. She had been furious with him for spiking her drink, but when she'd tackled him about it he had just told her to chill out.

'It was no big deal, babe. I bet you felt really mellow, then went home and got your Rabbit out. Next time I promise I'll be there.'

She couldn't believe he was being so casual about it, but as she could hardly say what had actually happened, she just snapped angrily, 'Just don't ever do it again, okay?'

Worse than that, he didn't seem to understand why Angel wanted to meet her real mum.

'You've already got a mum, what do you want another one for?' he said unsympathetically on one of Angel's visits to see him on his tour. The band were in Glasgow for a couple of gigs and Angel had hoped they'd patch things up a bit, would spend some time together, just the two of them. But when Angel flew in first thing in the morning in order to spend as much time with him as possible, Mickey didn't even bother to come and meet her at the airport, but sent his car instead.

In the early months of their romance, if they hadn't seen each other for a few days he would have pulled her straight into bed with him, and that was what Angel was hoping for. But when she walked into his hotel suite, Mickey was busy getting ready for an interview with a journalist and only gave her the briefest of hugs.

'I've got to talk to this guy, then I'll be free, babe. You can come with me if you want.'

As the whole point of her trip had been to see Mickey, Angel decided she might as well tag along.

'Okay, I think that's all the information I need right now,' the lad-mag journalist said at the end of his interview with Mickey.

Mickey looked peeved. 'But you haven't asked me about the next album, Dean.'

Dean shrugged. 'That's all I need for now.' He hesitated. 'Well, seeing as you're here, Angel, would you mind answering a few questions?'

Angel was reluctant. 'Well, isn't this article supposed to be about Mickey?'

'Oh yes,' Dean replied hastily. 'This would just be a small part at the end.'

Angel looked at Mickey to get his reaction, but he muttered something about needing to use the bathroom, got up from the table and walked out of the hotel bar.

Dean didn't just have a few questions. His interrogation of Angel ranged from whether she was going to be the new Bond girl (news to her) to what underwear she found most sexy on a man. It lasted an hour, double the length of time he had spent with Mickey, and Mickey himself didn't come back. Every time she tried to stop Dean, he would say, 'Oh, just one more little one.' Finally Angel exclaimed, 'Enough!' and Dean, realising he couldn't push his luck any further, thanked her profusely and left quickly.

Wanker, Angel thought, and reached for her mobile. 'Hey, Mickey, where are you? I couldn't get rid of that journalist.'

'Oh, come on, Angel,' Mickey replied nastily, 'I bet you had a great time, talking about your favourite subject – yourself.'

'Hey, that's not fair!' Angel was stung by his accusation. 'I didn't want to do it in the first place and if you had bothered to come back it would have been a damn sight easier to get rid of him.'

'Whatever,' Mickey replied. 'I'm in the room.'

'How about I take you out for lunch?' she asked when she saw Mickey lying on the bed, drinking wine. And that wasn't all, she realised, noticing the telltale white powder marks on the bedside cabinet.

Mickey shrugged. He obviously wasn't going to make it easy for her. She tried again. 'I asked at reception and there's a great Italian nearby. I've booked a table.'

'If that's what you want,' he answered off-handedly.

'Oh, for fuck's sake, Mickey,' she said. 'Can't you just forget it?'

'I suppose so, but I can't help feeling pissed off that a journalist would rather talk to someone who is only famous for getting her kit off than a serious musician,' Mickey said abruptly, getting up to collect his jacket.

Angel stared at Mickey in disbelief; he had never spoken to her so harshly before.

'That's such a horrible thing to say. I'm a model, and you're making it sound like I'm some kind of prostitute!' She felt tears of hurt and anger pricking her eyes and Mickey seemed to realise that he'd gone too far.

'Babe, I didn't mean it to sound like that. I was angry with the journalist, not you,' and he got up from the bed and hugged Angel, but she didn't feel comforted.

They were polite with each other over lunch, except when Angel brought up the subject of his drug-taking. He'd gone to the bathroom again and was so long that Angel just knew he was taking another line, and when he returned to the table she challenged him. 'You seem to be taking a lot of coke at the moment, Mickey. Is everything okay?'

'I'm not,' he snapped back, then added, 'Okay, I probably am taking more than usual, but it's this tour, I'm sick of it.'

'I know, Mickey, but you want to watch it, you don't want to end up with a problem.'

'I'll be the judge of that,' he said abruptly.

They spent the rest of the afternoon shopping for clothes for Mickey and pretending to be the perfect couple. Angel had been so looking forward to seeing him. She wanted him to show her some affection, to take her mind off what she'd heard about her real mum, but, if anything, being with Mickey made her feel even worse.

Mickey's mood seemed to improve after his gig,

which went down a storm with all the screaming girls, but instead of wanting to spend the rest of the night with Angel, he insisted they go out clubbing with the band. They barely said a word to each other the whole night, because they were constantly surrounded by people and fans. And it wasn't until they got into bed together that they were finally alone. Angel wrapped her arms round him, longing to feel close to him, wanting the release that making love would bring her, but Mickey just gave her a quick kiss, turned over and fell straight asleep. She lay in the darkness, unable to sleep. She had been trying to tire herself out so much these past weeks so that she wouldn't have any time to think about Cal and what had happened. But lying next to Mickey and feeling so alone, her thoughts returned to Cal with painful inevitability. She felt a surge of shame. Gemma and Tony were getting married in a few months' time and Angel could only pray that Cal would have forgotten all about what had happened. Realising she was never going to be able to sleep, she got up and channel-surfed, finally going to bed at six. At nine, Mickey woke her up, saying he had to do a radio interview.

She pulled him towards her. 'Haven't you even got time for a cuddle?' She slipped her hands around him.

'Sorry, babe,' he replied, pulling away, 'got to go.'

'Okay, I know you can't keep Radio Glasgow waiting. See you soon, I guess.' Angel couldn't help the sarcastic edge in her voice; she was fed up with coming a poor second to Mickey's pop ambitions.

'Don't be like that,' he told her. 'I'll be back in London soon and we can spend loads of time together. Love you, babe.' He kissed her lightly on the lips and was gone before she could reply.

Does he, though? Angel wondered. It didn't really feel like it any more.

She had her first TV appearance the next day. She was going to be one of the contestants on a musical quiz show. Carrie told her it would be 'good for her profile' to take part, but Angel had her doubts. The regulars on the quiz were all comedians who liked nothing better than taking the piss out of the other panellists and the last thing she wanted to do was make a complete fool of herself. Gemma agreed to come with her as her make-up artist, and, more importantly, to try to keep her calm.

As soon as they arrived at the studio, Angel regretted her decision. She felt totally out of her depth. She and Gemma were directed to a dressing room but before Gemma could get started on her face, Angel had to pour herself a large glass of white wine to steady her nerves.

'Why did I agree to take part, I must have been mad!' she groaned.

'You'll be fine,' said Gemma. 'I bet you know more than you think.'

'And I bet I know why they wanted to have me on – so they could make lots of tit jokes.'

Both girls jumped as there was a knock on the door.

It was the host, Derren Sylvester. He was a DJ in his twenties, from Manchester – good-looking in a laddish way, renowned for his put-downs and womanising. He was *so* not the kind of man Angel found attractive, though he thought he was God's gift, and after kissing Angel and giving her a lecherous once-over, said, 'Glad you could make it, I've been wanting to have you for ages.'

'Yuk!' Angel exclaimed after he left. 'How oily was he? And did you see him looking at my tits?'

Gemma agreed, pretending to throw up.

'Do you know what?' Angel exclaimed. 'If they want tits, they can have them!' She had planned to wear one of her little vest tops and her very low-cut jeans, but suddenly she decided to have more fun. She put on a white shirt, knotted just above her navel, and unbuttoned to show maximum cleavage and a hint of her black lace bra, a short black pleated skirt (longer than her usual ones but still indecently short), black over-the-knee socks, which looked like stockings, and trainers. Gemma completed the look by plaiting her long blonde hair in pigtails. She looked like a very naughty schoolgirl.

'Knock 'em dead, kid,' Gemma ordered her as the PA came to take Angel onto the set.

As Angel took her seat next to the two other

panellists on her team, she was very aware that she was the only woman there. She had definitely been booked so she would make a fool of herself and make the rest of them look clever.

'I'm really nervous, I've never done telly before,' she told Nick, her team captain, a flamboyant gay comedian with an acid tongue.

'Don't worry, darling,' he told her, patting her hand patronisingly. 'No one's expecting you to know all the answers. Love the outfit by the way – very Britney. We always have drinks after the show, you must stay for those.' Her other team-mate was a moody indie musician who barely acknowledged Angel.

Then the theme music started. *It's only TV*, Angel told herself, *nobody dies*. Derren introduced the teams, cracking jokes about their large assets. *Hilarious*, thought Angel – *not*. And then the game started. To Angel's enormous surprise and to everyone else's judging by their expressions, she got every single one of her questions right, and buzzed in with the right answer several other times when the other team couldn't answer. When it came to singing the melody of a well-known song for the captain to guess, she was pitch perfect. Her team won and that was largely down to Angel. Nick obviously realised that she wasn't a dumb bimbo because at the end he insisted that she came for a drink to celebrate. Angel made her excuses – all she wanted to do was crack open a bottle of wine with

Gemma and have a good laugh, not spend the next few hours in a room full of comedians all leering at her and trying to outdo each other with their witty remarks.

'You were fantastic, Angel,' Gemma told her friend. 'I'm so proud of you and you looked bloody gorgeous.'

'You say the best things, but I know I only looked okay because you did such a good job of my make-up.'

'Bollocks, you looked fab, now come on, let's have a drink!' The two of them piled into a cab and hit the very stylish Blue Bar, where they ordered champagne to celebrate Angel's TV debut.

Angel was delighted with how the show had gone but she was secretly upset that Mickey hadn't even called to wish her luck – she was sure she had told him about the TV show. She couldn't help thinking that she always remembered his schedule and made sure she watched his TV appearances. It wasn't something she wanted to reveal to Gemma, though.

'Tony still hasn't spoken to me,' Angel confided after several glasses of champagne. 'I've texted him and left a message saying sorry; I just don't know what else I can do.'

Gemma sighed. 'You know how stubborn he is. I'm sure he'll come round, just forget it for now. I've had a go at him about it as well.'

Two bottles of champagne later, Angel stopped

worrying about her brother and Mickey. It was fantastic having a girls' night with Gemma. She was laughing more than she had in ages.

'So what are you doing this Saturday night?' Angel asked as they got ready to leave, hoping she and Gemma could crash out in front of a DVD, get a takeaway and generally veg out. Gemma seemed slightly evasive and muttered, 'I think Tony's got plans for dinner. Sorry. Another time, babe.'

'Never mind,' Angel answered quickly, trying not to look too disappointed.

She might have said *never mind*, but she woke up on Saturday morning with a feeling of dread at the prospect of a whole weekend on her own. Mickey had told her he was knackered and that it wasn't worth her flying to see him in Newcastle. Finally, she decided to spend the day riding, and then she would chill out on her own. A glorious blue, cloudless sky greeted her when she opened the curtains. She quickly showered, grabbed some breakfast, dressed in her jodhpurs, T-shirt and riding boots and jumped into her new silver Mercedes CLK 55 AMG Cabriolet to drive out to the stables. Manda, the stable girl, had Star ready for her and Angel wasted no time in heading out into the countryside. She loved being out in the open, not watched or judged by anyone, just being herself. She rode for hours, stopping only to share an apple with Star. *See*, she told herself, *I can survive on my own*. By the time she decided to head back to the stables, the weather had changed dramatically. Ominous purple clouds dominated the sky and the wind had suddenly picked up.

'Let's get home before it rains, boy,' she urged Star. The last thing she wanted was to be caught in a thunderstorm with him; he could be a bit skittish around loud noises and was liable to bolt. Galloping across the field, they made it back before the thunder but couldn't avoid the torrential rain and Angel was quickly soaked to the skin. Manda was there to look after Star and after thanking her, Angel jumped into her car.

'Shit,' she said out loud, realising that she had absolutely nothing to eat or drink in the flat, so she'd have to stop off at the shop. Miraculously she found a parking place on Hampstead High Street and dashed through the rain into the store.

She kept her head down, quickly walking through the upmarket deli, but she could sense people staring at her as she filled up her basket. She was dripping great pools of water wherever she walked and her white T-shirt had become totally transparent, showing off her pink lace bra. She prayed that no one recognised her but, typically, just as she was putting a couple of bottles of wine into her basket, a young lad came up and asked for an autograph.

She was in the middle of loading her shopping onto the conveyor belt and fantasising about a hot bath and a large glass of wine when, to her horror,

Cal and Simone wheeled a trolley stuffed with luxury food right behind her.

Shit shit shit, she thought, *talk about being caught at a disadvantage*. She ducked down, piled the last of her stuff onto the belt and looked on impatiently as the checkout girl slowly pushed her groceries across the scanner. It would only be a matter of seconds before Cal saw her. She mentally urged the girl to move faster, got out her purse and pulled out her credit card, ready to make a run for it.

'Hi, Angel, how are you doing?' The voice came from behind her. She turned round slowly, composing her features into a casual smile. Cal smiled easily, as if he had completely forgotten their humiliating last meeting, when she had tried to molest him and he had ended up undressing her. But Angel was still so embarrassed that she could barely bring herself to look him in the eye. She mumbled something about being fine, then she looked up at Simone, who was a glamorous vision in a white trouser suit, and muttered, 'Hi.' Simone gave a barely audible reply and looked Angel up and down as if she was something the cat had dragged in.

Why, oh why, did she have to bump into them now? If she had to see them at all, why couldn't it have been when she looked her best? *Somebody up there definitely doesn't like me*, Angel thought grimly. She carried on unloading her shopping, but Cal was determined to engage her in a conversation.

'I saw you on TV last night, Angel. You did really well.'

'Cheers.' She shrugged. 'I think I was lucky with the questions.'

'I didn't realise it was fancy dress, though,' said Simone cattily.

'Well, you know me, I like to make a spectacle of myself wherever possible,' Angel said, and immediately regretted it, not wanting to bring back memories of the last time she'd seen Cal.

'So, are you out tonight?' Cal asked, obviously keen to change the subject.

God, she wished he would stop asking her questions.

'Ah, no, crash night tonight. I'm all clubbed out. How about you two?'

'Cal's cooking dinner for Tony and Gemma,' Simone replied, with a knowing grin on her face. Angel immediately wished she hadn't asked. Now she knew why Gemma had been so cagey when she asked her what she was doing on Saturday night. She couldn't help feeling excluded, even though Cal and Simone were the last people she would want to have a cosy dinner with.

Cal cleared his throat. 'Yeah, why don't you come as well?'

The look on Simone's face would have had most other grown men running for the hills.

'That's really nice of you,' Angel said, 'but I need to crash and I promised Mickey we'd have a long chat tonight; he's still away on tour.'

Thank God Angel had to concentrate on paying for her shopping and so didn't have to talk any more. As soon as she'd done so, she said a hasty goodbye. Waving at Cal and ignoring Simone, she walked towards the exit as swiftly as she could. But just before she pushed open the door, Cal strode up behind her, holding out his denim jacket.

'I really think you should borrow this,' he said quickly. 'I've just seen a photographer outside and they'll think Christmas has come early if they see you like this.'

They both looked down at Angel's transparent T-shirt.

'I'll be fine,' Angel protested.

'No, really, take it,' Cal insisted.

'Thanks,' Angel muttered back, putting on the jacket. 'Taking your jackets is turning into a bit of a habit.'

'And I did want to ask you round for dinner tonight. I know you haven't spoken to Tony for ages and it's time you guys buried the hatchet. It's not just the four of us, there are going to be some friends of mine there as well.'

'Cal!' Simone shouted sharply from the checkout. 'I need you here!'

'I'd better go,' Cal told Angel. 'Why don't you have a think about it and call me later?'

*

Back at her flat, Angel showered and changed, poured herself a large glass of wine and decided to call Gemma to tell her what had happened.

'I definitely think you should come,' Gemma told her. 'It's about time you and Tony started talking again and it would be good for you to put that night behind you. And I'm so sorry I didn't mention it yesterday. I didn't want you to feel left out.'

'Oh, God, Gemma, I don't know. I could barely even look at Cal, never mind spend a whole night with him.'

'Yeah, but there'll be loads of other people there. And think how much it'll wind up Simone!'

'True, the look on her face when she sees me will be priceless.' The thought perked her up a bit. She took a deep breath. 'All right, I'll come if you promise to sit next to me, and promise you'll make sure I don't drink too much.'

'Done,' said Gemma. 'Now you'd better phone Cal.'

It took Angel several attempts to summon up the courage to ring him. When she finally did, Cal was obviously in the middle of cooking and sounded busy and preoccupied.

'Hi, it's Angel,' she said quickly, wanting to get it over with. 'I'd love to come tonight, if that's still okay?'

'Of course, great,' he replied. 'See you later.'

Well, she hadn't really expected him to say he

was looking forward to seeing her, had she? *Get real, girl*, she told herself sternly.

Next Angel faced the task of deciding what to wear. She didn't know whether she should be smart or casual, but after trying on a number of outfits, she decided to go for her favourite jeans, a gold silk camisole and a black cropped puffed-sleeve jacket, accessorised by a gold love heart on a long chain. By now it was getting close to eight and, paranoid about turning up late, she only had time to slap on some tinted moisturiser, a brush of bronzer, mascara and lip gloss.

'That will just have to do,' she said, taking one final look at her reflection and grabbing Cal's denim jacket and a bottle of champagne.

Cal's house was a twenty-minute walk away from her flat, just off Hampstead High Street on one of the most sought-after roads in the area. Stunning four-storey Georgian houses lined the avenue. Cal's was painted white and a beautiful purple wisteria hung round the door. To her huge relief, Gemma was already there and answered the door. Through the enormous living room, Angel could see Cal and Tony out in the garden chatting. Feeling butterflies about seeing them, Angel followed Gemma outside. Cal was charming and kissed her cheek, then said he had to check on something in the kitchen and needed Gemma's help, leaving her alone with Tony.

The two looked at each other for a moment, then spoke at the same time.

'I'm really sorry,' Angel said quickly, trying to get out her apology before he had a chance to speak.

'No, *I'm* really sorry,' said Tony, much to her surprise. 'I was out of order saying those things to you. I was so angry with that jerk slipping you those drugs. Have you dumped him yet?'

Angel grimaced. 'No, but let's not talk about him.'

'Come here then,' Tony said, holding out his arms and they hugged.

Reconciled, they walked towards the house, Tony updating her on the news from Brighton. As she listened, Angel was free to observe Cal's house and garden. She liked what she saw very much. The garden was stunning, with gorgeous plants and flowers surrounding a decking area for sitting and chilling out, steps leading down to a patio built round a large pond with koi carp. Tucked along the side of the house was a sauna and hot tub. Inside, Cal had kept all the original features: the fireplaces, the coving and the cornices. Beautiful crystal chandeliers hung from the impressively high ceilings and the oak floors had been stripped and varnished. He had wonderful taste, she thought, and he had furnished the house with a few simple but stylish pieces of furniture. It was a bit minimalist for Angel's liking but the overall feeling was one of space, clean lines and luxury. *My God, he's come a long way*, Angel thought, remembering all too clearly the grotty, cheerless two-bedroom flat he'd shared with his mum.

They joined the others in the kitchen, and both Gemma and Cal smiled in relief when they saw them.

'The others are in the dining room,' Cal said. 'Why don't you go through and I'll get you a drink? What would you like, Angel?' He handed Tony a beer. Cal was casual in a tight black T-shirt and combats – he looked sexy and athletic and it took all Angel's willpower not to openly stare at him.

The spacious dining room was painted a delicate pale violet and was dominated by a large oak dining table with solid-looking chairs grouped around it. Through the double doors to the living room, Angel could see comfortable sofas arranged around the fireplace.

'He's definitely in touch with his feminine side,' Gemma whispered to Angel as they made their way over to the others.

'Does Simone live here?' Angel asked.

'Some of the time, but mostly she's away filming,' Gemma answered.

Cal's friends turned out to be two of his Chelsea team-mates, the Spanish Antonio and French Jean-Paul, and both were absolute charmers. Angel sat next to Antonio, who was clearly very taken with her and flirted outrageously all evening, even when she said she had a boyfriend. Cal was at the far end of the enormous table – at which Angel felt a mixture of disappointment and relief – with the lovely Simone at his side. She had finally made her appearance halfway through the starters. Everyone else had gone for the smart-casual look, but Simone had gone for all-out glamour and was wearing a turquoise silk dress with a plunging neckline, no back and an enormous slit up one side. She looked stunning, but slightly out of place. Simone had done a double-take when she saw Angel, and for a moment looked so furious that Angel was sure she'd make a scene, but instead she watched Angel closely and suspiciously. Angel felt self-conscious at first, but several glasses of wine made her mellow enough not to care. She had made things up with her brother, and Cal wasn't looking at her like she was the Antichrist. Perhaps she could put that night behind her.

The dinner was amazing. Cal was obviously a man of many talents, because he had been responsible for it all: a delicious asparagus soup, followed by a seafood risotto that impressed even his foreign team-mates, and home-made mango sorbet for dessert (*blimey*, thought Angel, *is there nothing this man can't do?*). Cal showed them all into his huge living room where he poured out brandies for the boys and Baileys for Gemma and Angel. Poker-up-the-arse Simone demanded camomile tea.

Despite Angel's best intentions, she and Gemma were now feeling slightly tipsy and sat on one of the large cream sofas, gossiping quietly.

'I bet Cal was gutted when Tony walked in on you and him. It was probably the closest he's been to getting a BJ in ages! Madam probably worries about the calories,' Gemma whispered cheekily.

'Ssssh!' Angel told her, smiling in spite of herself. She sipped her Baileys and realised that she was enjoying herself. But it was a feeling that was short-lived as she overheard Simone's conversation with Antonio and Jean-Paul.

'No, I'd never even consider it!' she heard Simone say emphatically. 'Anyway, I don't think I need them, do you?' She showed off her cleavage to the men's obvious admiration, and took a pointed sideways glance at Angel.

'I think there's something rather cheap about them, and Cal doesn't like them. Do you, darling?'

'What's that?' Cal had been on his way to top up Gemma's and Angel's glasses and half turned to look at Simone.

'Implants, darling, you don't like them, do you?'

'Um,' replied Cal, avoiding Angel's eye, 'I've never really thought about it.'

Immediately Angel felt her hackles rise. How dare Simone be so obvious in her put-downs. Did she really think that not having silicone implants made her a better person than Angel?

'Bitch,' murmured Gemma.

'More Baileys, girls?' Cal asked.

'No, thanks,' Angel replied coolly. 'I'd better go, actually, it's been such a long week.'

'Sure?' Did she imagine it or was his tone disappointed?

She nodded, said her goodbyes and even managed to give Simone an air-kiss, quite an achievement when really she longed to slap her smug face.

Cal showed her to the door.

'Thanks so much for asking me,' Angel said, looking into his eyes for the first time that night. 'I had a really nice time.'

'I'm glad you could come, and I'm really glad you made it up with Tony,' Cal answered.

He opened the door and just as Angel was leaving he kissed her lightly on her cheek. She paused in the doorway, summoning the courage to say the next thing.

'Cal, I wanted to apologise for that night. I feel awful about what happened. It was the drugs – I would never behave like that usually,' she mumbled, her cheeks flaming with embarrassment.

Cal bowed his head. 'Don't worry, I've already forgotten all about it,' he said. And then he gave her an incredibly cheeky smile and added, 'Though some of it I remember quite enjoying!'

Angel's cheeks burnt even hotter, but suddenly Simone's shrill voice came from the living room and the smile was wiped off Cal's face. 'Goodnight, Angel,' he simply said. 'Take care.'

Chapter 13

Betrayal

Angel had turned off her phone while she was out and when she got home she discovered several urgent messages from Mickey. She was still in a good mood from the evening and called him back right away. He sounded agitated, totally unlike his usual laid-back self.

'What's wrong?' she asked. 'Is everything all right?'

'There's a story coming out in the paper tomorrow,' he gabbled. 'I wanted to let you know, but it's not true, I swear. Nothing ever happened. She made it all up.'

'Hey, slow down,' Angel said, starting to feel sick inside. 'Who made what up?'

Stuttering and stumbling over his words, Mickey finally told her that a girl he'd met when he was in Germany had sold a story to the paper saying that they'd slept together.

'But it's not true, babe, I promise. She had a few

drinks with us in the bar, that's all.'

'Are you sure?' Angel asked coldly, remembering only too well Mickey's odd behaviour when he returned from that weekend in December, and how he had accused her of seeing someone else.

'I swear on my life, Angel. I love you, I would never be unfaithful to you. You have to believe me.'

'I don't know,' Angel replied slowly. 'I need to see you.'

'I'll drive down first thing tomorrow, I love you.'

She barely slept that night, unable to stop thinking about what Mickey had told her, and, much as he had protested his innocence, she really wasn't sure she believed him. She had seen for herself how much he loved getting attention from his female fans and she could just imagine how he might react to some fit bird coming on to him, especially if he'd taken a little too much coke.

She tossed and turned. What was wrong with her? Why wasn't she enough for Mickey? She felt empty and hollow.

But that was nothing to how she felt the following day. The press were already camped outside her flat at seven the next morning and she woke up to them ringing her buzzer. 'No comment,' she shouted down the entry-phone, then disconnected it to stop them ringing again. Desperate to read the story, she called Gemma, told her what had happened and begged her to get a paper and come over. While she waited for her friend she paced round the flat, feeling more and more wound up as the minutes ticked by. Finally Gemma arrived, looking grim. Silently, she handed Angel the paper. It was the front-page story.

Angel read it, the words swimming in front of her as her eyes filled with tears. According to the paper, Mickey and the girl had met in the bar of the hotel the band were staying at. Mickey had been eyeing up the girl all night, then finally approached her and suggested she come up to his hotel room for a drink. He'd filmed her doing a striptease, then they'd taken coke and drunk champagne. The girl claimed she hadn't wanted to sleep with him, but Mickey had promised her it was the start of something more, so she'd given in. They'd had sex three times that night, twice the next day . . . Apparently, Mickey couldn't get enough of her.

Even though it was written in typical lurid tabloid style and could be exaggerating what had actually happened, it seemed to Angel that it could well be true; the detail about him filming what they'd got up to made it all too believable. She finished reading and looked up at Gemma. 'I'd only just started going out with him when this is supposed to have happened. What's wrong with me?'

'Oh, for God's sake!' Gemma exploded. 'One – it's probably not true. Two – if it is, then it's about him being a total fuck-up. It's not about you!'

'I thought he loved me.'

At ten, Mickey called her and, protesting his innocence again, begged her to meet him at Claridge's, where the press couldn't bother them. Angel was all set to leave her flat dressed in her tracksuit bottoms and a hoodie, with no make-up, when Gemma stopped her.

'Come on, don't be a victim! You've got nothing to be ashamed of. Put something on that makes you feel good, and I'll do your make-up.' Reluctantly, Angel changed into a pair of skinny jeans, a tight black T-shirt and pumps and she allowed Gemma to do her face. Then she put on the largest pair of Chanel sunglasses she owned.

'That's better,' Gemma told her as she prepared to leave, giving her a hug. 'Now go and get the truth out of him.'

The two of them had to elbow their way through the scrum of journalists shouting questions at Angel. How did she feel about what Mickey had done? Was she going to stand by him? *Come on, Angel, talk to us, we'll make it worth your while.* Flashes were going off in her face and Angel felt cornered, hunted. She could sense the start of a panic attack coming on, but somehow she managed to push her way to the taxi and shut the door on the shouts and the cameras.

As soon as she walked into the hotel suite, Mickey rushed over and tried to embrace her. 'I'm so sorry, babe.'

She pulled away from him. 'I just want to know the truth, Mickey,' she said coldly.

'I told you, I swear that nothing happened! Yes, I met the girl, yes, I probably flirted with her, but it was nothing more than that.'

'So you didn't ask her up to your hotel room?' Angel demanded. 'You didn't have sex with her?'

Mickey's blue eyes looked pleadingly at her. 'No, babe, I swear. She's made it all up.' He sounded genuine, but Angel didn't know what to think. Her head was spinning and she felt sick.

'I love you!' Mickey told her. 'I'd never do anything to hurt you. I know I've been really crap lately because of the tour, but I'll make it up to you, I promise.'

He took her in his arms and this time Angel allowed him to hold her. *I do love him*, she told herself. *I do, and the papers are always printing things like that. The girl probably just wanted to make some money.* But suddenly she had a thought. 'If it's not true, then why don't you sue?' she said slowly.

Mickey looked uneasy. 'I already suggested that to my management but they said no, it looks bad and creates bad feeling with that paper, which means they might stop running positive stories about the band.'

They spent the rest of the day and night holed up in the hotel room, ordering room service and watching TV to pass the time. It was more time than she'd spent with Mickey in ages, but all she could feel was trapped and caged in. She longed to get out, but she really couldn't face seeing any more journalists. Carrie called her, wanting to know the truth about the allegations, and when Angel told her they were all lies, she asked if she'd do a story saying that she was standing by Mickey.

'No,' Angel said firmly. 'I don't want to talk to the press about this – it's private.' Carrie tried to argue, saying it was all good publicity, but Angel was having none of it.

'I've got something to cheer us up,' Mickey said when she got off the phone, and he pointed at the two lines of coke he'd laid out on the bedside cabinet. 'Make you feel better, babe.'

Why not? Angel thought. It couldn't make her feel any worse. She took a line. And, yes, she did feel better. Lounging around on the hotel bed, she and Mickey drank champagne and took several more lines of coke and eventually, Angel didn't care about anything much.

Early the next morning, Mickey had to rejoin the band for the rest of the tour. He said all the right things when they kissed goodbye, that he loved her, would miss her, and he promised they would go away when the tour had finished.

The press interest lasted a couple of weeks. Angel couldn't go anywhere without several journalists pursuing her and trying to get her to talk. It got her down. But Mickey couldn't have been more attentive: he phoned and texted her whenever he could, telling her he loved her, and he sent her flowers every other day until she begged him to stop because she was running out of places to put them and people to give them to. Her friends told her they were sure that Mickey was telling the truth, but she didn't think they really meant it. She kept remembering the way they had warned her about Mickey when she first started seeing him.

'How would you feel if a story like that came out about Tony?' she asked Gemma, when they were out one night.

'Tony's not famous, so it's not likely to be in the press, is it?' Gemma replied evasively.

'Okay, well, what if someone told you something like that about him, what would you think?'

'I'd know it wasn't true,' Gemma replied. 'I trust Tony one hundred per cent and I know he'd never be unfaithful. Why are we talking about this again? I thought you said you believed Mickey.'

Angel sighed. She so wanted to believe him, she just wasn't sure. 'I think I do. What do you think?'

She wanted Gemma to reassure her, but Gemma never said things she didn't mean and her answer wasn't what Angel wanted to hear.

'It doesn't matter what I think, it's what *you* think that matters. Anyway, I thought you wanted to talk about tomorrow.'

Angel nodded, trying to put the whole thing with Mickey out of her mind. The next day, she was finally going to see Tanya, her real mum and she was feeling very apprehensive about it so had asked Gemma for a drink.

'Yes, you're right, sorry. I've got her address and she knows I'm coming, but the social worker said she was still using drugs and that I shouldn't expect too much.'

God, I'd hate to live somewhere like this, Angel thought to herself as she walked swiftly through the run-down South London council estate on her way to her mum's tower block. Everywhere she looked, all she could see was concrete and graffiti. She felt a wave of claustrophobia grip her as she got into the grey metal lift that stank of piss and the door slid shut. *Please don't let me get stuck in here*, she thought anxiously, as the lift started moving. She got out on the fifteenth floor and slowly walked towards number 55. It was hardly home sweet home – the windows in the hallway were boarded up and there was an iron gate in front of the door. Angel took a deep breath. She could walk away now or she could go ahead and meet her mother.

After a moment's hesitation, she reached through the bars and rapped on the door. It seemed like ages and Angel had to resort to shouting 'Hello' until she heard the sound of bolts being undone. The door swung open and she was face to face with her mother. It was the moment she'd been waiting for ever since she'd found out she was adopted, and she was filled with both hope and fear; but not even the social worker's warning had prepared her for the shock when Angel saw her. She knew that her mother was only thirty-six, but the woman in front of her looked much closer to fifty. Her face was deeply lined, her skin looked sallow and her eyes, which were the same colour green as Angel's, looked blank and defeated. Her lank brown hair was scraped off her face in a ponytail. She was wearing a black hoodie and black tracksuit bottoms that hung off her.

Angel tried to muster a smile. 'Hi, I'm Angel.'

Her mother stared at her for a few seconds suspiciously, then said, 'You'd better come in,' in a flat South London accent.

Angel followed her into the flat. It was dark, dirty, barely contained any furniture and there was no carpet on the concrete floor. Her mother shuffled her way into the lounge, where there was one grotty floral sofa, a cheap-looking table and a TV. No pictures on the walls, no photographs, and the wallpaper was peeling off. The room stank of stale cigarette smoke and sweat. Angel stood awkwardly in the middle of the room, feeling claustrophobic.

'Got any fags on you?' her mother asked hopefully, lowering her skinny body onto the sofa.

Angel shook her head. 'Sorry, I don't smoke.'

Her mother tutted, then took the last remaining cigarette from her packet. She lit it and inhaled deeply, then turned to look at Angel, who had sat down next to her.

'Couple that had you, they looked after you okay?'

Angel nodded. 'Yeah, they did.'

'I reckon you did better than my other kids, they all ended up in care.'

'Oh,' said Angel, 'I've got brothers and sisters?'

'Two brothers, but you've all got different dads.' Her mother's voice took on a more self-pitying, whining tone. 'I really tried to get off the gear when you was all born, but it was hard for me, I didn't have no one to help me.'

'What about my dad? Who was he?' Angel asked, thinking, *Do I really want to know*? Her mother was in a far worse state than she could ever have imagined. God knows what she would find out about her dad.

She thought of Frank and Michelle, the home they had created for their family, how hard they had always worked to give her and Tony what they wanted, and how they loved their children and would have done anything to protect them.

'I reckon he was Robbie. I met him when I was working in a pub. He was a photographer, I think. Nice lad, but it was never serious and then he moved away and I didn't know where he'd gone, so I could never tell him about you. I thought I might be able to keep you, but then it all got too much . . .' Her voice trailed off.

Don't expect me to feel sorry for you, Angel thought bitterly.

'What was his second name?'

'No idea, darling. D'you fancy making us a cup of tea? Three sugars in mine. Ta.'

Angel got up and walked into the kitchen. She was no fan of washing-up herself, but her mother seemed to have abandoned it altogether – the sink and surfaces overflowed with dirty crockery. She looked in vain for clean mugs in the cupboards, then resorted to rinsing out two of the least stained mugs. She thought with a pang of Michelle's pristine kitchen, made the tea and walked back into the lounge.

'So you've done all right for yourself, ain't you, with all that modelling? Got your own place, have you?'

Angel nodded.

'And you've got me to thank for those looks, I looked just like you when I was your age.'

Angel pretended to sip her tea. Even when she had discovered her mum was a drug addict, she had still held on to the fantasy that their meeting would be special and life-changing. She had imagined her mother throwing her arms around her, begging for her forgiveness, and that in spite of everything there would be a connection between them. Now she looked at her mother and felt nothing except pity, and, if she was really honest, disgust. She was just about to make her excuses and leave when someone opened the front door.

'That'll be Lee, my boyfriend,' her mother told her.

A man in his late thirties, big built, with a shaved head, a tattoo of a dragon on one meaty forearm, a cobra on the other and a mean look in his eye, walked into the room.

'Who's this, then?' He glared at Angel.

'She's Angel, my daughter.'

He carried on staring at Angel, then there was a sudden flash of recognition in his hard eyes. 'Oh, you're that glamour bird, ain't you?'

Angel just nodded, then turned to her mum. 'I've got to go, Tanya, it was good to meet you.'

She started walking towards the door, desperate now to leave and get away from these people, but Lee was still in the doorway, blocking her exit.

'Excuse me,' Angel said to him.

'Didn't you bring nothing for your poor old mum, then?' he demanded, his alcohol- and cigarette-loaded breath making her feel sick.

Angel hesitated.

'I bet your house don't look like this, does it? Your mum could do with some new things.'

Angel bit her lip. He was a bully and she didn't like him one little bit. She turned and faced her mother, who was hunched on the sofa with an eager glint in her eyes. Angel opened her bag and pulled out five hundred pounds in cash, which she handed to her. She'd got into the habit of carrying around quite large sums with her because she was fed up of being hassled at cashpoints by people wanting her autograph or sneaking pictures of her with their mobiles.

Immediately, Lee legged it across the room, grabbed the money from Tanya and counted it.

'That all? I bet you could take out more with your cash card. I could take you to the cash point down the road.'

Wordlessly, Angel got out her purse and showed Lee that there were no cards.

'I don't believe in them,' she lied, thankful that something had made her leave her cards at home. 'And now I've got to go, I'll be late for work. Thanks for seeing me.'

She walked out of the room as quickly as possible. Once she had slammed the front door shut behind her she ran to the lift, hit the button and looked fearfully back at the flat. Dreading another encounter with Lee, she decided to run down the stairs instead, not stopping until she'd run all the way through the council estate.

As soon as she hailed a taxi she rang Gemma, but frustratingly, she was on voicemail. She then tried Mickey, who was back from tour at last.

'Can I see you?' she asked.

'Sure, babe, come on over.'

Chapter 14

Angel Lost

What Angel really needed was someone to talk to, someone who'd help her make sense of the meeting and her own conflicting emotions, but Mickey was far too preoccupied with getting ready for a glossy magazine awards ceremony, where he was going to be presenting one of the awards. He barely paid any attention to Angel's account of what had happened and she finally lay on the bed knocking back wine in a desperate attempt to numb her feelings, while Mickey tried on numerous outfits and demanded her opinion.

Honestly, she thought, *he's worse than a girl!*

Finally he chose a white suit and a black shirt, then exclaimed, 'Aren't you going to get ready?'

'Oh, Mickey, I've had such a shit day, I really don't want to come.'

'But they're expecting you!' he said angrily. 'Come on, we'll get a cab to your place right now.'

'I'm too pissed.'

'Well, why don't you have some of this, it will sober you up.' Mickey flung a small white packet at her.

Not giving herself time to think about the irony of snorting coke, just hours after leaving her junkie mother, Angel laid out a line on Mickey's bedside table. She just wanted to forget that today had ever happened and she didn't want to be alone.

The awards night passed in a blur. To the outside world Angel must have looked like she was having a ball, dressed to thrill in one of her revealing outfits. She was wearing a white shirt of Mickey's, pulled in at the waist with a big black belt, tiny gold shorts and gold Gucci heels. She deliberately messed up her hair to give it that 'just got out of bed' look and emphasised her eyes with false eye-lashes and lots of liner – slutty but sexy. She chatted and laughed and flirted her way through the night. She drank steadily and periodically retired to the bathroom with Mickey for more of the other stuff. She didn't want to think, all she wanted was to close the door on her feelings, terrified of what might come out if she didn't. Mickey's presentation went well and he was pleased with himself. When they finally got back to Angel's flat in the early hours of the morning, they made love for the first time in ages. Angel longed for him to tell her that he loved her, but as soon he had finished he turned over and fell straight asleep again.

In the morning Angel felt like hell. Her raging hangover was made worse by the fact that she was flying out for a really important shoot today for *M*, a gig Carrie had been trying to get her for ages. It was the most upmarket of the lad mags, more sophisticated and stylish than its rivals. She was due to fly to the South of France later that morning.

'Oh, God, Mickey,' she groaned, trying to force down a slice of toast. 'What am I going to do?'

'Hair of the dog, babe, it's the only way,' he said, laying down a line of coke on the bedside table.

'But I've never taken it in the morning – that's the slippery slope, isn't it? I don't want to end up like my mum!'

'Don't be soft,' he replied unsympathetically, more concerned with arranging his hair in the mirror. 'It's only one morning.'

He's right, isn't he? Angel told herself. It was an emergency, it would never happen again. She took it without further hesitation and was able to shower, get dressed and make it to the airport on time. Gemma was already waiting at the check-in.

'Why didn't you call me back last night? I was really worried, you sounded so upset on the phone.'

'I went to an awards night with Mickey, I'm sorry, we got back late.'

'Oh, is that why you look like shit?'

Angel groaned. 'Just promise me you can put me back together again, please.'

'I'll do my best,' Gemma replied tersely. 'And

when we get on the plane I want to hear how it went with your mother.'

But when they boarded the plane and were settled in business class, Angel was reluctant to tell her friend. Partly because she was worried about being overheard and partly because she didn't want to reveal just how awful the meeting had been.

'Let's wait until we're at the villa, I don't want anyone hearing us.'

Gemma seemed to understand and listened to music while Angel flipped through a pile of celebrity gossip magazines. Suddenly she froze, looking at a picture of Simone and Cal, photographed leaving an exclusive London restaurant. Cal had his arm protectively round Simone and they were both smiling away. ARE THEY OR AREN'T THEY? demanded the headline in huge letters. Feeling sick, Angel anxiously read on. The article was asking if Cal and Simone were engaged; apparently the 'love-struck' couple had been seen poring over rings in Tiffany's, and had then been spotted at a number of stately homes – allegedly looking for wedding venues. When Simone was asked directly by a journalist if they were engaged, she would neither confirm nor deny the rumours. *A sure sign*, Angel thought bitterly, *that the rumours were true*.

She held up the page for Gemma to see.

'Is this true, then?'

Gemma scanned the article quickly.

'God, I've got no idea.'

'Oh, come on, Tony's Cal's best friend, he would know!'

'He hasn't mentioned it to me, and I would think he would, don't you? You know you can't believe some of the stuff those magazines come up with.'

Angel flung the magazine away from her. The thought of Cal marrying Simone was like a knife in her heart. She knew she didn't stand a chance with him, and she was with Mickey anyway, but that didn't mean she could bear the thought of anyone else becoming Mrs Bailey. Depression washed over her. Gemma would soon be married, several of her other friends were also engaged, but there was no hint that Mickey had plans to ask her – not that she was sure if they even had a future any more. And meeting her mother and now this picture of Cal and Simone. All of a sudden she felt horribly alone and the hangover was making her feel so much worse that she wanted to crawl back under her duvet and pull it over her head.

'Cheer up!' Gemma exclaimed. 'It's probably not true. I bet you the journalist asked Simone and she's so desperate for Cal to ask her that she planted the whole story.' Angel hung her head miserably. 'Come on!' Gemma told her: 'This is the shoot you've been wanting to do for ages, don't blow it because of some stupid article.'

They were staying at the place where the shoot was taking place the following day. It was a stunning

location. The white modernist villa was built round
a dazzling aquamarine infinity swimming pool and
the surrounding gardens were full of orange trees
and purple bougainvillea. As soon as they got there,
the people from the magazine fussed around them,
pouring them ice-cold drinks and showing them to
their luxurious rooms. Once she'd had a quick
shower, changed into a bikini and hit the pool,
Angel felt slightly better. Her head cleared and as
she surveyed the beautiful gardens and breath-
taking views of the Côte D'Azur, it almost felt like
the meeting with her mother had never taken place.

They all had supper outside on the terrace in the
warm night air and Angel made sure she stuck to
water. She really didn't want to blow the shoot
tomorrow and at ten, she decided to hit the sack.
She had to get up at six to get ready and this was òne
night that she definitely needed her beauty sleep.

She slept for nine hours, but instead of feeling
refreshed when she woke up, she was strangely
agitated and unsettled. Thinking it was just the
consequence of meeting her mum, she tried to
block it out. But at breakfast she had very little
appetite and could only manage orange juice and
some fruit salad instead of her usual bowl of
porridge. Then it was off for hair and make-up.
Naomi, the stylist, wanted her hair poker-straight
and so the hairdresser spent a long time blow-
drying it and using straightening irons to achieve

the look. Then it was Gemma's turn to get started on her make-up.

'You're very quiet,' she commented to Angel, brushing foundation on her face. 'Are you okay?'

'Yeah, fine,' Angel muttered, feeling anything but. She really needed something to perk her up, otherwise this was going to be a bitch of a day. She and Gemma still hadn't had their chat about Angel's mum.

Half an hour later, Gemma had done her usual fantastic job. Angel's skin looked golden brown and flawless, her eyes were stunning with shimmering eye shadow and long lashes, and her lips were seductively glossed.

'See?' said Gemma. 'You'd never know how trashed you were.'

Next the stylist Naomi came in holding up the first outfit for the shoot – a tiny white bikini, which Angel was to wear with a gorgeous emerald neck-lace. Gemma went to get some water and Angel took the opportunity to whisper to Naomi, 'I'm feeling a bit strung out, do you have anything?'

Knowing exactly what Angel meant, Naomi told her to go to the bathroom and she would find what she wanted in the cabinet. Seizing her opportunity before Gemma returned, Angel rushed into the bathroom, found the coke and quickly took a line. She sniffed and rubbed her nose and almost at once the agitation she had felt disappeared. *It's because of seeing my mum*, she told herself. *This is just to get me through the day, I haven't got a problem.*

Angel gave one of her very best performances in front of the camera that day; she oozed sexuality as she posed in the different bikinis and jewels. After the white bikini and emeralds came a tiny black one, which she wore with a diamond choker and matching bracelet; a hot-pink one, which she wore with a gold chain around her waist; and a silver one, which she wore with a pair of diamante heels. Finally the photographer wanted to do a series of topless shots. Because they didn't want to get Angel's hair wet, she was sprayed with water so her skin glistened, then photographed emerging from the pool – a twenty-first-century Venus, the water cascading off her beautiful body.

'I think those are some of the best pictures you've ever done,' Gemma told her friend when the shoot was finished.

'You think so?' Angel asked, but feeling inside that it was true. Later that night, after another alfresco supper, everyone involved with the shoot went to a chic club in Nice. To celebrate the day's success, Angel drank quite a bit of champagne, expecting to feel relaxed and mellow, but once again the nagging feeling of agitation returned. So when Gemma was chatting to someone else, Angel quietly asked Naomi if she could get her something.

'I'll give you the money,' she said, discreetly handing her a wad of cash. Looking over at Gemma still talking, Angel got up and followed Naomi to the bathroom, where the two locked themselves in a cubicle. Naomi laid down two lines and handed Angel a small package of her own.

For the rest of the night, Angel felt fantastic. She hit the dance floor and danced for ages, flirting with the journalists from the magazine who were there to interview her. Then she rejoined the group at the table and carried on drinking heavily. At one point she noticed Gemma looking at her warningly, but Angel just smiled back, raising her glass to her friend.

The next morning she felt rough, but she had her emergency supplies and was able to laugh off her hangover. After breakfast she and Gemma were driven back to the airport. Angel couldn't help noticing how unusually quiet Gemma was being.

'Are you okay?' she asked her friend.

'I'm fine, I was thinking about you.'

'Why? I'm okay,' Angel said quickly.

'You seemed so different last night,' Gemma replied, still thoughtful.

'I was just letting my hair down, you know, after all that shit with my mother.'

'Well, I don't know, because you still haven't told me.'

Realising there was never going to be a right time, Angel quickly told Gemma about the meeting with Tanya. Gemma looked shocked but Angel felt strangely detached.

'And how do you feel now?' Gemma asked, concerned.

Angel shrugged. 'I'm all right, I just want to forget about it.'

'Don't you think you should talk to someone about this? What about Michelle?'

'No way. Like I said, I just want to forget it. I don't want to give her any more head space, she doesn't deserve it,' Angel told her friend abruptly.

As soon as they landed at Heathrow, Angel texted Mickey to let him know she was on her way round. She couldn't wait to see him, although deep down she knew that this was less about wanting to be with him and more about getting her hands on his supplies of coke.

She had barely embraced him when she asked if he had anything on him.

'Of course, babe, it's in the bathroom, help yourself.' He tried to kiss Angel, but she was a woman on a mission and pulled away, hurrying to the bathroom, desperate for a fix.

Mickey laughed at her when she re-emerged. 'Babe, you're going to have to get your own supply sorted, I'll give you my dealer's number. He'll deliver to your house.'

'No, I don't want it! I just need some now, because I'm tired and still stressed out from seeing that vile woman,' Angel replied hotly.

'Okay, whatever.' He shrugged.

'So what are we doing tonight?' she asked. Now

she'd had her fix, she was up for some partying.

'We could go to Buddah if you like.'

'Cool, I'll go home and get changed and get the car to come and pick you up around ten.'

Back home, Angel slung her Louis Vuitton overnight bag in the corner of her bedroom; she couldn't be bothered to unpack. She poured herself a glass of wine and took a shower. She was a beautiful golden brown from having been in the sun and decided to make the most of it by wearing as little as possible. She chose a white midriff-baring halter-neck top and white pleated mini and her gold Guccis. She called the chauffeur service she always used to book a driver and limo for the night. Half an hour later, Chris came and picked her up in the limo and they drove round to Mickey's. As soon as he sat down next to her in the car, he checked that the screen separating them and Chris was closed and pulled a small package out of his jacket.

'Thought you might like something for the journey,' he told her, cutting her a line.

For a split second Angel hesitated, then took the coke.

Buddah was already packed by the time they arrived. The theme was East meets West with huge low-slung velvet sofas to recline on, ornate gold tables, fat-bellied Buddahs lit up in alcoves and the sweet smell of incense in the air. Usually Angel would have hated the crowds, but tonight she was oblivious to them. She stayed close to Mickey, feeling loved up and mellow. Halfway through the night they bumped into Desiree, a backing singer the band had used a couple of times, he said. Desiree was a beautiful mixed-race girl in her twenties. She was very friendly to Angel, telling her what a fan of hers she was and how beautiful she was. When it was time to go, Mickey asked if they could give Desiree a lift.

In the back of the limo all three of them took another line and Mickey whispered to Angel, 'How would you feel about Desiree staying at mine tonight?'

'Cool,' Angel replied, thinking nothing of it.

As soon as they arrived back at the flat, Mickey opened a bottle of champagne and put music on. Angel was feeling increasingly out of it and was getting tired. She sank into the sofa and Desiree sat down on the other sofa, lighting up a cigarette. Mickey sat down next to Angel, kissed her lightly on the lips, then whispered, 'You know that thing we talked about a while ago? Now seems like a good time, don't you think?'

'What thing?' Angel asked, not having a clue what he was talking about.

'You know,' Mickey murmured, 'the threesome. You promised you'd try it when the time was right. Now seems perfect. Desiree's definitely up for it, she told me earlier.'

Slightly shocked, Angel pulled away from his embrace and looked over at the girl. 'I'm not sure I want to, Mickey.'

'Oh, come on, babe, it's just a bit of fun,' Mickey urged her, kissing her again. 'Go on, try it, for me.'

'I don't know.' Angel got up from the sofa and went into the bathroom. She'd taken more coke and drunk more champagne than she ever had, and she wasn't capable of thinking clearly. For a few moments she tried to focus on herself in the mirror, trying to gather her thoughts. *Was it such a big deal? If it would make Mickey happy, shouldn't she try it?* She returned to the living room, where Mickey was laying down more lines of coke, and sat back down. Still sitting on the other sofa, her long legs crossed, Desiree looked at her knowingly and smiled.

'I'm still not sure,' Angel whispered to Mickey.

'Just have another line then, babe, let yourself go,' Mickey replied. His voice was soothing and she relaxed a little, feeling comforted by being close to him.

Angel took another line, then Desiree moved next to her and Mickey. Mickey kissed her again and Angel tried to lose herself in his kiss. *What would be so bad about it?* she asked herself. It was no big deal really. Suddenly she was aware that Desiree was gently stroking her leg. Angel tensed, then relaxed; it felt good. When Desiree slid her hand up Angel's thigh and started caressing her through her silk thong, Angel pulled away at first, shocked, but Mickey pulled her back, telling her to relax. Angel closed her eyes and gradually surrendered to the pleasure. Desiree certainly knew what she was doing. As her slender fingers tantalisingly caressed Angel, sending waves of pure pleasure rippling through her body, Mickey kissed her more deeply.

'Come on, let's go into the bedroom,' he murmured, scooping Angel up in his arms and carrying her through. He laid her on the bed, stripped, then slid off Angel's clothes. Desiree joined them on the bed, now naked herself, her body firm and lithe. Mickey kissed Angel, first her lips, then her breasts, and Angel closed her eyes, feeling aroused. Suddenly, she was startled as Desiree slid down the bed and started caressing Angel with her brand-new, 24-carat-gold-plated Little Gold vibrator. She tried to move away, but Mickey held onto her.

'Just enjoy it, babe, enjoy it.' Angel tried to resist but Desiree persisted and Angel felt her inhibitions melt away, more waves of pure pleasure surging through her. She pulled Mickey towards her and went down on him, stopping only when Desiree brought her to the most amazing orgasm. It had been worth spending £200 on the toy.

'Take another line,' Mickey ordered. They switched positions so she was on top of Mickey while Desiree caressed her breasts.

Their sexual marathon seemed to last for hours, punctuated by more lines of coke and more champagne – so much that eventually Angel passed out.

*

She woke up as someone roughly shook her shoulder.

Struggling to surface from her alcohol- and drug-fuelled sleep, Angel blearily opened her eyes to see Desiree hovering over her, fully dressed and looking extremely pissed off.

'Mickey's already left for the studio and he hasn't paid me.'

'Hasn't paid you for what?' Angel asked, her head pounding as she attempted to sit up.

'For last night, of course!'

'What do you mean?' Angel asked, a horrible realisation starting to dawn. 'I thought you were a singer!'

'Sometimes,' Desiree replied with a hostile look on her face. 'Sometimes I get my money in other ways.'

Shock turned to anger. Angel hated Mickey for putting her in this situation. She'd gone along with his threesome suggestion to please him and, yes, much to her surprise she had enjoyed herself. But discovering that the third party was a prostitute put a whole different slant on the affair. Getting out of bed and reaching for her robe, she demanded to know how much Desiree was expecting.

'He said two grand.'

'Two grand!' Angel exploded. 'I'm going to phone him right now.'

Desiree shrugged. 'Suit yourself, it's what he agreed to.'

Angel grabbed her mobile and marched into the lounge.

'What the fuck's going on, Mickey?' she hissed down the phone as soon as he answered. 'That woman,' she couldn't bring herself to use her name 'has just demanded two grand for last night. Did you know she was a hooker?'

'Babe,' Mickey pleaded, 'I had no idea it was going to cost that much. Come on, you enjoyed yourself, didn't you?'

'I can't believe you did that to me, you fucking bastard!' Angel was shouting now. She started as Desiree appeared in the doorway, coolly watching her and dragging hard on her cigarette.

'Come on, Angel, just give her the money and I'll pay you back.'

Angel moved away to the far side of the room so Desiree couldn't hear. 'I haven't got two fucking grand on me, I'll give her what I've got and you'll have to give her the rest.' She snapped her mobile shut and, feeling humiliated and furious, she grabbed her bag, counted out a grand and thrust it into Desiree's hands.

'That's all I've got on me, you'll have to get the rest from Mickey.' She could hardly bring herself to look at the woman, mortified knowing she had been paid to do all those things.

'Cheers,' Desiree muttered, then sauntered towards the front door. There she paused, turning round to face Angel, and said, 'If you want to do it again, Mickey's got my number, or if you fancied a one-to-one, I'd be up for that. It would be less than for the threesome, of course.'

There were all kinds of things Angel wanted to say to her. Instead, she chose to ignore her and slam the door in her face. Desiree's laughter seemed to echo in the flat long after her departure.

Angel took a very long shower, as if she could somehow wash away the humiliation. When she got dressed, she received a text message from Mickey, thanking her for bailing him out and again promising to pay her back. He also left her the number of his dealer. Angel's lip curled in disgust.

'What a wanker,' she exclaimed, suddenly glad he was going to be away with the band for a few days and he would miss her birthday. She grabbed her coat and left the flat, slamming the door behind her.

She wanted to get back home right away, to a place that didn't carry the memories of what had happened last night. Her head was buzzing. In the taxi back to Hampstead, her mind kept replaying what had happened last night over and over, feeling a mixture of shame and anger – ashamed that on some level she had enjoyed it and angry that Mickey had lied to her. Then just to torture herself further, she recalled the awful meeting with her mother. She couldn't believe that her mother had shown no interest in her at all except when money was mentioned.

As soon as she got back home she paced around

her flat, unable to settle. There were several messages from Gemma and from Carrie. But Angel didn't feel like speaking to anybody. She picked up the pile of celeb magazines that had been delivered that morning. Now Cal and Simone's supposed engagement was front-page news in several editions. She scooped all of them up and flung them in the bin without reading them, just imagining what Cal would think of her if he knew what she'd been up to last night. Feeling desperate, she picked up her mobile and found Mickey's message with his dealer's number. She wrote it down, then took a deep breath and rang him.

Two hours later, after a visit from Mickey's dealer, Angel decided she felt up to phoning Gemma. Her friend wanted Angel to come and look at bridesmaid dresses and they arranged to meet later that day. Angel really didn't feel like bridesmaid material after the events of the previous night, but agreed, for Gemma's sake. She killed time before they met up by going to the gym, but found she could only manage thirty lengths and in the end went and sat in the steam room.

'You look knackered,' Gemma said, kissing her friend as they met up in the bridal boutique.

'Yeah, well, it was a late night,' Angel muttered, thinking, *If only she knew what I'd been up to.* She knew it wouldn't be the threesome that Gemma didn't approve of, but the drugs that led up to it, and Mickey's behaviour, too. She could only pray that Gemma never found out.

A romantic at heart, Gemma was going for the full-on traditional wedding. She was wearing a stunning strapless floor-length cream silk dress and she wanted her bridesmaids to be in pale pink. She planned to have the dresses made and wanted to get some ideas, so she had Angel try on a number of different outfits and model them for her. By now Angel was feeling decidedly jaded, so while Gemma was deep in conversation with one of the assistants, she quickly nipped back into the fitting room and took a line of coke, praying that the music would drown out the noise of her sniffs.

Three more dresses later, Gemma finally declared herself satisfied.

'Let's go for a drink – Tony said he might meet us later.'

They wandered along the King's Road in Chelsea and ended up at Max's, a trendy bar that had just opened. Gemma quickly texted Tony to let him know where they were.

'You seem to have livened up,' Gemma commented as they sipped their drinks.

'Must be the alcohol,' Angel replied, praying Gemma didn't think it was anything else.

'How are you feeling now about seeing your mum?' Gemma asked her.

Angel definitely didn't feel up to a heart-to-heart. 'To be honest I'm trying not to think about it. It was a mistake and I just want to forget it.'

Gemma was about to ask her something else when she caught sight of Tony. She waved at him and Angel's heart missed a beat when she saw Cal walking behind her brother.

'You look knackered,' her brother told her bluntly, giving her a quick peck on the cheek.

'Thanks, that's just what Gemma said. Are you going to join in the criticism as well, Cal?'

Cal gave her his slow sexy smile, which turned Angel to jelly. 'No, you don't look so bad.'

'Well, I think I'd better try and repair the damage,' Angel joked, making her way to the loos.

She considered herself in the mirror. The others were right, she did look knackered; she had dark shadows under her eyes, and her skin, which usually glowed with good health, looked sallow. Immediately she reached for her Touche Eclat. *That's better*, she thought, disguising the dark circles. Then she put on blusher, more eyeliner and mascara and lip gloss. She was sorely tempted to take a quick line, but her fear of being found out overrode her need and she returned to the table.

'Hasn't worked,' her brother told her. 'You've got more make-up on but you still look knackered.'

'Shut up,' Gemma told him, putting her arm round Angel. 'You look fine now, babe, we've just been worried about you.'

Angel frowned; she wasn't prepared for this. It looked like a set-up.

'Gemma told us you met your real mum and it didn't go so well,' Cal said gently. Angel took a deep breath, willing herself not to cry.

'Yeah, well, it wasn't quite what I had hoped for,' Angel said in a brittle voice, anxious not to break down in front of them. 'Anyway, I really don't want to talk about it, so can we change the subject – where have you two been?'

'Getting measured up for our wedding suits,' Cal replied.

At the mention of weddings, Angel's spirits plummeted still further – was she going to discover that Cal really was engaged? That would be the perfect end to a perfect day. She waited for him to say something but he just talked about the preparations for Tony's wedding and stag night.

'Oh, that reminds me,' Gemma said, 'I want you to be in charge of organising my hen night, Angel. Of course it would be you, who else would I want?'

'Yeah, but I don't want you doing anything too outrageous,' Tony put in.

'What, no strippers, no getting hideously drunk and shagging some lads? What am I going to arrange then?' Angel asked cheekily.

'I'm sure you'll think of something,' Tony replied.

'That's not fair, because I bet Cal's going to take you all lap-dancing, aren't you?' Angel looked challengingly at Cal, who tapped his nose mysteriously.

'That would be telling.'

After a couple of rounds, they decided to go for something to eat. Angel kept expecting Cal to mention Simone and the engagement, but he didn't. Instead the four chatted about the wedding, Cal's team-mates and news from Brighton. As always, conversation between them flowed easily and even Tony seemed to lighten up and was nicer than he'd been to Angel in a long time. Angel loved spending time with Cal, though she was very aware that this might be the last time she saw him without Simone. But even though she felt more relaxed, halfway through the meal she still felt compelled to take a line of coke. She tried to be as quick as possible and pretended that Mickey had called her and that's why she was gone for a while, but even so, she was aware of Cal looking at her quizzically when she returned to the table.

At the end of the meal, Cal offered to share a taxi back to Hampstead with Angel.

'That's a good idea,' Gemma put in before Angel had a chance to reply. She and Tony took the first cab home after saying their goodbyes.

'I'll speak to you later!' Angel whispered to her friend, half appalled, half excited about the prospect of spending time alone with Cal again.

But if Angel thought she was in for a cosy ride home, with perhaps a little flirtation thrown in, she was very much mistaken. As soon as they were sitting in their taxi and it pulled away, he was on her case.

'I know what you were up to when you went to the bathroom, Angel.'

Angel tried to feign surprise.

'What do you mean? I talked to—'

But Cal was having none of it. 'What's going on, Angel? You told me you only took it when you went out clubbing, now and then. I wouldn't say having dinner with friends counts, would you? That looks to me like someone with a problem.'

'Look, I'd had a bad day, that's all – a bad week, actually, meeting my mum and stuff. It's my birthday tomorrow, couldn't you just be a bit nice to me?' Angel could feel herself growing sulky. The last thing she needed was for Cal to have a go at her.

Cal's voice took on a softer edge. 'It must have been rough seeing your mum and I'm sorry, but taking coke isn't going to make it better. I could introduce you to someone who could help you.'

Angel shook her head. 'I don't need to see any-one. I haven't got a problem. You're right, I shouldn't have taken it tonight, but it won't happen again.'

Cal didn't look too convinced. When the taxi pulled up outside Angel's flat, he said, 'Happy birthday for tomorrow, Angel,' and kissed her goodnight on her cheek. Desire washed over her as she breathed in his scent and felt his warm lips on her skin. Then, all too suddenly, they had said their goodbyes and she was back in her flat, wanting Cal so badly it hurt.

Chapter 15

Kiss and Tell

'Happy birthday to me,' Angel said bitterly to herself as she woke up alone. Her mobile rang and she grabbed it, thinking it would be Mickey wishing her many happy returns, and she was itching to have another go at him about the threesome. He was in Scotland where his manager had pressurised him into appearing on a kids' TV show where Mickey had ended up having to sit in a bath full of baked beans, having green slime poured on his head in spite of his protesting that he was an artist and shouldn't have to do that kind of thing. But instead it was Carrie and she didn't sound happy.

'Good of you to actually answer your phone, Angel,' she snapped. 'I've been trying to get hold of you since yesterday. We've got a problem.'

Oh, God, what is it now? Angel thought wearily. She hadn't forgotten to turn up for a shoot, had she?

'I had a tip-off from a friend of mine who works on the *People* and tomorrow they're going to be running the story of your threesome. That girl, whoever she was, has sold the story. Apparently she didn't get paid.' Carrie took a deep breath and carried on ranting. 'Honestly, Angel, why did you have to go and get yourself involved in something like that? It's so fucking tacky.'

Carrie went on to say a whole load of other things that Angel could barely take in. Everyone was going to find out about that night – her parents, Tony, Gemma, Cal . . . The thought of it was so awful that Angel suddenly threw down the phone and ran into the bathroom where she retched into the toilet.

When she'd wiped her mouth and picked up her phone Carrie was still in full flow. Angel interrupted her. 'Well, what do you think I should do, Carrie?'

'I'm coming to that,' Carrie snapped. 'I've arranged with Mickey's agent that the two of you fly out to Spain this afternoon. I've got an apartment in Malaga, and you can stay there for a few days until this whole thing blows over. A car will pick you up in two hours. Now, get packing.'

Feeling totally shell-shocked, Angel put down the phone and did as she was told. As she started shoving clothes into a suitcase, her mobile rang again. It was Cal.

'Hi, Angel, I know you said you weren't interested but I've got the name and number of this guy I know and I'd really like you to have it.'

'Okay,' Angel just about managed to get out.

Cal reeled off the details and Angel pretended to write them down, but her hand was shaking so much she couldn't have held a pencil anyway.

'Well, happy birthday, Angel, I hope you enjoy your day.'

Cal was obviously about to go and Angel found her eyes full of tears.

'Wait, Cal,' she sobbed.

'What is it?' he asked, his voice full of concern.

'Nothing. Everything. I'm going away for a couple of days and something bad's going to come out in the press tomorrow about me.' As the tears streamed down her face, she struggled to carry on speaking. 'And I wondered if, when you see Tony and Gemma, you'd ask them not to judge me too much and that I'm sorry for showing Mum and Dad up.'

'Tell me what's wrong, I'm sure it can't be that bad. I can help you.'

'When you find out tomorrow, you won't want to. Goodbye, Cal.' He rang straight back but Angel just switched off her phone.

Three hours later, she and Mickey were at the airport, checking in. Neither had anything to say to the other. Mickey had been given a bollocking by his manager – threesomes with prostitutes and cocaine didn't exactly go down well with the clean-cut boy-band image he was supposed to promote – and he looked sulky and anxious. He didn't attempt to apologise to Angel for misleading her about Desiree, nor did he try to comfort her. They ignored each other through the flight, each pretending to watch the movie. Although Angel hadn't eaten all day she felt too sick to have any food. Instead, she drank champagne, each sip making her feel more and more depressed. Mickey hadn't even remembered that it was her birthday. She had thought her sixteenth had been her worst one yet, but how wrong had she been – with her nineteenth she'd hit an all-time low.

They were met at Malaga airport by a car and driven straight to Carrie's apartment. It was ten o'clock at night, but still incredibly hot. Any other time Angel would have been impressed by the luxurious surroundings. Carrie's spacious and elegant apartment was on the top floor of an expensive-looking complex, with its own swimming pool on the roof. But Angel felt like she was walking into a prison. Carrie had ordered her maid to stock the fridge with wine and food and had already warned Angel not to go out. The press would easily track her down if she did. Instead, her maid would buy them anything they needed. She'd also left Angel a new mobile phone with which Angel could communicate with her, so that she could switch off her other phone, which the press were bound to call the next day. There were already dozens of messages from journalists wanting to know her side of the story. Angel deleted every one without bothering to listen to it. There were several from Cal, but she couldn't bear to hear his voice so she deleted them, too.

That done, she poured two large glasses of wine. Mickey took his without even bothering to say thank you.

Fuck you, thought Angel bitterly; *it was you that got us into this mess*. But she didn't have the energy to argue, and, after calling Carrie to let her know that they'd arrived safely, she changed into her bikini and went swimming. She swam two miles, desperate to tire herself out and to dull the craving for coke that was already starting to take hold of her.

When she finally got out of the pool, Mickey was lying on one of the sun loungers, chain-smoking. He'd given up two years ago but obviously this crisis had proven too much for his willpower.

'Don't suppose you've got any gear on you, babe?' he asked hopefully.

'Oh yeah, because it would have been such a good idea to smuggle some on board the plane!' Angel snapped.

'I was just asking!'

The two of them sat there drinking wine. Angel's plan to tire herself out hadn't worked; she was still desperate for a fix.

'Don't you know anyone out here?' she finally asked Mickey.

'I've just been trying to think. I suppose Si might, it's worth giving him a call.'

It was midnight back in England, but luckily for Angel and Mickey, his dealer was still 'working' and, yes, he did have a contact in Malaga.

'How much cash have you got on you, babe?' Mickey demanded as soon as he got off the phone.

'I've got about one and a half grand,' Angel replied. 'And by the way, you still owe me a grand,' she snapped, feeling fresh anger at the memory of why they were here in the first place.

'Yeah, yeah, you'll get it. I'm going to call up this guy and get us a grand's worth. We don't know how long we're going to be here.'

Angel could only hope it wasn't for long – she was already starting to feel claustrophobic.

An hour later, Mickey had handed over Angel's cash to the dealer who arrived at their apartment, in exchange for a large supply of coke for him and Angel. As soon as he shut the door he quickly laid out a couple of lines.

'Fuck the tabloids!' Mickey declared after taking his line.

Then he tried to give Angel a hug. 'It'll be all right, babe, I'm sure.'

Angel let him, but she wasn't at all sure it would be.

Carrie phoned at seven the next day. Angel and Mickey had stayed up most of the night taking coke and Angel felt totally wasted.

'I'm going to fax over the article. I think it's best that you know what it says. The phone's been going crazy here, with people wanting to talk to you. I've issued a statement saying you have no comment; you're emotionally exhausted and are resting. I don't, repeat, *don't* want you to leave that apartment until I tell you. We just might be able to salvage something out of this by selling your side of the story, but I want a lot of money for that.'

When Angel tried to protest that she wasn't into doing kiss and tells, Carrie snapped back, 'You slept with a hooker, for God's sake, it's a bit too late to come over all coy.'

Angel and Mickey passed the day as they had passed the night, taking coke and drinking. Angel still hadn't eaten anything and she felt totally spaced out, unable to focus on anything. Carrie faxed the article, but Angel couldn't bring herself to read it. Mickey read it quickly and then told her it wasn't as bad as it could have been, although even he seemed a bit shaken by the way Desiree had described their drug-taking. At five, Carrie called to say that she had made a deal for Angel to sell her side of the story to a leading Sunday tabloid for a hundred grand. The journalists would be round first thing in the morning. When they arrived, Mickey was to stay in his room and not come out – his manager had signed a deal for forty grand with a rival tabloid for his side of the story. Angel paced round the apartment, unable to sit still, unable to relax. Part of her longed to speak to Gemma, but she couldn't face it. She felt so ashamed and humiliated.

Mickey was on the phone to his manager for most of the afternoon. Angel thought it was pathetic the way Mickey was sucking up to him, endlessly apologising and promising it would never happen again, and then whining that Angel was being paid more for her story than he was. 'Why is that?' he kept asking. *Go figure*, thought Angel. *Loser*. Then the moment he was off the phone, he was taking more coke. She was mildly shocked to find that all the love she had felt for Mickey was gone. She hated him for setting up the threesome with a hooker, she hated the way he had sponged off her, she hated him for betraying her with the girl in Germany. She didn't have any doubts about that one any more, certain now that he had been unfaithful. And she hated him for his self-obsession. But most of all she hated herself for wasting over a year of her life with him. She looked at him as he sprawled on the sofa dressed only in his white Calvins, and everything about him that she had once found so attractive – his blue eyes, his perfect features and his toned body – disgusted her now. He was just a selfish, vain, spoilt little boy, who didn't care about anyone except himself.

All Angel wanted to do was sleep, but she had taken so much coke that she was completely buzzing. She swam, flicked through magazines and channel-surfed on the TV, willing the day to be over. When she finally did get into bed, Mickey tried to put his arm round her, but Angel pulled away from him and moved to the edge of the bed to be as far away as possible.

'Come on, babe, don't be like that.'

'What! You think we can kiss and make up?' Angel sat up in bed. She couldn't lie next to him and pretend everything was okay any longer.

'You lied to me, Mickey, about that girl and I think you've lied to me right from the start. I bet you did shag that slag in Germany.'

Mickey tried to cut in, but Angel was in full flow. 'What kind of shit relationship is this? All you ever do is go on about yourself, you don't give a fuck about me. You just use me like a fucking cashpoint. Well, I've had enough. You owe me over ten grand and I want it back – now.'

'I'm expecting a cheque soon,' Mickey mumbled.

'Bullshit,' Angel shouted back. 'You own that flat, that must be worth over a million. You can get a loan based on that or you can fucking well sell the Porsche.'

Mickey looked down. 'I don't own the flat, it's my record company's. And I've had to give the car back, I couldn't make the repayments.'

Angel could hardly believe what she was hearing – he had borrowed from her knowing he couldn't pay her back. She didn't think her opinion of him could get any lower, but it just had.

'You don't understand what it's like,' Mickey complained. 'After we've paid the song writers and the management and divided up the rest between the band, we don't get that much.'

'Oh, my heart bleeds!' Angel got off the bed and marched into the other bedroom. She didn't want to spend another second in the company of that loser.

The journalists buzzed the apartment promptly at ten the following morning. Angel had made a half-hearted effort to tidy, clearing the empty bottles of wine and vodka from the table and throwing them in the bin. She'd made an equally half-hearted effort to make herself presentable, but had no energy. In the end she'd pulled on a white hoodie and a pair of white tracksuit bottoms over her bikini, tied her hair in a ponytail and put on a pair of huge dark sunglasses that covered up half her face underneath a baseball cap. She couldn't be bothered to put on any make-up. She knew she looked like shit, but for once she didn't care.

She led the journalists onto the roof terrace, not wanting them to snoop round the apartment. One was a hard-faced, overly made-up woman called Sue, the other a surprisingly young man called Keith. *Good cop, bad cop*, Angel thought grimly, though as it turned out, she was wrong, they were both bastards. They wasted no time in firing questions at her.

'Whose idea was the threesome? Did she enjoy it? How many other threesomes had she been involved in? What was her sex life like with Mickey? Was she into bondage?'

'Mickey's, no, just this one, great and no,' Angel replied wearily.

Then they got onto the part that Angel had been dreading. 'How long had she been taking drugs for? Did she have a problem?'

Angel knew she was a terrible liar, but found herself saying that she had only taken drugs once – the night of the threesome. She knew they didn't believe her and they kept pressing her on it.

At one point Sue leant over to her and touched her arm. 'Look, Angel, it would be far better if you were honest with us now. Either we'll find out or someone else will and it won't look good. The public hate a liar.'

'Well, Sue,' Angel replied, trying and failing to look her in the eye, 'I'm sorry to disappoint you, but I really don't take drugs. I'm a vodka girl, that's all.'

Sue raised her perfectly-shaped eyebrows in disbelief and tapped her long red nails on the table in irritation. 'Okay, have it your way, Angel. Now, let's get back to the threesome – there are one or two more details we need.'

After three hours they were through with Angel. She dreaded to think what they were going to write about her. She had pleaded with Carrie to get her copy approval of the piece, but Carrie had snapped that that had never been part of the deal. As soon as

Angel had closed the door on them she dashed into the bathroom, desperate for a line.

That's funny, she thought, as she took out the bag of coke from its hiding place in the laundry basket, *I'm sure we had much more than this*. There was barely enough for three lines, she calculated. She took a couple of lines and then wandered towards the bedroom to ask Mickey about the coke. When she opened the door, she stopped abruptly, gazing around her in disbelief. Mickey wasn't there. Furiously, she pulled open the wardrobe. None of his clothes were there. The bastard had obviously done a runner. Where would he go, though? Back to England? She shrugged – she didn't really care – but she was frantic now for the rest of the coke. Quickly, she searched through the bedside cabinet, but there was nothing. She picked up her phone and there was a text from him: *Sorry babe, had 2 go back 2 London 4 work, hope press shit went ok x*. Angel threw her phone on the sofa in a fury; she was certain he was lying. He was hardly likely to board a plane with a great stash of coke in his suitcase. He'd probably checked into a hotel and kept the drugs all for himself. Coke had been the one thing making her stay in this place bearable; she simply didn't think she could remain here without it, but Carrie had told her not to leave until her side of the story was published in a day's time. She counted her money: she had five hundred pounds. She reached once more for her phone and dialled Si's number, begging him for his Spanish contact, explaining that Mickey had left.

After several frustrating attempts, Angel tracked down Si's contact. He refused to deliver again as it was only five hundred pounds' worth this time and said instead that he would meet her at the Tiger Bar in an upmarket part of Malaga. Angel knew she shouldn't leave the apartment, but decided she had no choice. Realising she would stand out more in her scruffy clothes, she showered, put on make-up and chose a red silk dress with spaghetti straps and a pair of jewelled flip-flops. She completed the look with her huge dark glasses and a prayer that there were no journalists hanging around the bar.

She felt quite giddy as she stepped out of the front door and onto the street. It was nine o'clock at night and Malaga was buzzing with people all out to have a good time. She managed to hail a taxi. As she sat back, all she could think about was the dealer and the coke. It was five hours since her last fix and her nerves were jangling. The contact had told her he would be sitting at a table just inside the bar. Feeling apprehensive, she got out of the taxi and made her way inside. It was dimly lit and for a moment she had difficulty seeing anything, so reluctantly she took off her sunglasses. The contact was sitting on his own and he raised his glass to her. Nervously, she sat down at his table.

'You've got the money?' he demanded in strongly accented English.

'Yes,' she replied. 'Five hundred.'

'Okay, I'll get you a drink, make things look normal, and then we'll do the exchange.'

He nodded at the waiter and Angel ordered a Diet Coke.

'You must be pretty pissed off with your boy-friend doing a runner like that. He must be stupid to leave a beautiful girl like you all on your own.'

The very last thing Angel wanted to do was to make small talk with this man, whose eyes kept flicking greedily up and down her body, making her wish she'd worn her hoodie.

She shrugged, grateful when her drink arrived. The dealer obviously wanted to carry on talking, but Angel cut across him.

'I'm sorry but I have to get back to the apart-ment. Do you think we can do the exchange now?'

Reluctantly, the dealer nodded. Angel reached into her bag and pulled out the envelope of cash, passing it to him under the table. He slipped it inside his magazine and surreptitiously counted it. He nodded his head once he'd finished, then passed a package under the table back to Angel, which she put straight into her large beach bag. Just as she was getting ready to leave, a camera went off in front of her, the flash temporarily blinding her.

Shit, she thought, panicking. *Press*.

'Who's your boyfriend then, Angel?' a voice called out. Sue must have been watching Angel's apartment. The dealer pushed Angel out of the way and ran out of the bar muttering Spanish expletives. Angel tried to follow him, but saw to her horror that the street outside was crawling with press. She turned back into the bar and tried to push her way past Sue. 'Come on, Angel, you can see them all outside, why don't you and I have a nice little chat and then we'll get you somewhere safe, where no one else can bother you.'

'Fuck off,' Angel spat.

'We know he's a dealer. Getting your fix, were you?' Sue wheedled.

Angel was saved from having to reply as two security guards appeared and manhandled Sue out of the bar, much to her great disgust. 'You can't do this to me,' she shrieked, 'I'm press!'

Trembling, Angel sat at a table as far away from the window as possible. Tears pricked her eyes as she wondered how on earth she was going to get out of the bar and back to the apartment. She put her head in her hands, feeling totally lost.

Suddenly a voice she recognised called out her name. She looked up and to her complete amazement she saw Juan standing before her.

'I thought it was you! This is such a coincidence. It's like that line in Casablanca – of all the bars in all the world you had to walk into mine! What are you doing here?' Juan beamed at her, but Angel's face crumpled as she burst into tears. Juan immediately sat down next to her and put his arm round her.

'What's wrong? Why are you crying?'

'Oh, Juan, I'm in such a mess,' she sobbed.

Somehow she managed to tell Juan something of what had happened to her. If he was shocked about the drugs, he didn't show it, but instead held her hand and stroked her hair soothingly.

'Listen, you can come back to my apartment and stay there, the press won't find you; we'll go out of the back entrance.'

Drying her tears, Angel murmured, 'Thank you.'

Half an hour later, Angel was curled up on Juan's sofa while he made her a hot chocolate and an omelette, refusing to take no for an answer, saying that she looked far too skinny and pale. All Angel could think about was that she hadn't had her fix yet. Checking that Juan was busy in the kitchen, she grabbed her bag and nipped into the bathroom. *This is the last one*, she told herself, *the very last one*. When she emerged, Juan was setting the table.

'Won't my being here be a problem with Rosa?' Angel asked.

'Rosa's away, but I will tell her. And, no, it won't be a problem.'

Angel smiled and sat down. Just being close to Juan and seeing his warm smile lifted her spirits slightly; it seemed ages since she had seen a friendly face. To her surprise, she actually managed to eat the omelette and finish the hot chocolate. But when she caught Juan looking at her, she was taken aback by his serious expression.

'I think we should get rid of the drugs you bought tonight, Angel. You've got to stop.'

Angel felt cold and sick. 'Juan, I can't, please don't make me. I'll do it tomorrow.' She wasn't even convincing herself.

Juan shrugged and said, 'The trouble is, tomorrow never comes, does it?'

Angel tried to disagree, but Juan suddenly seemed weary and told her he was going to make up a bed for her.

As Angel pulled on one of his T-shirts and crawled into bed, she felt sadness wash over her. She was alienating everyone she was close to. Juan used to adore her but now seemed disappointed in her. What was she doing? She longed for reassurance, for love. She longed to feel someone's arms around her. She was lost.

Chapter 16

Rescue Me

She didn't wake until eleven the next morning. Juan was drinking coffee and reading the paper when she walked into the living room. After he asked her how she was feeling, he told her he had called Jeanie in Brighton at her salon to let her know Angel was okay, got Gemma's number and then called her.

'What?' Angel exploded. 'You had no right to do that!'

'She's been worried sick about you, Angel – all your family have. They don't care about the story in the press; they just want to know that you are all right. They want to help.'

'I don't need anyone to help me, there's nothing wrong with me!' Angel shouted, but even as she spoke she was aware of how empty her words sounded. She did need help. Pretending to storm out of the room in tears, Angel rushed to the bathroom, quickly took out her stash and laid out a line, hating herself for doing it, but at the same time unable to stop. She was startled by Juan knocking at the door, and, quickly hiding her stash once more, she opened the door.

'Listen, Angel, I have to go and open up the bar, but I'll be back in a couple of hours. I'll go to your apartment and pick up your clothes. I've made you some hot chocolate. Please phone Gemma.'

Angel nodded, thinking, *No way*.

After Juan had left, she took a long shower and put on her red silk dress. It was hot outside and Angel went and lay on a lounger on Juan's balcony. It was good to feel the sun on her skin. After a while, making sure that she couldn't be seen from the street below, she slipped off the dress and lay back down on her stomach. She felt herself drifting off to sleep, only surfacing when someone called her name. She looked up, rubbing her eyes. Expecting to see Juan, Angel had the shock of her life when it was Cal who walked onto the balcony. Feeling completely disorientated from the sun and the sleep, she sat up, forgetting that she was naked.

'What are you doing here?' she demanded, then, realising her compromising position, she quickly grabbed her silk dress and slipped it back on. Cal had turned away and she said, 'It's okay.' *Yet again Cal had her at a disadvantage*.

'I've come to take you home,' Cal replied.

'I'm perfectly capable of getting on a plane by myself,' Angel snapped.

Cal sighed and sat down on a chair facing Angel. He was wearing dark glasses and she couldn't see his eyes.

'I don't think you are. Unless you stop now, you're bang on course to ruin your life.'

Angel forced a laugh. 'Oh, come on, don't be so melodramatic. This is just a blip.'

'Don't you remember what your real mum was like when you met her?' Cal said seriously. 'Christ, what about my mum? Do you really want to end up like them?'

'I'm not like them!' Angel retorted.

'Okay, prove it to me. We'll get rid of the drugs right now – this stops here in this apartment.'

'No,' Angel said quickly. 'I just need a few more days to get my head straight, and then I'll stop.'

'You never will if you have that attitude.' Suddenly Cal got up from the chair and headed back into the apartment. With a horrible realisation dawning, Angel ran after him, but he was already in the bathroom, rifling through Juan's things, clearly searching for her drugs.

'No!' Angel shouted as he opened the bathroom cabinet and found her stash in the bag of cotton wool where she'd hidden it. He held the drugs over the toilet bowl, ready to drop them in. She grabbed his arm, frantically trying to reach for the drugs, but Cal was too strong for her and he shook the powder out of the plastic bag and flushed it away. Angel slumped back against the bathroom wall, sobbing hysterically.

'What did you do that for? I was going to stop.'

'Be honest, Angel, you weren't,' Cal said gently, then walked over to her and took her in his arms.

'Shush, it's going to be all right. I've got flights booked for tomorrow morning and I've booked you in at a clinic.'

Angel buried her face in his shoulder and sobbed harder.

'Here, drink this; it will make you feel better.' Cal handed Angel a cup of tea. She sat curled up on the sofa, suddenly feeling cold and shivery. Juan had dropped off her clothes before going back to his bar, but she hadn't brought anything warm with her.

'I've found this as well, thought it might take your mind off things.' Cal held up a Scrabble board and Angel couldn't help smiling.

'Yeah, right, like my addiction to a class-A drug can be beaten by Scrabble. Thanks, Cal, but I really don't think so.'

'Come on, it would be better than moping on the sofa, or are you afraid I'll beat you?'

An hour later, the pair of them were fully into the game and to Angel's secret satisfaction, she was winning by ten points. Cal was sitting at the other end of the sofa and every time it was his turn to come up with a word, Angel found herself gazing at him. He had recently had his already short hair shaved close to his head, making his rich brown eyes, with their long lashes appear even more striking. He was taking care of her. The contrast between him and Mickey came home to her and she realised that she'd been having a relationship with a boy. Cal was a man. He'd even interrupted his training to come over and bring her home. Angel thought he had never looked so handsome or so unobtainable. How could he have any respect for her now? He had seen her at rock bottom, he knew about the threesome and the drugs. What chance could she possibly have with him?

'Hey, no need to look so serious, you're winning.' Cal suddenly looked up at her.

Not wanting to show how upset she was, she quickly made up an excuse. 'Actually, Cal, I'm knackered, I'm going to go to bed.' She got up from the sofa and walked towards the bedroom. At the door she paused, turned round and said, 'Thanks for everything.'

'We all just want you to be okay, Angel,' he replied.

Why, she thought as she got into bed, *couldn't he have said* I *want you to be okay? Because,* said a mean little voice inside her head, *he's only doing this for Tony and Gemma. He doesn't care about you, and why would he? Look at you: you're pathetic.*

Three hours later, Angel was still unable to get to

sleep. She felt cold, anxious and paranoid. It had been six long hours since her last fix and she felt as if she was unravelling. She needed something to calm her down. Unable to lie still any longer, she got out of bed, tiptoed past Juan's bedroom, past Cal lying on the sofa and into the kitchen. She opened the fridge and poured herself a glass of wine, took a deep slug and was just about to go back to the bedroom when Cal whispered, 'You can't sleep either, then?'

She started and replied, 'No, I feel too wound up. What's your problem?'

'This sofa is killing my back.'

Angel considered her reply for a few seconds, then said, 'Well, you can share my bed if you like, it's a double.'

'Thanks. If I stay on this sofa much longer I doubt I'll ever walk again.'

Angel got into bed first and curled up on the far side of the bed, hardly daring to breathe. Even with the curtains drawn, the room was still light from the street lamp outside, so she was able to surreptitiously observe Cal getting into bed. He was wearing black Calvins that hugged his body and barely left anything to the imagination. His naked torso looked muscular and smooth and she longed to touch him. She had made sure that she was occupying as little room in the bed as possible, but as soon as he got in she could feel his warmth.

'Goodnight then, Angel.'

'Goodnight, Cal.'

Half an hour later, Angel was still awake and acutely conscious of Cal lying next to her. If only she dared, she could reach out and touch him. She listened to him breathing. Was he asleep?

'Can't sleep still?' Cal whispered.

'No, I feel too stressed,' she lied.

Cal moved towards her. 'I could give you a shoulder massage, if you like. Our physio's taught us how to do them – they're good for getting rid of tension.'

It was probably the last thing in the world that would help Angel relax, but she found herself agreeing and turned over onto her tummy. She was wearing a vest and French knickers, but as soon as Cal slipped the straps from her shoulders and touched her back, she felt as if she was lying there naked. As his strong hands massaged her back she felt consumed with desire. She longed to turn round and kiss him.

'You feel really tense and knotted up,' Cal told her, pressing hard on her shoulders. Angel willed herself not to think about Cal touching her skin. *Imagine it's a really old man who's doing it, a really old, ugly man*, she tried to tell herself, but Cal's hands didn't feel like an old man's . . .

'How does that feel now?' Cal asked after a few more minutes of massaging her.

She turned round to face him. It was now or never, she decided, as she reached up and, putting her arms round his neck, pulled him towards her and pressed her lips against his.

Don't resist, she willed him, *please don't*. And he didn't. He kissed her back, she definitely wasn't imagining it. Their kiss started off slow and tender, built up and became hot and deep. Now Angel could caress his body, and she ran her hands down his back, pressing her body against his, and she knew he was as aroused as she was. But suddenly Cal was pulling away; he was sitting up on the bed, his head in his hands. He sighed deeply and muttered, 'Angel, this is a really bad idea – it's not what you need right now. Sorry.' And to Angel's intense disappointment, he got up and walked out of the room.

Needless to say, Angel didn't sleep for the rest of the night. It wasn't until six that she finally drifted off; her last thought before sleep finally came to her was how on earth was she going to be able to face Cal in the morning? After what seemed like ten minutes but turned out to be two hours, she woke to Cal telling her they had half an hour to get to the airport. Angel had a hurried shower – there was no time to put on any make-up or agonise over what to wear, she just had to grab her jeans and a vest and tie her hair up in a ponytail. Cal was waiting in the lounge when she emerged from the bathroom. Angel could hardly bring herself to look at him.

He cleared his throat. 'About last night—'

'I'm so sorry,' Angel butted in. 'It was all my fault—'

'No,' Cal cut across her, 'I don't want you to think that. It was both of us – in fact, if it was anyone's fault it was mine. The last thing you need at the moment is for me to behave like that. Can we just forget it?'

Angel nodded, but inside she was thinking it was like a cruel rerun of their encounter in the Brighton club. Was he interested in her? Or did the fact that she so obviously wanted him seem like too good an offer to turn down? And how would she ever forget that kiss, or what his body had felt like, or his touch? She wasn't ever likely to forget the experience – it was burnt into her skin. As they drove to the airport and checked in, Angel kept hoping that Cal would have something else to say about last night, that he would admit that he couldn't just forget what had happened either. But he said nothing. He was withdrawn and serious and Angel didn't know how to reach him when he was in that mood, so she pretended to watch the in-flight movie and read a magazine.

'I've arranged for you to go straight to the clinic when we land – a car will be picking you up,' Cal finally said when they were half an hour away from Heathrow. 'It's better to start the treatment as soon as possible, I believe.'

Cal sounded so cold and detached that Angel couldn't believe he was the same man as yesterday, who had comforted her and made her laugh and then kissed her like no one else ever had before.

'Sure,' she replied, suddenly frightened about what to expect.

'Don't worry,' Cal said, as if he had read her mind. 'You'll be fine. You're a strong person, Angel, and I know you can beat this.' And he gave her the briefest of smiles.

And that smile was all Angel had to go on for a month.

The first week in the clinic was the hardest. She didn't want to confront her problem; she didn't want to take responsibility. But one thing she did take responsibility for was ending her relationship with Mickey, and the first night she was in the clinic, she asked to use the telephone (she'd had to hand in her mobile). They let her use it, and while someone hovered close by to make sure everything was okay, she rang Mickey. He didn't answer his phone, so she had to leave a message. *Pity*, she thought, because she had wanted to tell him exactly how she felt and hear his reaction.

Her message was simple and to the point; she spoke calmly and firmly. 'It's over, Mickey. I never want to see you again.'

Over the next few days, she was helped by Jim, one of the other patients, a thirty-year-old TV producer who had been in the exact same place two months earlier. He had been to several rehabs in the past and relapsed straight afterwards and he painted a grim picture of what life could be like if she didn't get treatment.

'I lost all my friends, because they hated what I'd become. All I ever did was borrow money or steal from them so I could buy drugs. My girl-friend left me and took our son with her – I haven't seen him for a year. All I cared about was my next fix. It isn't a life, Angel.'

Michelle also came to see her, which helped greatly. Angel was expecting her to be horrified by what she'd done, but she simply hugged her daughter and said, 'I love you, Angel. I know that your dad and me aren't very good at expressing how we feel, but never forget that we love you and are there for you and we only ever want you to be happy.'

'How can you love me, when you know what I've done? I've let everyone down. I'm such a bad person,' Angel sobbed.

'You're not a bad person; you're a wonderful, beautiful girl who just took a wrong path. I know you were upset finding out about your mum and I'm sorry it came out like that. We should have told you the truth years ago. And seeing you here, being brave enough to get treatment, has made me realise I'm going to get help about my depression. It's not been fair on any of you.'

'I know you might feel like this, Mum, but I bet Dad doesn't. He must really regret ever having adopted me,' Angel cried. For so long she had been suppressing her emotions, trying to pretend she was all right, but suddenly everything came flooding out all at once.

'Your dad does love you, Angel,' Michelle said calmly. 'He was the one who rescued you. I never wanted you to know the real story of your adoption, but I can see now that that was wrong and it would be better for you to know the truth.'

Angel sat, numb with shock, as her mum talked. She had been taken into care when she was six months old. Frank and Michelle had fostered her until she was a year old, when the courts decided that her real mother was now fit to look after her. Frank and Michelle were devastated; they had formed an incredibly strong bond with Angel and really didn't want to let her go, but they had no choice. Frank in particular was convinced that Tanya had not come off drugs and feared for Angel's welfare. He managed to find out where she lived and decided to watch the flat, gathering evidence if necessary. He saw Tanya go out one night, but without Angel. Desperately worried about the child, he rang the doorbell, expecting to speak to a babysitter. When there was no reply he broke into the flat and discovered Angel alone, curled up in a cot with no bedding, in filthy clothes and shivering with cold. He waited until Tanya returned home several hours later and confronted her, telling her he could either get her arrested for neglect and Angel would be taken back into care, or he would pay her two thousand pounds to tell social services that she could no longer cope and that she had handed Angel to Frank and Michelle for good and would never see her daughter again. There was no competition for Tanya. She agreed to sell her daughter right there and then.

'So Dad rescued me, then?' Angel said, her voice trembling with emotion, tears streaming down her face.

'He did, my love. When you came home to us, he was always the one who got up in the night to look after you when you had nightmares.'

'I remember,' Angel replied. 'But when I got older it seemed like he didn't care. I felt he was always criticising me.'

'I think he was just worried about you and that worrying came out as criticism. He loves you, he always has.'

A few days later, Frank came up to see Angel with Michelle.

'You haven't got any more bombshells to drop, have you, Dad?' asked Angel lightly, trying not to betray the emotion she felt at seeing her dad again.

Frank looked at Angel, his face full of emotion and said, 'We messed up, Angel.'

'Let's start again, then,' Angel said, hugging her dad. 'It's never too late, that's what I'm learning here.'

They spent the rest of the visit talking about what had been happening while Angel was in the clinic.

'Cal's been phoning us regularly to find out how you're doing,' her dad said suddenly.

'Really?' Angel tried to say as casually as possible. She had thought of Cal endlessly during the last month, replaying their last night together. She might have sorted out her addiction to coke, but her addiction to Cal Bailey was in a different league altogether and she had absolutely no idea how to tackle it.

Chapter 17

I Want You

A month later . . .

'You've done so well, babe, we're so proud of you!' Gemma cried, hugging Angel tightly. 'And I've missed you so much!'

'I've missed you, too,' Angel replied, trying not to show how disorientated she felt now she was out of the clinic. She'd been "free" for two days, and while she had longed to see Gemma at the clinic, now she couldn't help feeling afraid. It was all down to her. Now she was out she could do anything she liked: she could phone up Mickey's old dealer and order some coke or she could choose not to. She chose not to, but that wasn't to say she didn't think about it. A lot. And here she was, round at Gemma and Tony's flat pretending that everything was just peachy.

During her treatment at the clinic the press had had a field day, as she'd discovered from the cuttings Carrie sent her when she got out. Some were sympathetic and wished her well, but they were outnumbered by the ones that seemed to gloat and imply that she'd had it coming to her. She also read that Mickey's band had lost their recording contract, which made her even more relieved that he was no longer in her life. Sam, one of the other band members, had just leapt to number one with his new solo single, but there was no sign of Mickey's. She had a few shoots lined up but several had been cancelled. Cocaine addiction might be considered par for the course in fashion modelling, but the tabloids really didn't like it and it was with them that Angel had built her career.

'Tony will be back in a bit. He just had a few things to get from the supermarket. We thought you'd be happier eating in rather than going out,' Gemma chatted on. She opened a bottle of wine and went to fill two glasses, but Angel stopped her.

'I'm off alcohol for a bit, actually. I think it's a bit soon to risk it.'

'Sure,' said Gemma hurriedly. 'I won't have any either.'

'I don't mind,' Angel insisted, but Gemma wouldn't hear of it and poured them both a glass of mineral water.

As the two friends caught up and Gemma updated her on the wedding plans and what had been happening at work, Angel was longing to ask about Cal. She hadn't heard from him and she was desperate to see him again. She was just about to ask her question when Tony came through the door, closely followed by Cal. Angel's heart raced and her mouth went dry and she felt as if she couldn't move. Fortunately, she didn't have to, as Tony came over to where she was sitting on the sofa and gave her a hug.

'Good to have you back,' he said.

'How are you doing, Angel?' Cal asked.

'Okay, I think I'm getting there.' Making a supreme effort, Angel forced herself to look at Cal, who was even more gorgeous than ever – especially after a month of absence. Swiftly, Cal bent down and kissed her on the cheek, murmuring, 'Good to see you.'

'Cal offered to cook for us all,' Gemma put in. 'And knowing how crap Tony and I are in the kitchen, it was too good an offer to turn down.'

As soon as Tony and Cal disappeared into the kitchen, Angel turned to her friend. 'Why didn't you tell me he was coming?' she demanded.

'I didn't want you getting all stressed out,' Gemma replied.

'And is Simone coming too?' Angel asked tentatively.

'Of course not! She's away filming, but even if she wasn't I wouldn't ask her.'

'Do I look okay?' Angel asked anxiously. Thinking it would just be Tony and Gemma, she hadn't made much of an effort – she was hardly wearing any make-up and was dressed casually in jeans and a green silk camisole.

Gemma assured her that she did, but Angel insisted on dashing to the bathroom to check for herself.

She put on another layer of mascara and some lip gloss and brushed back her hair. She had just had her platinum-blonde hair dyed back to its usual brunette, and while she was pleased with how it looked, she wished she was wearing a more glamorous outfit and heels instead of flat pumps.

When she walked back into the living room, Gemma smiled at her. 'You look great, stop worrying.'

'It's all so stupid anyway,' Angel sighed. 'He's still with Simone.' She hadn't told Gemma what had happened that night in Spain; to be honest, there were times over the last month that she'd thought maybe she'd imagined it all.

'Yeah, but they hardly ever see each other. He's always training, and she's away filming. I really don't think it's a relationship that's going to last.'

'Dinner is served!' Cal called out from the kitchen, putting an abrupt end to the girls' conversation, and Gemma and Angel walked into the dining room. The boys had really gone to town, with flowers on the table and candles all round the room, and Angel couldn't help feeling touched by the effort. Cal sat opposite Angel and several times she caught him looking at her, but every time they both looked away awkwardly.

God, I want him, she thought, remembering only

too clearly what it had felt like to kiss him. Before, she would have knocked back the wine to give herself confidence, but now she only had mineral water to keep her going, a fact that hadn't escaped Cal. Was he impressed by her willpower? Everyone seemed to be sensitive to her situation and even the boys barely drank. Angel was worried that they would expect her to talk about her experiences at the clinic, but they seemed to understand that she was reluctant and spoke instead about Gemma's and Tony's hen and stag nights, which were only three weeks away.

After dinner, the four of them went into the lounge. Tony and Gemma snuggled up together on the sofa as they all watched Cal playing on *Match of the Day*. Angel felt a pang of longing to have that closeness with someone again. She and Cal were sitting on the sofa opposite them, but with a gap so big you could have fitted three other people between them. *Well*, she thought to herself bitterly, *what do you expect?*

'Jesus, Cal, that's gotta hurt!' Tony exclaimed, watching the Manchester United defender launch a brutal tackle against Cal, which left him lying on the ground in agony and clutching his right knee. A few years ago he'd had surgery on it after an injury.

'Yep,' Cal replied, 'it fucking hurt, but my physio reckons it's okay, I've just got to watch it.'

'He's sure it's okay, though?' asked Angel, worried for Cal.

He smiled at her. 'Take more than that to bring me down.'

By eleven thirty she was exhausted – she'd been used to getting up at half six at the clinic and going to bed at ten. Cal saw her yawning and offered to drive her home.

'No, it's okay, I'll get a taxi,' she replied, thinking, *Why on earth did I say that, of course I want him to give me a lift home!* But Cal insisted and after saying their goodbyes, she found herself installed in his navy blue Bentley Azure. They were quiet on the journey back, Cal concentrating on driving, Angel staring out of the window to avoid looking at him. To cover the awkwardness, she asked if she could put on some music. Cal nodded and switched on the stereo. Sinead O'Connor's 'Nothing Compares 2 U' blasted out of the speakers and only intensified Angel's self-consciousness.

'It must be hard to be out of the clinic,' Cal finally spoke, 'and back to temptation.'

Angel shrugged and said, 'It's okay. Like us addicts say, I just take one day at a time . . . And I feel so much better now I'm clean. I hated that horrible paranoid feeling I'd get the morning after. It was like spiders in my head and I didn't know what I'd done,' she said, feeling awkward.

'You're doing really well, Angel,' Cal said softly. 'I always knew you would.'

As they pulled up outside her flat, Angel said, 'I

haven't got anything alcoholic, but I could make you a coffee if you like.'

She was expecting him to say no, but to her surprise, he replied, 'A coffee would be great.'

Inside, Angel went to the kitchen, switched the kettle on and started getting cups out of the cupboard. Suddenly Cal was behind her, leaning against the doorway.

'You didn't really think I wanted a coffee, did you?' he said softly. Angel froze. She looked at him and he looked at her and this time there was no barrier, there was no attempt to hide the desire in his eyes. He pulled her into his arms and kissed her hard. In between kisses he said, 'Angel, I haven't been able to stop thinking of you since that night in Spain.' By way of an answer, Angel kissed him back. He started caressing her breasts through her camisole and her nipples hardened at his touch; she undid the buttons on his shirt and caressed his flat, hard stomach. Suddenly Cal stopped. *Oh God*, thought Angel, *not again*. But instead he whispered, 'Let's go to the bedroom.'

'I think he was well out of order,' Gemma exclaimed two weeks later, when Angel found herself unable to hold back any longer from telling her friend. 'You've just come out of the clinic, for God's sake! You're vulnerable. Did he say anything about Simone? Is he going to leave her?'

'No,' Angel replied. She was shocked by the

vehemence of Gemma's reaction. 'And I haven't asked him. Anyway, it's early days.'

'Or he just fancies a no-strings-attached shag with you!' Gemma retorted. 'You're worth more than this.'

Angel hung her head, unable to look her friend in the face.

'Oh my God, it's happened more than once, hasn't it?' Gemma exclaimed.

Angel nodded.

'How many times?' Gemma demanded, looking appalled.

'Every day for the last two weeks,' Angel whispered, bitterly regretting having told her friend.

'I just can't believe he would behave like this!' Gemma seemed livid.

'Please,' Angel begged her, 'it's just between Cal and me. I shouldn't have told you. And it's not what you're making it out to be, there's more to it than sex. We're . . .' she hesitated, trying to find the words that would make her friend understand '. . . connected. I feel so close to him and I know he does to me as well, even though he hasn't said it.'

Gemma looked so sceptical that Angel didn't want to carry on. What she had with Cal was so precious to her – she didn't want it to be trampled on by anyone who didn't understand.

Her first night with Cal had been amazing, the most awesome sex of her life. Cal was an incredible lover. He knew exactly how to turn her on, and whereas Mickey's attempts to please her had always played a minor role in their lovemaking – it was mostly all about him – Cal wanted to give her pleasure. He was the most sensual and erotic lover she had ever had. At first she had felt shy, and every time she kissed him or caressed him she kept worrying whether she was doing it right, but then desire took over and she stopped thinking.

The next day she woke up to find his arm still round her and, at first, she couldn't move for the sheer pleasure of being next to him and feeling his warm body pressed against hers. Then reality kicked in and she carefully moved out of his embrace and dashed to the shower, wanting to look good for when he woke up. Her whole body tingled deliciously from their lovemaking, which had lasted most of the night. Her face felt slightly sore from where he had kissed her so hard, but she loved the feeling. Her shower over, she walked back into the bedroom. Cal still seemed to be asleep and she watched him for a moment, mesmerised by his beauty – she couldn't quite believe that he was in her bed. Then suddenly his eyes opened and he made a grab for her. 'And where do you think you're going, young lady?' he asked huskily, pulling her towards him and slipping off her robe . . .

By four o'clock they were both starving and Cal finally got out of bed and headed to the kitchen. Angel couldn't help smiling to herself, knowing there was absolutely nothing to eat in there. She could hear Cal opening and closing cupboard doors and making sounds of exasperation, and a few minutes later he returned to the bedroom.

'Where's the food?'

'I think I might have some noodles somewhere,' Angel replied, laughing.

'Oh my God, I'm not having any of this anorexic model crap. I'm fucking starving. We're going to have to order a pizza. Even though, I have to tell you, it's not the kind of food I usually eat – my body being a temple and all that.' Cal showed off by flexing his muscles and Angel reached across the bed and whipped off the white towel he had tied round his waist. Suddenly she wasn't hungry for food any more . . .

An hour later, Cal insisted on phoning for pizza and garlic bread and ice-cream. While he was in the shower, Angel frantically checked her appearance in the mirror. Her cheeks were flushed, her lips swollen, her usually straight hair was wild and tangled, but she couldn't stop smiling. She quickly brushed her hair and slipped on a white shirt-dress, then went into the lounge and lit candles. Cal emerged looking fresh from the shower. He too had got dressed, and Angel felt a jolt of desire run through her even though they'd made love three times already that day and, frankly, she was knackered and quite sore in some places! Cal sat next to her on the sofa and put his arm round her. 'You look gorgeous, Angel, but I think I need a rest.'

The pizza arrived and both of them devoured it hungrily. Then they lay back on the sofa. But even though she'd had the most perfect time with Cal now, the doubts started creeping in. Was he going to stay the night? Was this just a one-off shag? She couldn't believe that it could be – there seemed to be such a strong bond between them.

'Is it okay if I stay tonight?' Cal asked. 'But I'll have to be up early for training.'

'Of course,' she replied, thinking, *Yes! Stay!* She was hoping that this would lead to their talking about what had happened between them, but Cal clearly had other ideas, as he began kissing her again and unbuttoned her dress. It seemed that Cal was a four-times-a-day kind of guy. And luckily, as Angel was discovering as Cal caressed her, she was a four-times-a-day kind of girl . . .

'What time is it?' Angel asked sleepily, seeing Cal getting dressed.

'It's half five, I've got training. What are you up to today?'

'I've got a shoot – it's my "comeback" one. You know – straight out of rehab, can I still cut it as a model and all that bollocks.'

'Do you want to come over to mine when you've finished and I'll cook dinner? At least I have food in my kitchen.'

'Ah, but will it be as good as that pizza?' Angel asked cheekily.

'So much better,' Cal replied sexily, leaning over the bed and kissing Angel. Then he was gone and Angel was wide awake.

Fucking hell, I've just spent the night with Cal. Am I dreaming?

Her shoot wasn't until two, but there was no way she could go back to sleep. Instead she took a quick shower and drove to the stables. But even after a two-hour ride her mind was still in turmoil, and when she saw Manda coming to untack Star, Angel could barely string a sentence together. She felt totally wired. She was desperate to tell Gemma, but something stopped her. She knew Gemma would be protective of her and would ask awkward questions – the ones Angel wanted to ask Cal but couldn't – like was he planning on leaving Simone? Did he want a relationship with Angel? Or was it just about sex?

At the shoot, Angel was dressed in white or silver for every single picture – the tabloid planned to run the headline THE RIGHT WHITE STUFF! So she was in a white tutu, naked save for a white cashmere wrap, and, with a cheeky take on her recent spell in the clinic, dressed as a saucy nurse in a tight white uniform, unbuttoned to the waist. Angel tried her best to appear normal, but she was restless and every time there was a break for a costume change or a make-up touch-up she kept checking her phone to see if Cal had texted her.

'What's up?' Gemma demanded.

'Nothing,' Angel lied. 'I guess I'm just nervous about the shoot going well. I don't want to fuck anything up. Carrie really laid it on the line after I came out of the clinic and said I wouldn't get work if I ever used drugs again.'

Gemma snorted. 'Like she's one to talk. I'm sure she's a bloody cocaine queen herself. Personally, I think you'd be better off without her – all she cares about is making money out of you.'

'Well, I feel I need her at the moment.' The thought of being washed-up before she was even twenty was not a good one. A few weeks before everything had gone so spectacularly wrong in her life, Carrie had hinted that someone in the States was interested in her, someone big, and Angel was anxious to find out more.

'Told you that you needn't have worried – you're doing great,' Gemma told Angel towards the end of the shoot as she retouched her make-up.

'Well, that was one good thing about being in the clinic. I lost weight because I couldn't drink any wine.'

Angel surveyed herself in the mirror. For the next set of pictures she was wearing a diamante G-string – she just hoped that the pictures didn't take too long as it wasn't the most comfortable garment in the world – and nothing else except a strategically placed arm. She still hadn't heard from Cal and was desperate for the shoot to end so she could text him to find out if he still wanted to see her that night. *Please let him text me*, she prayed. *Please*.

Bruce, the photographer, wasn't someone Angel had worked with before and he wasn't someone she warmed to. So far he seemed to be going out of his way to make the shoot as hard work as possible – ordering Angel to pose in positions that were supremely uncomfortable and then shooting end-less rolls of film when Angel was sure he had the picture he needed after the first take. The poses in the diamante G-string were no exception: he had her lying on the white sofa with one hand hooked under the diamante strap and the other arm across her breasts, but he kept trying to get her to pose topless and she knew perfectly well that this hadn't been the deal her agent had set up with the magazine, so she kept resisting. He was obviously used to getting his own way with his models and his tone grew more and more bullying. Finally, Angel snapped.

'Will you fucking stop trying to get me to show my tits, because I'm not going to. End of.'

Bruce just glared at her and got his revenge by deliberately taking his time, so by the time they finished, it was eight o'clock. Immediately, Angel grabbed her robe and dashed to the dressing room to get her phone. There was a message from Cal.

Still on for tonight? See you at mine at 8 x

Anxious that Gemma didn't see her, she nipped

to the loo and texted him back saying she would be there at nine.

'Fancy going for a drink?' Gemma asked her as Angel walked back into the dressing room.

'I think I'm just going to go home and crash – I'm knackered.' Angel had never felt less tired in her life. She was so keen to see Cal she could hardly bear to spend another minute talking to anyone, not even Gemma, but she forced herself to wait while her friend packed up all her make-up. Angel had been hoping to go home and get ready but there was no time, so she had to settle for wearing the outfit she'd put on that morning – the flirty little white pleated skirt, the sweet pink and white polka dot shirt and the pink peep-toe suede shoes.

'Thanks for today.' Angel hugged Gemma goodbye. 'I'll call you tomorrow.' She jumped into the waiting taxi. On the way to Cal's, she checked out her appearance. Fortunately, Gemma was such a fantastic make-up artist that although Angel was wearing far more make-up than she would usually, it still looked natural. She was willing the taxi driver to go faster, but he seemed to be taking the most indirect route possible. Angel found herself getting more and more wound up and was just on the point of ordering the cab to stop so she could get out and walk when she finally arrived at Cal's road. Not wanting the taxi driver to see where she was going, she got him to drop her off at the top of the road and only when she was sure he had driven off did she walk swiftly to Cal's house. With a pounding heart, she rang the doorbell.

'Sorry I'm so late,' she said as soon as Cal opened the door.

He smiled. 'Doesn't matter – you're here now.'

All Angel wanted to do was tear off Cal's clothes and make love with him, but he led her to his dining room where he pulled out a chair for her at the elegant table. Even though food was the last thing on Angel's agenda, she had to admit that Cal had prepared a delicious meal. He asked her about her day and she asked him about his. It was all very civilised and suddenly Angel felt shy. He still seemed so distant and unobtainable. It was no good, she couldn't keep up the pretence that they were just good friends any longer, and so, halfway through her buffalo mozzarella and tomato salad, she put her fork down and stood up.

'Cal, can the main course wait a bit longer?'

'Sure,' he said, slightly surprised.

'Because I don't think I can.' And, summoning all her strength, she walked over to him and kissed him. 'I've been thinking about you all day,' she told him.

'I've been thinking about you as well,' he replied, kissing her back. He pulled her onto his lap and started caressing her. 'I just didn't want you to think that it was just about sex, but now you're here . . .'

'It's not just about sex,' she murmured. 'But now I'm here . . .'

By way of an answer, he unbuttoned her skirt and kissed her breasts, and after that neither he nor Angel cared about what was for dinner.

Later, as they lay in his bed, he gently traced his fingers over her face.

'You're so beautiful, Angel.'

'No, I'm not.' She laughed, secretly thrilled that he had paid her such a compliment.

Then suddenly she was serious. She needed to know what was going on between them. Was she just a fling while Simone was away? She so wanted to ask him, but at the same time she couldn't bear it if he told her that's all she was. So she said nothing. When she went to the bathroom, she tried not to look at Simone's expensive cleansing products on display, feeling a sudden pang of guilt. She didn't like Simone, but that didn't mean she thought what she was doing was right. It's just that she was powerless to stop.

For the two weeks that followed, they were lovers in the way that Angel had only dreamt of. Fearful of being photographed by the press if they went out together, they spent every night at Cal's. Angel invented Narcotics Anonymous meetings when Gemma asked her why she couldn't meet up. For two weeks, Angel couldn't have been happier, but by the end of it she was still no closer to figuring out Cal's feelings for her. Yes, he said she was beautiful, yes, he held her all night, made love to her in a way which Angel felt sure must mean that he loved her. But he didn't say it, and even though Angel longed to throw caution to the wind and tell him that she loved him, something held her back. What if she ended up pushing Cal away?

On their last Sunday together, Angel was suddenly desperate to be outside. She felt if she stayed in the house any longer she would end up blurting out the questions she most wanted answered: was he going to leave Simone and be with her? Did he love her? They'd spent most of the day in bed and outside it was a beautiful summer afternoon.

'Shall we go for a walk on the Heath?' Angel asked. 'I've got a hat and sunglasses and I promise I won't jump on you in public.'

Cal considered and seemed reluctant, but then he agreed.

It wasn't her best idea, and even though she knew she wouldn't be able to hold Cal's hand, she couldn't help wanting to. They were surrounded by couples going out for romantic Sunday afternoon walks, arms draped round each other, whereas Cal marched briskly, so fast that Angel had to practically jog to keep up with him. She couldn't read his expression behind his sunglasses and he was subdued and barely said a word.

'D'you think we could sit down for a minute,' she panted, out of breath from the pace he'd kept up.

'There's a bench under that tree over there,' he said.

'You're very quiet today,' she observed as they sat down.

'I know, I'm sorry. I've got things on my mind. Simone's back tomorrow.'

Angel felt cold. Was this it? The moment he was going to tell her that he didn't want to see her again? This possibility had been torture *before* the two weeks they had spent together – she couldn't imagine what it would be like now they had made love.

'I really need to sort things out with her.'

Angel was expecting him to continue, but he looked at his watch and sighed. 'I'm going to have to get back now, I've got a dinner appointment with my agent.' They walked back to his house in silence. Once there, Angel hurriedly packed her things. while Cal made tea. But Angel didn't feel like drinking tea and pretending everything was okay.

'I'm going to head off now, Cal,' she said as he walked into the living room.

'I made you some tea.'

'It's okay, I'm going to go to the gym.' A whopping lie – she was going to go home and have a very large glass of wine – her first in nearly two months – and have a good cry. She so wanted him to take her in his arms as she said goodbye, but instead he simply gave her a kiss on the cheek.

'I'll call you when I can. Take care.'

What the fuck's going on? she thought angrily as she stomped back to her apartment. She'd hardly been there for two weeks and the place was unbearably hot. She opened all the windows, then poured herself a glass of wine. But as she sipped it, her mood darkened. She had felt so close to Cal and being parted from him, not knowing what was going to happen, was like a physical pain – she ached with longing for him. She kept hoping he would call that night, and so many times she was on the point of ringing him, but somehow she stopped herself. Two days later, when she still hadn't heard from him, she found herself confessing everything to Gemma.

'I don't know what to do, Gemma – I can't bear not knowing what's going on,' Angel said miserably, and Gemma's face softened as she took pity on her.

'Well, I guess you've got a choice: you can either wait for him to call, or you can call him and find out what's going on.'

'I can't call him,' Angel exclaimed.

'Well, you'll just have to wait for him to call you, then.'

Chapter 18

Truth or Dare

But Cal didn't contact her. Angel felt wretched, unable to concentrate on anything. She went through the motions of working and going out with Gemma and other friends, but she felt as if she was sleepwalking. It took all her will power not to take coke again; she felt so miserable that she was sorely tempted several times.

This weekend was Gemma's hen weekend and the last thing she wanted to do was to ruin it, so she tried her best to put on a brave face. She wanted to give her best friend a fantastic time, but she was also dreading it. Worst of all, Simone was coming too. Gemma really hadn't wanted to ask Simone to the party, not just for Angel's sake, but because none of Gemma's and Angel's other friends liked her. But Tony had insisted, saying it would look really bad if Gemma didn't ask her.

'It was Simone's birthday on Wednesday,' Gemma said meaningfully to Angel as the hen party travelled in the Chrysler Voyager to the first surprise Angel had planned for her friend.

Is that the reason I haven't heard from Cal? Angel wondered. *That he didn't want to be a total bastard by dumping his girlfriend on her birthday? Even so, he could have called me, or texted me or something. He must know how much I want to hear from him.*

From the moment the car had picked her up, Simone had moaned, wanting to know where they were going and why they were leaving so early in the morning.

'I can't say,' Angel kept repeating. 'It's a surprise.'

First the girls were off to Alton Towers – Gemma was such a thrill-seeker that Angel knew she would love all the rides. Then the car was driving them to a luxurious spa hotel where they'd be staying the night and having dinner, and the following day they'd be able to chill out in the spa and have treatments. Angel was paying for the majority of the trip, she'd just asked for a small contribution from the others – so far Simone was the only one who hadn't coughed up – to buy a cake and champagne for Gemma. Also with them were Cheryl and Tamzin, who went out with two of the players in the team Tony worked for, Zoë, who Gemma worked with, and Andrea, their glamour model friend – all lovely down-to-earth girls, up for a laugh. All except Simone.

'I wouldn't mind,' Gemma whispered to Angel,

'but I didn't want her to come anyway.'

They passed the time by singing along raucously to eighties CDs: The Human League's 'Don't You Want Me', Soft Cell's 'Tainted Love', Spandau Ballet's 'Gold', Culture Club's 'Do You Really Want to Hurt Me?' Madonna's 'Like A Virgin' – well, everyone except Simone, who complained that they were giving her a headache.

Finally they arrived at Alton Towers. Everyone, with the exception of Simone, squealed with delight when they realised where they were.

'That is so cool, Angel! What a great idea,' exclaimed Cheryl.

'That is *so* not my thing,' muttered Simone, moodily. 'I suffer from vertigo, there's no way I can go on any of those rides. I'll have a latte – that's if they make them in a place like *this*. Call me when you've finished.' And with that, she flounced off, leaving the other girls giggling at her high and mighty behaviour.

'She's such a stuck-up cow, she probably didn't want her hair messed up,' exclaimed Zoë. 'I can't believe she's with Cal, he's so gorgeous!'

Cal was the very last person Angel wanted to talk about, so she quickly said, 'Who's for Nemesis?'

'Yeah!' the girls all exclaimed, fizzing with excitement and rushing to take their places in the queue for the roller-coaster.

The girls were up for everything – as far as they were concerned, the more terrifying the better. By mid-afternoon everyone had screamed so much they could barely speak.

'I'm starving,' Gemma announced. 'Let's get some chips.'

As they sat in the restaurant, gossiping and laughing about their experiences, Gemma got a call from Simone. She pulled a face and held the phone away from her ear as Simone droned on.

'Okay, I'll just check with Angel.' Gemma finally managed to get a word in.

'She says she's freezing cold and wants to go to the hotel, so can the driver collect her and take her there and then come back for us?'

'Sure – that's the driver's number.' Angel found the number on her phone and showed it to Gemma. 'She'll have to call him.'

Gemma gave Simone the number and then came off the phone. 'What a waste of space she is. I wish I'd asked my mum instead of her, she'd have had a great time.'

'Wow, Angel, this is so gorgeous, thank you so much!' Gemma exclaimed, walking into the luxurious hotel room she was sharing with Angel.

Angel smiled. She was glad Gemma was enjoying her day. Seeing Gemma so happy helped make some of the pain about Cal go away, for a short while, at least.

They had arrived back at the hotel to discover Simone sipping a champagne cocktail at the bar and looking glamorous and smug. 'I decided to have a massage and get my nails and hair done; I want to look good for Cal tomorrow. Did you lot have a good time?' she asked patronisingly. 'You look so windswept, especially you, Angel. I wonder how on earth you're going to get a brush through your hair!' She gave a little laugh, showing off her small pearly-white teeth, and Angel resisted the temptation to throw her champagne cocktail all over her shiny, freshly-washed hair.

'Just as well that we're going to get ready for dinner then, isn't it?' Angel replied icily. 'Seems like you'd better have something to eat soon to soak up all that champagne you've been drinking.'

'Don't let her get to you,' Gemma advised Angel as the two of them put on their make-up.

'You don't think she suspects that there's been anything between me and Cal?' Angel asked.

'I don't think so, I just think she knows that you're better-looking than she is and she doesn't like the competition.'

All day Angel had tried to push thoughts of Cal out of her mind, but now they came flooding back. The thought of sitting at the same table as Simone made her feel almost sick with jealousy.

'Honestly, Angel, don't let her get to you, she's not worth it.' Angel smiled as Gemma put on an *EastEnders* accent.

'You're right,' she replied. 'Am I bovvered?'

Fortunately, dinner wasn't as bad as Angel had

been expecting. Poor Cheryl had the misfortune to sit next to Simone and had to listen to her going on about her acting ambitions, how she was so much better than everyone else in the soap, how she should get her own series, blah blah blah. After dinner Angel had arranged for a cake and champagne to be sent up to her suite so they could give Gemma her presents. Angel had bought her friend some gorgeous lingerie at Agent Provocateur; the others had bought a huge bag of saucy supplies from Ann Summers, including a Rabbit.

'Oh my God, Gemma, that's the platinum version – you'll never want to leave the house,' joked Zoë.

Simone looked at them all giggling and said, 'I don't see the point of vibrators. I've got Cal. He's so good in bed I don't need anything else.'

Angel felt a sharp pang of jealousy at the thought of Simone in bed with Cal and couldn't think of anything crushing to reply with. Gemma, though, had no difficulties.

'Yeah, but what about when you're away filming – I'm sure this—' she waved the Rabbit in Simone's face '—could come in very handy for all those lonely nights.'

'No, it's so tacky,' Simone snapped.

'There speaks a girl who's never used one,' Gemma laughed. 'Even Cal can't be that good!'

Everyone with the exception of Simone laughed, and she really didn't like it.

'Anyway,' she said nastily, 'I expect Angel knows the whole range of sex toys. I'm surprised she hasn't asked one of us for a threesome so she can demonstrate her knowledge.'

Angel stared at the floor, her cheeks burning with shame and anger. Everyone looked angry at Simone's comment and Gemma immediately leapt to her friend's defence.

'There's no need to be so bitchy, Simone, you're not doing yourself any favours here.'

'Oh, come on,' Simone retorted, 'I was only joking.' But seeing the stony looks on everyone else's faces, she huffily got out a package and thrust it at Gemma, who unwrapped it to discover a small travel pack of the Spa products on sale at the hotel. *Hardly the most imaginative of presents*, Angel thought. Sensing that she'd lost some ground, Simone said she was tired and went off to bed, but she couldn't resist making a last snide remark as she opened the door to go.

'Enjoy your goodie bag, Gemma, I'm saving myself for tomorrow night when Cal's here. We always have such good sex after we've been away from each other.' And before anyone could reply, she shut the door.

'Thank Christ for that!' Gemma declared.

'Ding dong, the witch is dead,' exclaimed Andrea, adding, 'She's such a bitch, Angel, don't let her upset you.'

Angel forced herself to smile, and, not wanting to

give Simone any more headroom, she opened another bottle of champagne and turned the music up.

'I've had a great time. Thanks again, Angel,' Gemma slurred as the two finally crawled into their beds. Gemma quickly fell asleep but Angel, who hadn't drunk anywhere near as much, was awake for hours, obsessing over Cal.

The next day, the hen party recovered from the night before at the luxurious spa, swimming, lying by the pool and having treatments. By five o'clock, everyone, including Angel, was feeling totally chilled out – well, everyone except Simone, of course, who complained that the facial wasn't up to the ones she had in London.

'Do you have facials very often then, Simone?' Gemma asked sweetly as Simone droned on and on about it.

'Every three weeks.'

'Well, I guess that's a good idea, because you are a little bit older than the rest of us, aren't you?' Gemma asked, still putting on her sweet voice.

'I'm twenty-five,' Simone snapped back.

'Oh, really?' Gemma answered in mock surprise. 'I thought Cal said that you were twenty-nine?'

Simone was too angry to speak. Angel had to bite her lip to stop herself from laughing and when she found that she couldn't, she quickly dived into the pool.

*

The girls were being joined by the lads later that evening. It would be the first time Angel had seen Cal for a week and suddenly she was gripped with nerves. She didn't think she could bear it if he rejected her. As soon as they arrived, Gemma and the others shot downstairs to see them and inter-rogate them about where they'd been – Gemma was convinced that Cal had taken them to Amsterdam. But Angel couldn't face seeing Cal and Simone happily reunited, so she stayed in the suite and slowly got ready for dinner. An hour later, Gemma burst into the room, grabbed her bag of Agent Provocateur lingerie, winked at Angel and told her she was going to Tony's room and that she'd see her at dinner.

Angel sighed; she hated to think of Cal being alone with Simone in their hotel room. How was she going to get through this evening, seeing the pair of them? She tried to occupy herself with getting ready. She was wearing a knee-length green silk dress that moulded to every curve of her body, sheer black stockings with seams running up the back and green suede peep-toe shoes – her grown-up look. The hotel hairdresser had come to the room earlier and put her hair up, which showed off Angel's beautiful long neck. If she had to face Cal with Simone, she wanted to do it in femme fatale mode and, if she was honest, she damned well wanted to show Cal what he was missing.

She was just making a last-minute check of her appearance when there was a knock at the door. Thinking it would be Gemma, she opened it to discover Cal.

Immediately, her throat went dry and butterflies exploded inside her.

'Can I come in?' he asked quietly.

There were so many things she wanted to ask him. Why hadn't he called her when he said that he would? What was going on between them? But she didn't have time to speak before Cal took her in his arms.

'Hi, beautiful.' He was ever so slightly drunk, she realised, as he kissed her.

She pulled out of the embrace. 'Where's Simone?'

'Oh, I don't know, having her nails done or something. Let's not talk about her now. I really missed you.'

He carried on kissing Angel, and with every kiss and every caress her barriers weakened and the questions in her head went unasked. When he unzipped her dress and let it fall to the ground in a silken pool, she didn't resist, and when he led her to the bed she didn't stop him either.

'I thought you were having your hair put up?' Gemma asked her friend, looking puzzled as Angel took her place at the dinner table.

'Yeah, I did,' Angel replied shiftily, 'but it looked

like shit, so I had to take it down again.' She hated lying to her friend, but what other explanation could she give, surrounded by people and sitting opposite Simone, who, as usual, was looking daggers at her?

Earlier Angel and Cal had made love – passionately, intensely, urgently, in a way that simultaneously thrilled Angel and left her wanting more. She still hadn't been able to ask him what was going on between them and he'd left in a hurry, promising that they would talk soon. Now, as she sat down for dinner and Cal barely acknowledged her presence, she couldn't help feeling used. She was sitting next to Antonio, Cal's Spanish team-mate, who clearly hadn't got over his crush on her and who was very attentive throughout the meal, but much as Angel liked him, she really didn't want his attention.

Over dinner the hen and stag party compared notes about their trips. Tony tried to pretend that they hadn't been lap-dancing, but it didn't take long for Gemma to prise the truth out of him. All the other girlfriends took the news with a pinch of salt, but Simone muttered something under her breath to Cal, who didn't look too pleased.

'Come on, Simone,' Antonio called out, 'it was just a bit of fun, and I promise you we did nothing more than watch.'

'Well, I just think it's tacky,' she replied crossly. 'Almost as tacky as where we ended up yesterday – Alton Towers.'

'Come off it, Simone,' Gemma cut across her, angrily. 'We all had a great time.'

'I was just wondering, Angel, weren't you worried your implants might explode on some of the rides?' Simone said cattily.

You hard-faced bitch, thought Angel, but not wanting to sink to Simone's level, she pushed out her chest and said, 'I think they're still in one piece,' and then something made her add, 'Cal can always check them out and report back to you.'

Simone looked absolutely furious, Cal wouldn't look at Angel, and Tony quickly changed the subject, asking everyone if they were ready to order.

'Just ignore her,' Antonio muttered under his breath to Angel. 'She's just jealous of you.'

'Oh, I don't care,' Angel replied, taking a large sip of wine and wishing the night was over. To get through it, she drank much more than she had in a long time and longed to crash out in bed. But after dessert, Tony said that everyone was invited up to his suite for champagne and Angel knew it would look extremely odd if she didn't go.

Once up there, to her very great surprise, Simone handed her a glass of champagne, and then said to everyone, 'I'd like to give a toast to Angel for organising Gemma's hen weekend – and although we had our differences, she did a really good job.'

It was so out of character that Angel couldn't help wondering if Simone had an ulterior motive.

She raised her eyebrows at Gemma, who also looked confused by Simone's announcement.

'And now I've got a suggestion to end the weekend,' Simone declared. 'Why don't we play spin the bottle?'

Angel couldn't think of a worse idea, and by the look on Cal's face, he thought the same, but everyone else was drunk enough to be up for it.

As they all sat round in a circle, Antonio leant across to Angel and whispered, 'That's a pity, I was hoping for strip poker!'

Angel laughed, then caught Cal's eye. She thought he looked a bit pissed off to see her talking to Antonio again. Simone gleefully spun the bottle and it pointed to Cal, which meant he had to choose between truth or dare.

'Dare,' he replied.

Simone reached for the card in front of her and read out the challenge. 'You have to spin the bottle again and kiss the person it points to.'

'Bloody hell,' Gemma muttered next to Angel. 'Now I don't think this is such a good idea.'

Cal spun the bottle and it pointed to Angel. She felt her heart beating wildly and didn't know how to react.

'Go on then, Cal,' Owen, one of Tony's stags, called out. 'If you don't, I will!'

And so Cal crawled across the circle to Angel and gently kissed her. She kept her eyes lowered and tried not to think about everyone watching them.

'Rubbish,' called out Owen. 'The rules say it's got to be a proper one!' But Cal had already returned to his place.

Angel was dreading her turn. Tony was dared to down three tequila shots, Simone went for the truth option and Andrea asked the question, 'What is the most sexually adventurous thing you've ever done?'

'Oh,' Simone simpered, 'I'll have to check with Cal, but I think it was when we made love on the beach in the Maldives.'

Angel felt something snap inside. She felt humiliated and hurt and she was starting to feel very angry over Cal's treatment of her. Andrea was dared to take her top off, Owen kissed Simone, Gemma had to perform 'Like A Virgin' and then spun the bottle and it pointed to Angel. To give her courage, she had finished her champagne and now felt quite drunk. 'Dare,' she declared, praying for an easy one; she didn't think truth would be such a good idea at this precise moment in time. Simone picked up a card and smirked as she read it. 'Perform a strip-tease. Right up your street then, Angel.'

'What?' exclaimed Angel, grabbing the card and discovering that it did indeed say that.

Immediately, everyone started clapping their hands and chanting, 'Off, off, off!'

'Fuck it!' Angel exclaimed, thinking it would be better to get it over and done with. She asked Gemma to unzip her dress, then she stood up, and,

looking into the distance, she slipped first one strap
from her shoulder, then the other, then she let the
dress fall to the ground, to cheers from the lads.
She undid each stocking in turn and rolled them
down her long legs, unclipped her bra and
whipped it off, but covered her breasts with her
long hair. Then she slipped one hand under the
side of her briefs as if to take them off, paused for
effect, then declared, 'That's all you're getting!'
Everyone clapped and Angel quickly got dressed
again. In the meantime the bottle had spun to
Antonio and he had also asked for dare.

'Kiss the person you fancy,' Simone read out.

'That's easy,' he replied and crawled over to
Angel and started kissing her. So far everyone else
who had played the game had given fairly innocent
kisses, but Antonio was passionately kissing Angel.
She tried to pull away, but he was very persistent, to
the group's enormous delight. When he finally let
her go, Angel happened to look up at Cal. He
looked angry, but was obviously trying to hold it in.
Suddenly Angel felt giddy and spaced out, as if
she'd taken something. *But I haven't*, she thought
blearily as the champagne glass in front of her
multiplied.

'Gemma,' she murmured, 'I feel ill, will you
come with me to my room?'

'Course, babe,' she replied, 'I've had enough of
this game anyway.'

But as Angel tried to stand up, she felt very

unsteady on her feet and thought she would fall. Immediately, Antonio and Cal stood up and grabbed her.

'Are you okay?' Cal asked, holding onto her arm.

'I just feel a bit giddy, I'm going to bed.'

Both men then spoke at once. 'I'll come with—' but Simone cut across them and said to Cal, 'Darling, I think Antonio can cope. And, anyway, you wouldn't want to be a gooseberry, would you?'

For a split second Cal hesitated, then let go of Angel and muttered, 'Hope you feel better,' and turned away before Angel could speak to him.

Antonio and Gemma then walked Angel to her room and at the door it was clear that he was expecting to be invited in.

'Thanks, Antonio, but I really don't feel too good. I'll see you in the morning,' Angel told him. He made a bad job of hiding his disappointment as he said goodnight. Angel managed to open her door and then collapsed on her bed. Gemma poured her a glass of water.

'It's weird, Gemma, I feel as if I've taken something, but I haven't. I know I've drunk a bit too much, but not that much.'

'Your tolerance is probably really low after not drinking for so long,' Gemma told her. 'Just drink lots of water and you'll be fine in the morning. I'll stay if you want.'

'God, no, I'll be fine,' Angel lied, not wanting to keep Gemma away from Tony. Once her friend had gone, she lay back and tried not to think about the room spinning round.

'Hi, I'd like the bill please,' Angel said to the receptionist. She still felt a little fuzzy and light-headed this morning. Suddenly, Cal was by her side.

'Enjoy yourself last night, did you?' he asked in an uncharacteristically cold voice.

'Not really,' Angel replied, wondering what the hell his problem was. She was the one who should be pissed off. He looked at her and shook his head.

'What's the matter?' she demanded. 'I didn't want to play that stupid game last night.'

'It didn't look that way to me. I've never seen anyone so quick to get their kit off, or to kiss someone. What was he like in bed, then?'

'What the fuck are you on about?' Angel asked, hardly believing what she was hearing.

Seeing that the receptionist was eavesdropping, Cal grabbed her arm and practically pulled her outside, where she ended up pressed against the wall with Cal leaning over her.

'You and Antonio. He was all over you and it was obvious where it was going to end up.'

'Do you seriously think I would sleep with him?'

'You seemed off your face at the end of the night, it looked like you'd been using again. Jesus, Angel, I thought so much more of you.'

'I didn't take anything, I swear. I think someone

must have spiked my drink,' she shouted back, cut to the quick by his accusation.

'What, again? Don't be so pathetic, who would do that?'

'I can think of a few people,' Angel said sulkily, thoroughly pissed off by Cal's attitude. 'Anyway, why didn't you call me?' she demanded, anger making her bold.

'Yeah, well, I'd forgotten it was Simone's birthday and things got difficult. So you didn't sleep with Antonio?' he asked again.

'If you really don't know the answer to that, then you're not the person I thought you were,' replied Angel, suddenly finding strength that she didn't know she possessed. How dare he speak to her like this? Suddenly, a flash bulb went off in their faces. They both turned and saw a photographer a few metres away, his camera focused on them.

'Shit!' shouted Cal, running after the photographer and trying to grab his camera.

Fearful of what might happen, Angel ran after Cal and tried to reason with him. 'Just leave it, Cal,' she shouted. 'Come back inside.'

Once she had managed to get him back into the hotel lobby, they were confronted by a furious-looking Simone. Ignoring Angel, she spoke only to Cal. 'Have you paid yet? I want to go now.'

Without even saying goodbye to Angel, Cal marched over to the desk. Angel took the lift back to her room and tried to gather her thoughts. She felt completely shaken by what Cal had said to her and horrified that they had been photographed together. Suddenly, her mobile rang. Praying it was Cal, she was disappointed to discover it was Carrie. 'Fantastic news, darling!' she gushed. '*LA Dreams* want you on their cover!'

'Great,' Angel replied, feeling too upset about Cal to be excited about anything else.

'Come on! Where's your enthusiasm? This could be your big break in the States. They want to see you next week.'

Everyone else travelled back to London with their partners and so Angel was alone in the car with Chris, her driver. Sensing her mood, he didn't try to make conversation but simply put the radio on, for which Angel was grateful. She gazed out of the window. She should have been delighted at Carrie's news. It proved that her career hadn't been finished by her recent drug problem; it looked like it was only just beginning. She tried to drum up some excitement, but felt too numb and too bruised from her recent conversation with Cal. As they neared London, Carrie called her again. She was expecting an ear-bashing about how she must get in shape for America, but she received entirely different news.

'Who's been a naughty girl, then?' Carrie said slyly.

'What are you talking about?' Angel demanded, suddenly feeling panicked.

'I've just spoken to a journalist and he tells me that you've been seeing Cal Bailey. You lucky thing, he's gorgeous! They're going to be running the story tomorrow. This is such good PR for your American trip! I couldn't have planned it better myself!'

Angel felt her world crashing in around her. 'But I haven't been to the press. How did they find out?'

'Who knows, who cares, it doesn't matter, it's great publicity – everyone will forget about that sordid threesome now—'

'Look, Carrie, I've got to go, I'll speak to you later.' She cut Carrie off mid-sentence and frantically texted Cal: *Please call me, I need to speak to you. It's urgent.*

But Cal didn't reply, and when Chris pulled up outside her flat the press were already camped out, anticipating the next day's story. As the car slowed, several photographers advanced on her, cameras at the ready.

'Oh my God,' Angel exclaimed. 'I can't get out, please take me to Gemma's.' Chris put his foot down, denying the photographers their shot, as Angel called her friend.

Angel didn't dare leave Gemma's flat once she arrived there, she didn't want the press tracking her down. To her relief, Tony had already gone away with the team; she didn't feel up to his judging her, which he undoubtedly would. Carrie kept calling her with the latest update from the tabloids of how much they would pay her if she agreed to sell her story. She just wouldn't take no for an answer – obviously thinking of her percentage from the very large sums of money Angel was being offered.

'Look,' Angel finally shouted, 'I'm not talking to anyone about what happened, not now, not ever, so you tell them that once and for all.' And without allowing Carrie the chance to reply, she switched her phone off. She had left several text and phone messages for Cal, but he still hadn't replied.

'He's going to blame me, isn't he?' she said miserably to Gemma as the two girls sat on the sofa, supposedly watching a DVD, although neither was following the slushy RomCom plot.

'Well, he shouldn't do, because it takes two people to have an affair and he should know that you would never talk to the press,' Gemma replied.

'But I did, didn't I? I did do a story after that incident with Mickey and now Cal is going to think that I'm behind this one.'

There was nothing Gemma could say to that.

Angel woke with a feeling of dread the next day. It was only six a.m. but there was no chance of her going back to sleep. She got out of bed and made herself a cup of tea, then was feeling so anxious she couldn't even drink it. At half six, Gemma woke up.

'I'll go straight out and get the paper,' she said.

As Angel had feared, it was front,page news – with the picture of Cal and her outside the hotel, arguing. Inside was the story – told by a 'friend' – of how the couple had started a passionate affair when Simone was away filming. It said that Angel had been pursuing Cal for a while and this had been her moment.

'Who the hell is this "friend"?' exclaimed Angel as she urgently read through the paper, feeling sicker and sicker with every word.

'God knows,' replied Gemma. 'Did you tell anyone else apart from me and Jez?'

Angel shook her head. This had to be the worst day of her life. She thought she'd already experienced that when she met her real mum, but this was nothing in comparison to how she felt now. She felt humiliation, along with overwhelming sadness. Her privacy had been completely invaded and Cal must think that she had gone to the papers, or else why hadn't he returned any of her calls? Gemma kept trying to cheer up her, making her snacks and cups of tea, but Angel couldn't eat or drink anything. She just sat on the sofa in a state of complete shock. Somehow the day passed in a blur of misery. But the next day brought even worse news.

When Gemma returned with the papers, she didn't want to hand them over to Angel.

'I really don't think you should read it. Let's go away, forget about all this,' her friend pleaded with her.

'I've got to know,' Angel replied, taking the papers from Gemma.

For a few seconds she stared at the front page, unable to take in the headline: I'M HAVING CAL'S BABY! AND I FORGIVE HIM!, which was accompanied by a picture of a smiling Simone reclining on a sofa, with one hand protectively over her stomach.

Angel let the paper fall. That was all she needed to know. That was it. Any dream she'd had that she could be with Cal had been shattered by that headline. He would never abandon his child, never. She knew that without even having to read the story.

'I'm so sorry, babe.' Gemma put her arms round her friend, tears in her eyes. But Angel didn't cry. She felt her heart was broken and tears didn't seem like nearly a good enough response. She wanted to scream, find some way of letting the pain out. Instead, she found herself comforting her friend.

'It's okay, Gemma, I'm fine, really. I think I'd like to go out now. Let's go to the stables.'

But she'd reckoned without the persistence of the British press, and just as she was tacking up Star two journalists appeared and started firing questions at her: 'How do you feel, Angel? Have you spoken to Cal? What are you going to do? We can do an exclusive deal with you, it'll be worth a lot of money. Come on, don't you want to put your side of the story?'

Angel did her best to ignore them, but they kept

going on and on at her. She clenched her jaw and tried to keep calm and carry on getting Star ready, even though her hands were shaking so much she could barely make them do anything. Gemma was shouting at the journalists, telling them to leave Angel alone, and Star was getting agitated. Somehow, she managed to put on his saddle and do up the girth and then she put her foot in the stirrup and swung herself on. The journalists moved out of her way pretty sharpish when Star advanced towards them, but carried on shouting at her. As soon as she was out of the stables and on the bridle path she urged Star into a gallop, but even then she still thought she could hear their questions echoing in the air. Minutes later, Gemma caught up with her on her own horse and they slowed down, looking across the fields.

'I've spoken to Tony and we're going to postpone the wedding for a couple of months.'

'Oh my God, no!' Angel exclaimed.

'We think it would be best, that way the press might have got bored of the story. Otherwise they'll be all over the wedding and I don't want that – not just for me and Tony, but also for you. And we can't afford the security to keep them out.'

'Gemma, you don't have to do that,' Angel replied, feeling terrible that her friend was having to change her big day.

'I want to, Angel, and it really isn't a problem. I want to spend the rest of my life with Tony and two months isn't going to make a difference to that. And it means that I can come to America with you now.'

'Are you sure?' Angel asked – she had been dreading the America trip without Gemma's support.

'Totally, and I spoke to Carrie yesterday, by the way, and managed to persuade her that it would be a good idea if we go to the States tomorrow – that way you can get away from all this.'

Yes, thought Angel. *Yes, get away, start again.* The girls rode in silence for the next hour and a half. Gemma made a call to Ray, someone Angel had very occasionally used for security, and he agreed to go over to the stable with a couple of his mates to make sure the press were kept out. But when they returned, journalists were swarming all over the place and although they were being prevented by Ray and his guys from getting into the stables itself, they were camped outside. As soon as they saw Angel the shouting and flashes started up again. Star got very skittish. 'Get out the way,' she called out to them. 'You're scaring the horses.' But all they cared about was getting Angel's picture. Star reared up, terrified by the lights and noise, and it took all of Angel's strength to reign him in. She felt such anger and hatred for the people out there. She wanted to scream at them to fuck off and leave her alone, but knew they would love to get that reaction from her. Somehow she managed to control Star and get him back to the stables, where Manda was waiting to grab him.

Angel quickly dismounted and thanked Manda, then she and Gemma got into Ray's blacked-out Range Rover. Even as the car moved out of the stables, the journalists stood in its way, still trying to take pictures.

'They'll be outside your house as well, Angel,' Ray warned her.

'I know, but I've got to get my passport and pack.'

'I suggest you do that and then I take you and Gemma to a hotel – somewhere these arseholes can't get in.'

Three hours later, she and Gemma were shown to their hotel suite in the Conrad Hotel in Chelsea Harbour.

'You have got to have something to eat now,' Gemma insisted. 'You haven't eaten for two days and you'll end up getting ill.'

Food was the last thing on Angel's mind. Over and over in her head the same soundtrack kept repeating: *you've lost Cal for ever*.

She shrugged. 'Okay, I'll have a sandwich, and let's have some wine. I really need a drink.'

A bottle of wine later and the tears finally came.

'I love him so much, Gemma, what am I going to do?' Angel sobbed.

'You're going to be fine. Not yet, I know, but you will be eventually. And one day you're going to meet someone else.' Gemma tried her best to reassure her.

Angel wanted to shout that there was no one else, there never had been, there never would be, but she knew Gemma was only doing her best to comfort her and so she said nothing at all.

Chapter 19

LA Dreams

'Okay, Angel, if you could just pick up the receiver and raise your skirt,' Carl, the photographer, asked as if it was the most natural thing in the world to do.

Angel took a deep breath. She had already revealed more in this photo shoot than she ever had before. Here she was, dressed in a silver corset with the cups cut out so she was topless, fishnet pop socks, sky-high heels, a sheer black skirt and nothing else, standing in an old-fashioned British red phone booth, on set in the *LA Dreams* studios.

'Okay, but all you'll get is a flash of a landing strip and that's it. I'm not showing off anything else!' she shouted back.

Carl had been pushing her for the last two days of the photo shoot to reveal more. Couldn't she lie back on the bed and just open her legs a little – it would be very tasteful, he promised.

No no no! had been her reply every time he asked.

He'd had her sitting in a black cab in her corset and nothing else, with just her hand covering herself, sitting up wearing a silver thong and nothing else and pretending to touch herself, with her eyes shut and her mouth parted.

And finally, against a white grand piano with a crystal chandelier in the background, she had to perform a strip-tease. She started off in a pair of sheer cream French knickers trimmed with diamante; in shot two she was slipping them down and in shot three they were off altogether and she was naked.

'That's beautiful. Look down, now at the camera, part your lips more, great, great,' Carl called out as he snapped away. Angel allowed herself to go into a kind of trance, where all she focused on was the camera, trying to block out everything and everyone else around her.

'Okay, Angel, that's a wrap,' Carl finally called out.

Immediately, Gemma walked up to Angel and gave her a white towelling robe to put on.

'You did good,' Carl told her. 'I see things happening for you out here.'

Angel smiled. To her surprise she liked it in LA, although she knew that probably had a lot to do with being away from the press, away from home where everything reminded her of Cal. Here, she could start again. No one had heard of Cal and her affair with him. To the Americans, she was a beautiful British glamour girl, nothing more. It helped that she had been busy from the moment she'd arrived. She'd done photo shoots and publicity events and Carrie had also arranged for her to meet several casting directors. She thought Angel might well be able to have an acting career out here and to Angel's surprise, the directors had seemed to like her – not that she seriously thought anything would come of it. All in all, she'd had barely a minute to herself and the two weeks had flown by.

Tonight was her last night and she was going to one of Larry T. Chance's famous parties. Larry T. Chance was the multimillionaire owner of *LA Dreams* and his parties at his pink mansion were legendary – crammed with film stars, pop stars, sports icons, as well as scores of beautiful women, and absolutely anything went . . .

As one of Larry T. Chance's 'babes', Angel was expected to dress up in something suitably revealing. She decided to go as a naughty angel and she and Gemma had tracked down the perfect outfit: a skintight pink bodice, which revealed an eye-popping amount of cleavage, with a tiny pink tutu skirt, a pair of pink fluffy wings, a pink diamante halo and a pair of pink suede thigh-length boots.

'What do you think?' Angel asked Gemma, giving a little twirl in front of her.

'Just don't bend over,' Gemma advised, 'or you'll

be giving everyone an eyeful of what you were trying to cover up at the shoot today!'

'Yeah, the skirt is a bit short,' Angel admitted, 'but seeing how lots of the girls won't be wearing anything at all, I think I'll be okay!'

Three hours later, as Angel hung out with two of Larry T. Chance's girlfriends (he actually had seven in total – *One for every day of the week?* Angel wondered), sipping champagne cocktails, she decided she felt okay, too. It was such fun star-spotting, although she wished Gemma could have been with her.

'Hey,' said a sexy American voice behind her, and she turned around to find herself face-to-face with Jackson Black, the gorgeous Californian film star and legendary bad boy. Angel knew three things about him: 1) he was a terrible womaniser, 2) he had a fiery temper which had got him into one too many fights for his agent's liking, and 3) apparently he was very well endowed . . .

'I'm Jackson. And you are?'

'Angel,' she replied, wanting to giggle because she had never met anyone so famous before.

'I can see that, but what's your real name?' Jackson demanded.

'That's my real name.'

'Well, it sure suits you,' he answered, looking her up and down appraisingly. 'Can I get you a drink, Angel?'

'I'll have another champagne, thanks.'

Jackson only had to turn his head and raise an eyebrow in the direction of one of the topless waitresses (well, topless except for some pink nipple tassels) and she instantly came over with a tray of drinks.

'So, what are you doing here?' Jackson asked, handing her a glass of champagne.

'I've just done a shoot for the magazine,' Angel replied.

Jackson looked very interested. 'And what kind of outfit were you wearing for that?'

Angel smiled. He was such an outrageous flirt but she didn't take it seriously. 'Oh, you know, the usual.'

'No, I don't.' He moved closer. 'Why don't you tell me? Better still, why don't I show you the games room or the Jacuzzi and you can fill me in on all the details.'

Angel laughed. 'Thanks, but I've already seen them,' she said, knowing full well what people got up to in there. Jackson was gorgeous, but there was absolutely no way she was going to be another notch on his already over-crowded bedpost.

He looked momentarily surprised. Angel was sure he didn't often get turned down. She thought that it would be his cue to leave her and find a more willing playmate, but to her surprise he stayed with her for the next two hours, chatting and flirting with her.

He was very easy to talk to and very easy on the

eye, with his handsome face, knowing green eyes and fit body (recently extra buffed, for a leading role in an action film). Angel couldn't deny the attraction she felt for him, along with most other women on the planet. When she told him she had to leave, as she had to catch a plane the next day, he kissed her and she didn't resist; she kissed him back and it was a very sexy kiss, too.

'I've got to see you again, Angel,' Jackson murmured in her ear. 'I've got a premiere in London in a couple of weeks. I'll call you and we can meet up for dinner or something.' The 'or something' was loaded with possibilities.

Lying back in the luxurious seat of the pink limo driving her back to the hotel – Larry had a fleet of them for his babes – Angel had to smile. Jackson was so arrogant, he just assumed that she would meet him. Although, she had to admit he was right – she probably would. She smiled again, but as soon as she closed the door of her hotel room and started packing, her spirits plummeted. She was going home, she was going to have to face the truth again: that Cal was out of her reach for ever. Suddenly, all the enjoyment she had felt flirting with the Hollywood star vanished, and she was left once more feeling empty and lost and longing for Cal so much that she didn't think she could bear it.

Chapter 20

London Again

Back in London, the tabloids were busy splashing the latest celebrity scandal on their front pages – this time a certain A-list film star's passionate affair with his children's nanny. Famous as she was, film stars' private lives tended to overshadow glamour girls', and to Angel's relief, she discovered that journalists were no longer camped outside her flat in hordes. Still, there often seemed to be one or two lurking around, so she resigned herself to wearing huge dark glasses and a baseball cap again every time she left the house, even if the sun wasn't shining. She had no desire to reveal her emotions to the waiting photographers.

Carrie seemed to have forgiven her for not selling a story about Cal, because the news from America was very good. Larry T. Chance loved the pictures and wanted to do another shoot with her, and a TV series wanted her to audition for them. It really looked like there might be amazing possibilities for her on the other side of the Atlantic. At first she was resistant to the idea of moving to the States, which she would have to do if she got the part, plus she had never seen herself as an actress, but when she flicked through the copies of *heat* and *OK!* that had piled up in her flat while she had been away, she began to think that the States would be a good idea after all. Every single one was full of pictures of Cal and Simone, bursting with speculation about their wedding: would they tie the knot before or after the baby was born?

On the third night she was home, Angel finally had to face Tony, an encounter that she really wasn't looking forward to. She expected him to blame her for the whole Cal affair, but as it happened, he was sympathetic and didn't criticise her at all.

'I love him,' she simply said when he asked her about it, 'Or I suppose I should say I loved him, because I'm really trying to get over it.' And then, because she couldn't resist, she asked, 'Have you seen him?'

Tony shook his head. 'I haven't seen him since the stag weekend. He says he's really busy. But I get the feeling he's avoiding me. There's a chance he might be going to play for Madrid.'

Angel couldn't help thinking that anything that took Cal away from London was a good thing. Since she'd been home, she could hardly bear to spend time at her flat in Hampstead, dreading every time she walked down the High Street that she would bump into him and Simone. She spent as much time as possible in central London and when she wasn't working, she went out for dinner with friends or clubbing – anything to avoid being alone with her thoughts. She almost thought it was working, except on those nights she dreamt of Cal and woke up crying.

'Angel, great news,' Carrie gushed down the phone. 'You've just been booked to present one of the music awards in a week. It's going to be televised, so make sure you learn your lines and don't fuck up. I can't tell you how relieved I am. It shows people are forgetting about what happened. So get something sensational to wear and we'll speak soon.'

As Angel put the phone down, she felt relieved. Carrie had been so down on her since the drugs. It was nice not to have her criticisms for a change. She was just about to call Gemma and tell her when her mobile rang again.

'Hi, remember me?' Jackson's sexy American voice drawled down her mobile.

I'm hardly likely to forget, Angel thought, but deciding to have some fun with him, she feigned ignorance.

'Sorry, do I know you?' she demanded.

'Ha ha, very funny,' Jackson replied. 'Listen, I'm over in London now and wondered if you wanted to meet for dinner tonight.'

'Actually, I have plans, but I could meet you tomorrow night,' she replied, thinking *Cheeky bastard, how dare he assume that I would just drop everything for him?*

They arranged to meet at a very exclusive restaurant and when Angel ended the call, she couldn't help feeling slightly excited by the prospect. He was such a big star and he was gorgeous.

'I hardly recognise you without your angel kit on,' was the first thing Jackson said as they met the next night. Even though they were meeting at The Ivy, a restaurant so exclusive it was the kind of place no one was supposed to stare at celebrities, Angel noticed that the other diners, women mostly, kept taking surreptitious looks in their direction, clearly willing Jackson to notice them. She didn't blame them – Jackson was very, very handsome. *As handsome as Cal*, she thought with a pang.

'I've ordered champagne, I hope that's okay – it's what you were guzzling at Larry's.'

'Excuse me!' Angel replied in mock indignation. 'I was not guzzling!'

'I remember thinking,' Jackson continued his teasing, 'that woman can certainly put it away!' And then he took her hand in his and kissed it. 'But I do like that in a woman,' he murmured suggestively. Angel almost squirmed in her seat, half with embarrassment and half enjoying his attention.

They ordered traditional English fish and chips

(Jackson said that he loved it), but Angel couldn't eat very much, she felt too self-conscious in front of Jackson. He continued to flirt with her and once the champagne had taken hold, she flirted back. He was making his attraction to her very obvious.

'I'm getting kind of tired of everyone staring at us in here,' Jackson said after they'd eaten, or rather, he'd eaten and Angel had rearranged the food on her plate. 'Why don't we go back to my hotel suite and have a drink in private?'

Oh God, she thought, thrilled and scared in equal measure. Part of her wanted to go straight home to her flat, but the other thought, *Cal's not interested any more, you may as well see where this leads.*

'I could come for one drink,' she replied. 'I've got a shoot tomorrow.'

'Okay, Miss Control Freak, just one drink,' he answered, and then leant closer to her. 'Though don't think I'll be letting you go that easily.'

Outside the restaurant the paparazzi had obviously been tipped off that Jackson was there, as flash bulbs immediately exploded in their faces. The couple got into the waiting limo, but Jackson seemed totally unconcerned. He simply shrugged and said, 'Occupational hazard. I'm surprised you're not used to it by now.'

Jackson had the luxury penthouse suite at The Dorchester. There was champagne waiting for them, candles had been lit around the room and music was playing. *He was obviously expecting me to come back with him*, she thought wryly. He expertly opened the champagne and poured them each a glass.

'Here's to you, Angel – quite the most beautiful woman I've seen in a long time.'

Angel couldn't help laughing – he was such a smooth operator.

'I'm serious,' Jackson insisted. 'I was dreading doing this premiere in London, the press here always give me such a hard time, and now meeting you has given me something to look forward to. Why won't you take me seriously, Angel? I really like you.' He gazed at her with his dark green eyes and Angel almost felt convinced, but then she remembered he was an Oscar-nominated actor and a serial shagger.

She shook her head. 'You hardly know me.'

'I like what I see,' he replied, taking her champagne glass from her and leading her to the bed, where he pulled her down next to him.

His kiss was just as good as she remembered from the party. Angel felt desire building up within her and she touched his body back. *See*, said a voice inside her. *Why not? What's wrong with this?* But suddenly it was all going too fast and he had unzipped her dress so roughly that she heard the silk tear, had pulled it off her, had unfastened her bra and was sucking her nipples so hard that it hurt.

She wriggled in pain, and he took that to mean

she was enjoying herself and moved down her body. He pulled down her lace briefs and began caressing her with his tongue, except it didn't feel like a caress, more like slobbering, and he had no sense of which spot to hit.

Bad oral sex is just the worst thing, Angel thought, all desire for him gone. Again she tried to move away from him, but again he took that to mean that she was writhing in pleasure.

'Oh yeah, baby,' he murmured, lifting his head up and unbuttoning his jeans. 'You ready now?'

'No,' she said, crossing her legs and trying to sit up. 'I can't do this.'

But he didn't seem to register and now he was lying on top of her, kissing her, biting her lip, touching her body with greater urgency and forcing her legs apart.

'Jackson! Stop!' she said again, trying to push him off her. He was starting to scare her; it felt as if he wasn't going to stop even though she was saying no.

'Get off me!' she was shouting now, and, struggling frantically, tried to twist her body away from his.

'Come on, Angel.' He stopped what he was doing and looked at her. 'You know you want to, you wouldn't have come back with me if you didn't.'

Angel took her chance and, using all her strength, pushed him off her and leapt off the bed, grabbing her clothes and her bag and heading for the door.

'Oh, run off home, then, little girl,' Jackson snarled from the bed, frustration and rejection making him nasty. 'You're not that special, you know. I could go out right now and pull ten girls who look like you – better than you.'

'Yeah, well, your last film sucked,' Angel replied, anger replacing fear. Not wanting to stay in the same room as him for another minute, she opened the door and stepped out into the corridor even though she was dressed in nothing but her briefs. She quickly put on her dress and ran to the lifts, desperate to get out of the hotel.

'Oh my God!' Jez exclaimed, his eyes wide in amazement two days later when she filled him in on what had happened. Jez could always be relied on for his larger-than-life reactions. 'What a class A creep!'

'It was really scary; I thought he was going to rape me. And it was horrible when he said I'd asked for it by going back to his hotel room,' Angel replied, still a bit shaken.

'Well, I'm never going to see one of his films ever again!' declared Jez. 'And I'll rip up that poster of him I've got in the loo as soon as I get home. The bastard.'

They were meeting Gemma for coffee in Soho and when she arrived she looked very excited and immediately thrust a tabloid in front of Angel.

'Look! It says here that you're seeing Jackson

Black and that he's very taken with you! What's been going on between you?'

Both Angel and Jez groaned, and Angel said, 'Jez, please tell her, I can't bear to go through it again.'

As Jez filled Gemma in on the details, Angel couldn't help shuddering; she really did feel that she'd had a lucky escape. She imagined all the other women who had found themselves in the same situation with Jackson and had wanted him to stop, but couldn't make him. *Bastard*.

'Let's not talk about it any more, please! And, anyway, I want you two to come and look at some outfits with me. I still don't know what to wear for the awards tomorrow night,' Angel told her friends.

So, after coffee, the trio hit the boutiques. Angel always liked to choose something that would make her stand out – she never wanted to look like anyone else. Two hours and many outfits later, Angel finally found something she liked: a show-stopping, floor-length silver halter-neck dress with a tight bodice showing off her tiny waist and a plunging neckline. She hoped to make a night of it with Jez and Gemma, but both of them had other plans and, for the first time in a while, Angel had to go home on her own. As soon as she shut the door on her apartment, she felt consumed with longing for Cal. All the frenzied socialising and working she'd been throwing herself into had done nothing but temporarily numb the pain. The encounter with Jackson hadn't helped. She wanted to feel Cal's arms round her – nothing had ever felt so good as being held by him. She put on the Al Green CD that she and Cal had listened to during those two weeks when they were lovers, and curled up on the sofa. She allowed herself to remember what it had felt like being with Cal – how good they were together, how he made her feel and how she had never felt so close to anyone before. Suddenly, she longed to speak to him, to hear his voice one last time, and almost without thinking about what she was doing, as if something else was guiding her, she picked up her mobile and called up his number. It went straight to his voicemail. For a second she paused, then said: 'Hi, Cal, it's Angel. I just wanted to say good luck with the baby and everything. Take care of yourself.' Somehow she stopped herself from telling him she loved him.

'And now give it up for Angel, who's presenting the award for best British band!' Derren Sylvester, the DJ and presenter of the music awards, shouted into his mic. Angel walked on stage to thunderous applause. Even though she was only going to be reading out a few names, she couldn't help feeling nervous and she was sure she was going to get some stick from Derren, who loved taking the piss out of celebs. She certainly hadn't warmed to him when they'd met on his TV show and, sure enough, he waited until he'd kissed her to deliver his killer punchline.

'Three bands have been nominated, all with lovely young men in them, Angel, but their girlfriends have asked me to tell you that they're all taken – so hands off!'

Angel forced herself to smile sweetly, all the while thinking, *You little shit.*

'But there is someone who is available, someone who I think you've already met, who's going to present the award with you. Everyone, please give it up for the bad boy of film, Jackson Black.'

Fuck! thought Angel. He was the last person she wanted to see again. He came bounding on stage dressed in a dark purple designer suit and he immediately grabbed Angel and kissed her full on the lips, to the delight of the audience. When she tried to pull away, he held her tighter and kissed her harder – much to her disgust.

'Okay, you guys, get a room!' joked Derren. Finally Jackson let Angel go and she was furious, sure he had done it deliberately to humiliate her.

'Yeah, gorgeous, isn't she?' drawled Jackson, draping an arm round Angel's neck and pulling her closer to him. 'Although usually she prefers soccer players, I hear. But that's okay because usually I prefer blondes.'

Everyone laughed and just when Angel wondered how much longer this piss-taking of her would go on, Derren seemed to be given instructions down his earpiece to speed things up and he quickly asked Angel to read out the names. Clips of the bands were playing on the large screen behind them and when Angel knew the cameras wouldn't be on her, she took the opportunity to whisper in Jackson's ear, 'Fuck you!'

'Missed your chance, babe,' he drawled back. 'Got a bigger, better model to suck my dick after you left.'

Angel was itching to continue trading insults with him, but the clips stopped and she had to open the envelope and announce, 'And the winner of best band is . . . Kaiser Chiefs!'

The five lads came running up the stage, where they kissed Angel and hugged Jackson. Angel couldn't wait to get away from Jackson and off-stage, but just as they were both leaving, Jackson shouted out, 'Right, the lads have got their award, here's mine!' And he picked Angel up and carried her off, to shouts and whistles from the audience.

Furious as she was, Angel knew it would look even more ridiculous if she tried to resist him, so she smiled as if she was loving every minute of being held in Jackson's arms and thanked her lucky stars that for once she was wearing a long dress, so was in no danger of flashing her arse to millions of viewers. Off-stage, Jackson practically dropped her without warning, slapped her on the backside and sauntered off. Shaking with rage and wishing she could jump in the shower right away to wash herself clean where he had touched her skin, Angel went straight to her dressing room. There, Jez and Gemma were waiting, both suitably appalled by what had happened.

'Come on,' Angel told them. 'Let's go to the after-party now, I don't want to risk seeing that wanker again backstage.'

In the car, Angel examined her face. Her lip gloss had come off, but everything else was intact. She couldn't help shuddering to herself as she re-applied it, hating the memory of his lips on hers.

'Tell me the truth,' she demanded. 'Did he make me look a total tit?'

'Of course not!' the pair reassured her, but Angel wasn't entirely convinced by their reply, and it was only after quickly downing two glasses of champagne at the party that she started to feel a little less murderous. Fortunately for Angel, one of the celebrities presenting an award after her, a soap star heart-throb, had been hitting the free booze and made a complete fool of himself, unable even to string a sentence together and falling over when he tried to exit the stage, so that's what everyone at the party was talking about. However, just as she came out of the Ladies, she bumped straight into Jackson – a coked-up Jackson.

'Well, well, look who it is, little Miss Frigid. Found anyone else to pricktease lately?'

Angel made to walk past him, determined to ignore him, but he grabbed her arm and before she was able to stop him, he pulled her into the Gents.

'Get off me,' she shouted, frantically struggling, but he only held her tighter.

'I don't appreciate being turned down by anyone, least of all a fucking whore who strips for a living.' She could tell from his eyes that he was off his head.

She tried reasoning with him. 'Okay, okay, let's just forget it.'

But Jackson was beyond reason and Angel found herself being dragged towards the nearest cubicle.

'Get off me!' she shouted again, desperate to attract someone's attention, but the music was very loud.

'I'm going to show you what you're missing now,' Jackson declared maniacally.

Angel resisted with all her might, kicking at his ankles and screaming, until he clamped his hand over her mouth. She felt a huge surge of panic. This was it. Suddenly, a familiar and longed-for voice shouted, 'Let her go!' and Cal burst through the door of the Gents.

'Fuck you,' roared Jackson and, shoving Angel away from him, he charged at Cal, pushing him against the door and drawing back his fist. Angel watched in horror, trying to see how she could slip by them to run for help, but they were blocking the exit. Cal neatly sidestepped Jackson, who hit the wall with his fist, then turned in even more of a fury and came towards Cal again. Cal stood his ground this time and punched Jackson in the face, a blow that had him reeling to the ground. There was blood streaming from a cut above Jackson's eye, but still he got up and charged at Cal once more. He was like a man possessed. Cal managed to deflect him and Jackson ended up on the floor. For a few seconds he didn't move and seemed unconscious. Just as Cal was asking him if he was all right, Jackson reared up and head-butted Cal, knocking him to the ground, where he proceeded to kick him viciously, making contact with Cal's right knee, which had only just healed after the recent violent tackle on the pitch.

'Get off him,' Angel screamed, seeing Cal writhing in agony and clutching his knee. She ran at Jackson and tried to stop him, but he punched her in the face, knocking her to the ground, then turned his attentions to Cal again, kicking him with such force that Cal was knocked back towards the wall. Angel could hardly see through the tears of pain, but she picked herself up and once more hurled herself at Jackson, desperate to stop him hurting Cal, resorting to dirty tactics, digging her nails into his face. Nothing seemed to make any difference to the violence of Jackson's attack. Who knows what he might have done next, but suddenly the room was full of security guards.

'Phone an ambulance!' Angel screamed. She knelt down next to Cal, who was curled up in agony.

'It's going to be okay, Cal, I promise.' He barely seemed to register her presence.

While they waited for the ambulance, the security guards bundled Jackson out of the Gents. When the paramedics turned up they refused to let Angel go with Cal, so she, Gemma and Jez had to jump into a taxi. *Please let him be okay*, Angel kept saying to herself over and over again. *Please, please, please*.

'You should get someone to look at your face, Angel, when we get there,' Gemma said gently. 'It's bleeding, you might need stitches.'

'I'm fine, there's nothing wrong with me. I've got to see Cal. Have you phoned Tony and told him? He'll know the name of the doctor who operated on Cal last time. We must call him and Cal's agent,' Angel gabbled on hysterically.

'Yes, I told you, I've called Tony and he's onto it, you don't need to worry.'

Angel put her face in her hands and sobbed. 'It's all my fault. If I hadn't met that bastard none of this would have happened.'

'It's not your fault, Angel,' Jez put in. 'The only person who is responsible is that wanker, and only him.'

At the hospital Gemma did all the talking and managed to persuade the nurse to let Angel see Cal. Immediately, she rushed over to him. He seemed to be asleep. He looked pale, a purple bruise developing over his right eye, his bottom lip swollen and split. She had never seen him look vulnerable before and it frightened her.

'Cal,' she whispered.

His eyes opened and he looked at her and murmured, 'Angel, are you okay?' He reached out and she put her hand in his.

'I'm fine, and you're going to be fine too, I promise, Cal.'

Angel saw the tears in his eyes and she gripped his hand more tightly. 'You are going to be okay, Cal, do you hear me?'

Just then, the door opened and the consultant and his team marched in purposefully. Angel got up to leave, but Cal held onto her hand, saying urgently, 'Stay with me.'

She held tightly to his hand as the consultant went through the risks of surgery and the chances of Cal making a full recovery. Apparently, there was a forty per cent chance of his knee recovering well enough for him to play football again, but that didn't seem like great odds to Angel. After the consultant and his team left, Cal gently stroked Angel's face where Jackson had hit her.

'Does it hurt?' he asked.

She shook her head. 'Don't worry about me.'

Cal stared at her. 'But I always have.'

Angel was desperate for Cal to say more, but the nurse and porters arrived to wheel him down to surgery. She squeezed his hand tightly. He managed a small smile and then was gone.

*

Gemma and Jez tried to persuade Angel to go
home and get some rest, but she wasn't having any
of it. She was staying at the hospital and that was it.
Around four, Gemma and Jez went home, but
Tony stayed and the two of them took it in turns to
pace up and down the visitors' room and fetch cups
of tea.

'Will he be all right?' Angel kept asking.

As usual, Tony was realistic. 'He could make a
full recovery or he might never play again.'

'Oh God, Tony, what would he do if he had to
stop playing?'

Tony didn't have an answer for that one.

It was the longest night of her life. Cal didn't
come out of surgery until seven the next morning.
A nurse came in to tell them that the operation had
gone well, but they weren't allowed to see him. At
eight o'clock the door of the visitors' room burst
open and Simone stood in the doorway. As usual,
she was immaculate, with perfect make-up and
hair, dressed in an expensive-looking white mac
pulled in tightly at the waist, skinny jeans and heels,
a designer bag on her wrist – in stark contrast to
Angel, who looked exhausted. She had taken off
her high heels many hours ago and was now
barefoot and wearing Tony's hoodie over her
evening dress.

'What the hell are you doing here?' Simone
demanded, her eyes furious.

'How is he?' Angel asked urgently.

'Do you seriously think I'm going to talk to a cheap little tart like you?' Simone spat back. 'It's all your fault that he got hurt.'

Tony leapt to her defence. 'Don't talk to my sister like that, we just want to know how Cal is.'

'The operation went well, though of course we won't know for a while whether he'll ever play again,' she answered coldly, looking accusingly at Angel.

'Can we see him?' Angel asked, desperate to be with Cal.

'Absolutely not!' Simone retorted. 'You're not family. I'm the only one who can stay with him.'

For a moment Angel stared at her, too emotionally shattered to take in what Simone was saying, but then she saw it on her finger. A huge princess-cut diamond on a platinum band.

Simone saw her looking. 'Yes, we're engaged.'

Then she turned to go, a triumphant smirk on her glossed lips.

'Send him our love, won't you?' Tony called out as Simone marched off, flicking her long hair as she went and giving no indication that she had registered Tony's request.

'We may as well go home, then,' Tony said to Angel. Reluctantly, she agreed; she was never going to be able to see Cal while Simone was around.

Tony wanted her to come back to his flat but she refused, saying that she would be okay and would go straight to bed. As soon as she got home she texted Cal. She knew that he probably wouldn't have his mobile switched on, but she was desperate to get a message to him. *Hope you're okay, thinking of you, Angel x.*

The next day she cancelled her shoot and went back to the hospital. But there she discovered that Cal had been transferred to a private clinic and the hospital wouldn't tell her where.

'Oh, come on!' she said in exasperation. 'I'm a really good friend of his!'

The nurse on duty just looked at her and shrugged. 'We don't give out personal details to anyone unless they're next of kin. For all I know you could be press.'

Seeing that it was futile to argue, Angel got straight on the phone to Tony, who promised to find out from Cal's agent where Cal was being looked after.

Two hours later, Angel was driving to the private clinic in Hertfordshire. All she wanted to do was see Cal and she couldn't rest until she did; not even the news that he was engaged changed that. She had to see him. But when she arrived at the clinic, she was immediately told she wasn't welcome. First by the nurse and then by Simone, who came down to reception when Angel said she refused to leave until she'd seen Cal.

'Why don't you get it?' Simone said to her. 'Cal doesn't want to see you.'

'I don't believe you,' Angel said hotly.

Simone sat down next to her. 'Get the message! He's far too nice to say it to your face, but he really doesn't want to see you any more. So why don't you go home and concentrate on your "modelling",' (she said as if it was the lowest kind of profession) 'and find another member of a boy band to shack up with. It's what you do best, isn't it? Cal is out of your league, he always has been and he always will be. He just tried to help you because he felt sorry for you and because of what your mum and dad did for him. And he admitted that he only had that affair with you because he was lonely. Please don't embarrass yourself any more. We're engaged, we're going to get married, there's no room in his life for a little tart like you.'

Angel wanted to protest, to say it wasn't true, that Cal did care about her. But something held her back. He had never told her that he loved her, hadn't called her after their brief affair and now he was engaged. Without giving Simone the satisfaction of an answer, she picked up her coat and walked out of the hospital, trying desperately not to cry. Simone was a jealous, spiteful bitch, but maybe, just maybe, she was right and Cal really didn't want to see her.

As Angel drove back to London, Carrie called her in a state of high excitement, telling her that one of the American TV producers she'd met in LA wanted her to audition for a new series at the end of the month. 'This could be your big break, Angel. You could become an international star!' she exclaimed. 'You'll have to spend the next couple of weeks at the gym – everything has got to be perfect!'

Angel tried to sound enthusiastic, but she felt too full of sadness to care.

Chapter 21

Make Or Break

Over the next couple of weeks, Angel tried to follow Carrie's orders. She went to the gym every day and worked out with a personal trainer; she stopped drinking and cut out junk food; she had regular facials and body wraps. Physically, she had never looked better. But her emotional state was another matter. Even Tony hadn't been allowed to see Cal, and so Angel still didn't know how he was. She prepared herself for the fact that she probably wouldn't see Cal until Tony and Gemma's wedding the following month and she just prayed that he was recovering well. The reports in the press about him were all frustratingly vague; no one seemed to know whether he would ever be able to play again.

But there was plenty of speculation – that he might lose his place in the first team, that his manager was already shopping for his replacement. Angel could only hope that Cal hadn't read them.

In desperation, Angel phoned Cal's Chelsea team-mate Antonio to find out what he knew about Cal, but he couldn't tell her anything either. It seemed that Simone was keeping everyone away from Cal.

'I'm sorry I can't be more helpful, Angel, but I'll keep asking and maybe have some news for you soon. Actually, I was going to call you, because I've been invited to open a new Spanish restaurant in Soho and I wondered if you would like to come with me?'

Angel hesitated. She liked Antonio well enough as a friend, but she really didn't want to go on a date with him. Her encounter with Jackson had taught her one thing and that was to be crystal clear about her feelings from the very beginning.

'I'd love to come to dinner with you, Antonio, but it has to be as friends.'

'Don't worry,' Antonio said a little sadly, 'I understand.'

As it turned out, Angel enjoyed her non-date with Antonio more than she expected to. Because there was no pressure on either of them, they could both relax. In Angel's case that meant confiding in Antonio about her feelings for Cal, and he proved to be a sympathetic listener.

'I wasn't surprised when the story of your affair came out,' Antonio told her. 'I always thought you had feelings for each other. I could tell from the way he looked at you and the way he spoke your name that he was in love with you.'

'Really?' Angel was desperate to know more. 'He's never said that to me.'

'He's afraid of his feelings for you. You threaten this strong image he's built up and he doesn't know how to handle it, so he ends up pushing you away.'

'Christ, Antonio, I didn't realise you were a psychologist as well as a footballer!' Angel replied.

'It's obvious,' Antonio replied.

'It makes no difference, anyway,' Angel said sadly. 'He's with Simone.'

And there was nothing Antonio could say to that.

The following morning she received a phone call from her dad. 'Is everything all right?' she asked anxiously, immediately thinking that there must be something wrong with her mum, because her dad never called her.

'Why haven't you been to see him, then?' her dad demanded, ignoring her question.

'Been to see who?' Angel asked, totally con-fused.

'Cal, of course. I've just phoned him and he said neither you nor Tony had been to see him. Never heard him in such a state – the poor lad is seriously depressed and the two people he cares most about in the world haven't even bothered to visit. What the hell's going on?'

'Hang on a minute!' Angel exclaimed. 'Simone

told me he didn't want to see me and she told Tony the same.'

'Well, she's a conniving little cow. She's buggered off filming and left Cal on his own. He's out of the clinic now and I think it would be a very good idea if you paid him a visit.'

'But what if he doesn't want to see me?'

'You'll never know unless you try. But I rather think he will. He told me he was only in that club on the night of the attack because he wanted to see you. So get your arse over to his house right now.'

When Angel put the phone down, her heart was racing. She grabbed her bag, rushed out of her flat and ran all the way down Hampstead High Street, not caring that people were staring at her. Cal wanted to see her! For the first time in weeks she was filled with excitement and hope. But when he opened the door, he barely acknowledged her. He looked like shit: he had bags under his eyes and obviously hadn't shaved for days. He looked totally dejected.

'Hi,' Angel said, 'How are you?'

'I'm fine,' he replied. 'Don't you think I look great? Come in and you can watch me hobbling round the house.'

With a sense of disbelief, Angel followed Cal in. His usually immaculate house was in a complete state of chaos – dirty coffee cups, takeaway pizza boxes, old newspapers, empty bottles of beer were strewn across the floor and table. She picked up one of the boxes and said in amazement, 'It's not like you to eat food like this.'

'Yeah, well, I haven't felt much like shopping. So do you want a coffee or a beer? I'm having a beer.'

Angel sneaked a look at her watch. It was eleven a.m. 'I'll just have water, thanks,' Angel replied, hardly able to believe Cal's transformation.

He limped into the kitchen and came back with a glass of water for her and a beer for himself, then lowered himself onto the sofa.

'So how's the knee?' Angel asked.

'Not great,' Cal muttered. 'I'm supposed to be doing physio every day but I don't know if it's even worth bothering.'

Angel had never heard Cal so down before and she didn't quite know how to deal with him.

'Simone told me that you didn't want to see me or Tony,' she finally said. 'In case you're wondering why we haven't been round. I did try to see you.'

'Whatever,' he muttered. He looked at his watch. 'My physio's coming in a minute. Thanks for coming by, Angel, can you see yourself out?'

Hurt by his abrupt dismissal of her, Angel quickly got up, turning her face away so he couldn't see the tears in her eyes. 'Tony said he would come round after work.'

'Whatever,' Cal said again, concentrating on drinking his beer and staring at the TV.

'See you then, Cal,' Angel said sadly.

Outside she started walking home, then stopped.

She remembered Cal flying out to Spain to bring her home, Cal preventing Jackson from hurting her, and here she was now, walking away from him when it was clear he was in a complete mess. He needed help, that was obvious. She turned on her heel and marched back to the house. As soon as Cal opened the door she walked straight in.

'Your physio isn't coming, is he?' she demanded.

Cal shrugged. 'So? It won't make any difference. I'm never going to be able to play again.'

'You don't know that!' Angel replied passionately. 'Surely you owe it to yourself to give it a try. You can't just give up.'

'Why not?' Cal muttered, slumping back down on the sofa. 'From where I am at the moment, that looks like a pretty good idea.'

God, what the hell can I say to shake him out of this, Angel wondered despairingly. Then she had a sudden thought.

'If you can't do it for yourself, what about for your baby?'

For the first time since she had come to his house, Cal looked at her – and she was shocked by the look of pain in his eyes.

'There is no baby. Simone had a miscarriage. Or at least, she said she did. I'm not even sure if she was really pregnant.'

'Oh my God,' Angel exclaimed. 'Why would she lie?'

'I can think of several reasons and it really

mattered to me before all this.' He pointed to his knee as if he couldn't bear to look at it or mention it. 'Now it just seems pointless.'

Angel's mind was racing with questions she wanted to ask him, but before she had the chance, the doorbell rang and Cal limped off to answer it.

It was Tony. He'd obviously received the same SOS call from Frank.

He was visibly shocked at the state of Cal. 'Mate, what's going on?' he asked in disbelief, and he got the same shrug from Cal that Angel had. Tony and Angel looked at each other helplessly, then Angel spoke.

'Cal says his physio isn't coming today, but why don't you work through some exercises with him and I'll tidy up?'

Cal tried to protest, but Angel and Tony weren't having any of it, so, extremely reluctantly, Cal agreed to do some exercises with Tony. The two of them went into the basement where Cal had a gym and Angel busied herself with loading all the rubbish into bin bags and stacking the dishwasher. An hour later she'd made some progress and Cal's beautiful house was looking less like a dump. She checked out the fridge and saw he had no fresh food, called out that she was going to the shops and then dashed to the nearest supermarket to load up with fruit and veg and fresh meat and fish. She was a woman on a mission and the mission was to get Cal well again.

By the time she returned, Cal and Tony had finished and Cal had showered and shaved and was looking more like his usual gorgeous self. Still, he seemed depressed.

'You didn't have to go shopping for me,' Cal told her. 'I'm not a complete invalid.'

'You're not an invalid at all,' she replied. 'I just wanted to help.'

'Yeah, well,' he mumbled. 'How much do I owe you?'

'For God's sake!' Angel retorted. 'All the things you've done for me, can't I just get you some food? And now I'm actually going to cook lunch! So let me get on with it!'

'Your cooking's improved, Angel!' Tony exclaimed, tucking into the lunch of grilled fish, salad and steamed vegetables she had cooked for everyone.

'Even *I* can grill fish, Tony!' she replied. The two of them niggled good-naturedly and bickered their way through lunch as they always did. Cal was quiet, but Angel was pleased to see that at least he was eating something. She wished she could spend the rest of the afternoon with him, but she had a shoot she knew she couldn't cancel, so reluctantly left after lunch. Cal had still said barely a word, but he walked over to the door with her to say goodbye.

'Thanks for coming over, Angel. I do appreciate it, even though it might not look like it. And good luck with . . .' He paused and Angel assumed he was going to mention her America trip, but he said awkwardly, 'Well, you know, at least it's one choice I approve of and I understand.'

'Who knows what will happen,' Angel replied, thinking, *What does he mean he understands? What's there to understand?*

'I can come round again tomorrow, if you like?' Angel said.

Cal nodded. 'That would be good, thanks. Even though I'm sure you've got better things to do.' He still looked sad, as if something had been broken in him. Putting it down to his injury, Angel gave him a quick kiss and said, 'It will be okay, Cal, you have to believe that.'

'You didn't tell me you were seeing Antonio,' Gemma said to her accusingly as she got Angel ready for her shoot.

'I'm not!' Angel answered, completely taken aback. 'What makes you say that?'

By way of explanation, Gemma picked up one of the tabloids that were in a pile on the table in front of them and flicked it open at the celebrity gossip page. There was a picture of Angel and Antonio arriving at the Spanish restaurant together. The accompanying article was hot with speculation.

'We're just friends!' Angel exclaimed in exasperation.

'Thank God for that,' Gemma replied. 'I was thinking I was going to have to re-jig all the seating arrangements at the wedding for your new boy-friend.'

Gemma and Tony's wedding was now only a week away and Angel couldn't help feeling nervous. In fact, she probably felt more nervous than the bride. She so wanted the day to be perfect for Gemma and for her brother, and felt guilty about the fact that they'd had to postpone it once, even though Gemma had assured her that she shouldn't.

She went round to see Cal as she'd promised, and although he looked better, he was more detached than she had ever known him. It was evening and he was sitting by the fire in his living room, listening to Joy Division's 'Love Will Tear Us Apart' (not the cheeriest of choices when you're feeling blue). He poured her a glass of wine – her first drink in a while – and she sat on the sofa opposite him. They had spent so many intimate moments in that room during their brief affair and it was very nearly unbearable to Angel that there was such a distance between them now. But she could see no way of bridging it.

'So how's the physio going?' she finally asked.

'A little better,' Cal conceded, 'but I still don't hold out much hope.'

'You can't think like that!' Angel told him. 'You can't just give up. I could have given up about the drugs but I didn't, because you didn't let me and you were right.'

'Well, maybe you're stronger than me, Angel,' Cal said, draining his glass and pouring himself another.

'So are you still seeing Simone?' Angel finally asked the question she'd been longing to ask ever since Cal had told her there was no baby. She tried to ask the question as casually as possible and steeled herself for the worst.

'No, it's over,' he replied. 'Funny, isn't it, that whenever I'm single you're not and vice versa. Is it going well, then?'

Angel frowned. 'Is what going well?'

'Your new relationship,' Cal replied bitterly, as if the words cost him a great effort to say. 'He's a good bloke, Antonio. There's just one thing I need to know – did it start that weekend at the hotel?'

For a moment Angel was so shocked that she couldn't quite grasp what Cal was talking about. Then she realised. 'Antonio and I are just friends, nothing more.'

'Oh, come on,' Cal replied, 'you don't have to spare my feelings. I know how badly I've treated you but I would rather you were straight with me, that way I can start to get over you.'

'I am telling the truth! There is absolutely nothing going on between Antonio and me. There never has been and there never will be. I went out for dinner with him, that's all. As a friend,' Angel said passionately, now desperate for Cal to believe her.

'So, you're single, then?' Cal said. 'How ironic. At last you're free and all those times I wished we both were and here I am, a fucking useless wreck who will never be good for anything again.'

'I had no idea you ever wished I was single!' Angel said in astonishment. Cal was saying all the things she had longed for him to say so many times, but it was in such a sad, final way that it made them seem hopeless.

'Well, I was quite good at fucking everything up – quite spectacularly good, don't you think?'

'Cal, what are you saying? I need to know, tell me!' Angel was quite literally on the edge of her seat, gazing at Cal.

'Isn't it obvious? I love you, Angel, and I always have, even though I seem to have spent the last few years doing everything I can to make you hate me.'

All Angel could think was that Cal had said that he loved her. She was on fire. 'But I love you, too,' she burst out.

'How can you? I've treated you so badly,' Cal said bleakly.

But Angel had had enough of talking. Within a moment she was next to Cal, wrapping her arms round his neck and kissing him for all she was worth. Cal tried to speak, but she wouldn't let him. 'Shush,' she whispered. 'Haven't we talked enough for now?'

Chapter 22

Just Say Yes

'Hi, Cal, it's Angel, where are you? Are you okay? Call me *please*.'

Angel put down her mobile, sighing with frustration and worry. Two nights ago she and Cal had made love and she thought they had never been closer. He had told her that he loved her; surely this was the start of the relationship she had wanted for so long. But suddenly it all seemed to be going wrong. Cal hadn't turned up at the restaurant where they had arranged to meet and he wasn't returning any of her calls. Angel felt the all-too-familiar despair grip her and she couldn't even tell Gemma. The wedding was only three days away and she had no intention of burdening her friend with her problem. What could she do? She couldn't just sit at home waiting for Cal to phone her – if he was ever going to call her. She had to know what was going on. It was midnight, but she had to see him and get the truth from him.

When she arrived at his house the lights were on
and she could see Cal in the living room. She pressed
the buzzer and heard the sound echo through the
house, but he made no attempt to answer the door.
Feeling increasingly frustrated, she forced open the
letter box and shouted through it. 'Cal, let me in. I'm
not going away until you see me.' She had to call out
several times and eventually Cal, realising that she
wasn't going to go away, opened the door.

'What's going on?' Angel demanded, walking
into the house. 'Where were you today?'

He shrugged. 'Something came up, sorry.'

He didn't sound sorry, just cold and distant. He
made no attempt to kiss Angel, but returned to the
living room, picked up his drink and looked away
from her, as if her presence bored him.

Angel went and stood in front of him, forcing
him to look at her. 'What the hell is the matter? I
waited for two hours in the restaurant. I thought
you'd had an accident. Why didn't you call me?'

Cal still wouldn't look at her. 'I saw the surgeon
today and the knee doesn't seem to be healing as
well as it should. So I went out and got pissed. I'm
sorry I let you down, Angel, it's the last time, I
guarantee it.'

'Too bloody right!' Angel exclaimed, and was
about to let rip about how he might have bothered
to let her know, when he said:

'It's the last time, because I don't want to see you
again.'

Angel felt the room spin round. She grabbed the sofa to stop herself falling. 'What?' This couldn't be happening, Cal couldn't be saying this, not after telling her he loved her. What could have changed in two days?

Still not looking at her, Cal said, 'I'm not sure you'll understand this, but I can't be with you if I can't play football again. You deserve to be with someone who can give you the world.'

'Is it because of Jackson? You blame me? Angel asked in desperation.

'Of course not, the only person I blame is myself. I've got to get through this somehow and I've got to get through it on my own. That's the only way I know, Angel. And it's not good enough, I know. So please go now, fall in love with someone else, forget you ever knew me.'

Angel wanted to cry out, to throw her arms round him, to beg him to change his mind, but she knew it would be hopeless. Instead, summoning all her strength, Angel managed to answer, 'Okay, I'll go if that's what you want, but you're making a mistake, Cal. l love you and I always will.'

As she walked out of the room and out of the house, she kept thinking that Cal would come after her any second and tell her that it had all been a mistake. But by the time she reached her flat, she knew he wasn't coming.

*

'Oh my God, Angel!' Zoë exclaimed as Angel arrived at the hotel room to get ready for Gemma's wedding. 'Have you been ill? You look like shit.'

'Thanks for bigging me up, Zoë! I know I look like shit, but you're the artist, can't you do something about it?' Angel sat down at the dressing table and had to agree with Zoë's analysis. Her eyes were puffy and bloodshot from all the crying she'd been doing since she saw Cal; her skin looked blotchy and there were dark circles under her eyes. Not so much bridesmaid, as bride of Frankenstein . . .

'Just do something before Gemma sees me, for God's sake.'

By the time Gemma arrived to get ready, Angel had been transformed into Britain's favourite glamour girl, and she made a supreme effort to smile and hide the sadness in her eyes.

'Here comes the bride!' she exclaimed, making a big fuss of Gemma and pouring her a glass of champagne. Angel thought that Gemma had never looked more beautiful. Her long black hair was coiled on top of her head in an intricate design, held in place with diamante pins; she was wearing a strapless cream silk dress, which showed off her beautiful back and shoulders, with a tight bodice that emphasised her tiny waist and a full skirt. The bridesmaids – Angel, Cheryl and Tamzin – were all in fifties-style prom dresses in delicate pale pink, their hair in sophisticated French pleats. Putting on the bridesmaid dress helped Angel put on an act that everything was okay, even though inside she felt broken.

'How's Cal?' Gemma asked her as they walked down to the cars that were going to take them to the church.

'He's been really busy with his physio, I haven't seen him,' Angel lied, the mention of his name making her feel sick to her stomach, and then changed the subject by telling Gemma yet again how beautiful she looked.

Just as they turned the corner of the street leading up to the church, Angel suddenly felt like she couldn't hold it together. She shouted at the driver to stop the car, then leant out, retching into the gutter. When she climbed back into the car, she told the others that she was still getting over a bug. The thought of seeing Cal again and having to pretend that he hadn't broken her heart was almost unbearable.

Her heart sank still further when the car turned into the church driveway and Cal was the first person she saw. He was dressed in a grey morning suit and looked impossibly handsome. It took all of Angel's willpower not to look at him. Seeing the bridal cars pull up, Cal walked into the church. Angel took a deep breath and dug her nails into the palm of her hand, forcing herself to think, *This is Gemma and Tony's day, just focus on that and on making it happy for them. Don't think about anything else.* She handed Gemma her flowers, smoothed down her dress, wished her luck and took her place behind her as the bridal march started up on the church organ.

Tony looked overwhelmed when he saw Gemma for the first time. He didn't seem able to take his eyes from her, and despite her heavy heart, Angel smiled. But then she looked up and saw Cal, and for a fleeting moment they held each other's gaze before Angel quickly looked away.

The ceremony was so lovely that most of the guests were in tears, but Angel remained dry-eyed, fearing she would lose control completely if she cried. It was torture when it came to the exchanging of the rings and Angel had to stand up and hand Gemma the box containing Tony's ring. Opposite her, Cal was doing the same for Tony. She looked everywhere but in Cal's direction, willing the ceremony to be over so she could sit back down. Now that she had seen him and he seemed to be so unconcerned by what he had done to her, the hurt she felt was being overtaken by a slow-burning anger. *How dare he treat me like that – picking me up and then dumping me?* she thought bitterly.

Mentally she was ticking off parts of the day in her head – the first ordeal was the service, the second was the photographs. She knew Gemma had booked someone to do a few formal shots and then make the rest of the pictures informal, and she just prayed that the formal ones didn't take too long so there wouldn't be much standing around and trying to avoid Cal. She found herself caught up with Jeanie and her mum, who were comparing notes over who had cried the most during the service.

'Doesn't she look beautiful?' Jeanie said proudly.

'Stunning,' Angel replied sincerely.

'And you look beautiful, too,' Michelle put in, and then, to Angel's horror, Cal walked over and she had the total embarrassment of hearing her mum say, 'Doesn't Angel look beautiful, Cal?' At any other time during her long history with Cal, Angel would have been thrilled by her mum's comment, but now she wanted the ground to swallow her.

If Cal felt awkward he didn't show it, and simply said generously, 'Yes, she does and I'm sure she'll make a beautiful bride one day.'

That did it! Angel wasn't going to hang around to be patronised by Cal. She gave him a scathing look, then marched off as far away from him as possible. How dare he make a comment like that after all he had put her through? Did he really think she was going to stand there simpering and hanging on his every word?

Suddenly he was by her side, saying urgently, 'Angel, I really need to talk to you.'

She looked over his shoulder and pretended to be studying the church. 'Well, I don't want to talk to you! How dare you fucking patronise me like that!'

'I wasn't patronising you, I meant it. I need to

tell you—' but Cal was interrupted by the photographer calling them over. Tony and Gemma wanted a picture of the four of them together. Angel swiftly walked on ahead of Cal, determined not to say another word to him if she could help it.

'So now you're avoiding me?' Cal said at the champagne reception in the country hotel, as he finally managed to track Angel down.

'Sorry,' Angel said curtly, 'I've just remembered that I've got to go and talk to someone who isn't a total bastard. Excuse me.' And she started walking away.

Cal grabbed her arm and whispered urgently, 'I really do need to talk to you. I know I was a total bastard to you and that's what I need to talk about.'

'I don't want an apology from you,' Angel said angrily, pushing his hand from her arm. 'I just want you to piss off!'

He grabbed her again to stop her from leaving and this time she saw red, spun round and slapped him round the face as hard as she could, drawing shocked gasps from the guests around her.

'Got the message now?' she shouted and ran away from him, praying that neither Gemma nor Tony had witnessed the scene.

Angel hid in the toilets for fifteen minutes, too embarrassed to face anyone, but then she heard one of the ushers calling the guests to the wedding breakfast and she knew she would have to go back in. She was sitting with the bride and groom and her family at the top table, which looked out over the room, and she was at the opposite end to Cal, so she could avoid all contact with him. Word of what Angel had done didn't seem to have reached the bride and groom and Angel could pretend that everything was just fine. That was until Cal got up to deliver his best man speech. All eyes were turned to Cal, except Angel's – she stared fixedly at the arrangement of pale pink roses in front of her.

His speech was charming and witty and warm, full of good wishes for Tony and Gemma – so far, a typical best man speech. Then his voice suddenly seemed charged with emotion. 'They're so lucky to have found such a love. Seeing them today has made me realise that when you find love like that, you should hold onto it. It's more important than anything.'

Angel found herself compelled to look up at Cal and she discovered that he was gazing directly at her.

'I know this is Gemma and Tony's day, but I hope you won't mind if I say a little bit about myself and someone who means the world to me. A week ago I told the woman I love that I didn't want to see her any more.'

Oh my God, Angel thought, *what's coming next?* She was aware that all the guests were riveted by what Cal was saying.

'I told her that if I couldn't play football again, then I couldn't be with her, even though I loved her. And it was stupid of me. I pushed her away when I needed her most. I've spent the last few days trying to get hold of her to tell her that I was wrong, and, understandably, she doesn't want to know. But I'll give it one more try.'

And to Angel's astonishment, he walked towards her seat, got down on one knee, took her hand and said, 'Angel, will you marry me?'

There were gasps of astonishment and delight from the guests. Angel was speechless. She took the pale pink leather ring box he was holding out to her and opened it to reveal a stunning pink diamond ring. She looked at Cal.

'No pressure, Angel,' he said, 'but if you turn me down I've just humiliated myself in front of two hundred people.'

'Yes,' she whispered in a voice full of emotion, 'I will marry you.' And as Cal took her in his arms and kissed her, the room erupted into cheers and applause. It had taken a long time and it very nearly hadn't happened at all, but Angel had found her happy-ever-after at last.

The End

Angel Uncovered

By Katie Price

Angel Summer looks as if she has found her happy ever after. She's married to the love of her life, sexy footballer Cal, they have a beautiful baby girl and Angel is Britain's top glamour model. But all is not as it seems and there is heartache in store.

When Cal is transferred to AC Milan, Angel feels isolated being so far away from her family and friends instead of embracing the WAG lifestyle of designer shopping and pampering. Surrounded by beautiful people, will Angel and Cal pull together or will they turn elsewhere to seek comfort? Angel's worst nightmares come to life when an old flame of Cal's comes back on the scene and suddenly Angel is fighting to save her marriage, and herself . . .

'Glam, glitz, gorgeous people . . . so Jordan!' *Woman*

'A real insight into the celebrity world' *OK!*

'Brilliantly bitchy' *New!*

arrow books

ALSO AVAILABLE IN ARROW

Paradise

Katie Price

It's six months since beautiful model Angel Summer found herself having to choose between a life with Ethan Turner, the laid-back Californian baseball player, or giving her marriage to football star Cal Bailey another go. Her friends and family were stunned when she picked Ethan, but it looks like Angel made the right decision: Ethan loves her and she loves him.

But nothing is perfect. Ethan has secrets in his past that could threaten their relationship and when he faces financial ruin the couple are forced to star in a reality TV show about their life together. Despite everything, though, Angel is convinced that Ethan is the man for her. So why can't she stop thinking about Cal?

As the tabloids have always been quick to point out, the path of true love has never run smoothly for our sexy celebrity, and when her dad falls dangerously ill Angel rushes back to England to be by his bedside, throwing her and Cal back together. But Ethan loves her, Cal has a girlfriend, and Angel has made her choice. It's too late to go back now . . . isn't it?

'A fabulous guilty holiday pleasure' *Heat*

'Peppered with cutting asides and a directness you can only imagine coming from Katie Price, it's a fun, blisteringly paced yet fluffy novel.' *Cosmopolitan*

arrow books